Fifteen

Fifteen

A Novel by

CAROLYN DOYLE

skydance
press

Skydance Press, LLC
Piermont, NY
2014

Copyright ©2014 by Carolyn Doyle (Carolyn Doyle Winter)

    Fifteen : a novel / by Carolyn Doyle. -- Piermont, NY : Skydance Press, 2014.

    pages ; cm.

    ISBN: 978-0-9915305-0-2 ;
          978-0-9915305-1-9 (ebook)
    Summary: Set in the Bronx in 1967, the revolution of the 60's is not only an exterior uprising in the world, but an upheaval at home in this traditional second-generation Italian-American family. The story is told from the viewpoint of the mother, Maria, and the daughter, Angelina. Maria married young, to a man 15 years older and set in his ways. Angelina is a typical teen of the turbulent era. When Pasquale, the sultry Italian stallion enters the picture, sparks fly and nothing in the Campisi family is ever the same again.--Publisher.

    1. Italian-American families--New York (State)--New York--Fiction. 2. Bronx (New York, N.Y.)--Fiction. 3. Nineteen sixty-seven, A.D.--Fiction. 4. Mothers and daughters--Fiction. 5. Intergenerational relations--Fiction. 6. May-December romances--Fiction. 7. Marriage--Fiction. 8. Fashion--Fiction. 9. Women's clothing industry--New York (State)--New York--Fiction. 10. Families--Fiction. 11. Chick lit, American. 12. American fiction--Women authors. 13. Bildungsromans. I. Title.

PS3604.O95473 F54 2014
813/.6--dc23   1410

Library of Congress Control Number: 2014916814
SAN: 920-8968

All rights reserved. No part of this publication may be reproduced, stored in a retrieval system, or transmitted in any form or by any means-electronic, mechanical, photocopying, recording, or otherwise-without prior written permission from Skydance Press, LLC.

Published in the United States of America by
Skydance Press, LLC
Piermont, New York
www.skydancepress.com
Facebook connection Is: https://www.facebook.com/SkydancePress

Printed in the United States on acid-free paper
First Edition

Please note: This is a work of fiction. Names, characters, places, and incidents either are the product of the author's imagination or are used fictitiously, and any resemblance to actual persons, living or dead, businesses, companies, events, or locales is entirely coincidental.

For:

Madison Taylor Hall (11) & Isabella Rae Hall (8)

With love in my heart:

"It's not about the difference of our ages;
it's about the sameness in our hearts."

CHAPTER ONE

Maria

I've been here before. I know the fabric of the place—each blade of grass, each cricket chirp and song-bird melody of the place. It's my vision of serenity—far-away from the clackety-clack of the sewing machines and the chatter of my busy household; this lush Eden of trees and bushes, thick mossy grass with spiky ferns in the background. A scattering of fuchsia, saffron and periwinkle wildflowers dot the landscape, just like the ones on the bolt of fabric ready to be cut into a summer sundress for Angelina. The scent of crisp-and-mossy drifts in the air, and the purr of a nearby stream tumbling over rocks dances to the tune of my cherished tranquility. No, it's passion, my passion. Tranquility and passion—do they ever exist in the same thought?

We're alone in this paradise, away from the clatter of everyday life. On a grassy mound perched above a glass-like lake stands a weather-worn picnic table with carved initials and love-hearts, the promises from years past. "M.C. loves L.C., Our love forever." My transistor radio sits atop the table softly playing Frankie Valli's new hit, "Can't Take My Eyes Off of You," while an ant parade toils with left-over crumbs. And, just beyond, tucked behind a bushy area, my red and cream blanket is spread. It's the one I curl up with at home on my brocade wing-back chair. Wine glasses with the trace of crimson lipstick, a single red rose, and an empty bottle lie on the grass.

With the straps of my yellow sundress freed from my shoulders, and the pearl buttons down the front undone to my waist, I lie sprawled on the blanket. My shirtless lover leans over kissing me with passionate desire. I grasp his thick dark hair as he plants kisses on my neck and face and chest. I feel drugged by sexual urgency. How do I look to him with my long, wavy hair encircling my face, and my ecstasy impossible to hide?

I barely notice the soft dream-like glow drifting over the grassy knoll, for I am completely seduced by his muscular body and his sensual touches. Our legs entwine. I respond to my sexy lover as I melt into a vulnerable state. At this moment nothing else exists in the world; nothing else matters.

"Maaaa," a boy yells. Snap, it's gone.

The lush greenery is replaced by heavy clothes lines, abandoned toy trucks, and an old swing set. The sexy lover has vanished, a phantom of my imagination and yearning. The tattered picnic table in my imagined Eden dissolves into the chipped, but vividly painted table on the patio of our Bronx back yard. The transistor radio at the edge of the table concludes the Frankie Valli song. A basket of folded towels sits beside me and piles of freshly folded laundry are arranged on the table. I reach over and switch the dial to an Italian ballad, and then to a chirpy DJ who announces, "93.5, New York City," before airing "Yesterday" from the Beatles. Family chatter permeates the neighborhood. The serene rippling of flowing water and romance has evaporated.

It's my ten-year-old son, Johnny. His twelve-year-old brother, Louie, chases him past me, heading to the back door, knocking through a line-dried sheet, and tangling it into a bunch. The boys, just visible inside the kitchen, are screaming at each other. This is not unusual. I ignore them, wad up the dirtied sheet, and wipe my forehead with the back of my hand, just as the rambunctious boys run past me again around the side of the house. Louie grasps a baseball bat and Johnny juggles a ball and two mitts.

Everyone in the neighborhood must hear the group of boys out in the street. I clunk my elbows down on the picnic table and drop my chin into my hands. "What a fantasy," I say out loud to the swaying sheets and boxer shorts on the clothes line. I continue to fold clothes, stacking them in the basket, then, I head into the kitchen through the back door. Why rush on this dreadfully hot day? Propped up on the wall, just inside the back door next to a picture of the Virgin Mary, is the bolt of fabric for Angelina's dress. I wink at the Blessed Mother as I enter the house. She seems to be watching me, judging me. What would she think of my lustful fantasy? And below the idyllic image is a calendar with days marked off. It's Friday, June 2, 1967.

• • •

In my entire thirty-four years, I don't think there has been a Sunday afternoon that my Italian-American family has not had a traditional Sunday dinner together. There's no questioning this unspoken Sunday rule. It's never to be broken without consequence. Attendance is mandatory unless you're hospitalized on your death bed. Funny, it's my least favorite day of the week. Maybe it's because I've never much cared for cooking. Oh, I don't complain, at least not to anyone in the family. I take it for granted, being the mama that this is my responsibility. Every Sunday I just do what needs to be done. It's ingrained in my brain. First, there's mass at our parish—Our Lady Mt. Carmel over on 187th Street and Belmont, and then the family gathers. It's the same every week—antipasti to start and fresh baked bread from Terranova Bakery. There's always macaroni with fresh-made gravy, and then the roast chicken or veal from my sister-in-law, Francine's brother Giovanni's butcher shop. For dessert, it varies, there's cheese, nuts and fresh melon or seasonal fruit on regular Sundays, and if there's a special occasion, we get cannoli for dessert.

I grab my apron from the hook in the pantry, sling it over my head and tie it around my back in a floppy bow so I don't stain my floral silk Sunday dress. I fill our largest pot with water and set it on a flame on our black-and-white enamel stove. Slowly, with a worn wooden spoon, I stir a second large pot of tomato gravy, and I daydream.

Curiosity tickles my mind as I gaze into the swirling liquid. I wonder if all families are like this, with the traditional dinner and all, and I contemplate the lifestyles of some of the girls that come into Tia's boutique where I work, the ones who wear all the make-up and dress in miniskirts with their hair straight or wild. I wish I was as sophisticated as these girls. Then, I think of my signature beauty mark next to my right eyebrow. That's sort of something interesting. Marilyn Monroe had a beauty mark, but she wasn't Italian like me. Maybe I should try wearing make-up once in a while. And my hair, I'd have no idea how to fix it like they do. I just pull my thick hair into a twisted bun, even though it makes me look older, like Francine. I look over at my sister-in-law standing at the counter next to the kitchen table. We're dressed similarly except that Francine's dress size is quite a few sizes bigger than mine, and her hair is limp and streaked with grey. I keep stirring. I'll probably look like her in another ten years, but for now I'm proud to be almost the same size as my fifteen-year-old daughter, Angelina. I get a kick out of the fact that we are often mistaken for sisters. That probably has a lot to do with the fact that I'm married to a man who is forty-eight-years old—that's almost fifteen years older than me. Luigi even looks older lately, and some people might think, oh, you know, that he's the papa. If someone says something, I have to hold back my snicker or his anger might blow a hole in the roof. Funny, when we first met, our age difference was an attraction to me, but now as the years pass, he seems older and older, and I feel an uncontrollable urgency to act younger and younger. Poor Luigi feels he's had a tough life. He really is a good man. But my once romantic husband has become stout and toughened with salt-and-pepper balding hair and a pudgy stomach from all the pasta he's stuffed himself with over the years. And, no matter what he or his brother, Giuseppe, does or says, their mama, who everyone calls Nonna, sticks up for them. And, no one wants to get into it with her. Even though she's not much more than five feet and one-hundred pounds, she's a living firecracker!

Francine prepares antipasti with a scowl on her face. I can almost visualize the bitterness seeping through her pores. After all these years, I'm still not used to how she fills the kitchen with negative energy. Am I staring at her? She turns with a grimace, suddenly interested in my progress with the gravy. Yes, I'm daydreaming again. It's the stirring. I get caught up in the swirling gravy.

"Check the pasta," Francine barks.

Our mother-in-law, Nonna is always next to us in the kitchen, like she has to make sure we do everything right. Francine pulls items out of the refrigerator and hands her provolone cheese, olives, peppers, *cappicolo*, *mortadella* and *sopressata*. Nonna sits at the table in the center of our tiny kitchen and ignores both of us as she arranges the antipasti platter with one hand and grips her special wooden spoon like a sword in her other hand. Every once in a while, she carefully sticks the wooden spoon in her apron pocket and focuses on the platter. Then, she grasps the spoon like a security blanket holding it ready to attack. Yes, it's a little crazy but I think she sleeps with that wooden spoon tucked under her pillow. I always hear the boys whispering about sneaking in and stealing the spoon from her while she's asleep, but honestly, I think they're afraid of what she'll do to them if she catches them.

"The pasta, Maria," Francine stares at me with disapproval. "It's never al dente over here."

"Bah," Nonna says shaking her head.

I taste the gravy and check the pasta then wipe my hands on my apron. I can't help but notice Nonna's scowl directed straight at me. No wonder, for me, preparing Sunday dinners is not particularly enjoyable. One Sunday it's at me and Luigi's house, then the next week it's at Giuseppe and Francine's down on 185th Street. But, when the family gathers for dinner at our house, I have never felt like it's my kitchen.

Our small two-story house is just off Arthur Avenue on 183rd Street, right in the center of the Italian section of the Bronx. Vito Campisi, my late father-in-law, proudly purchased the home in 1933 with his gambling winnings. This was when he had just gotten off the boat from Italy and the men in the Bronx neighborhood were clueless of his card-shark abilities. Luigi was only fourteen and anxious to work in the new country, but his papa had other ideas for him—"an American Education." But this never really ended up happening, at least not to the extent that old Vito expected. Giuseppe was seventeen—old enough to work, and old enough to get Francine pregnant and have the first American wedding for the Campisi's. The young couple continued living in Vito's house after the wedding until there were one, and then two babies. When their second son was born, Giuseppe moved his growing family down a few blocks to their own apartment above Carlo's Candy Shop on Arthur Avenue.

This was around the time that Luigi married me. I was like a kid to him back then and he called me *Piccolina*, his Americanized teen lover. Every day he told me how beautiful I was and how he must marry me so that none of the *ragazzi* got a hold of me and spoiled my virginity. Honestly, back then, I didn't even know what he meant. As a high school sophomore, I thought Luigi was dreamy and out of this world. I couldn't help myself. At night, I snuck out to meet secretly with him. He was the most romantic man I'd ever met, nothing like the boys in school. My papa would never let me date any of them anyway, so basically, I guess you could say that Luigi was the only man I ever got to know other than my papa, and I never really got to know him. He was the silent type. And now, I wonder how much I actually even know my own husband, and what's funny is, he's definitely not the silent type.

It was just before my junior year in high school that I found myself pregnant and married, and the mama of a baby daughter. Then, as the years piled up, two sons were added to our little family. I still felt like a girl back then. When was it that I became a woman? I often think it's a trick life plays on teenage girls—to make them dream of being scooped up by an adoring husband into a fairytale life of love and happiness. Now, in actuality, I'm here, stuck in this family and it seems like no one even wants me. It seems like I never do anything right. It feels like no one cares what I feel or think, especially Luigi's mama who I've never known by any other name than, Nonna. Everyone in the neighborhood calls her that. I've given up the desire for us to get along, for her to teach me to cook, sew, and take care of a family, and for me to have a mother-in-law to confide in. Truth be told, living with her after being brought up by my own gentle soft-spoken mama, is agonizing.

Nonna, almost eighty, is especially difficult now with Vito gone, and Luigi has grown miserable having to take on the responsibility of caring for her along with me and the children. But most of all, my husband struggles with living up to his father's reputation, and striving to make Vito's beloved home our family home in the same flavor of the past. I know it's a lot of pressure but, you would think after more than fifteen years of marriage, I would at least feel like master of my own kitchen. But, Nonna remains a nosy, dominating, tough old bird. I could count on one hand how many times she's actually smiled at me over the years. Once in a while you'd think she could simply say, "good job" to me, but that will never happen. And, by the way she treats me, you would think my becoming a part of this family ruined her cherished son's life, and her life, as well.

Now that the kids are getting older, the household feels cramped—two wild boys and a teenage daughter. In the living room just off the kitchen, the television blasts the Sunday news. From the kitchen we hear the distinct, loud voices of our men, competing with the volume of the TV. Giuseppe, grayer and stouter than his younger brother, argues that he knows better no matter what the subject is. Those two brothers, for as long as I know them, have always argued endlessly, even if they feel the same way. They somehow find an argument in every little thing. But, without fail, there is one thing they always agree on, and that is their mutual desire and dream to take their families back to the town in Italy where their father, old Vito grew up. Somehow, the subject of being able to visit Italy together comes up on a regular basis, and then, as much as they agree that that is their main dream in life, they manage to find an argument in the hoped for trip to Italy someday, too.

But recently, Luigi has cooled in his bickering with Giuseppe a slight bit. Everyone feels a little sorry for Giuseppe and Francine. Their oldest son, Aldo was downed in gunfire over in Vietnam a year ago—his body shipped home in a box. That incident catapulted Francine right over the edge. Before that, her younger brother, free-spirited Carmine, who she had practically raised when her mama died suddenly, abandoned her and ran off to California to make a life on his own. It was less than a year later that the family lost Aldo. To lose her eldest son to the devastation of war can't be easy for any woman. Francine was always stubborn and critical, but now, she's intolerable.

Their second son, sixteen-year-old, Rudy sits in the living room with his papa and uncle completely ignoring their ranting, engrossed in the news on the new color television. He leans with his elbows on his knees straining to hear the current news report about the state of the country, the ongoing war, the riots in Detroit, and the hippie marches on college campuses.

"Six a' stones since a beginning of a year," Luigi says in broken English, "You know how painful is?"

"Kidney stones?" Giuseppe says with a snort. "You was a

chicken shit when you was a kid. Still a chicken shit. How can a little stone in your gut be so painful?"

Louie, a young image of his father, Luigi, and his brother, Johnny, with skinny softer features, come racing into the kitchen in a rowdy game of tag with their twelve-year-old cousin, Rocco. Louie grabs a hunk of *sopressatta* off the antipasti tray. Nonna swats at him with her spoon. The spoon becomes her weapon. You'd think it was a precious gem at times, and at other times it's her defense against the world.

"Tell Angelina and the girls to come set the tables," I tell them. The three boys run out and clomp up the stairs. In less than a minute all the kids are in the kitchen milling around.

And there, with her two younger cousins is my daughter, Angelina standing on the worn linoleum floor with her hip jutted out in defiance. I study her features for a minute as I stack the plates for dinner. Yes, we look like sisters, but her style is definitely of a teenage girl in America with her long black hair parted down the center and ironed straight; a rawhide band around her forehead. Dark make-up encircles her eyes. She wears a midriff top with no bra and a mini skirt and moccasins like in the cowboy and Indian movies. Her two younger cousins, Lita and Rosa, are her minions. In their early teens, the two cousins are still dressed in their church clothes—simple dresses with lace collars and hair combed with barrettes in page boy styles. My independent daughter's eyes signal, "Why are you looking at me like that?" I pick up the stack of plates angrily observing her outfit. Francine gawks at Angelina, too, as she carries a bowl of meatballs into the dining room. I dread the confrontation from Francine that I know is inevitable.

"You don't wear a bra yet?" Francine says to my daring daughter on her return to the kitchen, scanning Angelina's appearance from head to toe. Francine tries to fiddle with Angelina's hair, but she pulls away without responding to her aunt. "What happened to your hair?" Francine barks with disapproval.

"Ironed," she answers and her cousins giggle.

"Don't get no ideas," Francine instructs her girls with a serious expression. As the men walk in, Francine whispers to me, "Angie needs a bra. Look how big she is. It's embarrassing."

I ignore her and focus on the dinner preparations. The men mingle in the door to the dining room rubbing their bellies with hunger. Giuseppe has his arm slung over, Rudy's shoulder.

"This summer I take Rudy to work with me," Giuseppe says, "I teach him to cut a pattern like Papa taught us when we were boys."

Luigi ignores him and gives Angelina a rigid stare. "You couldn't keep your Sunday clothes on, just for a dinner?"

"It's the style, Papa."

"I won't take you to a' *Italia* like that."

"By the time we go to Italy I'll be twenty, at least."

Luigi stands rigid and points towards the stairs at the edge of the dining room. His nostrils flare and he juts out his chin. "Go up an' change. You can't sit at a table with no under-garments." Lita and Rosa watch Angelina to see how she'll react. Suddenly, Angelina's face reddens and she storms out tearing up the stairs. Luigi turns to me, "You let your daughter dress like a *putanna*?"

"I don't dress her. She's fifteen not five."

Luigi bites the side of his hand to control himself. "Aaarrrrrr," he growls. I visualize steamy anger rising out of his bulging neck. Nonna rushes to his side glaring at me like it's the worst thing in the world to speak to her son in such a tone, provoking his anger. She raises her wooden spoon and sets a stern frown on her face. Francine ushers the rest of the family to their seats. The adults plus Rudy, the oldest of the kids, take their seats at the dining room table. The three girls and the younger boys have place settings at the kitchen table, separate but visible through the open archway between the rooms.

Angelina slowly descends the stairs in a longer skirt and is clearly wearing a bra. Luigi glances at her as he takes his seat. "Head of a household," he mumbles, "Bah."

Angelina stops and stares at the adult table. "Why do I have to sit at the kid's table? I'm almost as old as Rudy."

"It just works this way," I explain in a calming manner, "with the numbers."

Nonna perks up. "Numbers?" She looks around like she's suddenly heard something interesting. No one notices her mumbling comment except me. She clutches her wooden spoon and gives me a cold stare like she's half dead. I sneer back.

Angelina pouts as she plops down in her seat in the kitchen, just as I enter and lean against the counter out of sight of the dining room table. I untie my apron and toss it on the hook by the sink, feeling defeated, like I can never please them all. From the dining room Francine hollers, "Maria, more gravy."

As I return to the dining room with more gravy, Luigi does not acknowledge me as he slouches over his plate with what I call the "eating scowl," shoveling the penne in his mouth like it's a bitter race. The pasta has to be penne at our house ever since he slopped spaghetti on his white shirt and Giuseppe laughed at him, saying that he should learn to twist it in his spoon. "Too messy like worms wiggling the gravy all over," he had snapped back. Of course, it was my fault. I should have known better.

"These kids today, no respect," Giuseppe says, "Call themselves 'freaks.' What, they think that's a good thing?" Giuseppe looks down at his plate for a minute and Francine dabs her eyes with her napkin. We all know what they're thinking. If poor Gino was alive, he'd never be a crazy "freak."

"It's the mother's fault," Luigi grumbles. "They off at a' work all day."

I skip the pasta course and finally sit down in my seat to dish up my own plate with the main course, some roasted peppers and a slice of veal. I look over at Luigi, "I work only three days a week."

"I was speaking to Giuseppe," he scolds. They all ignore me with a stinging wordless silence. The moment is forever—only the sound of knives and forks and eating in the dining room. Suddenly, Luigi slaps his utensils down and glares at me. "Not enough meat for this gravy."

That's it. I have no more appetite. No appetite for this nonsense, for this food or for any of it, just sadness in my heart. I wonder if it's showing in my eyes, but who cares. I stand up to fetch more meat. Francine attempts to get it but I motion for her to sit. Rudy reaches across the table for the cheese. He knows he should ask for it to be passed. Nonna swats him with the wooden spoon.

"Owww," Rudy says. He holds his hurt hand and glares at Nonna who out stares him with a frightening wobbly eye.

I have escaped the fury of my husband's bitterness in a kitchen that feels like it belongs to someone else. Slowly, I dish up more ground veal for the gravy, noticing the chitchat nonsense at the kid's table.

The phone, mounted to the kitchen wall by the refrigerator, rings. I reach to answer it, but Angelina leaps off her chair and grabs the phone from me before I am able to say "hello." Her reaction spurs my curiosity. I take my time dishing up the gravy to eavesdrop on the conversation.

CHAPTER 2

Angelina

Mama's listening to me like a spy, so I whisper into the phone to Celia, "Call you back later," and I dramatically slam the receiver down. She rolls her eyes and returns to the dining room.

Sunday dinner at our house is really a drag. It used to be fun when I was a kid. Honestly, I can hardly stand it anymore. My papa, you should hear him. He's at the table ranting and raving to Uncle Giuseppe accentuating his opinion with his hands.

In front of everyone, my papa bellows, "It's not right, like a *putanna*."

My own papa announces to the whole family that I'm like a slut. Oh, man. I'm standing there thinking like, is he complaining about me? I'm looking right at him with my chin up and arms crossed. I'm just so sick of this family, and they've got me still eating at the kids' table with my two bratty brothers and cousins. The boys are rough-housing around in a loud annoying argument, throwing food and stuff.

"Stop kicking me," Johnny yells to Louie. "Ma, tell him to stop."

"I didn't touch you," Louie argues, "You little wimp."

I stomp over to my seat on the other side of the table next to Lita just as Louie scrapes his antipasti onto Johnny's plate. Then, Louie smacks Johnny on the side of his head. Here we go, I think. He bends over his plate pretending he didn't do anything just as Mama returns to the kitchen to referee the fight. Johnny punches Louie in the arm and they really get into a wrestling match. I just sit there with my head plopped in my hands, bored. Mama grabs a hold of both the boys. I'm telling you, its nuts around here.

"If you boys don't..." Mama is practically in the match with them until Papa appears at the head of the kitchen table. Now they're really in for it.

Papa glares at the boys and he doesn't have to say a word for them to straighten up. But then, he turns and glares at me. Why me? I wasn't fighting and making a mess.

"God Papa, I put on a bra," I say. I'm thinking maybe it's my ironed hair. Maybe it's the headband.

"You have to talk about this female stuff in front of the boys?" Papa says with his hands balled up into fists. The boys hunch over in full belly laughs and Lita and Rosa blush.

No one "gets" me in this house. I push my chair back and stand up to leave the table. "You don't understand nothin'," I cry out.

"Sit down," Papa demands, "Listen to your papa." He puffs his chest out with authority like a general commanding his troops. Well, I'm not in his army. I dart out of the room knocking over Johnny's chair in my haste. Poor Johnny is petrified of Papa. He scurries to pick it up and seat himself. Louie reaches to jab Johnny and the bowl of gravy tips over. Papa smashes his fist on the kitchen table glaring at the kids as they quiver in their seats. I don't care what he says, I trudge up the stairs sobbing out loud, but I can still hear them.

As usual, Papa turns his anger on Mama, "Enough!" he yells and the house is silent except for Johnny's fork bouncing on the linoleum floor.

I've escaped to my pink bedroom where I can see out my window to the sidewalk in the direction of Celia's. When I spot her heading to our house, I grab the transistor radio and scoot out of my room making sure I close the door to my room with the door stopper right behind it so I'll know if the boys sneak in here to snoop around. Then, I remember. They were talking about going down the street to play ball after dinner. I tip-toe down stairs, peek into the dining room to make sure they're all finished with the clean-up in the kitchen, and I sneak out the front door and around the back to meet Celia outside. We're on the back patio when Jen joins us a few minutes later. We set up the radio on the picnic table, and soon, Lita and Rosa come out to join us.

"So, I was on the kitchen phone when you called," I tell Celia. "Mama was hanging around pretending not to hear me. She must think I'm stupid or something. She's standing at the stove dishing up something and it's like taking her half an hour.

I had to plead with her. I gave her the puppy-dog eyes and the slouch so she'd feel sorry for me. When she whispered to me, to ask Papa, I almost died, like I'm going to ask him, like he'd ever let me do anything anyway."

"Yeah, my parents, too; they were out front saying goodbye to Alberto and the kids when I called. They think I'm coming to your house to watch *Movie of the Week*."

"Jeez," I giggle, "Hope your ma doesn't call over here later."

"Naw, she won't."

Rudy comes out on the patio to join us. I have to watch what I say about our plans for later. He's sure to report back to the adults.

"Satisfaction" by the Stones comes on the radio and I leap off the picnic table. "Show me that step you were doing the other night." Celia and Jen start dancing and I join them. Pretty soon we're all dancing and even Rudy joins us.

CHAPTER 3

Maria

After dinner, I remove my wedding ring and the opal that was my mama's birthstone ring. Whenever I slip off the delicate token of my mama's love, I think of that tender moment, years ago, when she slipped it off her finger and placed it in my trembling palm. She died less than an hour later. I put both rings in the miniature ceramic bowl on the window sill like I always do when I'm cleaning up the kitchen. I scrape out bowls and sauce pans of leftover food and hand the dishes to Francine, who scours the pots and pans and washes the dishes in an overflowing sink full of soapy water. I cover and stack food in the short, squat Frigidaire arranging it with an experienced eye so the abundance of food will fit. Lita and Rosa have cleared the table and brought the final serving bowls and used dishes to the kitchen. There is no sign of Angelina to help in the kitchen, but from the patio, the sound of rock-and-roll blasts so that it's annoying to all of us in the small house. With so many people in such a tiny space, no one has much privacy and, for the most part, everyone knows what the others are up to. I just wish Angelina would join the rest of us women and help out in the kitchen, instead of sitting on the patio while the other girls are so helpful. I know Francine will rub it in my face about Angelina's behavior.

I march over to the back door and yell, "ANGELINA. ANGELINA, TURN DOWN THE RADIO." The music is slightly lowered. "Probably had homework," I say picking up a dish towel to dry the serving bowls. I try to act like it's no big deal that my once angelic daughter behaves like a demon.

"On the patio?" Francine scowls at me. "What could be so important for homework? School's out in a week."

Finally we finish the dishes and I see that Lita and Rosa have joined Angelina and her friends out on the patio. Out of the corner of my eye, I glimpse Nonna as she tip-toes through the kitchen with eagle-eyes obviously hoping no one notices her. Lately, she has become a pro at "sneaky-and-quiet." Dressed in her light spring coat, she carries the large leather handbag that Luigi got for her down in the garment center more than ten years ago. I notice her wooden spoon sticking out of the side of the bag as she heads to the back door. I spot her just as she's opening the squeaky screen door, like a dog spotting a frantic squirrel that's itching to make a run for it.

"Where you going, Nonna?" I ask. Francine looks on with judgmental eyes. Nonna's guilty expression causes me some concern especially when she scowls and waves her hand at us in a "go away" motion and doesn't answer. The door swings shut behind her. Screech and bang.

"Where's that old lady go all the time?" Francine asks. "Always in a hurry to go nowhere." She removes her apron and heads into the living room where the men are seated. I just shake my head. It's a mystery where the old woman goes, but there's no stopping her. She probably just wants to get some air; claim her independence. That's where Angelina must get it.

Luigi lounges in his worn brown leather recliner with his feet kicked up on the round foot stool. It has a circular patchwork pattern on top—the first patchwork I ever made when we were newlyweds. Everyone has their spot in the living room, like assigned seats. Giuseppe sits across from his brother smoking a cigarette and Francine, like a robot, takes her seat on the couch next to him. She picks up her canvas tote bag with knitting and begins to knit.

The television blasts a commercial announcement for the *Ed Sullivan Show*. "Stay tuned this evening for our special guests, The Doors," the announcer says with enthusiasm. A short clip of the band playing entices viewers, but certainly not the Campisi brothers.

Giuseppe snubs out his cigarette and coughs. "This show's goin' to crap."

Luigi hollers, "Maria, bring my pipe."

I bring Luigi's pipe into the room, and I stop to watch the preview of the The Doors. I'm not usually a fan of television but this new band catches my eye. I smile with interest wondering what it would be like to be a teenager—all the carefree excitement, and I'm amazed at these boys with the long hair and tight leather pants. When the announcement finishes, I glance at Francine who's engrossed in her knitting project. Funny, its 85 degrees and she's knitting a wool scarf. I return to the kitchen where I toss my gravy-stained apron over a kitchen chair and lean over the sink looking out the window. To me, the scene on the patio is more interesting than TV, especially since the men decided not to watch *Ed Sullivan* after all. The older kids are outside with Angelina's transistor radio listening to music. I hear them say it's by Jimi Hendrix. Angelina's friend, Celia, a petite Spanish girl with a new shag-style hair cut has arrived and the young cousins, Rosa and Lita appear awestruck by everything the older girls say. Celia flirts with Rudy who is definitely embarrassed that his sisters are listening to his conversation with Celia. I watch with interest and giggle to myself at Rudy's expression. The other girls laugh at Rudy who has turned lipstick-red but tries as best he can to act cool. The kids begin to dance on the cracked cement patio as another song comes on. I don't remember having this much fun when I was their age.

I look down at my faded five-year-old dress thinking how out of style I've become these days. Then, I unpin my hair so it rolls down free on my shoulders. I cock my head to one side gazing at the free-spirited teenagers and try my best to imitate their dancing from where I stand alone in the kitchen. I really try to get the step they're doing and fail to notice the back door open. It's Angelina coming in for another Coke. Now, from the patio, the radio broadcasts a news report. Hippies are declaring "MAKE LOVE, NOT WAR," as the reporter speaks in the background. The hippies chant, "NO MORE WAR" and "FREE LOVE." In the kitchen, Angelina stops with hand on her hip and snickers at me. I immediately stop dancing, or, should I say, trying to dance.

"Ma, you like Hendrix?" Angelina asks.

"Who's that?" I say.

"The music you were dancing to."

"Dancing? I wasn't dancing." I pretend to straighten up the kitchen as "Light My Fire" by The Doors comes on the radio. Who am I kidding? She's on to me.

Angelina takes my hand and pulls me out the back door. "Come on, Ma. Dance with us."

A smile sprouts on my face, with reluctance, and at first I refuse and shake my head, but, why not? What would it hurt?

Curiosity draws me out to the teen-agers. Was I ever this open and uninhibited? Or, did Luigi sweep me off my young feet and into an adult world before I had any chance to let loose?

Before you know it I'm one of them—I'm dancing freely with the teenagers on the patio. I kick off my shoes, along with Jen, Rosa and Lita, and imitate their dance moves. Rudy maintains a stiff dance style like he doesn't dare lose control of his masculinity. Angelina cranks up the radio. "Light My Fire" stirs them into a frenzy of wild dance. The girls swing their long hair to the beat, arms stretched and pumping in the air. I imitate them as best I can—mostly just thrilled to be accepted by my unpredictable daughter. When the song finishes, we all laugh and jump around being silly, hugging and teasing each other. This is probably the first time I've laughed all day.

In the corner of the yard, the younger boys toss a baseball to each other. There are four of them: Louie, Johnny, their cousin, Rocco, and a neighbor boy. The music blasts so loud that we don't even notice when the ball veers off course and is accidently hurled through an upstairs window of the house. The glass shatters. Almost as fast as the ball was tossed, all four boys dart around the side of the house dodging sure punishment. The radio music halts abruptly and the teenagers and I stand frozen to see Luigi next to the radio with crossed arms glaring. Francine and Giuseppe stand behind him by the back door with gaping expressions.

"What goes on out here?" He points up to the broken window. Everyone looks up except me. I don't even want to know. "You don't see the broken window? What kind of a wife…"

Giuseppe looks disgusted as if a crime has been committed. "We don't have this problem at our place."

Luigi turns his angry attention to his brother, "Shut up. You think you so smart." I keep my head down as he approaches me and roughly grabs a hold of my arm. He reaches his other hand up as if he will hit me. I can't help but crouch, but mostly, I feel embarrassed for the teenagers who sit quietly at the picnic table with their heads bowed. Maybe they won't be dancing so freely on the Campisi patio again so soon.

Luigi reeks of anger and frustration as if it's the most difficult thing to control; as if he could not help it if he hurt someone, specifically me. But, he has never really hurt me physically. His bark is bigger than his bite.

"I, I was, we were just dancing," I mutter softly.

Luigi stomps his feet but will not let go of me. "Dancing? Crazy. No wonder my Angelina is wild. She learns from her mama."

I feel so humiliated in front of everyone, but then my heart dances in my chest when my brave Angelina rises and hugs me, even while I'm in the clutches of her papa. "It's not fair, Papa. It was the boys that broke the window."

"Francine," Giuseppe says, "Get the kids. Let's go."

Rudy and his sisters approach the back door. Celia and Jen head off around the side of the house. Celia turns back and mouths to Angelina, "nine o'clock" and holds up nine fingers. Angelina nods as she picks up the transistor radio and slides the antennae down and in place. I pretend I don't notice.

"Where's Mama?" Giuseppe asks.

"Out for a walk," Francine answers.

"Are you crazy, woman?" Giuseppe says. "You just let her go out alone to walk?"

"Maria says she always goes…"

Luigi still grips my arm. I gaze up at him helplessly feeling like a child being reprimanded. He lets go of me with an enraged push like he wishes I'd dissolve. I reach into my pocket, pull out hairpins and pin my hair back into a bun as if it will make me more acceptable to my raging husband.

"Just like a child," he says glaring at me. "Can you do nothing right?"

Just then, Nonna creeps around the side of the house looking guilty. She stops when she sees that everyone is astonished to see her sneaking around to the back door.

"Where you been, Ma?" Luigi says releasing me. Nonna quickly darts in the back door. The rest of us follow her into the house.

Luigi stands alone, like a bewildered soul, out on the patio. He peers up at the shattered window. There are loose shingles visible along the edge of the roof and part of the gutter is coming apart. When he focuses on it, the house looks a bit shabby and in need of repair.

"Look at this," he mutters to himself. "This house is falling apart." I watch my husband from the open kitchen window in his white Sunday shirt, open enough to see his gold cross and the thick carpet of curly chest hair puffing out. His perfectly tailored black linen pants, held up by suspenders, are creased from sitting all day. He ruffles his thinning hair. It's not often that one sees Luigi's vulnerable side, but I notice it now for just an instant, and can't help thinking he looks like a lost child who has no clue how to get his own way in an argument. He's falling apart, I think, just like the house.

* * *

Once evening has fallen on our household, the kitchen is dark and the only sounds are of window fans whirling in the summer heat and the television in the living room. Angelina, dressed in a midriff top and no bra, slips in from the front staircase preparing to make an unnoticeable exit out the back door, just like Nonna. The boys are up in their room and Giuseppe's family has gone home. Me, Luigi and Nonna are in the living room in front of the television. My chair is right by the door to the kitchen so I easily spot Angelina. Our eyes meet. She halts her carefully planned escape—caught. Her eyes reveal her calculating brain as it ticks away to figure out how to get out that door. With a blank expression, I quietly rise, careful not to disturb the old grouch and his mama, as I enter the kitchen. Angelina slips outside the back door and I follow.

"Ma, Please?"

"You going to Celia's?" I ask, pleading with my eyes for my daughter to stay.

"Don't tell Papa," she says softly with relief in her voice knowing she can get her way with little trouble from me.

"Don't be late," I tell her with authority, "10:30."

"Eleven," she replies. She is already around the corner at the side of the house. I stand at the back door with my hand over my mouth. How is it that Angelina gets her way so easily with me? Luigi would blow his top.

I creep back to my seat in the living room where Luigi breaths deeply on the edge of sleep and Nonna slouches in her seat engrossed in *The F.B.I.* on channel 2. The newspaper rests in Luigi's lap. He snorts awake and picks up the paper barely skimming through the news. He rolls up the paper, tosses it on the coffee table and glances over at me. Now what, I think.

"Go turn on the news," he orders. He sounds angry, but angry at a bitter life, not necessarily at me.

I get up and go over to the television to switch the station to channel 7 *ABC News*. The grandfather clock in the hall bongs an echoing nine gongs.

"It's not on yet," I say, as the familiar music to Nonna's show signals the end of the program. "Want to watch *Bonanza*?" He mumbles something and I return to my seat.

I silently observe my husband wondering what makes him tick. Luigi likes to feel like he's the boss. He's not a mean-spirited man, but I wonder how I ended up with a man like this. I daydream staring at the television. My papa was not like this, like Luigi. My papa was so jolly. There was no TV as the center of entertainment in my childhood home. The family played Canasta or Hearts. We sang to Papa's wild and lively accordion tunes. Papa hugged all of us—my brother and sister and me and especially my sweet mama. Wasn't it natural for me to expect to have a husband like Papa, who loved his wife so much that he could hardly contain himself of joy to be in the same room with her? And, sometimes he was silly. He came home from work with maybe a few drinks in him, but there was always something to celebrate—a raise at work, a cake from the neighbors, an outing planned for the family, a gift for Mama. Sometimes he barged in on a Friday night sweeping Mama off her feet and twirled her around until she lovingly scolded him. There was lots of laughter. We thought that was how life was in a family; in a marriage. But, what happened to my marriage? Was it my fault? It wasn't always so grim and solemn and bitter.

I watch Luigi as he nods in his chair with the TV blasting and remember how romantic he had been, but that was a long time ago. He is never like that anymore. What is he so angry about? And, there's never any time alone with him. Nonna is always right there in the house. And then a silly thought pops into my head. I chuckle out loud. I quickly cover my mouth with my hand and look over to make sure Nonna isn't watching me. I'm thinking what Luigi would look like in tight leather pants and long hair. I try, but can't picture him with a guitar. How ridiculous. I decide I will talk to him one of these days, when he's in a good mood. Maybe with a little convincing, he will lighten up a bit.

I look down at my hands and notice I forgot to slip my rings back on after cleaning up, and the dancing-and-baseball drama. I step out to the kitchen again and there in the dish is the opal ring, but my wedding ring is nowhere in sight. This has never happened before. I search all over the kitchen and then, I think about the kitchen drain. Did it fall down there? Luigi will kill me for sure. It is an heirloom—his papa's sister's ring. I'll have to find it later when he's asleep so he doesn't suspect anything like, what am I searching for in the kitchen when they're trying to concentrate on TV? If worse comes to worse, I will get Mr.

Rigoletto from across the street to come over tomorrow and open up the drain, but I figure it's got to be around somewhere in the kitchen, and I just haven't noticed.

CHAPTER 4

Angelina

Celia Rubino is my best friend for as long as I can remember—all through elementary school until now, almost the end of our first year in high school. For just as long, my papa has despised her papa. From what I gather, it's something to do with Celia's mom, but Papa doesn't ever say anything about her, it's just Mr. Rubino that gets on his nerves. I say, do your own thing, whatever, but we are like sisters since day one and nothing's going to change that. Then, on the first day of freshman year we meet Jen—Jennavieve Riley, properly speaking. She hates when the teachers call her by her full name. Anyway, she transfers in from some private school down in the city and grabs our attention right away. Celia and I envy her confidence and cool style. And, to top it off, all the boys love her, and even though she turns out to be almost a year younger with tons more smarts, she's the type of girl you want as a best friend. She's perfect with the straightest blonde hair (no need for an iron), a splash of freckles on her cheeks that she doesn't even try to hide, and the guts to wear the shortest mini-skirts and hip huggers, when all the rest of us would be worrying about getting a bad reputation for being a slut if we ever stepped foot out of our Italian households in such provocative outfits. Jeez. But, the thing about Jen is she always makes you feel special, like you're the only one in the world that she can count on to be there for her, and she makes sure you know that she's there for you no matter what, even though sometimes it's not true. Celia and I struggle constantly over who's the closest to Jen, always competing for her attention and approval, but most of the time, it's just the three of us having fun together, like tonight.

It's already dark out. We meet our boyfriends, me with Ford, Celia with Carlo and Jen with, oh I forget his name, some guy that Carlo knows from Yonkers—all new relationships in the past week, but we figure they'll last all summer, if not, forever. We take the long walk to the Concourse for the D train at 188th Street. Jen wears a large peace sign around her neck on a leather strap that everyone comments on. The medallion dangles between her enormous braless breasts. God, she's bigger than me. Celia is almost flat-chested which is a lot easier, believe me. As for Ford, I'm so proud he chose me to hang out with. When I look at him, I can hardly believe he likes me. He's so tall and German and lanky with real long dark hair, like a rock-and-roll star, even cuter than Mick Jagger. And, he's so romantic always holding my hand, even now he's cuddly in front of everyone, with his arm draped over my shoulder as we wait to catch the train.

On the D train ride to Manhattan, I don't know why, but Mama and Papa come into my mind. They would kill me if they knew I was on a dangerous subway train after dark. They just don't understand that I can take care of myself. And besides, I'm not alone. I'm with my two best girlfriends and even better, I'm with Ford. Ford and I talked about it—we believe in "free love," but we're still committed to each other, as of just last week. What could ever happen to us? We're all together—all six of us. It's already after 10:00 PM when we climb the steps going up to Times Square at the 42nd Street subway station. Ford leans down to kiss me and his hand stretches down sort of feeling my breast. What is it that guys like about breasts?

News cameras roll all around on the streets, but I don't think much of it, even when they're pointed at us, except that one rolling camera comes right up in my face, directly at me. Weird. What could I possibly say into a camera that would be so important? It's a harmless demonstration, an expression of people's rights, and who would watch this anyway? No one in my family would ever expect to see me at a protest like this. To them, a disturbance announced on the news would obviously involve criminals who are trying to cause trouble in the country, like communists or rioters. To me, there's something thrilling about being involved in a movement—a bit secretive and a little bit naughty. But, Jen keeps reminding us, "It's all about standing up for our rights, our freedom of expression—to be free. It's our responsibility."

The six of us wander along 42nd Street. I'm personally more interested in spending fun-time together than participating in the current protest in the center of Times Square, but before we know it, we're in the midst of the freedom march that Jen has been ranting about. There are hundreds of chanting hippies and protesters. They encircle an open fire lit in the center of the Square displaying signs that read, "BAN BRAS" and "NO MORE BRAS" and "FREEDOM NOW!" Some carry signs protesting the war, but tonight's protest is specifically about freedom from the norm of wearing brassieres. News cameras roll out of vans and police sirens pierce the area as the crowd swells. Me, Celia, and Jen pull out our bras from our shoulder bags and dangle them in the air like all the other marchers. We each brought old bras we were going to toss out anyway. I really feel a part of this and I can see in Ford's eyes that he has admiration for me just for taking part in this cool femininity freedom stance. Actually, I probably would never be here if it wasn't for Jen, but he doesn't know that.

Pretty soon the protesting group grows sort of angry. Celia and I exchange fearful glances. Ford is a little too much into it. All the chanting evolves into a much more determined and insistent growl. "NO MORE BRAS. FREE OUR BODIES.

NO MORE BRAS. FREE OUR BODIES." Gosh, what about the war? That seems like a lot more important than a bunch of "over-the-shoulder-boulder-holders." Jen points to the spot where the majority of the fury is developing. It's in a lesbian-looking biker chicks' group. Then we see some Hell's Angels arrive on their rumbling motorcycles, loud and angry, and we decide it's time to move on.

One guy stands up on a car and yells, "Free love. Burn the bras. Burn them NOW!"

Another guy yells, "Show us your tits." Yikes!

We hold up our bras twirling them around over our heads to massive cheers from the crowd. Then, one by one, we toss our bras into the soaring fire. The police start yelling more actively trying to halt the more aggressive marchers. One of the guys must be high on something. He strips off a piece of clothing, one item at a time. First, he tosses his T-shirt into the fire with the bras. Then, he pulls out his belt and slings it across his chest like a beauty contest banner. Into the fire, he throws his torn hip-huggers. He leaps up on a turned over garbage can and strips off his underwear twirling them in the air. My eyes are like popping out of my head. I never saw an adult guy completely naked so I try to act like it's no big deal, you know, free love and all. So, the police in patrol cars and on horseback go completely wild, yank the guy down and drag him away. I don't want to admit that I'm a little freaked out. I can tell by the expression on Celia's face that she is definitely ready to leave.

As the fire leaps into the steamy night sky from the blazing garbage pail, we head away from the main craziness of the demonstration. The whole point is peace and freedom. Most of the other teenagers begin to flee the area to avoid the wrath of the riled up police officers. Some of the crowd calls them "pigs," but I think of the nice cop, Mr. Ricci, who lives on our block, and I can't see where cops get that name.

The six of us pass a neighborhood strip joint where "Light

My Fire" filters out into the street. A perfect song on a night like this I think, as we scamper away from the mob. Soon, I realize I'm separated from my girlfriends, but Ford still holds tight to my hand. We run off toward the subway station on the corner of 8th Avenue.

CHAPTER 5

Maria

It must be after 11:00 PM since the news is on TV. I avoid waking Luigi because he might somehow realize Angelina's still over at Celia's. If he had his way, I swear he'd have it so she wouldn't go anywhere, especially on a school night—and especially not on Sunday night, the Sabbath. He keeps nodding in his chair and I try to act like I'm not concerned. I slip out to the kitchen every once in a while to poke around in search of my ring. No luck, but right now I'm more interested in when Angelina will return home. She should be here any time now and I'm spooling the thread of my brain around and around to all the things I'm going to talk to her about—how she can't keep me worrying like this, and going behind her papa's back, and how can she think it's okay for a teenage girl to be out on the street this late at night. Anything could happen. Oh God, I can't even think about it.

"Lazy bunch a freaks," Luigi grunts. "A free country an' they still complain and march about with no respect. They don't know what is like to be suppressed. Huh. They don't know nothin'."

Nonna sits on one end of the couch and I'm on my wingtip chair closest to the kitchen. I ignore the news and pick up a *Silver Screen* magazine from the magazine rack next to my chair.

I leaf through and focus on a picture of Sophia Loren, like a princess, and a gorgeous Latin man handing her a jewelry box with a diamond necklace inside. I curl my legs under myself and set the magazine on my lap as I unclip my hair letting it roll down my shoulders. I visualize my own hair like Sophia's silky hair in the picture. She must have a fascinating life, I think—anything to take my mind off Angelina. I turn the page to an article about a sexy male actor in a black turtleneck sweater and slim tailored pants—an American new comer, Steve McQueen. Maybe if Luigi would lose a little weight, or alter his pants a little, but no, as hard as I try, I can't picture my husband in anything modern.

Why does Nonna watch the news so intently? She never pays attention to current events, but there is some silly demonstration on with lots of police and people screaming about something or other that mysteriously interests her. Who can figure out that old woman? Suddenly, she turns to gape at me. I try to ignore her—another one of her dirty, unappreciative looks. I leaf through the magazine with an eye on Luigi. He sits there with his feet propped up on the footstool. He snores and grunts. A commercial break from the news catches my eye. A sexy woman in her thirties looking glamorous swivels her head around to display the glimmer in her hair—a Prell shampoo advertisement. It must be so exciting to be on TV. I watch the model with envy as she says, "And, you too can look gorgeous and attractive." Around here? Yeah, right, I think. But I'm thinking of doing something new with my hair, something more modern.

I can feel Nonna's eyes on me and I slap the magazine closed. She twitches her mouth in an odd expression. "What?" I ask.

"Where is our Angelina?" she demands.

"With her friend, Celia." I get up to rouse Luigi. He is snoring so loud now that he will wonder why I didn't scoot him up to bed earlier. "Go on to bed, the news is almost over."

"I watch a' the news," Nonna says. "You don't know nothin' jus' like Luigi say."

CHAPTER 6

Angelina

Ford and I wait at the 8th Avenue entrance to the subway station for an hour, but Celia, Jen, and the other guys never show up. Finally we decide we better get back. Even Ford has a curfew on school nights. Only one and a half more weeks left of school before summer break. I'm so excited to have Ford as my boyfriend for the summer. I'm envisioning us at Orchard Beach lazing around with suntan lotion lathered all over us as we make-out on the sand and listen to music on the beach. Maybe we'll get to go to Seaside down the Jersey shore, but mostly we'll be in the neighborhood of the Bronx. We'll definitely be at the park hanging out, maybe even at the zoo, and as usual, we'll be going every Friday night to movies at "the dumps" over on Arthur Avenue. The adults don't even bother to go there anymore on a Friday—it's all kids making too much noise for them to concentrate on the picture.

Ford tries to get me to sneak into his bedroom and stay at his house but I'm looking at him like he's out of his mind. "How much of that stuff did you smoke?"

"I just wanna be near you, Babe," he says wrapping his arms around me and kissing me right on the street. I melt in his arms until a police siren speeding around the corner where we're standing startles me. It reminds me of those angry cops at the protest and I wonder if any of our cops actually use those batons they carry around.

"I'm late," I plead. "I gotta go home."

Ford walks me to the sidewalk in front of my house. He stops next to a light post and leans on it securing me in his arms for what I'm sure he hopes is going to be a feely, touchy make-out session before he heads home. I lean into his delicious body and let him kiss me. I can't resist but we're right out in front of my house. What if someone peeks out a window? I look up at the house. Good, all the lights are out. But, it doesn't feel right for Ford to grope my breasts right out here on the street. I give him one last peck on the lips and push away in a playful way and say, "See ya at school."

I creep up onto the porch and reach into the flower pot by the porch swing for the key. Then, I almost jump off the porch. The front door key slips from my hand and down into one of the slats on the porch floor—gone forever. There's Mama sitting quietly not moving an inch. She pulls me down in the swing next to her and we sit swinging and gazing up into the navy blue sky. Mama lays her hand on my thigh, turns and looks at me. I can't read her expression, but this is not like her to be sitting out on the porch in the middle of the night. And, oh God, she must have been watching me and Ford kissing out front.

"I'm not going to tell your Papa," she says in an even tone. Is she mad? She must be. I nod. "But, you are grounded for a week. Don't even ask to go anywhere."

"Ok," I say.

And just like that, without another word, we both get up and go into the house. She follows me up the stairs flicking off the lights along the way. When I'm finally in my bed cuddled up, I remember that Jen's having her end of the school year party on Friday. I'll have to figure out something. There's no way I'm missing that.

CHAPTER 7

Maria

For a brief time, before Luigi's brother, Giuseppe, met and married Francine, he dated my very best friend, Tia Stafford. It makes me laugh to think about it, and if you saw them today, you would never in a million years believe that those two ever had anything in common. My conservative brother-in-law, Giuseppe, won't own up to it no matter what. He says I dreamed it up in my whimsical head. I mean, Tia is not even Catholic, or Italian. They call her "the floozy."

But, to me, Tia is like a sister. I've looked up to her and trusted her for as long as I can remember. Plus, she lived right next door to my childhood home in the "pink house" as everyone called her unusual family house. "It was bad paint my dad bought at that cheap hardware down on the avenue," she always told us as the reason the house was not a traditional color. It was always something funny or off-beat with Tia, and even though she was two years older and two grades ahead of me, we were inseparable. In fact, it was through Tia that I met Luigi all those years ago when I was as green and naive as a cucumber. Tia said she was like a pickle—ripe and seasoned and plenty spicy. She was always a little different from the other kids in our neighborhood, being only half Italian—the other half is Irish—and she flaunted every aspect of her Irish heritage in as outrageous a manner as she could get away with. Tia was the only one in the neighborhood with bright red hair and a face sprinkled with freckles. Instead of subtly blending to fit in, Tia hennaed her hair even brighter, orangey-red. She wore the label "easy" in high school, but Tia was anything but easy. She was wild and sexy and fun to be with, but she was also as tough as day-old bread at the bakery that her parents owned on the corner of 186th Street.

She married a guy on the rebound from Giuseppe, right out of school, but she's divorced now and proper Italian families like the Campisi's consider her an outcast. I still love her because, with Tia, everything is from the heart. It hurts me the way they put her down. And, Luigi hates that I still associate with "the floozy." But she pays no mind to what anyone says. She's liberated with a free love attitude, like the teenagers. When her divorce was final years ago, she used the alimony lump sum to invest in a fashion boutique, "Do Your Thing" where she sells all the vibrant-colored and wild-printed outfits that are in style. The unique merchandise that Tia buys for her boutique attracts younger customers for the most part, not the middle-aged standard Italian, Jewish, and Irish women who frequent the other shops meant for the middle class women of the Bronx.

So, once Luigi's father, Papa Vito passed away nearly five years ago, Luigi finally agreed to allow me to work at Tia's shop, but only three days a week and only temporarily while he works out the financial issues of taking on the extra expenses now that his papa is gone. It's really overwhelming to him, to foot the bills for the entire household. He's always carrying on about it like, "We'll never get to *Italia* now with all these bills." I try not to say much or he blows his top. My working remains a bitter subject with him. He likes tradition, and a wife and mother working is not traditional. The papa works. The mama takes care of the kids and the house and the papa comes home as the boss of everyone and everyone has to listen to him and do what he says. Okay, okay, I've heard it a million times, but why does it have to be so glum?

So now I have a purpose outside the house—a place to go and be myself and to earn a little extra. Actually, I was going out of my head in the house everyday with Nonna. The kids are all in school and have friends and activities, and this is perfect that

Fifteen

Luigi finally agreed to let me work at Tia's. No matter how tired I am with the kids and the housework, I always look forward to my work days, especially now that Luigi has grown grumpier and petulant over the years.

I kneel on the floor, pinning the hem of a pair of Halloween orange and sunshine yellow bell-bottom pants on a girl around twenty or twenty-one. Tia stands with hand on hip admiring the outfit on the young girl. She nods her head, then cocks it, as if deep in thought approving of the outfit on the girl. Tia's bright hair is frizzed to imitate an afro. Her trim body, clad in the newest style, is not quite the image of the hippie-style of the youth—she's a little too flamboyant and sexy.

She swoops up one armful of garments and takes a long drag from her cigarette with her free hand. "Sexy as hell, love," she comments. "Now take those off and try on these new hot pants and this halter top. No bra, love."

Two matronly women enter the shop wearing pill-box hats and dull floral printed dresses. They begin sorting through the racks and immediately look displeased at the girl being fitted, and when they look over at Tia, one turns to the other and the two whisper to each other. Tia's sales girl, Kate, a college student working at the shop for the summer, tries to assist the women.

"This shop is going right down the drain," one woman says. "Nothin' in here for me."

"Can I help you?" Kate asks.

I guide the bell-bottom girl to the dressing room with her new fashion choices and Tia joins the older women and Kate.

"Whadya mean, honey?" Tia asks the woman. "We got the newest styles in. Don't ya wanna be in fashion?"

The second woman speaks up bluntly, "What happened to those cute dresses from Donald Brooks and Bonnie what's-her-name?"

"Cashin, Bonnie Cashin," the other woman chirps.

"They went out with Lady Bird, honey," Tia insists.

"Lady Bird's in style," the mouthier one says.

"Not anymore," Tia insists.

The woman crunches up her face, glances at her friend and the two walk out.

I've always been good at sewing. I've even made a few things for Tia over the years, so that's what I do, mostly in the back room of Tia's shop. I alter garments, hem pants and skirts for the customers, and if I have time, I sew some cute little midriff tops that Tia had me cut out of psychedelic-patterned fabric that she found down in the garment district.

After the lousy Sunday I had with the family, I'm not in much of a mood to chat, plus it occurs to me that I still haven't found my wedding ring. I know my hair is messy and I feel distant from Tia and Kate. But, even though I try hard to mask my mood, Tia picks up on it right away. She sashays into the back room a little later holding her fluffy butterscotch dog, Pumpkin. I'm at my sewing machine fixing the items that were fit on the young girl earlier in the shop. My head is down, but I can feel her eyes on me. She lovingly sets down Pumpkin and opens the small refrigerator next to the tiny café table and three chairs. She pulls out a Coke.

"Want one?" she says to me. I don't answer but can see out of the corner of my eye that Tia shrugs. She plops down at the café table with her eye on me as she chugs the Coke and plays with Pumpkin. The crazy little dog runs in circles as she rewards him with treats. "My damn ex, still tryin' to get Pumpkin," she says, "He's just pissed about me and Freddie. Thank God we never had kids."

"Thought Pumpkin was driving you nuts, biting all your boyfriends," I mumble like she's annoying me.

"Hum, nah, you know I love my little pooch." Tia pulls out a few more treats and teases Pumpkin, making him do tricks and rewarding him. "Hey, what's buggin' you, love?"

I continue sewing and do not look up at her, "Same old

stuff, Luigi's attitude mostly." Kate walks in the back room and plops down at the table.

"Sounds like you need a little roll in the sack," Kate says, "loosen the old guy up."

"That boring old man might keel over," I say like I'm ready to burst. I accidently sew the seam of the garment right off the edge and throw my hands in the air.

Tia leaps off the chair and tosses the Coke bottle in the garbage container. "Honey, you gotta get some of these new styles, spiff your hair up and put on a little make-up. That's all ya need." She pulls a rolling rack over and selects a few items for me. I wobble my head, no, just as the bell over the front door rings and the chatter from a group of customers entering the shop interrupts our conversation in the back. Kate and Tia dart out to the shop, but I can tell Tia's still thinking about me.

* * *

The best patternmakers in New York City's garment district are Italian men trained in Italy, or trained by their fathers who trained in Italy. The patternmakers, from the smallest low-priced garment companies to the couture houses with "designer" names like Anne Klein and Halston, refer to themselves as, "designers." They are the ones who design the cut of the garment. To them, the designer is all about drawing and being artsy, and the designer name is all about business. It's a proud lot, these patternmakers. They insist that they are the true creators. It's an honorable career for an Italian man like Luigi Campisi who learned the trade from his father, and these guys take their jobs very seriously.

I've been accused of being an avid daydreamer, and I have to admit, that hits it right on the button. Button, I snicker to myself. Isn't the saying, "on the nose?" Whatever. I find myself thinking about my husband and imagining him at work.

Luigi stands at his pattern-making table wearing a work

apron, white dress shirt and dark slacks—the uniform of the Italian patternmaker. He finishes his sandwich that I had packed for him early in the morning, and removes his apron, tosses the garbage in the trash can, and removes his meticulously tailored blazer off a hook near his work area. He slides into the blazer, even though its 80 degrees outside. He carefully brushes off his clothes and smoothes his thinning hair back as he walks toward the door.

Luigi walks down the street—Seventh Avenue. He joins a similarly attired group of Italian men, including his brother, Giuseppe, who hangs out on the sidewalk, smoking and whistling at girls who pass by. They joke, laugh, and talk about guy stuff, like how important they are, how good they are at pool, and about how their bosses don't appreciate their expertise. When Luigi joins the group, his fellow patternmakers slap him on the back and shake his hand to greet him. One of his pals calls out something like, "How's yer stones, Luigi?"

"Don't remind me, eh?" Luigi says. He turns to another patternmaker, "Frankie, you say you gotta cousin up by me that works on houses, repairing a roof an' stuff?"

"Yeah, Anthony Corso, lives right near you," Frankie says. "He's primo." Frankie bunches his fingers together and kisses them dramatically, then tosses his splayed fingers into the air like throwing a kiss. From the inside pocket of his blazer, Frankie pulls out a piece of paper and pen, jots down a number and hands it to Luigi.

"*Grazie*," Luigi says.

"*Prego*. Goin' to the pool hall later?" Frankie asks.

"*Si*, I'll be there."

Another guy remarks, "Oooo. Looka this. *Bella*."

Frankie and Luigi stop and watch along with the group of patternmakers as a tall blonde model walks by wearing a mini skirt to the top of her thigh and obviously no bra. The group ogles her and whistles.

Later, I envision the same group of Italian guys hanging out at the pool hall but with no blazers, their dress-shirt sleeves rolled up, and ties neatly folded and put away in their blazer pockets. Luigi walks in looking miserable, as usual. Frankie holds a pool stick near one of the two pool tables. He watches as another guy makes a shot.

"Next," he says to the guys to indicate he's ready to play the winner and he heads to a barstool.

The bartender, Tony Tucci, a typical Italian middle-aged guy with a full head of silver hair and a potbelly, wears the classic white shirt and suspenders. "What'll it be? Tap?"

"Yeah," Luigi says pulling out a five dollar bill.

"Losin' yer money to these shysters again?"

"Awwww," Luigi looks at Tony as he serves him a beer on tap. Tony stands wiping the counter and together the two watch the game of pool. The Yankees are on the TV set at the end of the bar. "Good ole baseball. These kids today, they don't know what's important."

"I'll say," Tony agrees, "My kid's got hair like a girl. Don't have no respect."

Luigi spins his bar stool around to face Tony, "An' the women, they got no business working. My mama's work was to make a nice house, to discipline the kids."

"The times is really changed, that's for sure," Tony says.

"I tell you what I do," Luigi pounds his fist against the bar. "I put my fist down. I don't put up with it no more. They gonna know I'm the boss."

"You're up, Luigi," Frankie says, "Ready to lose big?"

Luigi gulps his beer and hops off the bar stool.

Suddenly I snap out of it and rush to get out of the shop and home to get the dinner fixed. It's been a long day at work and Luigi will be home soon and hungry as an old troll. Oh yeah, I've got to call Mr. Rigoletto. Rings don't just disappear. I picture my ring lying in the bottom of that curved part of the drain under the sink.

CHAPTER 8

Angelina

I am no longer a virgin. I say it over and over in my head because I just can't believe it. It wasn't supposed to be like this. I don't even care about all the free love and stuff. I want to be a virgin and I'm not. I'm not a virgin, my insides cry but no tears will form in my eyes. I wonder why. Why does this bother me so much? Celia and Jen—they both bragged that they went all the way with their boyfriends since last summer. I guess I love Ford, but I didn't feel like he is the one I wanted to have as my first. But, I am a woman now. I'll be sixteen in a couple of months. Mama was married at my age, but I just can't picture her doing it with Papa or anyone really. It's not how I thought it would be and my heart feels torn apart. I wish Ford hadn't forced me. Maybe it would have been better if he had been more tender, but I doubt it. It didn't feel good at all. Maybe I'm different from Celia and Jen. Maybe I'm different from everyone. They say it makes you feel whole, like a real woman once you do it, once you have sex. Love and sex is all that matters once you're a woman; that's what they say.

I'm curled up on my bed so grateful its Saturday. Just for today, I don't have to go to school and face Ford and Celia and Jen. I probably look different. They'll know I did it with Ford just by looking at me. For sure, Ford will tell everyone. Can Mama know just by looking at me? And, Papa, he would kill me if he knew.

I look out my bedroom window remembering last night. If only I would have stayed home. Mama never did tell Papa about the night we went to the protest, I don't know why, but I couldn't stand that I'd have to sit in the house and put up with my brother's obnoxious games and teasing while my handsome boyfriend and all my best friends were at the party of the year. I wish I hadn't done it now, but I was itching to get out and plotting every which way I could think to get out for the night. In the end, I snuck out the back door, just like Nonna. No one seems to notice her. What I didn't think of until it was too late was that the key fell down under the porch the other night. I was out for the night whether I liked it or not since the house was locked up safe and sound.

The night started out great. I had it all planned down to the simplest detail of my every move. I even had a backup plan where Jen would call if I didn't show up by nine and plead with Mama that she needed me to come help her with something to do with her mother. Mama would always give in to something like that. But I didn't have to go that route. I had everyday slouchy pants on over my mini dress so if someone at my house saw me sneaking out I could just say I was walking over to the candy store for a Hershey's bar. I tucked high heels, a comb and my makeup case in a grocery bag behind the prickly bush by the no-parking sign out front so I could grab it on my way to Jen's, and then slip into her bathroom and get ready for the party over there. I turned my transistor radio on low in my room so everyone would think I was in there reading or writing in my diary and they should leave me alone. I made sure it wasn't turned up too loud so Papa wouldn't come pounding on the door for me to turn it down. I crept down the stairs and out the back door while they were all watching TV in the living room—even the boys, and they were so focused on the program that they didn't even notice me. Perfect, I thought.

Everything was fine at Jen's party. I shed the ugly pants and fixed my hair and makeup before any of the kids arrived, then I just let loose. I had some beers and even got to try some pot. Far out, man. Kids showed up in droves once the word got out that Jen's parents were out partying at the annual swing dance contest in Manhattan. Only thing was, Jen and Celia both had other friends sleeping over and I was stuck with nowhere to go when Jen announced that her parents were on their way back and we all had to leave. That's when I remembered the dropped key. I glanced at Ford. He was 'gone' out of his mind on beer and pot. He said he'd be my protector. He said we'd stay out all night together. But I hung around to help Jen clean up biding my time, hoping Jen would insist I stay over and make it three of us for a girl's sleepover. But her parents arrived earlier than expected and were furious that she had a party without their permission. They made us leave immediately.

All the kids scattered including Celia. I was left with Ford feeling tipsy and tired. We walked up and down Arthur Avenue six times until he insisted we go up to the tree house in the square by his house, that a fat owl sat up there hooting all night. My stomach was feeling sort of sick from the beer and the thought of somewhere to sit down and try to figure out what to do was appealing to me. I didn't want Ford to think I was a prude or anything uncool.

"Tree house?" I laughed. "Owls? I don't believe you. Where's there a tree house in the Bronx?" I had to see this. I mean, I would have rather we waited to see it in the daylight but what else were we going to do?

"Come on, I'll show you," he took my hand and we stumbled along some side streets. Then, we were in a parking area by his house. Ford went up to an old Plymouth and reached for a key positioned on the back tire. He opened the car door and pulled a blanket out from the back seat. "To sit on in the tree house," he explained.

I couldn't stop laughing. When we got to the square there were a couple of drunks lying on benches, which made me nervous.

"Is this your owl?" I laughed indicating one guy sleeping on a bench.

"You'll see," he said.

It was pretty late, maybe one or two o'clock. All I could think was that Mama and Papa were going to kill me, but it eased out of my mind when Ford led me right to a big maple with a handmade tree house built up like what a full story would be in an apartment building. Ford helped me and we climbed up into the little house where he carefully laid out the blanket for us to sit, but we didn't sit. Ford began to kiss me with intensity. At first, I thought it was with passion but when he stripped his jeans off, I knew he meant business.

"I have to go home," I said in a quivering voice but he locked his lips onto mine and stuck his tongue down my throat. He began humping his pelvis against me in a way that made me realize he had this planned before he even mentioned the tree house.

"Come on, Babe," he urged. There was no way to say no. He was on me, holding me down, pushing my legs apart, kissing me and reaching into my hot pants and touching me, pulling at my clothes. And then, I was naked with him on top of me, rutting away like those two brown dogs over on the Rigoletto's lawn that I'd seen when I was a kid. Was I bleeding? All I could think of was the two scruffy looking dogs. And when he was finished, he just rolled over like it was nothing, just like those two dogs. Ford fell asleep and I just lay there listening to the hoot of the big fat owl I never did see, and staring at the rough wood ceiling for hours.

CHAPTER 9

Maria

When I first meet Pasquale Corso and his papa, my mind is entirely distracted. First of all, I'm contemplating how to get

Mr. Rigoletto into my kitchen to dismantle the kitchen pipes without anyone realizing my ring has been swallowed by the drain, and then, I simply forget the workers are coming. Life, for me, is a frazzled mess on this particular morning. I just want to make sure they are all doing what they need to do so I can go off to work in peace. And, I'm doubly annoyed at Nonna for riling up Luigi over a simple remark I made about having to keep an eye on her sneaky behavior.

"She don't keep her eyes on nothin'," she spouted out to her spoiled son.

Now, she gapes at me in bitter judgment as she rocks in her chair by the window, seeming to get a kick out of my frustrated morning hustle. Oh man, if she knew I misplaced the heirloom ring she'd really have something to complain to her son about.

I peek out the dining room window to see Anthony Corso, a rotund man in paint-stained overalls, bumbling out of his clunky Volkswagen van. On the side of the yellow van is a purple hand-lettered sign that reads, "Corso and Sons" in really large letters, and then underneath it, "Right Up Your Alley, Roofing and Home Repairs." Anthony Corso is gray-haired with sun-tanned muscles and exploding cheerfulness. He's been around the neighborhood for years, but we've never formally met. He belts out a lively Italian ballad as he opens the side doors of the van and pulls out a toolbox and some supplies. His son hops out of the van to help his papa. I don't pay much attention to him at first. There's a bunch of sons in the Corso family. I think this son is Pasquale, the one who is around thirty. I glance back out the window. When did he become so strikingly handsome, with that dark shiny hair and coy smile? There's something in those eyes that makes me know he's up to something intriguing. I can't help but stare. He's right at his papa's side, obviously with good intention, insisting on carrying the heavy toolbox up to our front door. The fact that I'm running late slips out of my mind at the sight of this father and son team—they're like a singing comedy act.

Although it's Saturday, Luigi heads out the front door ready for work. The dining room windows are open and I am just inside the door peeking out. Luigi yells back to me, "MARIA, THE WORKERS ARE HERE." I wave to my husband so he knows I hear his command. Luigi shakes hands with Mr. Corso, greeting them at the van and then heads off to work. Then, the workers approach our front door.

My attention is on getting the kids organized before running off to work. Although they intrigue me, I'm not prepared for dealing with these guys. There's no time. Luigi should have taken the time to deal with them. With irritation, I whip open the door and instantly freeze at sweat-glistened, sexy Pasquale, who cracks an impish smile, enough to melt me on the spot. I gape at Pasquale mesmerized, as if he's the only one there. My eyes are focused on him like a deer-seeing-headlights, and a reel plays in my head—my lake fantasy of my ideal man making romantic love to me. And Pasquale too, so close he can probably smell my lavender shampoo on my still damp hair. Does he think my hair looks like Sofia Loren's? What would it be like to kiss those lips and nuzzle up with his face on my cheek, in my hair? My crazy fantasies are messing with my head. I can hardly stand not touching him, even in the warm summer heat. What's wrong with me? It's just a hand shake. But, my breath stops as he smiles and stares at me so blatantly that I blush. Is he thinking the same about me? Mr. Corso chuckles and raises his eyebrows. Then, my mind snaps to something more in touch with reality, a bit out of my infatuation as if I just now realize that Mr. Corso is there, too; that these are the father and son workers that my husband has hired.

"Mr. Corso?" I say fixing my hair and straightening my house-dress with the realization that I haven't yet dressed for work. I reach out to shake his hand. "And, your son?" I hardly dare to glance at Pasquale. Is this what they call being swept off your feet?

Angelina bounds down the stairs behind me. She eases up beside me and curiously peers out at the workers. Pasquale's eyes are glued to me like magnets. And there, moved to the porch swing sits Nonna, silent and judging with a scowl on her face. She's ready for a fight, holding her wooden spoon upright.

"Please, you an' your sister call me Tony an' this is Pasquale, my middle son," Mr. Corso says with excessive pride in his son. Angelina is stuck to my side now, but it seems like Pasquale hardly notices her with her dark make-up and orange mini-skirt.

"Oh, no..." I begin to correct Mr. Corso. Or, is he just being complimentary referring to me and Angelina as sisters? "I..." Why correct him, I think, as he swaggers back down to the van for more supplies.

"Work to do, son," he says. Pasquale does not turn to help his papa until I smile and close the front door. Then, I hear him scuttle down to the van to help.

I stand on the opposite side of the front door with my forehead up against it. Angelina stares at me like I've gone nuts. "Ma, you okay?" She holds a pile of books and notepaper. She plops it down on the dining room table.

"Yeah, yeah, go on," I say. "I have to get to work."

I glance at my tiny Timex watch that Luigi bought for me on my thirty-second birthday. Already ten o'clock. I rush up the stairs to change into a nicer dress for work. In less than ten minutes I'm back down in the dining room ready to go. I reach for my shoulder bag and loop it across my shoulder. I take a deep breath before exiting. Angelina sits at the dining room table right next to the breezy window.

"Keep an eye on the boys today and let me know if Nonna goes out."

I exit the front door flustered to see gorgeous Pasquale again. What is it about him?

And, there's Nonna with her nose in everything. She has not moved from the porch swing with eagle eyes on the Corsos.

She sticks her tongue out at me and shakes her spoon, as she eases off the swing and enters the house. Angelina peeks out the window. She has a clear view of Pasquale and his papa, and it's obvious that she is more interested in them than in studying for finals.

The Corsos already have ladders and equipment set up at the front of our house as I step out and close the door behind me. As I step off the front porch, I look up to see Mr. Corso as he climbs up on the roof. I eye them curiously as Pasquale hands him a shingle to match up to the existing ones. Now, it is Pasquale who sings, and in a crispy crooning voice so melodic and soothing, enough to up-lift any mood.

"I knew this is a' right color," Mr. Corso says barreling down the ladder, humming along with Pasquale.

I step off the porch. With an armload of shingles, Pasquale steps towards me. "What a beautiful sight on a humid day like this," he says.

"Bella," Mr. Corso agrees, "Two sisters."

Angelina and Nonna watch me and the workers from the open dining room window. "*Pazzo*," Nonna says, so sure that I can hear.

Pasquale comes up close to me as I slowly head away from the house. I'm actually quivering and I feel a blush developing on my face as he looks into my eyes with admiration, bluntly flirting. I glance at my watch, then giggle absent mindedly and turn to leave. He stands watching as I walk away down the sidewalk. He begins to sing again. I turn around to see him still staring and we wave at each other like teenagers. I walk faster with a skip in the rhythm of my pace, and then it pops in my head that I forgot to call Mr. Rigoletto. So that's why the Corsos assumed Angelina and I are sisters—no wedding ring on my finger.

CHAPTER 10

Angelina

There's something in me that wants to be a little kid again. Whatever I can do to get Ford off my mind, I do. I simply want to pretend I'm still a virgin and the thought keeps gnawing at my brain. I wonder how many of the people I see every day have gone all the way. It's so gross to think about. And, to top it off, as if I had nothing else to worry about, Mama is acting crazy. She's just not with it, and blatantly embarrassing. Usually she's easy—I can do my own thing, not like Papa who is like on a different planet. He blows my mind the way he acts. But, it really seemed like Mama was flirting with the cute worker that Papa hired. If that young worker would grow his hair and not act so Italian, I could go for him. I'm thinking, I need an older man— a guy who knows how to treat a woman. I've had it with Ford. I just think he's wacked out on drugs or something. I may be into free love, but I'm not ready to have real sex with him on a regular basis, that's for sure. Doesn't he get it? He's just too immature like most of the boys in school. This Pasquale guy would get it. Man, look at how he was looking at Mama. I'll have to mention it to her when she gets home. She just doesn't realize what guys are like these days.

I open my algebra book. On Wednesday is our last test of the year, then, summer and the fun begins—the concert over in Van Cortlandt Park—to start with next weekend. Oh darn, then I have to deal with Ford. I sort of wish he'd disappear.

I'm just getting started on the practice questions when Nonna comes over and sits at the table right up close to me. She's practically suffocating me; she's so close. I push away from her, but then, she leans over and whispers in my ear like there's a room full of people who might hear, "I make a deal with you," she says with authority in her raspy old voice.

I look at her quizzically. "Whaddaya mean?"

"Your Nonna, she knows everything. Wanna me to tell your papa you was at a criminal meeting in a New York City burning your underwear?" I pull away, my eyes wide like I see a ghost as I shake my head. "Good," she says, "I go out now." I keep gawking at her as she slowly rises, picks up her spoon and purse and heads to the back door. As she exits, she glances back at me with narrow eyes. She scares me sometimes. Did she see me on TV at the protest? "Our little secret," she instructs waving the spoon as the screen door slams. And, I take it I'm supposed to keep it a secret about her going out. Maybe she's doing it with a crotchety old boyfriend. Yuck. I can't believe I could even think that. That would never happen in a million years. Oh man!

I lean over my book bored, with my head propped on my arm. I just can't get into algebra. I can't concentrate with the voice of Pasquale singing outside. It vibrates through the house blending in with the whizzing of the fan in the dining room window. At least he could sing something from the Doors or the Stones, and it would be more fun. I decide to skip algebra and turn on some rock-and-roll. I peek out the dining room window, and there goes Nonna quickly hurrying away. I pull my transistor radio out from the dining room chair where I tucked it next to me. I set it on the table, and flick it on. I watch myself with critical examination in the gold-trimmed mirror over the buffet cabinet and practice a dance step that Celia taught me. The mirror has Nonna's rosary draped over the decorative center of the frame. I remove it and sling it around my neck so that it swings from side to side, like the peace necklace Jen wore the other night, as I dance to "Paint it Black" by the Stones. I stare at my image repeating the mantra, "sinner, sinner, sinner" instead of the real words to the song, but when a commercial blurts through the airwaves, I switch the radio off and peer out the window at Pasquale as he climbs up and down the ladder singing that Frank Sinatra song that Mama likes. I'm annoyed by his boisterous voice, but I'm curious about him for some crazy reason. He's definitely not a "freak" or anything close to the boys I usually like. I dangle the rosary back on the mirror and go to the kitchen where I pull cookies out of the bread box and arrange them on a tray. I mix up a pitcher of lemonade with lots of ice and arrange everything on a tray like Mama would do. Hoisting the tray, I gaze at myself in the mirror before heading out the front door to where Pasquale and Mr. Corso sweat in the blazing sun. It might be fun to have an older boyfriend for the summer, but Pasquale would never be interested in me. He looks like the type who would not settle for any girl unless she was pure.

"Come sit in the shade for a cold drink," I holler up to them.

• • •

I must be really bored, you know, to sit with the workers and see what they have to say. But then, I've got my eye on Pasquale and I'm thinking he really looks too much like a greaser, definitely not with it. I wonder if he's married and if he ever went all the way with a girl, so I sit with them for awhile at the picnic table in the back as they munch every single cookie and drink the entire pitcher of lemonade. I purposely give Pasquale my Raquel Welch smile, the one Jen says you can hook any guy you want with, and I stick my chest out, but all they talk about is the different grades of shingles and how to tell how old they are on a roof. Boring. He's probably been doing it with girls for years and is sick of it by now.

CHAPTER 11

Maria

Tia glides around the shop wearing my favorite bell-bottoms, the purple ones with orange piping down the side and double pleats from the knee down to her ankle that open up in bright orange to match her front-tie sleeveless blouse. Even though I would never dare to wear anything that comes close to resembling this outfit, I love how she flaunts herself in such extravagant style. It makes me smile just to look at her. She breezes into the back room and lounges at the café table like she's on a beach chair in some exotic location. She kicks off her Keds, replacing them with leopard platform heels. I'm a little late and flushed from hurrying to work, and without realizing it, I'm humming. Me humming? These days, that's a rarity, to say the least. Tia fixes her hair in the mirror and spots my reflection behind her. Our eyes meet and she smiles, whips around, places her hands on my shoulders (with the platforms, she's now a head taller than me) and raises an eyebrow, determined to peek into my mind.

"So, what're you glowin' over?" The intensity in her eyes jiggles my brain. She'll get every single detail about the cute worker out of me. "A few days ago you were down, practically to the soles of your shoes, love."

"It has to be something?" I say sliding into my sewing apron as I sit down to work. "I can't just be in a good mood?"

Tia struts over to the door to the outer shop and I pretend I'm not paying any attention to her as I turn on my sewing machine. "Oh, Tia, those new outfits you got in last week..." I look up at her.

"Yeah?" she says with her hand on the doorknob.

"Maybe I'll try one."

"Sure, doll. Get the old guy's motor runnin'." She opens the door to the shop and turns to wink at me before exiting.

At lunchtime, Kate comes in the back for a break, followed by Tia with an armload of clothes. I'm wondering what I'd look like in an outfit like Kate's—a simple pair of black hip-huggers with a daisy-printed peasant blouse. She looks stylish but not so loud like Tia. The three of us take seats at the café table for lunch. I pull out a homemade sandwich from my paper bag. Tia grabs sodas out of the fridge for all of us. Then she lounges on a stool fanning herself with the *Cosmopolitan* magazine that must have arrived in today's mail.

"So, you and Mr. Grumbles get it on this morning?"

"You kiddin?" I say chomping on my sandwich. "That stuffy old man was wrapped up with the contractors."

"Contractors?" Kate wiggles her shoulders in a figure eight. "Any cute ones?"

"The son is handsome, around thirty."

"Wanna fix us up?" Tia asks as she opens the Tupperware lid of her homemade salad. "I'm sick to death of Freddie humpin' me. Thank God I'm on the pill."

Everyone knows the birth control pill is taboo according to the Pope. "Tia, really," I say.

"Let me guess," She positions her pointer finger on her chin. "The son's sexy and charming and he's what put a smile on your face."

Tia and Kate giggle as I blush. I wad up my wax paper and bag and toss it in the trash can. Both of them watch me like I'm gonna do a magic trick or something. I pull out some new outfits off the rolling rack by my machine. Tia and Kate watch me as they leaf through *Cosmopolitan* and *Harper's Bazaar*.

"Go ahead, try 'em on, doll," Tia says.

I unzip my baggie old-lady dress and let it fall to the floor.

I slip on bright colored bell-bottoms and a sheer swirly-printed Indian top. I spin around to model the outfit for the girls like I'm the lunchtime entertainment. I stop and look down at myself, suddenly uncomfortable.

"I look like a clown."

Tia leaps off the stool and straightens the top on me. "Like this," she corrects. "Honey, you look just fab. It's about time you get with it." She searches through the rack and pulls out a Pucci printed dress; not quite a mini but still pretty short with a key hole opening at the neck. I hold it up to my body and admire it in the mirror. I can't imagine walking into my house in something like this. Luigi would think I'd lost my mind. He'd blame it all on Tia, of course.

A rain storm rolls in and the boutique is pretty much deserted for the rest of the afternoon. Kate is itching to leave early and Tia has piles of paperwork, so I just stay around trying on the new styles, just to see how silly I look in some of them, even the hot pants with big wide black patent-leather belts. I feel like a kid in her mama's closet trying on clothes that I know I can never wear. Funny though, after a while, some of the garments feel right to me and I look at myself in the mirror with my baggie old dress and decide it is time for a change.

• • •

The storm passes on Sunday night littering the neighborhood with trash cans and garbage along with dead branches and all sorts of debris, but the glorious sun makes everything sparkle when Pasquale pulls up in the van alone to work. Luigi has already left for work and I'm there getting the kids off to school—only one more week. Angelina opens the door in her shortest plaid mini and a low cut top that I've never seen before. She must swap clothes with her girlfriends—there's always a new outfit on that girl. When Pasquale peeks in from the front door, he sees me and smiles. He doesn't seem to be interested in my sexy young daughter. He steps inside the door boldly.

"My father is sick. He goes to the doctor today so I will work alone."

"Gee, sorry," Angelina chirps. "Will he be alright?" I turn away and step into the kitchen but can still clearly hear their conversation. I'm afraid Angelina will see my expression or the heat oozing out of my pores at the presence of this sexy man.

"Oh, sure," Pasquale says. "It's an asthma attack. He's had them before."

From the kitchen I say, "Angelina, it's time to go."

"I'll see you this afternoon," she says to Pasquale like he'll be waiting here just to see her. I step back into the foyer as she leaves. The boys are already down the street tossing the baseball back and forth as they head towards school. Angelina turns to wave at Pasquale, and standing just in the doorway, I can see him checking her out from behind. Obviously, he did notice. He wipes his forehead with the cloth from his back pocket, then, he ties it as a kerchief around his neck.

I busy myself around the kitchen all morning with the faint melody of Pasquale's singing in the background making it very hard to ignore that this gorgeous man is right outside working. I check the calendar by the back door. My work days are marked along with important reminders, but for today there is only noted, "Nonna to Francine's." I peek out at Pasquale going up and down the ladder with shingles and begin preparing lunch with a smile smeared on my face like I've been into something forbidden. I pull the big tray, with the map of Italy printed on it, off the top of the cabinet and begin arranging dishes of food on the tray to take out to the picnic table. And then I remember my ring. I've been hiding my left hand from my husband so he doesn't ask why I'm not wearing my ring. I pick up the phone and dial Mr. Rigoletto. It's a perfect day for him to come over and check the drain, and yes, he says he'll be over in a few hours.

Fifteen

When the lunch is ready and the dishes and silverware are all set on the tray, I untie my apron and toss it over a chair before examining the tray of food—a basket of bread from Terranovas, antipasti, vinegar and olive oil, sliced cheeses, a plate of grapes, walnuts and chopped apples. It needs something. I take a small crystal vase off the window shelf and fill it with water. I zip out the back door to the lilac bush at the end of the yard and break off a couple of clumps of the fragrant flowers. Pasquale sees me from up on the roof. He stops and waves. I crane my neck to look up at him and shield my eyes with one hand. I yell up, "I made lunch if you're hungry."

"Starved," he says vigorously.

"You can try my family manicotti recipe."

Pasquale puts down his tools and wipes his hands on his coveralls as he gazes dreamily at me from the roof. As he rushes down the ladder, I dart in the back door, plunk the flowers in the vase and tuck a little sprig behind my ear. I carry the tray out the back door. Pasquale rushes to my side to relieve me of the heavy tray and I inhale his fragrant perspiration. It's not distasteful to me. He smells like a real man, the kind of man who could do anything.

"Nonna's over at Francine's today and there's plenty of food," I say as if it's an apology.

"Lucky me," he says untying the cloth from around his neck. He wipes his forehead and I pretend not to notice his perfectly cut muscles along his torso and shoulders. He removes his coveralls to reveal his glossy, sweat-covered muscular body even more revealing in his tank top and shorts. I hurry to the kitchen through the back door for the manicotti that I managed to forget. Crazy, I think, but I don't stop for a minute to reconsider my sudden lunch plan. I dart back out with the main course and there is Pasquale by the hose at the back of the house. When he turns it on, water squirts him in the face. He holds up the leaky hose to show me, then, washes his hands and face. He stops to straighten the small statue of Mary near the hose before sitting at the picnic table across from me.

"After we eat, I will fix that hose," he says.

"That would be nice, but eat now and relax." I am so nervous, afraid I will mess up a simple thing like dishing out our food. But, how silly of me. Don't I serve food to my family all the time? And then suddenly, maybe it's the way he's so carefree and easy. It seems so normal and comfortable to be sitting there as two friends enjoying a jovial conversation over lunch. I exhale all the tension out of my body and smile across the table at him.

"You're singing all the time, so beautiful. What a lovely voice you have."

"It's my passion," Pasquale declares with zest. "If it was possible, I would be a singing sensation. But, so far I only perform at Telly's Restaurant on Saturdays. You should come."

"So, if you are so crazy for singing, how did you get into this roofing business with your papa?"

"Oh, it's more than roofing. We do gutters and siding and, you name it. My papa's dream was to have a business with his sons. We are five sons, all of us born in Italy except the youngest."

I nibble at my manicotti but the conversation is much more interesting than any delicacy could possibly be on this glorious day. Well, I don't know about interesting. It's just that Pasquale is interesting to look at, and it's not just his appearance. He's got something I yearn for. He's got passion for life.

"How old is the youngest?"

"Gino is almost eighteen—still in school. I am the only son who works with Papa."

"Your papa must be so happy," I say with sincerity. "And, what about a wife? Are you married?"

Pasquale lays down his fork and turns his face away so that I get a perfect view of his masculine profile. "I was to be married just six months ago. But, our relationship is broken permanently."

I look down at my plate feeling embarrassed. Was I too inquisitive? "I'm sorry."

His eyes are away and down but then like a light switch is turned on, he brightens and smiles at me. "It's my dream to have a lovely wife just like you."

There is a moment between us that could have been a fraction of a second, or it could have been a lifetime. I know it isn't just me. It is electric and I absorb it, some of that zest.

Then, he picks up his fork and continues to eat. "I am so sorry. I have talked only about myself. What about you? Your family, what about them?"

What can I say? Does he really think I'm Angelina's sister, Luigi's daughter? But, it's only lunch and we're just talking about our families. "My mama died eight years ago," I absentmindedly blurt out. It is the truth, but the real truth about this family, the family that Pasquale is working for, is that it's a family where I am the mama. The mama, it sounds so old and finished, set in a fixed life of hum-drum. What is fulfilling about being the mama? More work, that's what. So, even if for only just a little while, I continue letting Pasquale believe that I am the daughter and I tell myself that it's okay. I am my dear late mama's daughter.

"So much for you to bear—a young sister and brothers. You're like a mother to them and you're such a beautiful young woman."

How can I tell him he's mistaken? I turn away. "You don't have to say that."

"But it's true. You remind me of…" He has finished and wipes his face with the cloth napkin as he stares at me. "Oh, never mind."

I allow myself to glance at him and our eyes meet again. He is smiling in that devilish irresistible manner of his.

"Well, thank you." I believe he can read my thoughts of overwhelming embarrassment.

"I should fix that hose now."

I stack the leftovers and plates onto the map-of-Italy printed tray, and he carries it to the back door for me like a perfect gentleman. I open the back door and he brushes against me initiating a shy smile from me. He sets the tray down on the counter below the large crucifix on the paneled wall near the dining room entrance. Before he exits to finish his work, we stare into each other's eyes with a rare yearning. And then, he is gone, out on the roof and all that I have left in the house is the resonance of his harmonious voice singing.

I'm cleaning the dishes when there is a knock on the front door. Pasquale, I think, and rush over to whip the door open with a smile, but there is Mr. Rigoletto. For the next hour I'm puttering around while he dismantles the pipes under my kitchen sink. There's no ring, now what?

CHAPTER 12

Angelina

I know it's wrong to go all the way before you're married, and I feel awful that I did it with Ford. I don't even like him anymore, at least not the way I thought I did. This summer was supposed to be so much fun. Everything is already ruined, and school's not even out yet. My stomach is actually sick. I'm wondering if going all the way can give you the flu, but maybe it's just the feeling of guilt and sin.

The creepy feeling of confessing to the priest clobbers me on the head as soon as I close my eyes to go to sleep at night. I end up sitting up reading old Nancy Drew books from when I was like twelve, just so I don't think about dealing with my worries. I still haven't confessed at church or to anyone else except Celia and Jen, but even though they asked me a million questions, they act like it's no big deal. Why do I feel like they never really did it with anyone? And, I don't really explain to them that Ford forced me. I don't dare tell them that if it had been my choice, I never would have gone all the way, especially not in a creaky old tree house with spiders and splinters and owls. What about the romance of making love? I think about the princess stories from when I was a kid—Cinderella and Snow White. I'll bet their gallant princes never even thought to mess up their beautiful dresses and steal their virginity in some bug-infested shack. Anyway, at Sunday mass, Father Milani preaches that we must forgive those who have caused us harm. I guess Ford caused me harm. It doesn't feel like something good, that's for sure. All the way home I think about what he said at mass, and now, in my mind, it's clear; I must forgive Ford. It makes me feel a little better, but that doesn't mean I want to go all the way with him again.

    We're all supposed to meet at the park after morning exams today. There's me with Ford, and Celia and Jen with Carlo and Pauly—this is the group that us girls thought would be the perfect summer group to bum around with. Funny, now I can't get it out of my mind about Celia and Jen, wondering if they actually did it with anyone. They are so evasive when I tell them about Ford, kind of easing off the subject when I ask. My enthusiasm for all the plans we had kind of fizzles. What made me think it would be fun hanging out with these guys anyway? It was just last fall when school started that I thought Ford and his friends were way too stuck up. First of all, I never thought he'd go out with me, figuring him for a guy who'd only date cheerleaders and that type. Why can't it be just the three of us girls? It's always so much more fun to be meeting new guys than to be stuck with one, especially one you don't really feel like you love.

I'm almost in front of Jen's house repeating the mantra in my mind to get over it or it'll ruin the day. I dash up the steps of her apartment building and ring the buzzer. Mrs. Riley answers like she's not expecting me, and when I ask for Jen, she says that Jen left like half an hour ago. Was I supposed to meet them at Celia's? No, Celia was spending the night here with Jen. Neither one of them had the history exam in the morning since they're both in Mrs. Wismer's class in the afternoon, and I hadn't seen them all day at school. I figure it must be me that mixed up the plans. I think about it, how I didn't even bother to confirm our plans, and how I'm so upset about Ford, that I didn't come to the phone when he called, like two dozen times in the past couple of days. I figure the best thing will be to tell him today at the park that I forgive him and that I'm not interested in doing it again.

I practically run all the way to the entrance of the park, and in the process, almost get run down by a car on Southern Boulevard. Celia and Jen are at the edge by the southern gate, and oddly enough they don't acknowledge me at first, like they aren't expecting me. When I run up to them complaining that I almost got killed, Jen snaps at me.

"Trader!" Her arms are plugged in at her hips like Mrs. DeLucci in algebra. "So, you're playing a game with Ford. What's that all about?"

"I told you, I don't think I like him as much as I thought."

"Oh, so you're a slut, then?"

I look from Celia to Jen. "Whaaaat?"

Celia hunches over and drops down on the bench by the ticket booth. "Thanks to you, Ford convinced Pauly and Carlo to go off and meet some other girls at the zoo; at the zoo for Christ's sake. God, Angie, what the heck did you do with him?"

"What did I do?"

Jen comes over in my face. "They all want a try at you now. Did you have to be so sexual? Where did you learn all the stuff to do anyway? We thought you were so naïve and all."

"Are you kidding? I don't know anything. That was my first time ever."

"Right," Jen says, "that's not what Ford said."

Tears are streaming down my face now and I can see that Celia feels bad for me. She comes over and puts an arm around me. "Really?" she asks.

"Oh come on," Jen storms on. "Ford said you weren't meeting us today cuz you wanted to do it with some guy you met down in the city. It better not be that cute guy we met on Easter break, just because he took both our numbers."

"What? That is so not true what Ford said," I say through gasps of hysterical tears. I pull away and head off away from the two girls I thought were my best friends. How could they treat me like this? How could they believe creepy, Ford?

Celia comes after me and I can tell she believes me and is there for me like she has been since we were kids. But, I'm out of my mind upset that they've turned on me like this. Jen follows and seems a little sorry at this point, too. Celia gets a hold of my arm before I dart out in traffic again, this time on Fordham Avenue. She forces a hug from me.

"I know you didn't do all that stuff Ford said. He's just jealous you wouldn't answer his calls."

"How could you believe him?" I whimper to Celia and give Jen a nasty look.

"I didn't really think you did anything," Jen admits. "He just got me so mad because Pauly would rather go off with him to flirt with girls. He was like, 'Free love, Baby.'"

"Those guys are just a bunch of jerks," Celia adds, but I know she really likes Carlo a lot.

I can't believe how messed up our plans for the summer have managed to get from my situation with Ford, and I'm feeling so sick now. The day is ruined, maybe the whole summer, and I just want to go home. They walk me all the way apologizing. They even try to get me to go over to the baseball diamond and check out some different guys for the afternoon, but I'm thinking that's all I need, to feel like crap and run into my bratty brothers to deal with on top of everything. I opt for spacing out in my room.

Nonna rocks in her chair by the dining room window eyeing me when I walk in. By the way she watches me I realize that she must know I'm not a virgin anymore. Well, the hell with it, she's not either, and I still find that almost impossible to believe.

Celia's at mass the next day and all nicey-nice to me. She acts so concerned about how they treated me yesterday, and I actually feel bad. I hope Carlo still likes her. Of the three guys, Carlo is the nicest one, but I don't really know Pauly that much except that he seems really swayed by whatever Ford says even though he's Carlo's friend from Yonkers. And, I don't know what the big deal is with Jen. She dumps a guy almost every week. What she sees in that Pauly guy, I have no idea. And, Ford, I know he has a big mouth, but who would have thought he could be so mean. He seemed like a nice enough guy—probably a little too cool for me, but now, I could care less. The best thing would be if I never saw him again.

I'm sort of glad when Celia asks me over for Sunday dinner since I can hardly stand to face Papa and Mama lately, these days after. It's like the days before and the days after. God, how can girls stand it? Maybe that's why some girls become nuns. This is like the first time I ever miss Sunday dinner, and with Papa, you'd think I committed a crime. And then I think, oh man, is having sexual intercourse at fifteen a crime?

At Celia's we talk about the boys. "Jen's at the park with Pauly."

"I thought they dumped us cuz of me and Ford. So, she's not mad anymore?"

"Ford told her he was sorry for yesterday and he really likes you."

"So what. He's a jerk."
"You didn't think that last week."
"That was before I knew him, before, you know."
"Did it hurt?"
"I thought you did it before? Don't you know?"
"Yeah, it hurt me a little. I just wondered how it was for you."

I could tell she never did it. She was way too inquisitive trying to pry information out of me. "Come on, Celia, did you really do it?"

"Sure I did."

"Really?" I say like I'm missing something here, and then she softens. She plops down on her bed and crosses her legs. We're in her bedroom with the door closed and her family is down stairs chattering away at the dining room table.

"Don't tell Jen," she looks seriously into my eyes. "I never did it. I was scared to, and I said it was with that Tony Raffela, but I couldn't stand kissing him. His lips were stale and his breath smelled like cat litter."

I roll on her bed in a fit of laughter. I love Celia. I don't think she'd ever do anything to purposely hurt me.

We're laughing so hard like we have lost control of our bodies and then suddenly out of the clear blue sky, Celia gets all serious and sits in the middle of her bed and stares at me.

"What did you tell Ford about Jen?"

"About, Jen?"

"Tell me. Seriously. Ford told Pauly, and he told all of us that you said Jen can't live without doing it every day, and he went into detail of what you said she liked to do, you know, naked."

"Celia, I never said anything like that to him. I would never do anything like that." I get up off her bed and reach for my shoes that have slipped under the bureau. She jumps off the bed and takes my arm.

"I knew you didn't say that. It's just that Jen was embarrassed and when he told us, and you weren't there and, you know, it made her look like a slut."

"Right." I get it, how Celia and Jen would have been upset. I put on my shoes anyway. "I didn't say a thing about you or Jen."

"I know," she said. "I really do like Carlo, though, and Jen—I know she likes Pauly. You think you can forgive Ford?"

"Yeah, I guess, if it means that much to you."

And, just like it was all planned out, Ford is suddenly a gentleman again all full of apologies to me like he didn't know what got into him, and he tells me that I mean the world to him and we can't ruin the whole summer's fun we had planned. I agree to just hang with them. But, I decide to make sure I don't catch myself in a situation where Ford will have any chance to try any intimate things with me again.

• • •

School's out for the summer. A few days later, the six of us are down at the park hanging out together like nothing happened between me and Ford—not like I'm still a virgin, but, the fact is, I'll never be one again. What is crystal clear is that Ford likes to get high on just about any substance from pot to booze to his grandmother's pain killers, and he really likes it when everyone around him participates. I guess it makes it all okay to him if everyone else gets all messed up, and so he's stoned most of the time. I don't know why I never picked up on it before. I realize that's why he forced me to go all the way. He says he couldn't control himself that he was just too out of it. Actually, that's probably the truth.

Things never do get back to normal between us. I try to make it seem like everything is cool, especially for Celia's sake. But, that first afternoon when I realize it is getting high that causes Ford to be like a Jekyll and Hyde personality, that's when

I see things more clearly. We plan to go see *Bonnie and Clyde* at the movie theater, "The Dumps," on Arthur Avenue. Ford is so out of it, it's like he forgot his promise to treat me with respect. First, he almost passes out while the movie is playing, then Pauly gives him a bottle of Apple Jack wrapped in a brown paper bag and he drinks the whole bottle during the second half of the movie. That's when he starts mauling me right in the theater. His hand is inside my blouse and he's pinching me really hard right on my left breast. I almost start to cry so he pulls his hand out and sticks it down my pants and suctions his mouth on me all slobbery so I can't scream and his tongue smelling like sour fruit from the Apple Jack is jammed almost down my throat. I am able to pull away when the lights come on but tears have formed in my eyes and when I glance over at Celia, it's obvious that she knows something is wrong between us. I decide right then and there that it doesn't matter about having a fun group to hang around with all summer. If Celia and Jen are really friends, they will understand.

CHAPTER 13

Maria

I step out on the backyard patio and notice a robin's nest tucked away in the curve of the drainage pipe that runs along the brick wall of our house exterior. And then I notice the neatly rolled up hose that Pasquale recently repaired. It's so early in the morning that no one in the house is up except me. I couldn't sleep. It wasn't the tossing and turning type of sleeplessness, more like exuberance and anxiety for the day to start. I sprawl out on the picnic table gazing up at the early morning sky, watching the summer clouds bumble and toss around. That's what I did as a kid. I got up before everyone, snuck into the backyard and stretched out on the potting bench where Papa used to transplant tomato plants. All summer those tomato plants lined the windows in our sunny back room. If anyone in my family saw me out here laying on the picnic table daydreaming like a kid, they would think I lost my marbles. At the thought, I pop up and notice the nest just as the mother robin lands on the edge with a long slimy worm. Baby birds chirp so loud they rouse the black and white tomcat from next door. I'm thinking and thinking and I can't figure out where my wedding ring could have gone. I get up off the picnic table and ease into the fresh early morning kitchen. I search around the sink, behind and in everything on the counters, on the floor, everywhere. I have done this a zillion times in the past week or so since I lost the token of my marriage and I'm still baffled.

Later, at Tia's, my mind drifts to Pasquale as I sit sewing at my machine. I don't realize I'm humming until Tia walks in from the outer shop. She has a large bag of take-out from the deli. I can smell the fresh ham and pungent cheese. I flick the off switch on the machine and join her at the table for lunch, but I have my own lunch packed from earlier in the morning. I pull it off the shelf and open up the bag. Dreamily, I munch on leftover manicotti with my eyes closed and when I open my eyes, Tia is gawking at me like I'm crazy.

"What?" I say.

"What?" she says. "What'd you put in that lunch?"

"Leftover manicotti from yesterday's lunch," I say.

"You had lunch at home with the old girl?"

"Nonna?" I ask. "No, I shared lunch with the worker I told you about."

Deli meat and sliced tomatoes drop out of Tia's sandwich splattering all over the table and floor. She gets up for a paper towel to clean up the mess without taking her probing eyes off me.

I take another bite and answer with a half full mouth. "It was just lunch."

Tia sits back down and sips her soda. "Tell me the details. I'm sure the butter was meltin' on the table."

"We just talked and talked," I say like it is absolutely nothing. "He thinks Angelina and I are sisters. Can you imagine?"

Tia nods her head like it's a bobbly doll. "Uh, yeah. And, you didn't tell him?"

"Oh, I will."

Tia dumps her sandwich remains in the take-out bag and opens a Twinkie all the while watching me with her brows raised. She takes a big bite consuming half the Twinkie and shakes her head. "Oooo. Weee. Talking, huh?"

• • •

It's our usual Friday night dinner of baked sole. I will grill some zucchini and toss a green salad, and of course, we always include a heaping bowl of Penne with gravy. I have most of the dinner prepared ahead of time. Friday's are a little tricky and I certainly don't need to listen to Luigi's whining and complaining. If I don't leave the shop a little early and Luigi doesn't stop at the pool hall, then he's home before me, and that puts him through the roof. He likes to smell the food cooking when he walks in from a hard day of toiling over that damn patternmaking table.

I try to get back ahead of him, but he beats me to the house. I enter through the back door, just in case he's home so I can go right in the kitchen and be cooking before he notices. Sure enough, I hear him, in unusual jovial conversation and laughter in the living room. I quickly ease into my apron and turn on the stove. Then, I peek into the living room. I almost slip to my knees. There is Luigi and Pasquale each drinking a beer and talking like old friends. Angelina is there on the couch just listening and the boys dart in and out excited asking baseball questions. They're asking Pasquale like he's an authority.

Nonna's eyes are closed and she sits snoring in her chair.

"Maria," Pasquale stands up.

"Pasquale's staying for dinner," Luigi announces.

"I, I, I'm making dinner," I mutter. I turn my back and close my eyes. He thinks I'm the daughter. I stay in the kitchen and cook, trying to figure my way out of this one. I'm a thirty-four-year old woman, a wife, a mother. I should know better than to play games.

In a little while, Angelina comes to help in the kitchen, a miracle in its self. I can't look into her eyes and I realize that I'm snapping at her. "Set the table," I bark. "No, this bowl for the gravy."

Once the dinner is ready and set out on the table, I tell Angelina to seat everyone in the dining room. Pasquale is directly across from me on the right side of Luigi with me on Luigi's left. I try not to look at him, but I can't help but notice how handsome he is all washed up and changed from his work clothes. The words are all caught up in my brain, the laughter and conversation between the two men, Luigi and Pasquale. The boys are unusually quiet and well-behaved listening intently to Pasquale like he has placed some sort of trance on them. Angelina sits next to Pasquale on the opposite side of where I sit with the two boys, and down at the end is Nonna with her wooden spoon. Angelina leans toward Pasquale so that their arms touch. I widen my eyes and then narrow them making eye contact with my foolish young daughter. I give her a "watch yourself" warning glare, and then revert to keeping my eyes down and my mouth shut.

"The roof looks good," Luigi praises. "You do a fine job, son." He glances over at Pasquale's plate and sees that it's almost empty. "What's wrong with you, Maria, Angelina? Get more food for our guest."

I am on my feet immediately and notice Pasquale smiling at me.

"You and your family are so kind to me," he says. "I will make your house the best in the neighborhood."

I rush to the kitchen for more fish. Angelina follows and I hand her the plate of extra food. I dish up more marinara sauce and rush in to the dining room where I place the bowl to Pasquale's side and offer him the spoon, but in doing so with such nervous slippery fingers, I slop the gravy all over his light khaki pants.

"Clumsy," Luigi reprimands.

Angelina and I both hurry to the kitchen and clamor around finding towels, club soda and soap to clean Pasquale's pants in a flurry. We both fuss over him as Nonna rolls her eyes. I'm stooped down wiping the sauce off Pasquale's pants as Angelina hands me fresh towels. Do they see that I'm blushing? I refuse to look into Pasquale's eyes.

"It's fine," Pasquale insists. "Fine, don't worry." He touches my arm with tenderness.

Luigi throws his napkin on the table and plops his arms down. "Can't you do anything right, both of you?"

CHAPTER 14

Angelina

Every time I look at an adult, or even think about someone, like Mama or Aunt Francine or even Nonna, I know they must have gone all the way at some time in their lives. The horrible fact that I have actually done it and I really know what it's like has taken over my brain. I'm sure none of them do it anymore, of course. I can't even imagine, but it has to be true. They've had babies. I think of Ernie at the deli, or even Butch who picks up the garbage. Have all of them done it? It doesn't seem possible. Now that I'm an expert on the topic, I can say to myself that it's true, that sexual intercourse is over-rated, but still, I can't help but be curious.

I'm getting dinner ready for Mama who shouts out orders like a sergeant ever since she started working at Tia's. "Watch the boys. Start the marinating. Blah. Blah. Blah," she says. And tonight it's, "Mix up the meatballs, roll 'em into the small balls like the Swedish ones, but put in more Romano this time so Nonna doesn't complain." She should be home anytime. I hear the front door. Did she forget her keys, but no, it's Pasquale.

I brush the sheer curtains aside and peek out the dining room window. He's got his toolbox and is fixing the screen door. Those hinges have been squeaking for months. Papa wouldn't have a clue how to fix something like that. I stare at Pasquale with the Rachel Welch smile and watch him repair the door as he hums some old-fashioned song. I think about him going all the way. He must have gone all the way like a hundred times. He must have a girlfriend and they're older so, yes, I'm sure he's done it. And then I think of Tia. I realize that she must have been doing it with Freddie and it grosses me out. I heard Mama talking about how she broke up with him. Maybe he was forcing her like Ford did to me. My thoughts about sex are like a broken record.

Johnny and Louie skip towards the house. They're throwing the baseball back and forth, so boring. Johnny yells, "Hey, Pasquale, catch."

Pasquale stands up and turns just in time to catch the ball in his bare hands. He unhooks his work belt and lays it by the door before stepping into the street to toss the ball around with them. I pull out a dining room chair and sit watching them for awhile. Obviously, my brothers have not gone all the way yet. I wonder if anyone has told them what to do. And then, I'm a little upset that Mama never told me a thing. I felt like a dummy when I was ten or eleven and Celia told me all the facts of life.

I didn't believe them at first, like she was pulling a joke on me. That couldn't be true: a man puts his thing inside of you. How does he get it in? Well, now I know. But, I was just a kid then, and I never would have believed Celia if I hadn't seen the dogs in the street, one on top of the other and then, the boy dog's pink thing disappearing back inside him.

I pull my transistor radio out and turn it on full blast. Even if Nonna is upstairs it won't matter since she can hardly hear. I pour two glasses of Coke and take them with my radio out on the stoop to watch them toss the ball. I'm keeping an eye out for Mama, too.

"Here's a drink for you, Pasquale," I holler.

"Thanks," he says.

Louie throws the ball up in the air and catches it and keeps doing that while Johnny wears his mitt like a hat doing a crazy jig like Russian dancing while Pasquale runs over to take a sip of the Coke. I smile and bat my eyes. He pats me on the head like a puppy dog—a puppy dog, can you believe it? He must think I'm a kid or something.

"We're having penne and meatballs," I yell. "Wanna stay for dinner?"

He turns back towards me, "Again? You sure?"

Just then, Mama comes up the sidewalk. She's loaded down with two grocery bags and her shoulder bag. I get up to help but Pasquale has already abandoned the game of "tossing the ball" to relieve Mama of the heavy bags, one in each of his tanned muscular arms.

"Pasquale is going to stay for dinner, okay?" I say.

"You're always welcome," Mama says, then turns to me with bitterness as we make our way up the front steps to the front door, "Angelina, turn down that radio."

Mama stops at the door where the toolbox is opened. She opens and closes the screen door and flashes a glittery smile at Pasquale. Oh my God, what is wrong with her? "First the hose, and now the door. This house will be like new," she says to Pasquale batting her eyelids. I wonder if she knows about the Rachel Welch flirty smile.

"It's no trouble," Pasquale says and we enter the house with the boys following.

"Let me help," I say, but Pasquale is wrapped up in a conversation with Mama like it's as important as life or death. I watch Mama to see what it is about her that has him all interested and excited. I even wiggle my mini-skirted butt as he sets down the grocery bags on the kitchen counter, but he doesn't even look at me.

The boys stand quietly at the back door. This is something monumental for them. I guess Mama notices too. "The boys have been behaving like young men since you've been around." We all look over at them.

"That's great," Pasquale says leaning against the counter as Mama and I put the groceries away in the refrigerator. I prance in front of him to the pantry with the rice, but he turns away and leans over the center island to listen to Mama.

"You've been good for them," she says. "Their papa doesn't play any sports."

"Hey, Pasquale," Johnny says, "Meet us out back when you're done."

Then Louie says, "If you wanna play ball some more." Pasquale nods and smiles at them, but his attention is focused on Mama.

"Pasquale has more important things to do than to watch those wild boys," I complain. "I watched them all day and Nonna was gone again." Mama shoots me one of her "looks" and I leave the kitchen with my radio. I figure I'll listen to my music as loud as I want from my bedroom so I can think about what to do about the situation with Ford.

I hear Mama so sugary to Pasquale, "We'll miss you once you finish this job."

"I'll come around when I can, to toss the ball with them," he says.

The phone rings and I stop half way up the stairs to see if it's for me. I stand patiently and then Mama yells up, "Angelina, its Ford." I carefully ease up to the top of the stairs like I can't hear her. She yells up a couple of times but I don't answer like I'm in the bathroom with the door shut. Then, she says, "I'll have her call you." I spin around toward my bedroom and run right smack into Nonna who holds her spoon up and the corner of her mouth curls up like she knows exactly what's going on around here.

* * *

We walk down the street together, the whole family heading back home after mass. It's gotta be the hottest Sunday of the year. I can't wait to peel off my horrific red and yellow floral dress with the three-quarter sleeves and white pique collar and cuffs. The hemline swishes down around my calves. I'm dying in this dress and even worse, I would be mortified if any of my friends see me wearing it. I'm trying to be agreeable since its Johnny's birthday and he's got a thing about all the family being picture-perfect. Even though he's a little neurotic, he's a much better brother than Louie who always tells on me if he sees me do a single thing wrong. Anyway, I've got a lot on my mind and I just wish dinner was over and I could go up, lie on my bed and think about what to do about my messed up life.

As we approach the house, I notice the porch swing swaying back and forth. God, I hope it's not Ford, and to my relief I see that it's Pasquale again on a Sunday waiting for us with a bag of fresh fruit. When we get closer, I can smell cannoli. He must have bought them for Johnny's birthday. He stands up and hands them to Mama.

"This is becoming tradition," Mama says. Everyone in our family just loves Pasquale, even Papa, and he has spent the last two Sundays at our house for dinner.

Papa pats Pasquale on the back as we enter the front door. "You did a fine job, son. I told your Papa he should be proud."

"Thank you, sir. I will finish this week."

Papa rushes us in the door. "Hurry now. Make us coffee and prepare the table. Boys, help Nonna up the steps."

Louie pushes ahead of me and Johnny tries to help Nonna, but she shakes that dirty old spoon at him, "I don't need no help." I could have bet a hundred bucks she'd say that.

Before I can get in the door, Ford comes rushing up from behind. Oh God, what am I going to do? But, I figure its good I don't get inside before he spots me. He would probably knock on the door and Mama would get me and I'd have to ask him in and then, oh forget it. It would be disastrous. Papa would make a fuss, especially that Ford is not Italian and in Papa's eyes, no good. I'm not even supposed to date boys until I'm sixteen. Papa's just so uncool. Mama's more with it but she's way too curious and has to know everything about everything.

While everyone is busy greeting Pasquale, I quickly shut the door and face Ford. "Go away. I can't talk now."

"Why won't you talk to me?" He stands there in his Sunday clothes with his hands open wide and sweat dripping down his face. Was he running or what?

"I'm confused, that's all." I cross my arms and then I look down at my ugly dress and wonder why he wants to go out with me anyway. I look like a frump. I untie the prissy bow fastened at the nape of my neck and shake my hair out. Even if I don't want to talk to him, at least he will think I'm a little bit hip. "You're too aggressive with me and I don't like it when you get stoned."

"Look man, I thought we were like together," he says in a defensive tone, "like you were my 'old lady'."

I stand my ground. I don't want to deal with him right now. "Well, yeah, but I just don't know, after all the stuff you said, and did. I can't talk now."

"So, do your own thing and all, man, but why you givin' me

a hard time? I told you I was sorry. I was just kiddin' around with you." Then he changes his tone to a lovey-dovey voice, which really turns me off. "Babe, I can't wait to get you in that tree house again."

I turn, open the door and go in. I tell him one more time, "Go away." I don't even want to be hanging out with him this summer. I can see him out the dining room window along with the rest of my family who suddenly all seem interested in my little spat on the front porch. Ford turns and marches down the front steps and paces in front of the house on the sidewalk.

I put on my mean face so no one will ask me questions, and I rush to the kitchen to help Mama with the dinner, just as Aunt Francine, Uncle Giuseppe and their family arrive at the front door. I'm all absorbed with frustrations about Ford but then I think how funny and odd it is that everyone is laughing and talking and competing for Pasquale's attention—everyone, the adults, the boys and even my cousins, Lita and Rosa.

CHAPTER 15

Maria

In a way, Pasquale has become almost a part of our family. Even though his own mama, papa, and brothers are right here in the neighborhood, it's obvious he'd rather spend time with us, especially on Sunday. And, today is one of those perfect Sunday nights where all you want to do is be somewhere outside, walking down Arthur Avenue or hanging around on the front stoop greeting neighbors as they meander along the street. Giuseppe's family has just gone home and the dishes are all finished. Pasquale has his guitar and we gather on the front porch as he plays for us. All except for Luigi, that is. He can't miss something on TV. But, the rest of us, even Nonna, sit on the porch. The kids and I sing along with Pasquale to some Italian ballads, a few Beatle songs and American songs like "Take Me out to the Ballgame." The boy's singing to that one is more like howling. To me, Sundays have not been that bad lately, but then, I remember that Pasquale must still think I'm Angelina's sister. What will it hurt to wait just a little longer?

Pasquale strums his guitar one more time, and then carefully sets it against the side of the house. He stretches his sexy limbs and leans back against the mesh lawn chair like a cat sprawling out. He is so full of life—so vibrant. I watch his robust laughter and envy how easily he is able to smile.

"How about ice cream?" Louie asks.

I know he's thinking of Angelo's Gelato down on the Avenue. From out on the porch, I lean in and gaze into the living room. Luigi lounges in his chair softly snoring with the newspaper covering him like a blanket.

"Okay, I'll take you," Pasquale jumps to his feet and so do all three kids. Nonna just sits on the swing keeping an eye on who's walking around in the street in front of the house. Suddenly, I think of Luigi as he coughs and stirs in his chair. I should really take Pasquale aside and tell him that I am the mama, but I let it fester in me a little longer. But, I don't dare act like one of the kids or Luigi, or Nonna will get suspicious and it would be embarrassing for all of us.

"Go ahead," I say. "I'll stay here."

Pasquale faces me inquisitively peering into my eyes. He rests his proficient hands on my shoulders and immediately I feel Nonna's eyes on me. I know she's holding the spoon. "You sure?" he asks and I turn away.

"I'm sure."

"I'll bring some back just for you." He glances over at Nonna. "You too."

A cloud of gloom lands on my heart. Why can't my husband

be more like Pasquale? "Oh, no. Thank you, no." I turn and walk into the house and then I watch at the door as the boys and Angelina rush to Pasquale's van with the big gaudy purple lettering on the side. Louie pushes Johnny away so he can sit in the front with Pasquale. I smile weakly and wave. Pasquale hesitates at the van and waves back at me. As they drive off, I see that boy, Ford, the one who comes around to see Angelina. It looks like he's headed towards our house. He stops and stands there watching the van pull away, and crosses his arms defiantly. Suddenly, I am curious about him. I should probably pay more attention to what my daughter is up to.

Like an army guard, Nonna is stationed on the porch. This is good entertainment for her so I leave her out there and join Luigi who is awake now and watching TV. I settle in my chair.

"Maybe you want to run along with them like a little child," he says. "You don't want to rub an old man's shoulders and be company to your husband?" This is the last thing I feel like doing. Yes, and when I think about it, what I truly would love to do, would be to revert back to Angelina's age with no worries and responsibilities and to run off to Angelo's Gelato, but, I get out of my seat, go around to the back of Luigi's chair and rub his neck and shoulders.

"You old fool," I say. "That's crazy. What is there that I don't do for you?"

Luigi grunts. He leans back in his chair and closes his eyes enjoying the massage. When *Bonanza* comes on the TV, I finish the massage. His eyes are closed so I slip out of the living room and into the kitchen like a mouse in the dark. I sit at the kitchen table looking out the back window at the picnic table. I listen to the guns shooting and horses galloping on TV but my mind is outside at the table with Pasquale.

CHAPTER 16

Angelina

From my seat in the back of the van, I watch Pasquale maneuver his way through the traffic over by Arthur Avenue. He lays his right arm along the back of the front seat, looking out the rear window to judge the distance to parallel park. I examine the muscles of his arm and the glistening black hairs on his fore arm. On his pinkie, he wears a gold ring with a 'P' in the center and I wonder if it was a gift from a girlfriend. I don't want him to see me staring at him, so I look out the window, and there's Ford hurrying down the street toward the van. How did he spot us?

Pasquale turns off the engine. The boys discuss what flavor gelato they plan to order and I'm calculating how I'm going to duck out of sight from Ford, but there's no hiding, even in the paneled van. I try to slouch down, but there's no way. We're all getting out and he spots Johnny and Louie. I open the door and he's right there next to the van scowling at me. Pasquale almost knocks him over with his door, by accident of course. I think quick, and grab a hold of Pasquale's arm like he's my boyfriend or something. I see in Ford's eyes that he's stoned and angry as hell. Pasquale seems baffled at my actions but I try to laugh it off like I'm just playing around. The boys are running way ahead, almost to the corner already.

I figure that's the end of Ford, at least for now, but once we get our gelato and go to sit at one of the outside café tables he's there with a couple of girls from school. It's not far from our house. He must have been lurking around since earlier. They're talking loud and pointing at me. Ford must be telling them some lie about me. I move my chair closer to Pasquale hoping

Ford doesn't come over and embarrass me in front of him. He is unpredictable when he's high. Who knows what he'll do.

On a beautiful Sunday evening, I should know that everyone would be out. The next thing I see is Jen and Celia who have just arrived and are standing over with Ford, who is leaning against the side of the building gawking at us.

"Do you know that boy?" Pasquale asks.

"Sort of."

"She knows him," Johnny says, "That's Rexford Coleman. I heard you kissed him and more, too."

"Who told you that?" I can't believe my little brother would have heard rumors. Now I'm really ticked off at Ford.

Louie licks his gelato and snickers. "Everyone knows."

"You don't know anything."

Louie asks. "So, tell me."

"Aw, my Angel," Pasquale says, and I swoon. I can't believe how he says "Angel" like I'm special. "These boys are just fooling around. Right, boys?"

"Uh, no," Louie moans just as Celia and Jen come over to our table. They are flirting and gawking at Pasquale like he's "God's gift" and like he's free for the taking, especially Jen. Celia just kind of looks stunned by his gorgeousness.

"You must be Pasquale," Jen says pulling a chair up. Celia sits on the edge of a chair and they focus on Pasquale. Johnny and Louie roll their eyes.

"Yes," Pasquale says.

"They know about you, you know, from working on the house." I'm sort of embarrassed by their childish blatant attention to him. He smiles at me and I feel just like my gelato—melting.

Jen barely glances at me with her eyes glued to Pasquale, "Ford wants to talk to you. It's important."

I look over and Ford's still there. He motions for me to come over and I'm so frustrated that I get up and go over to see what he wants. Pasquale's attention is on my two best friends now, so I might as well deal with Ford.

"What're you doing hanging around with Mr. Mafioso?"

"Who?"

"That your uncle or something?"

"My Uncle Carmine lives in California. What'd you want?"

"We're all going to a party. Why don't you come on with me and tell Mr. Mafioso to stuff it."

I turn to leave. "You're drunk or stoned or something. I'm not going anywhere with you." He takes a hold of my arm and I try to pull away. Pasquale must see my struggle because before I realize what's happening, he's right there by my side.

"I think you'd better take your hands off this young lady," he insists.

"You're not her father," Ford growls. "She's going to a party with me."

Pasquale motions for the boys to join us and then wraps his arm around me. "She's not going anywhere with you. She's coming with me. And, don't even think of ever bullying her again or you'll answer to me." With his free hand he digs his pointer finger into Ford's chest.

As he leads me and the boys back to the van, I notice the envious expressions on Celia and Jen's faces, as they stand there watching with their eyebrows raised.

CHAPTER 17

Maria

When I foolishly bought the Pucci printed dress from Tia, I had quickly hid it in the back of my closet behind my heavy wool pants and long-sleeved dresses. Now, I think it's the perfect thing to wear to appear somewhat stylish and attractive. Standing in my white slip, I part the clothes in my closet, searching for the dress. It's sort of casual but flashy at the same time. In my regular boring life, I have nowhere to wear it. I might as well wear it around the house; see how it feels, plus, Pasquale is working at the house today. It wouldn't hurt to look nice for once, instead of being so dowdy and old fashioned. I admire the dress, still in the plastic cover, then, I quickly pull it off the hanger and slip it on. I trot off to the bathroom and play around with my hair trying to figure out how to style it in something modern. I'm determined not to pull it back in a bun. I comb my full head of thick, dark wavy hair straight down, but it won't stay that way without some coaxing, so, I part it on the side letting it easily slip down across my eye. If I tilt my head just so, it makes me look younger, sexier, but no, it doesn't work. Nonna will be watching me like a hawk if I prance around the house like this. I swiftly pull it back in a knot. Then, I remember that it's Nonna's bingo day. She's gone with Francine. I shake my hair out and part it in the middle. The alarm clock next to Luigi's side of the bed says 8:55. Pasquale will be here any minute. He should already be here. That's it, I'm out of the bedroom and darting down the stairs to gawk out the dining room window, but, his van is not there. Maybe he's not coming. I pace back and forth in the foyer, and then I open the front door and look out with a worried expression. Where is he? I close the door and lean against it. Didn't he say he was coming on Tuesday, or was it Wednesday?

My heart thumps when I hear the sound of his van's squeaky brakes out front. A smile appears on my face, and I take a relieved breath to know that Pasquale is out front. What on Earth has come over me? I pull open the door beaming.

He's busy unloading his tools and supplies and finally looks over at me. "I'm sorry to be late. I had some things to do this morning but here I am." He stretches his arms wide with confidence to show he's all there. I laugh nervously.

"I have the day off. Maybe we could have some lunch later. I have fresh prosciutto."

"Great, but it looks like rain," he says. "I must get to work so I don't lose the whole day."

As I close the front door, I see the back door easing shut. It's Nonna slipping out alone. I thought she was gone with Francine, but I watch her sneaking out around to the front sidewalk and off she goes hobbling down the street on her own. I furrow my brows and sit down by the window to think about the old girl. Why is she such a mystery? Maybe I should go after her and make sure she gets to Francine's. But then I wonder why Francine didn't pick her up.

The morning hours drag, feeling like days instead of a few hours. The tray for lunch is ready setting on the counter with plates of prosciutto draped over fresh melon slices. Additional cantaloupe is arranged in a half moon on a plate with red grapes and sprigs of fresh mint. A plate of ripe sliced tomatoes alternating with wedges of *burrata* cheese are arranged on another small plate with fresh basil and drizzled with balsamic vinegar and olive oil. I wait to slice the fresh bread from Terranova Bakery that I sent Angelina out to buy earlier this morning before she went off to Coney Island with her friends for a special kick-off-the-summer trip. The bread is still warm, ready to be served in an oval basket wrapped in a freshly ironed napkin. There is a plate with olives and sliced fennel, and a cold rigatoni with roasted peppers in olive oil and fresh pepper. What am I missing? Is this enough food? Is it too much? I check the clock on the kitchen wall: 12:42. The sun peeks out of gray clouds. This is a good sign to me for a glorious picnic. I quickly slice up the bread, wrap it in the napkin, and discard my apron. I head out the back door with the plates and silverware. Oh no, drinks. I rush in and fill the green glass pitcher with lemons, mint and cold water. Maybe he'd rather have a Coke, but it's almost one o'clock. I hurry out with the pitcher to continue setting the table and look up at the sky. What if it rains?

Fifteen

As soon as Pasquale sees me, he waves. I rush in for the food and when he sees me struggling with the tray, he scoots down the ladder and rushes to carry the heavy load. He sets it on the table before washing up. As I arrange everything for our lunch, my heart suddenly flutters as he removes his coveralls. When I first made the meal to share with Pasquale I didn't really know him and it was just sort of a curiosity thing. Now I'm smitten even though I'm a married woman and I know what I'm thinking and feeling is wrong. I don't think I've ever been alone with a man this sexy. It's a little intimidating, but I let my guilty feelings slip away. We're just friends after all. Today I'll tell him I'm the mama.

The clouds roll in and the sky darkens just as the two of us have started on the pasta. And then, it begins to pour with rain. No wishing it away, it pours down in buckets. I screech at the drama of it. Pasquale sweeps the tray up and into the back door so quick it hardly spoils a thing. Suddenly, we are there at the kitchen table soaking wet and laughing. I pull out towels from the pantry cabinet and we dry off giggling like children. We finish our lunch chattering like two old friends before I notice that it must be obvious to Pasquale through my wet Pucci-printed dress that I'm not wearing a bra. He fixes his eyes on my chest and I blush.

"That hasn't happened to me since I was a child," I say strapping one arm over my chest and anchoring it on my shoulder to cover my breasts.

"It's good to be a child sometimes," he answers with a coy smile.

I laugh and let my arm free. "I don't think a child would thrill at being caught in a downpour with a charming..." What am I saying? I pause and look down at my plate. "Oh God." I roll my eyes. "I didn't mean to, I mean, I didn't mean anything by..." I look up and he's leaning over the table his eyes staring directly into my soul. His elbows are on the table and his arms stretch out toward me, frozen like I've been hypnotized. He reaches and lifts my chin with one hand. Then, he looks down, grasps both of my quivering hands and pulls them toward his face and kisses them with passion. We gaze into each other's eyes like statues, motionless, our hands locked together.

In an instant Pasquale pulls me to my feet. "Ummm. Now I'm done with working out in the weather for today. What shall we do?"

I am afraid to answer. "You left your guitar here on Sunday. Maybe you could play a few songs."

"I know, I will teach you. We shall play and laugh a little." He has a hold of my hand and we're headed into the living room.

For the next twenty minutes I am mesmerized by his charm and he manages to entice me into seriously trying to learn to play the guitar. I can't remember the last time I did something so foolish. He teaches me a few simple chords and instructs me how to hold the instrument. We are side to side with his arm around me and we laugh at my feeble attempts at "Twinkle, Twinkle Little Star." I'm really serious about learning the song, but then, he takes the guitar and plays an Italian love song. He mixes it up with some pop songs like I've heard on the radio into his own musical style and I'm his dedicated fan.

Without warning, he sets the guitar down against the couch and leans over me taking my face in his hands, and he kisses me so intensely that I feel as if my bones have turned to gelatin. Like a magician's trance, I am motionless and then I wrap my arms around him. He kisses and kisses and kisses me and I don't want to let go.

"I have wanted to do this for so long," he whispers and then gently licks the inside of my ear. I feel like I'm on an elevator soaring up to the top floor. And, I feel like we're going through the ceiling as he kisses my neck with his delicious lips.

I want this to go on forever—this passionate making out,

but when he gently leans me down to lie on the couch, I panic. What am I doing? This is so wrong. This is a sin. I push away and stand up abruptly. I turn away in tears.

"I can't," I sob unable to even look at him.

He stands up behind me and rests his passionate hands on my shoulders. "I'm sorry. I'm too fast with you. I can't help myself."

I twist my body around, first my head, then my shoulders and torso to face him and I rest my head on his chest. There's no way I can look into those fiery eyes. He wraps his arms around me like a comforting blanket. "You better go," I whisper with tears I try to hide. I don't know what he's thinking. If I would dare to gaze at that face of his, I might guess, but I'm in another world—in my own daydream. He releases me with a puzzled expression and heads out the front door. How could I let him go? I rush over to peek out the dining room window to see him heading to his van and there is Nonna rushing towards the back door. I see the two of them as their eyes meet and right then, I don't care.

I step into the kitchen and drop into a kitchen chair, an emotional mess facing Nonna who's dripping wet as she quietly enters the kitchen through the back door. Even though I just saw her out in the front heading towards the house, I am startled when she appears face to face with me. I snap at her, "What're you doing out in the rain? Look at you."

She strips off her raincoat and hangs it on the hook by the back door. "Is not your concern," she says to me.

I have had it with her. "Your son would not be so happy…"

But, it seems as though Nonna is having a bad day. She barks back at me, "My poor son would not be so happy to see his crazy wife keeping company with the young man." She does not wait around for my response. I never argue or raise my voice to her. She always gets the last word, but this time, as she darts out of the room, I follow her. She passes through the dining room and up the front stairs and I follow her to the landing where the stairs curve to ascend to the second floor. I stare up at her as she hobbles up the last few steps.

"What is it with you?" I demand. "Why do you hate me so?"

She glances back at me then continues around the corner and out of sight. I squeeze my eyes shut and hang my head as the tears stream down my cheeks.

I can hear Nonna up in her closet banging around, furniture moving. What the heck is she doing? I go up and peek through the keyhole as she moves a chair in front of her bedroom door. I can just slightly see her as she rummages around in the bottom of her closet until she locates a shoe box mixed in with other boxes. She takes the box to her bed and sets it down next to her purse. From her purse, she pulls out wads of cash, then, she sits beside the box on the bed and opens the box that is almost full of money. She counts the new amount from her purse, puts it in the box and scribbles a dollar amount on a piece of paper before carefully replacing the box in her closet. I freeze. What is she up to? Is she stealing money from somewhere? And I thought I had a secret. I tiptoe away from her door and down the stairs.

Luigi and the kids will be home soon so I try my best to dry my tears and prepare the supper, something simple tonight. Maybe Luigi will be late, going to the pool hall or visiting with his brother after work. How can I face him tonight? I have kissed another man, but I don't dare think about that now. And, what kind of trouble is Nonna involved in?

The boys dart into the house all dirty and wild. I shoo them upstairs to wash up, but I know they will stop at Nonna's room to get a silver dollar each. I knew she must have some money tucked away, always promising the kids a silver dollar if they behave during the day, but wads of money, I had no idea. I must make it a point to find out where she goes during the day.

She must hear the boys stomping up the stairs toward her room. Then, they are suddenly quiet and whispering as they near her door. Has she quickly removed the chair in front of her door and rushed to lie down on the bed so they'll think she's asleep? Huh. She's a sneaky old bird. I hear them barge in to her room. I start up the stairs when I hear Louie say, "Quiet, numbscull, can't you see her eyes are closed?" I hear them tip-toe out and towards their room. Surely they think she doesn't hear them, but I know she's awake. I can just see the tricky old bird still as a board next to the pictures on her night stand—pictures in old silver frames with tiny Mass cards of Jesus tucked in the corner, one of Papa Vito and a second of her parents in Italy. If they only knew she's up to no good.

CHAPTER 18

Angelina

Thank God for summer and no school. What a relief to spend a whole day out of the neighborhood and away from contemplating what I'll do when I run into Ford. And more important, or maybe crucial to my future, it's a break away from Pasquale. All of a sudden it doesn't matter that Pasquale doesn't have longish hair and wear bell-bottomed jeans. I guess I kind of have a crush. I know it's not realistic and all, but Ford is just so juvenile compared to Pasquale, and frankly, it's tiring the way my tortured mind is all tangled up thinking about him, wondering what it would be like to do it with him. It might be exciting. He's so much dreamier. He would be a good husband. Maybe it's my luck he hasn't found the right girl to marry. Maybe he won't care that I'm not a virgin. Maybe he'll see that we would be perfect together, and it would be so easy, he already knows all my family and they love him. That's another strike against Ford. Papa would never accept me dating a German, that is, when I'm ever old enough to date anyone, so it's good we're broken up. Well, we're broken up in my eyes anyway. I do really wish Pasquale would think about growing his hair a little, and those pants he wears are like right out of Papa's closet. Why does everything have to be so confusing?

It's the first beach day of the summer—like a mini vacation for me with Celia, Jen and Celia's cousins from California. They even met my Uncle Carmine out there. He is so cool and like an Italian hippie like her cousins say. He hasn't been back in the Bronx since I was like ten. Anyway, we decide to take a trip to a different beach—one we never go to, just for this one day. And, we plan to go to Coney Island, too. I feel like a normal teenager again. It's all girl talk at Brighton Beach in Brooklyn, no boy or parent pressures, just hanging out. Clouds are off in the distance and threaten to ruin our day, but for now it's time to lather up with our mixture of iodine and baby oil to make us nice and black in the sun so our legs will look sexy in minis and hot pants.

No matter what, as it turns out, there's no way to get Pasquale off my mind. Jen and Celia want to know all about him—every single detail. So, we end up baking in the sun and getting all hot about Pasquale, while I'm getting bothered by their interest. If anyone's getting him, it's going to be me. Yup, I'm "hot and bothered" like I hear Uncle Giuseppe always say.

"I bet he likes teenage girls, probably blonde ones at that," Jen wiggles down on her beach towel. "Is he still working at your house?"

"I think my parents have some repairs to do," Celia adds. "Maybe if I can get his number, I can ask them if they want to call him."

Jen sits up and glares at Celia. "Huh. All you want is to get his number for yourself. I can tell you're not his type. I'm ready to dump Pauly and go for it with him. I'd probably make him shorten his name to something cool like Patch."

"Patch?" I'm so irritated. "That sounds like a dog's name."

"Well, he is cute, as cute as a puppy," Celia says, "but, I'm sticking with Carlo. I think I'm going to do it with him this weekend."

"About time," Jen says. "I'd like to do it with Patch."

"He's like a grown man," I say. "Why would he be interested in a teenage girl?"

"Believe me, I could show him why," Jen says.

"Forget it," I say and lay down on my towel with my eyes shut. I slip on my shades to block out those girls, especially Jen. Now, I'm determined, if anyone's getting him, it's me.

"Don't tell me you like him," Jen says, "What about Ford? You promised you'd try to work it out with him for all our sakes."

I don't move from my towel. "How would you like to go out with Ford? He's a jerk. Plus, you're supposed to be with Pauly, remember—the six of us?"

Jen sticks her nose up then plops her shades back on her face and scooches down on her towel.

"Yeah, I can't imagine Pasquale would want to hang out with us anyway. He probably goes to bars and stuff," Celia says. "Plus, I'm into the stoners with the hip-huggers, boots and long hair, you know like Carlo. Ooooo, I can't wait 'till this weekend. He's really got what it takes for me."

Jen pops up from her towel and swirls around facing me. I can feel her breath of wintergreen mints on me and the baked smell of baby oil and iodine. I peek out of the corner of my eye to see her cross-legged smirking at me. "Sounds like you've got a secret crush."

"You're right," I say sarcastically, "He's like a greaser. All he needs is a little leather and a motorcycle." They laugh and under my shades, I roll my eyes just as Celia's cousins come up from the ocean and drip salt water all over our newly lathered bellies. We screech and then notice two really cute guys only a few feet away with a whole beach day set up—a cooler and umbrella on their sprawling beach blanket circle complete with cold beers and fragrant pot.

CHAPTER 19

Maria

I can't sleep. What have I done? I have betrayed my sacred marital vows. I have kissed another man. I drag around for a whole day thinking I'm the worst person in the world. But, by the next day, there's no more guilt about kissing Pasquale. I have it all worked out. It was just a misunderstanding. We're just friends and anyway, he must know that I'm Luigi's wife. I've got to find my ring. I can just slip it on and if he asks, 'What's this?' I'll say, 'Oh, didn't you know I'm Luigi's wife?' I wonder about it. Does he know? I haven't told him, but then I think of this vibrant man younger than me—but really only about four or five years younger. He must have all sorts of girlfriends, or certainly, after months since his break-up, there probably is one special girl. That upsets me more that there may be one instead of lots.

After work the next day when Pasquale is just finishing and I'm heading home from Tia's, we meet outside and he insists I go with him to Angelo's Gelato for a treat. Why not? I'm early and I'll fix the supper when we return. Nonna gives me the evil eye from the porch swing as the two of us climb into his van.

I roll down the window and say to her, "I'm just getting gelato for dessert."

We're seated at a corner table talking nonsense at Angelo's

and I'm thinking I could do this for the whole day. Yes, we flirt with each other but it's just goofing around. We're just friends. He tells me about a clown in a circus when he was very young. I wear a smile so enormous that my cheeks hurt from the laughter. Then, he reaches over and smears his chocolate gelato right on the end of my nose. It startles me, but I'm still laughing and reaching for a napkin when he leans over and licks it off—licks it off, amazing. It throws me off guard but I hoot with amusement until he moves his mouth to my lips. What am I going to do? I scan the area to make sure there's no one around that knows my family. Reality sets in on the van ride back to the house. I'm worried and rushed; its dinnertime and I should be home. While he's driving, he reaches for my hand in my lap. He pulls my hand close to his cheek and kisses it without letting go for the rest of the ride. I jump out of the van as soon as we pull up out front. I don't thank him or turn to look at him. I rush up to the house like there's a fire. Yeah, there's a fire alright—it's in my heart.

Of course, Nonna wants to know where the gelato is for our dessert.

"Oh, the gelato," I say like I must have misplaced it. If there really was gelato and it wasn't in the freezer, it would be melted into a pile of creamy liquid by now. "Oh, did I leave it at the store?"

For a few days I avoid him. I really wasn't expecting the confusion of an infatuation in my life, and I keep telling myself over and over that we are just friends. There's nothing wrong with being friends, but who am I kidding? The fact is, I can't wait to see him when we're apart. I can't wait to kiss those fiery lips and feel those arms cradling me. And, I hadn't thought about it, but the girls at Tia's mentioned that I'm dressing much more stylish these days. Yes, I have been spending my pay on new outfits from the shop when I should be putting that money towards our family's bills. I tell myself that I haven't spent money on clothes for such a long time that it won't hurt.

Pasquale raves about the joy of singing at Telly's Restaurant over on Belmont, and how he really wants me to come see him perform. How can I possibly go there in the evening? A woman alone in a place like that would not sit well with my family or anyone in the neighborhood. First I decide that I will definitely not go there, that this game has gone way too far and I must figure out a way to nip it, end it. But, no one my family knows goes to Telly's. No one will see me and the opportunity, like a piece of cake, presents itself for me. Angelina and Celia want to watch a movie at the house and the boys are playing upstairs for the night. That's a usual night, but there is something going on down at the pool hall and Luigi tells me the night before that he's going straight over there after dinner on Saturday night.

There are times, especially since I met Pasquale, when I think I have totally lost my mind. Is it because of Pasquale, or is it all the notion of free love that has taken over? I wonder about this as I sit alone at the table by the stage where Pasquale performs. My behavior is so foreign to me. Never have I done anything like this. I have never sat at a table in a restaurant alone anywhere especially not on a Saturday night at a nice restaurant with white tablecloths and filled with all couples enjoying a night out with their spouses. My family would be mortified if they knew, but why shouldn't I go to a place to see a friend perform? I tried to bring Tia, but at the last minute, she was not available. Everything happens so quickly with Pasquale—so quickly that I don't have a second to figure out that it's not a good idea. Before I know it, I'm here at a lonely table by the stage and he's singing to me so that the whole restaurant can see, like I'm his passionate lover, as if there's not a single other person in the room and he's singing his heart out to me.

The room is dark with a bluish-grey smokiness—a blur to me. All I see is Pasquale in the spotlight on the plywood stage trimmed in a red curtain. The passionate melody of his voice has me hypnotized. When he wraps up his set on stage, the lights dim. And then, with eyes away from the stage and me sitting there for everyone to see, I feel vulnerable. I'm embarrassed to be alone on a Saturday night and as I look around I notice that most of the room is a collection of small round tables with couples out for the night. I feel more secure when Pasquale approaches the table, kisses me on the cheek and takes a seat next to me. I'm a little concerned that some of the couples might recognize me, and can swear I see one of Luigi's friends, the bartender, Tony Tucci and his wife, at a table on the other side of the room. But why would Tony be here when there's an event at the pool hall? I don't dare do a double take. How would I explain Pasquale? For half a second, it occurs to me that it's time to come out in the open with everyone. What do I care if Luigi knows I'm going to a performance? He thinks the world revolves around Pasquale. We're just friends no matter how much fantasizing goes on in my head. And, Pasquale can't possibly still think I'm Angelina's sister. He can't possibly be interested in me, for real. Then, as soon as Pasquale is sitting with me and staring into my eyes like I'm better than chocolate gelato in July, I'm under his spell and I push the whole thing to the back of my mind and go with the moment.

• • •

    I know our relationship is spinning out of control and I know it's time to face the music really soon. Once I find the ring, it will be obvious to Pasquale, but I can't find the ring. I begin to wonder why Luigi hasn't noticed my bare finger. He couldn't possibly have something to do with the disappearance of the symbol of love and devotion between me and Luigi.
    I take the bowl of peas out to the patio and sit at the picnic table to snap the peas and daydream. I try to concoct the feeling I had when Luigi gave me the ring. I was pregnant with

Angelina and of course, he had to marry me. It was different in those days. I imagine what it's like for young couples these days, how they must be thinking about sex before getting married with all the free love going around. When I was a teen, it was all a big secret. The peas are all snapped and my daydreaming has gone full circle to my situation with Pasquale. I'm not proud that we have kissed, and made-out, but I tell myself it's under control. I will make sure that I never find myself somewhere private and alone with him. I don't know if I could resist him.

• • •

One of the things we've been doing together is meeting in the park when we get off work early, like today. It's a dreadfully humid day at the end of June. Angelina is with her friends, the boys are over at Francine's with their cousins, and I'm at Tia's, full of anticipation knowing I'm meeting Pasquale after work. I change into one of those sexy new slip dresses. It's too hot for most people, so it seems like we're alone over in Van Cortlandt Park, walking hand in hand. We talk poetry and song writing. He loves my ideas of writing song lyrics about things he's told me about his family, and his passion for life. I throw out words, and he creates them into songs. I'm so flattered that he sings my words out loud, as we walk along. We laugh and sing, sweating in the muggy weather. We're down by the stream now where it's a little cooler, and there, I see a picnic table near the lake. I stop in my tracks for a moment. My passionate daydream flashes through my mind like the dozens of butterflies that flit and fly around the park bushes. I've been having that passionate dream for years, and I stand in awe of an exact replica of my mind's Eden.

"Oh my God," I mutter. He takes my hand and we approach the table. He can't possibly read my thoughts, but this is dangerous territory for me. We sit on one side of the table, both of us facing the lake and he slings his arm around me. He toys with my hair—my weakness, and I put my arm on his sweaty bicep. It is as if we have no control of our actions—both of us. I am in his arms and he's kissing me and all I want is to be with him. I'm like a feather, light and floating with no control but from the wind. Pasquale is my wind. There is such passion between us, and God, what he does with his hands. I can't put it in words. They're everywhere on my breasts and legs and...

I move away swiftly and cover my face with my hands. I don't know what to say to him. And then, he takes my hand and we start walking back towards his van. I think he will just take me home and I will think about how to deal with this later, but he opens the back doors to the van and jumps inside. He reaches his hand out to me to jump in with him. He stoops down and scoops me up, his feather, and kisses me tenderly but when I realize what is happening, I panic. He has a cot-like pad on the floor of the van and all the tools are moved to one side. He spreads out an Indian blanket and pulls me up and on the blanket before carefully closing the van doors. We are alone in a steamy love den and we make passionate love. It is fiery sexual love and I have no ability to control it.

CHAPTER 20

Angelina

It's pretty obvious that Pasquale has finished working on our house. The adjustable ladders and extra supplies have vanished and now I panic to think I'll never see him again. But, that's probably not true. He lives nearby and he's usually around on Sunday with his bag of fruit or cannolis. I keep my eye out for him around the neighborhood thinking I'll see him on someone else's roof, but then, I think I must be out of my mind. There's a million other guys to obsess over, and cool guys closer to my age, but, when I stop to think about it, there's not one single guy in high school that I've seen over at Angelo's Gelato or "The Dumps" on Friday or at school, that I'd want to bother with. I used to think it was Ford who was the prize—yeah, the booby prize. I snicker to myself as I walk home from Celia's. I did make a promise to her that I'd try to work it out with Ford so the six of us could have a fun summer together. It's more fun in a group; everyone knows that.

    I drag myself home from Celia's after a Thursday night sleepover. We probably didn't get more than an hour's sleep all night. There's always something to talk about in the middle of the night. We didn't get back from the beach until late and all sunburned. We ended up meeting up with those guys with the pot and sun umbrella from the week before. They bought us pretzels on the boardwalk and even tried to get us to hang out in Brooklyn for the evening, but we headed back to the Bronx on the B train and made all these plans to meet again and spend the day at the beach. But I don't think any of us really likes them much. The only reason we met with them again after that first time was that Jen had "the hots" for the Albanian one with the pot. They got so stoned and sloppy. Plus, they live out there in Brooklyn—nothing like a long distance romance. Who knows what kind of trashy crowd they hang with? Give me the Bronx any day. I'd rather be hanging out at our usual beach spot at Orchard Beach. If some guy gets wise with you, all you gotta do is pop into a shop, and you probably know the owner or there's someone around always looking out for you.

    As soon as I walk in the house, the phone rings and its Jen complaining that Ford's fuming mad about our beach trip to Brooklyn again, meeting those guys and all, and especially venturing off to a beach that's out of our territory. Big deal. It was harmless. So, I figure we'll all be together tonight at the Savoy, "The Dumps" over on Arthur Avenue. It's getting kind of boring hanging out there every Friday night.

Into the phone she says, "He wants you to meet him over there early so he can talk. He's over there with the other guys for the horror matinee."

"I don't want to talk to him Jen. I'll just go over with you and Celia."

"Just go talk to him. What's the big deal?"

Mama walks in and I don't want to go into the whole thing about Ford and the guys at the beach so I tell her fine, I'll go over half an hour early and see them there. I hang up thinking Mama is going to want to hear about my day or question me or something, but she blurts out a quick hello and darts upstairs.

Mama is unusually quiet all through dinner and I'm wondering what's wrong with her, but its fine with me. I just go up and change and tell them I'm going to meet Celia and Jen, and I leave. Actually, I'm going alone. I'm anticipating the lecture I'm gonna get from Ford and all for just talking to some idiot guys. He thinks he owns me now that we went all the way.

He's waiting outside "The Dumps" for me. It's not dark yet, but there're lots of looming clouds from the three-minute storm that passed through during dinner, so it's kind of shady outside and eerily chilly for a summer evening, after such a major heat wave during the day. I see Ford alone by the side of the theater leaning against the wall. He's fidgeting with something—a pack of cigarettes. He lights one. When I get close enough I realize that something is not quite right about him. He has a frightening expression like he's uncontrollably angry. His eyes quiver darting up and down the street like he's afraid of something or someone. When he sees me, he stubs out the cigarette with his cowboy boot and approaches me. He grabs my arm and pulls me into the alley. I wasn't expecting this. We were supposed to just talk. What's the big secret?

"What's wrong?"

He frowns at me and shushes me until we are deep in the darkened alley and then I realize he's been drinking, heavily. The strong scent of alcohol and cigarettes oozes from his body but there's something else. His eyes are funny, bouncing around in his head like a madman.

"I'm in trouble cuz of you." He's angry and pushes me into the wall.

"Me?"

"How dare you whore around on me."

I try to pull away from him but he's got a firm hold on me and there's no one around when normally this place is crawling with people on a weekend night. I figure everyone's in the theater, that a movie is showing and it's still early for our regular crowd to be hanging out front.

"I didn't do a thing. Let me go."

"I need you to stay with me. I need an alibi."

"For what?"

"I did some stuff. I took some stuff. If you would stand by your man this wouldn't happen." He pats his hand on his chest like he's the man and I should be his little lackey. Boy, I sure didn't see this side of him before or I would have had nothing to do with him. He used to be all about "Flower Power" and "Make Love Not War." That was cool.

"What kind of stuff?"

"Bad drugs. I'm freaking, and I took a lot. Really evil guys from the Heights are after me. You gotta get me outta this. It's your fault."

"It's not my fault and you're not my man."

When I look into his eyes, I realize I should cool it. He's not messing around with me; he's very serious and stoned on something that is doing something weird to his head. I figure I'll try to go along with whatever he says and we'll be meeting with Celia, Carlo, Jen and Pauly in a little while and going in to the theater.

Right then and there even though I try to be nice so he doesn't flip out and hurt me, I realize that I'm done with him no matter what and this is the last time I'm ever going to go out with him. But, it doesn't matter because even after everyone arrives and we all go into the theater and we sit there like nothing's wrong, the police come barging in with guns and clubs. They make the owner stop the film and drag Ford out in handcuffs.

But, before the others arrived, it was clear that Ford was just scared, that he wasn't really going to hurt me. Something was wrong. He took something he didn't know would mess him up so bad and he needed someone to help him. Was I the only one he could count on? I don't want to be any part of it and it is clear that Jen and Celia and the other guys are clueless about Ford's dilemma when they arrive. They are as shocked as I am when the police come charging in after Ford.

I never find out exactly what Ford did but somehow in his concocted brain, he figures he wouldn't have done it if I would have been around to hang out with him in the Bronx instead of taking a trip out of the neighborhood to Brooklyn with the girls. Then, later, Carlo and Pauly tell me how messed up on drugs Ford has become in the past few months, and that he's been dealing lids of reefer and all sorts of weird drugs like animal tranquilizers and stuff that makes your mind spin around upside down. So much for our summer plans. Now, the main concern for me is to make sure Mama and Papa don't find out about the crazy stuff about Ford or I'll be in deep shit and I'll never be able to go anywhere for the rest of the summer.

CHAPTER 21

Maria

Adultress. *The Scarlet Letter* scorches my brain like the bright red "A" that should be etched onto my own chest. I have betrayed my husband. I have had sexual relations with another man. I can't possibly live with myself, not just because of Luigi, but Pasquale. He is frantic with confusion about me, why I'm so upset. He tries to console me, handing me tissues in his van. I let this happen. How could I be so weak? I'm slouched over weeping with swollen eyes and looking frightful.

"I must go home now," I wail. "Please drive me home now." I don't know what he must think, but he throws on his clothes.

"What is wrong? What did I do? Please, you must tell me."

My sobs are so out-of-control that I can't speak with clarity, and when he pulls onto the street to drive me home, I try to control myself. He gazes over at me with concern, with a look of total bewilderment.

"We have such passion. Why are you sad?"

"I know," I say through my tears. "I know. But, I must tell you…"

"What can possibly matter?" He interrupts as he pulls up in front of my house. He leans over to kiss me again, but I give him a quick peck on the cheek and bolt from the van. I tear up the front steps. With haste, I dry my tears. I turn to wave at him as he pulls away but then, I lean against the door unable to muster the strength to face my family. But it's late—time that the dinner should be on the table. I open the door and there in the archway between the dining room and kitchen is Luigi with hands on hips glaring at me. I look away to hide my red eyes as I march past him and into the kitchen. Nonna and Angelina are preparing dinner. They barely look in my direction. I can feel the friction in the air.

"Where you been?" Luigi growls. I turn from the kitchen and scurry out and up the stairs.

• • •

I don't know what happens in my house for the rest of the evening. I don't even know why anyone doesn't ask me what is wrong or demand I come down and help, or eat or anything. I fall asleep on my bed in all my clothes. Maybe they think I'm sick. They would be right. I am sick—sick about what I'd done, sick about what is going on in my life, sick about how I feel. What I do find out later is that Luigi stormed out as soon as he finished eating.

He went to Tony's Bar next to the pool hall on Arthur Avenue, his usual hang out where he consumed his lager beer, watched sports on the TV, and complained to everyone that he has no respect. I heard the bartender, Tony Tucci talking to Frankie the next Sunday at church. Frankie and Tony are out front in the street as I come out the door with Nonna. I realize they are talking about my husband, how he is so miserable and how Tony refilled his glass twice while he told him he saw me hanging around with Anthony Corso's middle son, all chummy. I don't think Nonna can hear the conversation, so I walk a little slower to try and listen. Tony is caught in the act of gossip right there in front of the church. I hear him, and I look away, but not until I hear him say that Luigi doesn't believe a word, that Luigi said, "That's a' crap, that the boy was just working at our house, that Tony should get his eyes checked."

When I'm heading out to the market for some *romano* the next day, my neighbor two doors down whose sister is married to Tony confirms that he is spreading this around about me and then, I remember thinking that was him staring at me at Telly's Restaurant when I was there watching Pasquale sing. God, what am I going to do?

CHAPTER 22

Angelina

I've been trying to figure out what to do for the rest of the summer. Everything and everyone around me seems to be so alive with excitement and activity, but for me, things have gotten so messed up—not at all what I planned. I even figure I'll try to get a part time job at the A&W with Celia. Of course, I can't tell Papa. Maybe Mama would understand but better to keep it a secret from them both, at least until I know if they'll hire me. I'm all set to meet Celia now. I'm dressed in something a little conservative for the interview—my white blouse with the forest green jumper that is also sort of stylish. Me and Celia have the whole day planned. First we're stopping off at the A&W to fill out applications, then we're going to a matinee at "The Dumps." All the cute boys go on Saturday and then maybe we'll find out if there's anything exciting going on for later in the evening. I skip down the stairs noticing that Mama has the local news on the kitchen radio up really loud, and there she is peeking out the dining room window like a spy or something. Is there someone suspicious outside? I creep up next to her and she jumps. I look out and all I see is Pasquale getting out of his van. He's with Mr. Corso who is really looking fragile these days. I take another look at Pasquale trying to figure a way to approach him. If I were a little older, I'd have no trouble. I'd get him to grow his hair and wear some hip-huggers. Maybe I could get him to go to the "Human Be-In" in Central Park that everyone's talking about. I try to imagine Pasquale as a hippie. That would be a tough one, but then I think maybe I'm not really cut out to be a hippie either. Maybe I'll be more like a frat or a greaser, but Pasquale doesn't fall into either of those categories, he's just in the category of "older."

"You'll be home all day, right?" Mama asks.

"Ma, its Saturday. I'm going with Celia—you know, to the movies."

"You've got to keep an eye on Nonna," she demands. "Make sure she doesn't go out, and the boys, too. I can't be late. It's a busy holiday weekend and the store is crowded. Plus, didn't you go to the movies with those girls last night? You need to be careful. I just heard on the news there was some violence over there last night. You hear anything?"

"No Ma." God, if she only knew. But, now, I'm really ticked. I cross my arms and stomp my sandaled foot. She doesn't even get it. I don't know what's gotten into her lately. She slips on gigantic dark glasses like Jackie Kennedy, and grabs her purse before hurrying out the front door. She's like hiding from someone. I've never even seen her wear sunglasses, even at the beach.

"Pasquale will be working. See if he needs anything."

"I thought he was finished with the house."

"Papa's got him doing some more repairs. Ridiculous."

"Come on, Ma." But, she's not listening. She quietly opens the front door, looks around, playing the spy again, and then whizzes out. I'm starting to wonder what the heck is wrong with her lately. I hear Pasquale out on the roof in the back of the house. He's always up on that darn roof. Mama looks up, and then she zips off down the street. I slam the door, but actually I'm thinking of how I can get Pasquale's attention, if he would ever seriously be interested in me.

I stomp through the kitchen, wink at Nonna and barge out the back door to the picnic table. I plop down on top of it, kick my feet up and stretch out on top like I did when I was a kid. My legs dangle off at my knees now that I'm fully grown. I shade my eyes and watch Pasquale on the roof. Jeez, what a boring job, but I watch him for a while before making a quick decision. There's no way I'm staying home on a Saturday, even for Pasquale. Papa will be home in the afternoon and Nonna is here peeling potatoes. Plus, the boys are old enough to stay alone for a while by themselves if necessary. I leap off the table and head over to Celia's hoping it's not too late for the job application.

Celia's got all the news about Ford. Why am I always the last to know?

"If you would listen to the radio, you would know practically as much as everyone else," Celia says.

"God, it was on the radio? With his name and everything?"

"Not his name. He's a minor, but we know it was him. We were there."

We're rushing down the street toward the A&W and she's out of breath telling me everything. Every two seconds I'm like, "What? You're kidding? They couldn't have said all that on the radio."

"Well, you know, Jen heard from Pauly, and she heard from Ford's little brother. The judge was like telling his parents they'd let him out if they'd sign him into a rehab somewhere upstate and he'd have to live there and maybe even go to school there and they were crying and didn't want anyone to know and they agreed and he's gone. Gone, can you believe it?"

I'm scratching my head, jogging along side of Celia. "Can they do that?"

"That's what I heard, yea, I guess so. He's not supposed to be allowed to see any of his old friends even when he gets out—that means all of us, too."

"I guess I don't have a boyfriend anymore." I smile, but in a way, I do feel sort of bad for Ford. The drugs must have messed him up. "That's the most unusual way to break up with a guy. He seemed like a cool guy, sort of, at first, at least." I'm kind of stunned to know a real live criminal that the police have arrested and sent to a rehab. "What's a rehab?"

We both stop in front of the A&W and straighten our hair. "I don't know for sure. It must be some kind of jail you go to where they have school."

"I never heard of that before."

We go in and fill out applications for the waitress or counter jobs. We meet the manager who is not much older than the two of us, and then we walk over to 'The Dumps.'

"We have to figure out what to do for the July 4th weekend," Celia glances over at me like she feels sorry for me that my boyfriend turned out to be a criminal.

"Yeah, there's fireworks at Yankee Stadium," I say but I'm thinking in my head about Pasquale. I wonder what he's got planned. I bet I can get him to go to Yankee Stadium, but I certainly don't want Celia to know that. She would think I'd lost my marbles.

CHAPTER 23

Maria

Somehow I manage to avoid Pasquale all week. It takes tedious planning on my part—like planning to work early at Tia's, or taking the boys to the dentist before September rolls around—whatever I can think of to be out of the house when I know he's coming to finish up the tidbits of work that Luigi has hired him to do. I have to figure out how to tell him but I have to admit, I'm a plain old coward. Then, on Sunday, I have no more excuses. Not only does Pasquale normally come around for dinner but it's the Fourth-of-July holiday and Luigi's around for four whole days. I won't even have a chance to take Pasquale aside and explain.

It's early in the morning and the boys and Angelina are still upstairs getting ready for mass. I'm in the kitchen, as usual and Luigi's out in back puttering around on the patio like he knows how to fix anything out there. "Aw heck, I wait for Pasquale.

Why should I get my good clothes dirty? He knows how to fix these old shingles," Luigi complains.

I cringe when I hear him, and he keeps going on about Pasquale. "He's a good boy, told me that every Sunday is special to spend it with our family and that's why he brings over cannoli—it's something special."

The back door is open with just the screen door shut to keep out the flies. I pretend like I'm not paying attention, like I don't hear what he's saying. I have this gnawing intuition that today's going to be a difficult day. I know I'll have to face Pasquale.

• • •

We're on the sidewalk heading towards the house, me walking behind Luigi and Nonna and the kids trailing behind, and there he is coming toward us with the bakery box, a huge smile plastered on his face. I hurry in front of everyone and hold my head like I've got the worst headache in the world.

I turn back to my family before rushing into the house. "I have to lie down," I moan, "My head is killing me."

I don't wait to take in their expressions of surprise, plus, they have just spotted Pasquale and they're all busy greeting him joyously. I run up the stairs to my bedroom and lay on the bed staring at the yellowing stucco ceiling. I stare at a brown spot and wonder if it's a leak from the attic. Maybe from the old roof before Pasquale did all the work. And then, I think that this will be the next job Luigi will have Pasquale doing—fixing the ceiling. Anxiety makes my head hurt for real when I imagine this sexy man in the bedroom that I share with my husband. I glance around at pictures on the bureau. There is one of each of the kids and of course, there's a big one in the center of me and Luigi on our wedding day. I cover my face with my hands. I have to figure something out and quick.

There's nothing to do but lie here and think. As my mind concocts all sorts of crazy things—worst of all, Luigi finding out about my sins, I realize that I don't dare face Pasquale in the presence of my family today or any day. First, I must figure out how to deal with it all in my own head, and it all comes down to the simple fact that I must confess to Pasquale that I'm Luigi's wife. But, somehow, in my mind, I figure that if I avoid him maybe the problem will just go away. Maybe he won't come over anymore, then, I won't have to deal with facing the inevitable. But, every time Pasquale finishes one job at the house, Luigi finds something else for him to do, and now with the ceiling. It's inevitable. But, maybe Luigi won't notice and a few weeks back he was working at Lucca's across the street. If he's not at our house, he is on Lucca's roof every time I step outside. Maybe he'll find work someplace else. But, as I lie here, it's not even Pasquale that I'm concerned about. It's really Luigi. I don't know why he hasn't noticed that my ring is missing. And, why wasn't I thinking of my husband during my transgressions? He's dealing with a difficult time in his life—all the extra financial burdens and all, and certainly, what he doesn't need is a cheating, betraying wife who has lost a family heirloom ring. And then, I realize that I'm lying there concerned about my own husband's feelings, and really caring and loving him. It hurts that I was so stupid to do something so selfish that would hurt him deeply—and embarrass him, too. Now, all I can do is pray that he'll never find out.

Even at work, Tia and Kate keep asking why I'm wearing my old dowdy clothes again. I think I will punish myself and look like crap. They say I'm reverting back to my old-fashioned old self.

"Get with it," Tia lectures me.

They're all perky since its summer and they're giggling about beach plans and family get-togethers while I tromp around in a glum mood. I need to find a happy medium. I need to put all this Pasquale business in the past and I need to find my ring.

Fifteen

• • •

It's Monday and I hear Pasquale up on the roof even though it's a holiday—the day before July 4. I know he's fixing the gutters this time since I listened to their conversation while I was hiding up stairs on Sunday. It's really tough to be alone in the house especially when I know he's up there. I try to be quiet but he must know I'm in here. At the end of the day when I don't hear him prancing around up there, I figure he's gone home, but then, the doorbell rings. I ignore it pretending I'm not home, while I'm sitting quietly in the kitchen like a mouse avoiding the cat. I peek into the dining room and see his outline walking off towards the sidewalk. He seems so sad and it makes me feel like a first class jerk, but now, it's getting late and I have to head to Terranova Bakery before it closes or there will be no fresh bread for dinner. I slip on my dark glasses in case I run into him on the street and head out the front door. He rushes out from around the side of the house throwing me off guard and startling me so bad that I drop my purse. He reaches up and pulls the glasses off my face and takes a firm hold of my shoulders so that I have no choice but to face him and glimpse into those eyes.

"You think you hide from me with these silly glasses?" He says this in a flirtatious voice edging on laughter that it's all a game of hide-and-seek and I'm found—caught.

"I have to go. I have to get to the store." What he couldn't possibly know is that along with not wanting to face him, I'm worried that Luigi will see us together and get suspicious.

"I have things to do, too." He holds me firm. There is nothing I can do but face him, but I bow my head and pull away from him. I stand there hugging my body and quivering. A seriousness spreads over us and we both pause. Then, he gently takes a hold of my arm.

"Please, you don't need to avoid me. Can't we talk?"

I am suddenly brave and I face this exciting man and wonder how things have gone so far with him. I smile at him. It is my fault and I must deal with it.

"Yes, we must talk, but later."

"This evening, after dinner. I'll be waiting for you. Just tell me where."

I nod, "At the lake, by the picnic table." I walk off thinking I will have to make it quick with Pasquale since the fireworks will attract a crowd. He smiles and I can feel his eyes on me as I walk away down the street. I turn back and notice that Nonna has been watching us, up there all the time on the front porch swinging in her swing and gripping her spoon.

CHAPTER 24

Angelina

What a lousy July 4th holiday—first, all the drama with Ford, but at least I don't have to worry about him anymore. I think I might see Pasquale at Yankee Stadium but there's no sign of him. Celia and Jen try to get me interested in Gianni, the new kid from Sicily who just moved in the neighborhood. I figure it won't be so bad. He doesn't speak much English and we can just sort of hang out. He doesn't smoke pot, just cigarettes. And, he doesn't talk much. The only trouble with that, with him, is that he smells like garlic and has slimy permanently wet lips. The six of us are perched up at the top row of bleachers for the fireworks. He licks his lips and then mauls me and kisses my neck when I'm not expecting it and rubs against me making sure I can feel his hard penis, so disgusting. I'm sure he thinks it's so cool. And what can I do? Celia's making out with Carlo like they're Siamese twins. She swears they really did go all the way this time. And, Jen and Pauly, they like make out and then fight like wild animals and then make out some more. Oh man, what a summer. And I'm feeling so tired lately, like I just don't care and would rather just stay home. They all want to go to the Viet Nam anti-war demonstration in the city, but then there're all the riots we've been hearing about. Sometimes I just feel like staying home in my room by myself. But, the big thing to look forward to is the "Human Be-In" in Central Park. I've been looking forward to that for months.

Jen says, "We should all wear hippie beads so we look cool, man."

I'm fine with that, but we're walking around Arthur Avenue with wilted daisies in our hair, which seems pretty retarded to me. I guess it's just that I have this bad attitude lately. I'm thinking I have the flu or something and really don't want to go anywhere in the awful heat. They say it's the hottest summer on record. I think maybe I should see a doctor but I definitely don't want to, then I think back to Aunt Francine when she was talking to Mama one time. She said how sick she got when she was pregnant with Lita. Oh my God, pregnant. That's just not possible. I've only gone all the way that once with Ford and that was not because I wanted to do it. But, I guess you don't have to want to get pregnant.

While no one is looking, I study the kitchen calendar and try to remember exactly when I had my last visit from my "friend"—my menstrual period. I'm sure it was the first of June and it's already July. I go to the bathroom and check. I think each day that it will come soon. And, I think back to a few months ago when I was late and everyone joked with me that I was pregnant. Funny, "I'm a virgin," I had said. Jen had said, "Well, look at the Virgin Mary. She got pregnant."

So now, along with the obsession of imagining what it would be like to be Pasquale's girlfriend, I have the thought of pregnancy pounding away at my brain like a baby's rattle smacking into my eardrums. I might as well just lie down and die right now. I find myself in tears at any little thing. What's wrong with me? I form my hands in prayer position.

"Please God; let my 'friend' come."

But, that doesn't help. More things enter my brain through cracks somewhere in there. If I am pregnant, what am I going to do? There's no father. I'll have to leave home. Maybe I can go stay with Uncle Carmine in California, or go find a hippie commune somewhere. I start to look forward to going to the Be-In. Maybe I can meet some hardcore hippies and help sell daisies and panhandle with them and have my baby with them to help me. Baby, what, am I nuts? My "friend" will be here any day. I look in the mirror over my bureau and I gasp. Tears stream down my face. No, I don't want to be pregnant. I can't be. And then, I force myself to be practical. Ford is gone. There's no papa. I have to find a papa for my baby, just in case there's a baby. I say the word out loud, BABY. I'm too young to have a baby. But then, there's an answer to my problems—Pasquale, he would be the perfect papa.

CHAPTER 25

Maria

My jaw is set in rigid determination as I fling open the front door to the shop. Tia is behind the counter fiddling with the adding machine and some receipts when I march in and remove my dark glasses. She sees the anguish in my eyes the second she glances up at me. I stand there in front of the counter staring at her. Her expression changes immediately at the sight of my seriousness. She knows me, probably better than anyone, and she knows that my stone face is a front, that I'm really on the verge of tears.

"I need to talk," I announce.

Tia abandons her work like it has no importance at all—like it's a crumb on the floor, and she wraps an arm around my shoulder. She walks me to the back room to hunker down over the café table. My head is bowed so low that the tears drip right into my hands wringing on my lap.

"What on Earth?" Tia asks.

"I sinned. I don't know how I could have done it, but, I did. I, uh, I did it with the worker, and I don't know what to do."

"Whoa. Slow down. You did it? You had sex with the worker?"

I can hardly speak, I'm sobbing in fits of practically a seizure. I nod my head up and down fiercely.

"Sweetie, it's not the end of the world. Guys do it all the time."

"But, he still thinks I'm Angelina's sister. I just kept playing along. I never thought it would go so far."

Tia hands me a tissue. I know her eyes are as big and popped out as Louie's pet frog. I should have told her before. Tia always knows what to do in situations like this. She lays a sympathetic hand on my thigh.

"He really thinks that? Doesn't he see you're married?"

"That's the other thing. I lost my wedding ring," I look up at her knowing she will tell me exactly what I should do.

"Oh Honey, your ring? Did you take it off so he wouldn't know you were married?"

"No, I thought it fell down the drain but it's not there and I've looked everywhere."

"It'll be okay. I'll help find your ring, but you gotta tell the worker, at least so Luigi doesn't find out."

I get up and hug her. She doesn't have to tell me this. I already know it.

I don't know how I make it through the day and especially during the evening dinner with my family. I'm so grateful that Luigi goes out to the pool hall after dinner and Celia and Jen come over to watch TV with Angelina. It's simple, like God knows I have to confess to Pasquale and he's just making a path for me. All I do is announce I'm going to walk the boys over to the park. Nonna looks at me with suspicion, but that's nothing unusual. I grab a light raincoat from the hall closet and slip out the front door behind the boys who already have their baseball mitts and ball and are excited to run out to play. I'm hoping it doesn't rain and ruin my intention.

We arrive at the park, my eyes darting around at each person I see. It's light out— close to the longest day of the year now. There are families out walking and lovers and a few people jogging along on the path, but when the boys veer off towards the baseball diamond, I take the less traveled path down by our spot and the picnic table where Pasquale and I had stopped to talk and make-out. My hands shake so intensely when I spot Pasquale perched on top of the table looking out at the view and singing a soft love ballad. I fiddle with the gold cross around my neck, the one Luigi gave me for Christmas last year and I wish I had my ring so that the sight of the ring would simply tell the story, so I would not have to form the words.

When Pasquale notices me, he jumps off the table and approaches me with worry in his expression. He can tell there is something wrong the minute he looks at me. He leads me to the picnic table and we sit side by side on the side facing away from the path.

"You must see that I can't do this," I say knowing there is no way I can look into his eyes. Not just his eyes, I cannot stand to look at his sun-tanned hand on my arm, the masculinity of his gentle but creative fingers. Then, with both hands, he takes my trembling hands away from my necklace and holds them with tenderness.

"But why? Is there someone else?"

"You've misunderstood from the beginning. I let you believe…"

From nowhere like soaring jets, my two boys fly to me. I

don't know why they never called me Mama in front of Pasquale before, but now it all comes out. Louie tugs on my arm and Johnny yells, "Mama, he's lying. I didn't do a thing."

"You hit me on purpose, you and that mean boy," Louie cries. Another boy appears with apologies and the boys turn away to sort out their own battle. But Pasquale is on his feet staring at me in absolute shock. It is clear that he did not know I am the mama. He looks over at the boys and points at them.

"They, you are…" He turns his back and covers his face with his hands. I am speechless when he spins back around facing me. "Mama? You are their mama?"

"Pasquale, I'm sorry."

"You are married, that is why?"

The boys have gone back to the baseball field and I am alone with Pasquale who stands there in front of me leaning over with a crinkled brow in disbelief.

"You are married to Luigi? Luigi!"

I look up at him just once, enough for the memory of the pain and disappointment in his expression to burn a spot in my memory forever.

"I'm sorry."

He leaves me there sitting on the side bench of the picnic table. I am frozen in sadness and Pasquale is gone. Now he knows, I'm not the sister. I'm the mama and I must face my life—that is what I am. That is my life.

• • •

Although I feel emptiness in my heart, I have a certain feeling of relief. This fake life I've been leading has been eating away at me and it was never right, how I behaved. But my life isn't right and I just can't figure what to do to get it back on track. Was it ever on the right track anyway? I'm glad that Pasquale has finished most of the work at the house and he hasn't been around lately. I don't know how I can face him anymore. He must hate me. And, he doesn't show up on Sunday, so maybe we won't see him anymore. But, I still have a dull ache inside my heart. I have such guilt of what I did to Luigi, and I pray he never finds out.

CHAPTER 26

Angelina

My "friend" has not arrived. I know I must be pregnant, and each day I tell myself to find a solution. Who can I ask? Who, that I trust, will know what to do? I need a father and I dream up all sorts of things I can do—elaborate antics that each time I suppose I have the perfect plan, I realize it's ridiculous. I chant to myself over and over like it will do some good. Ha.

"Father, Father, Father, Father," I say it out loud lying there on my bed and then I realize someone in my family might hear me and I clasp both hands over my mouth.

Maybe Pasquale's brother Gino—he's been hanging around with our group lately and he seems to like me, but then, I'd rather have Pasquale. None of the other guys even have jobs or could afford to support a wife and child. I zero in on options and it's definitely Pasquale who is the first choice of anyone. I concoct a plan. I remember how Ford's personality changed so much when he got drunk and in the tree house, he forced me like an animal. How can I get Pasquale alone and persuade him to get drunk? Unless I just happen to run into him and get him to take me somewhere and do it, the only other option is at the house on a Sunday. That's it. When he's ready to leave on Sunday, I'll walk out with him and tell him I need to talk. I'll get a bottle of one of Papa Vito's whiskey collection. I check the cupboard and those bottles sit there covered in dust. Nonna gives me the evil eye like I better not even think of touching any of Papa Vito's booze. Oh man, he's dead for ages. Sometimes I don't think she realizes it. I'll wrap a bottle up as a gift for helping our family and I'll walk him out and give it to him. He'll surely invite me somewhere to have a drink with him, or maybe to go out with him somewhere. And when he gets drunk, I'll let him go all the way with me. I'll tell him I'm into free love and if he wants some, I'm all for it.

I lie on my bed reflecting on this plan and I think it might work but then doubt creeps in and I don't think I'll have the nerve to go through with it. My brain is worn out, but I decide I will have to give it a shot. What other choice do I have? And then I remember he plays guitar. I can ask him to give me lessons. That will be the first step to hook him—to get him to want me, to like me. I will ask him on Sunday.

But, he doesn't come on Sunday. I panic. Something must be wrong, but what? I track down Gino at "The Dumps" and tell him I'm dying to reach his brother that I definitely have this incredible craving to learn guitar. That sort of works. Now I have to deal with Gino who seems to think it's him I like, and every time I turn around he's right there.

Suddenly, all in the same day, I get a job at A&W that I have to keep secret from Papa, and I meet with Pasquale to arrange guitar lessons. I tell him I can pay him from my wages at my new job, but that he has to promise not to tell Papa.

CHAPTER 27

Maria

The kids are totally into their summer routines and I'm busier than ever at Tia's. This is all a good thing under the circumstances I've put myself in. Yes, I'm so grateful to have plenty to keep my mind off my sins, and to try getting back to my regular life as a mama and a wife. As far as my vanished ring, I've decided to save up my earning from Tia's to buy a ring—one that looks something like my original wedding ring with the cluster of tiny chips of diamonds around the edge. Since Luigi's eyes are getting bad and he needs glasses to work at the patterns, maybe he won't notice. After all, he only wears glasses at home when he's reading the paper.

As I walk home from Tia's with fresh macaroni from Borgatti's, I'm still thinking of Pasquale, and I'm trying to think where I can purchase a look-alike ring. At the same time, I'm struggling to get my thoughts into normal things like making the dinner for my family.

At the front door, I see baseball stuff all over the sidewalk. What's wrong with these boys of mine? Some guy passing by who has a little boy might just decide to pick up a nice leather mitt and take it home with him. I turn to yell at the boys to pick up the baseball stuff when I'm already half way in the front door. That's when I hear a voice from the living room, which causes me to drop the bag of macaroni.

"Look, my Angel your mama is here," Pasquale chirps.

My jaw has dropped like I'm catching flies. There on the couch is Pasquale with Angelina and he's teaching her to play guitar, alone, the two of them in my living room, on the same couch that I couldn't resist the passionate kiss from this man only a few months ago. Like a statue frozen in disbelief, I listen to them laughing and talking softly and close together practically on top of each other. And then, I move into the room.

Angelina leaps off the couch where she is cuddled with Pasquale. He sits there smiling up at me, but I turn away and pick up the bag of macaroni trying desperately to compose myself.

"Ma, Pasquale is teaching me to play. It's so much fun."

I can't look at them. I scurry off to the kitchen, but they can see me from the couch. I turn my back. My heart hammers in my chest, like it's a wild animal in a cage, as I lean against the counter. My emotions are out of control now, like an angry mother lion protecting her cub, I'm ready to be set free to go for Pasquale's juggler. They are there together, my innocent daughter and my hot, sexy lover. They bop into the kitchen. I open the refrigerator practically pulling the door off the hinges and furiously pull food out—all sorts of food, anything I see that might make the dinner, celery, lettuce, tomatoes, cheese, olives.

I snap, "Wash up now, Angelina and help with the dinner." I spin around and face her. "And, Nonna, she's out?"

"How can I stop her? She sneaks out."

"Conveniently," I mumble, and turn my back on them. I busy myself at the sink re-washing clean dishes over again.

"Mama, Pasquale is staying for dinner, alright?" I'm wondering why she couldn't have called me Mama when we first met Pasquale. That might have changed the dynamics of things in our family. Would he have come every Sunday to butter up me and Luigi if he had an interest in seducing our teenage daughter? He never showed interest in her before. It was me he paid attention to, flirting with me, pursuing me, making love to me, leading me to believe that there was something special between us. But, it was not Pasquale that did the deceiving, it was me, and now his revenge is seducing my innocent daughter. How could he do this to me?

Pasquale must see my distress. He says sarcastically, "Thank you, no, my Angel. I promised my mama to join the family for dinner. Another night, maybe?"

I can't help but notice that he stresses the word, mama and points his seducing nose in my direction. The sound of his voice saying, "Maaaaammmmmaaaa" resonates in my mind.

"Sure," I say without turning to face him and I give him a glimpse of my sour expression.

"Oh no, Pasquale, it's no fun without you here," Angelina whines.

"My little angel, you flatter me. Go now and help your sweet mama."

She runs out of the room in a teenage tantrum, but it's only to fetch the guitar, and in that short second, Pasquale tiptoes around the side of the counter to where I stand by the sink. He leans down and whispers in my ear, "Only you hold my heart. You have turned me into a sinner."

My head is bowed but he kisses me on the back of my head and my cold expression softens slightly. The lion tamer's charms succeed.

Angelina returns with Pasquale's guitar.

"Ciao," he says stepping away from me.

CHAPTER 28

Angelina

I used to think Mama was the coolest, most understanding mother in the whole world but she's been acting so wacky lately and she's treating me like a kid. It used to seem like she understood me, like when I broke up with Ford, even though she didn't know all the circumstances, or when I came home late and she didn't tell Papa. But, she's been acting crazy lately. Maybe that's just what happens when you get older; you just don't understand what it's like, you know, like how hard it is to be a teenager. I'm almost an adult. I'm trying to live my life free. She needs to quit treating me like a kid especially with all the other things I've got on my mind.

The chanting is happening in my head again, "Father, Father..." Pasquale must think I'm weak, that I'm a wimp or something to put up with a family that I'm stuck with. I don't know what's going on in my head. It's like I'm obsessed with Pasquale more than ever. He acts like he wants to be part of our family, like he really likes all of us. Maybe it's just an act with him because he wants me to like him. Maybe he's just showing off by playing ball with the boys and coming to dinner and acting all sweet to Mama and respectful to Papa. But, I'll have to make a point to tell him that he doesn't need to do that anymore. I don't want to be too anxious, but he needs to know that he's got me in his corner—our corner. And, if it works out my way, a "love nest." It might be fun to just be together away from the family. I think I'm ready to go all the way on a regular basis, now that I'm experienced, and I sure would like it to be with Pasquale. He's a real man, but even though he's older, it's not that many years. Look at my mama and papa. She was married around my age and Papa was something like Pasquale's age. It's perfect, and so romantic. In comparison, Ford doesn't even come close. I don't know what I ever saw in him.

Sometimes my mind gets carried away. I'm thinking that Mama really did sort of embarrass me in front of Pasquale. She barged in right in the middle of me and Pasquale really starting to make a connection. And aside from the "father plan," I really was enjoying the actual guitar lesson. I was envisioning us like Sonny and Cher or something. Man, I have a lousy voice, but I'd play the guitar and he'd sing a love song on stage in front of a ton of people, but he'd ignore the crowd and sing directly to me. I'd be sitting there on a stool in a maxi dress with flowing sleeves and my hair ironed and parted down the center, the way Papa hates it.

I walk Pasquale to the door hanging on his arm so he can see that I'm interested. He says something about how I will be a guitar-playing sensation and I can't help giggling at his silliness, and there's Mama peeking around the corner of the kitchen door. God, is she really eavesdropping on us? I reach up and give Pasquale a hug and surprise him with a kiss right on the lips before he exits.

Mama's in the kitchen pretending like she's not listening to us. I'm down that Pasquale isn't staying for dinner, but, she doesn't have to be so rude to him.

"You make a fool of yourself with that man," Mama says to me like I'm ten-years-old. I don't even believe she's treating me like this. "You practically fall all over him. Here, wash the lettuce." She practically throws the lettuce at me and it almost goes tumbling to the floor like a soccer ball. Then, she heaves carrots and peppers and green beans towards me—green beans—we never put green beans in the salad. I'm sure not laughing anymore. In fact, I'm sick of this behavior from her.

"You don't know anything," I spit out. "He respects me."

"Oh really?" She stands facing me with her face all flushed and her hands on her hips, and I notice she's wearing that ugly old-lady apron that I hate. Pasquale must think I have a prude for a mother. "What must he think of a child acting like this? Respect, huh? You humor him."

"I'm not a child. You know that." I slam the lettuce down on the counter.

"I know enough to see you blatantly flirting with a man twice your age."

"What about you and Papa? He's older than you."

"He was from Italy. It's different now."

There's no use fighting with her, she's too old, she will never understand.

CHAPTER 29

Maria

I wonder how on Earth I could have allowed myself to fall for Pasquale's flirtatious compliments, to anticipate every possible second with him, and to actually deceive him into believing I was something I'm not. I drop my head into my hands and silently weep. How could I have sinned in this way? How could I have had consensual sex with this man? I am so tormented by my actions, and the worst is the repercussions. Not only do I suffer every minute of the day, but he will punish me by getting at Angelina. Now I begin to feel something else for him—anger and bitterness. What made him think it was okay to play with my daughter's emotions, a fifteen-year-old who is naive and immature, ready to believe in anything a charismatic hunk of a man would say. Did he make her trust that he feels something for her? Of course, she would believe it in her adolescent mind the way he carries on. But, maybe there's nothing to worry about. Maybe I'm making too much of the silly guitar lesson. I had forgotten about Ford. I know Angelina was excited about hanging around with him and her group of friends for the summer. It's probably nothing, that she just hasn't mentioned Ford lately. My mind plays tricks on me when it involves Pasquale, that's all. To think that Angelina would be even the slightest bit interested in an adult like Pasquale is pretty much ridiculous. One thing that's for sure—he hasn't been around for over a week and Angelina hasn't mentioned a thing about him. I'm pretty sure she's interested in another boy, other than Ford, or maybe not. I'll have to keep my ears open. She's been hanging around with Celia a lot this week, but I know she's boy crazy. Maybe it's someone new that Celia knows that has caught her fancy. It's time for me to quit acting like a teenager myself and pay attention to what's going on with my own daughter before it's too late.

It's dark at the kitchen table where I sit in my robe and slippers. The usual creaks and gurgles of the house are amplified against the silence—sounds that no one notices during daylight. The kitchen clock encircled in golden crosses that I never notice during the day, tick-tocks like a bomb. I can hardly see the hands that read 12:11am. It's much too late for Angelina to be out, but she would have called if she was staying overnight at

Celia's. I contemplate whether I should phone the Rubino house at this late hour.

The back door eases open as if a burglar is sneaking in. I exhale relief as I recognize its Angelina slinking in. She gasps, startled to see me at the table staring at her. Then, in her panic, she knocks over the boy's baseball bats that are propped up against the cabinet. The crashing clamor disturbs the silence. A dog barks at a neighbor's house and an angry holler disrupts the calm.

"Mama?"

"Shhh. Go to bed," I just stare like a figurine as she tiptoes towards the front stairs. In my heart I know I must approach my daughter with a mother-to-daughter talk. I contemplate it in my head, but don't know quite how to tackle this issue—this concern. One thing's for sure, Angelina is up to something and her attitude is not acceptable.

I'm still thinking about Angelina in the morning. I have just scooted Luigi out the door to work with a tasty lunch of leftover veal on a fresh roll and a container of fresh melon. I've been treating him extra special these days. The boys are out front playing stickball in the street with a group of neighbor boys and I'm considering what will be the best way to open up a chat with Angelina. I want us to get along, for her to tell me what's going on in her life like she used to do when she was younger—not so many years ago. She would tell me every detail of an afternoon with Celia—every single thing they did and what all the girls said and thought and what they dreamed and loved. I hear her coming down the stairs two at a time, in a rush. I'll fix her some breakfast and we can talk. It's my day off; maybe we can go shopping. I wipe my hands on my apron and walk over to the banister. She has her tote bag and purse and is all dressed with make-up ready to dart out the door. She glances over at me with a frown and heads to the front door. I hurry to her side and take a hold of her arm.

"You were out too late last night. I can't imagine that Celia's mother would let her be out so late."

She pulls out of my grip. "Ma, it wasn't that late." She opens the front door and exits. I'm so raging mad. I can't believe she thinks she can just walk out of the house first thing in the morning without an explanation of her whereabouts and not even so much as to tell me she's going to where ever she's going. I follow her out the door as she hops down the porch steps toward the sidewalk.

"It was after midnight, missy."

She turns around to look at me hesitating briefly. "School's out. What's the big deal?"

"A girl your age should not be out alone so late. Your papa would go nuts."

"Ma, I wasn't alone. You treat me like a child." She turns away again and I follow her to the sidewalk and grab her arm again. I turn her to face me as the boys chase around us with their friends in a game of tag.

"Nah, nah, nah, nah. Lina's in trouble," Johnny sings sticking out his tongue at Angelina.

"What do you mean?" I demand holding tight with an iron-claw grip on my daughter's arm. "You weren't with Celia, at her house? Were you with Ford?"

Then, I realize what I must look like to her and I think of my intention to have a nice talk with her before she blatantly darted out the front door. I let go of her arm and we gaze at each other, me with pleading and concern in my expression, but Angelina with boredom and annoyance in her eyes.

"I was at Celia's, Ma. I'll be back to help with dinner."

Before she turns and walks away down the sidewalk, she pats me on the arm as if to indicate that everything's okay. I stand there watching her thinking of myself at fifteen. That could have been me. She has my way of walking, slightly pigeon-toed on the right side, funny how that happens. As I turn back to the house, I notice the boys engaged in a stickball game and oblivious to my sadness.

CHAPTER 30

Angelina

Since I didn't care for that jerk, Gianni, Celia and Jen want me to hang out with Gino—of all the guys in the Bronx and they pick the little brother of the love of my life. If he only knew I'm probably pregnant and his brother is going to be the father, if I can figure out a way to make that happen. This thought provides momentary comedic relief to my stressed brain. I'm thinking, really, what am I gonna do? This is no joke. I have to be realistic. I can't follow Pasquale around or anything like that. But now, at least I've got him to give me lessons at his parent's house so Mama won't bother us. And, I plan it out so I will bring one of those whiskey bottles over when I know no one is going to be around. It's hard though with Gino on my case—always trying to kiss me and stuff. If it wasn't for my situation, I might be okay with going out with him. I mean, he's nice and all, just too young for me. I need a man, and even though he's two years older than me, it's not enough. And lately, it seems like every time I'm out with the group, Gino is there with us and we sort of get paired off unless there're some other girls or guys along, but now it's usually Celia, Paul, Jen, Carlo, Gino and me.

On the way to the movies on Friday night, it's the six of us and we're like paired off. We're walking down Arthur Avenue and Paul and Carlo have their bodies all wrapped up with Celia and Jen. I'm trying to walk as far away from Gino as possible, but then he slings his arm around my shoulder sort of casually and not too intimate, so I let it go for the time being. We're almost to the theater anyway, and I figure I'll try to sit at the end by Celia to avoid Gino. So, while I'm deep in thought about what I'm going to do about our seating arrangement, from around the corner Pasquale appears with his guitar case. I pull away from Gino. I don't want to spoil my plan. He's in a rush and says a quick hello and hurries off. I'm thinking maybe he didn't notice Gino's arm but I figure it won't help to worry about it. So a little later while the movie's playing I'm fantasizing about being with Pasquale, hurrying down the street with him carrying his guitar probably headed to his gig at Telly's, and maybe I'd get to hang back stage, hand him his guitar when he's ready for it on stage, or maybe even he would announce a special, very talented guest and he would announce my name and I would be a little shy at first but then I'd ease out on stage next to him and we would do a love song and then everyone would applaud like we were the best thing since our papas got off the boat from Italy.

But in reality, there I am with Gino. I glance over at him and suddenly feel hopelessly depressed. We end up sitting right next to each other. Oh man. How did I get into this? It's just that I don't want to encourage him or even carry on a conversation with him. As soon as the lights go out, he drapes his arm around my shoulder. Oh well, no one can see in the dark. I try not to think about it but then when I don't push it away, he starts creeping his fingers right down to my breast. Oh man, then, he leans over and kisses me right when Mrs. Robinson kisses Benjamin on the screen. I pull away claiming I have to pee.

In the bathroom girls are chattering about their boyfriends, two of them are smoking. It's almost all teenagers on Friday nights—the hang out for the neighborhood. I go in a stall and sit there thinking about what I'm going to do. When I come out some girl I met a few times, Janice, I think is her name, she says something about my boyfriend. I panic thinking everyone thinks Gino's my boyfriend. My plan is down the drain.

"Who, Gino?"

She smiles. "He's really cute."

"He's not my boyfriend. He's my boyfriend's brother." I wash my hands with a serious face.

Janice's friend comes out of a stall and they give me a wild look. "Free love? A little brotherly love?"

"Naw," I say, but I'm curious.

"He said you were his girl. You doin' it with both a' them?"

"Of course not," I snap and now I have a really bad case of the hiccups, the ones you can't control by holding your breath. I rush back into the darkened theater. I don't sit in my seat. I go straight to Celia and tell her I'm not feeling well that I'm going home. I avoid even looking at Gino who must think I'm nuts. But then as I'm trying to whisper to her, the loudest hiccup escapes my mouth and everyone turns to look and snicker. Oh man. It looks like Gino is getting up to come over by me. I turn and practically race out of the place.

I like Gino. Actually, I like him a lot, but he just doesn't fit into my life right now. The biggest problem is that somehow he finds out when I'm going for guitar lessons at the Corso house, and ends up hanging around instead of going out and doing something else. So, my plans to get Pasquale drunk and seduce him keep getting messed up. And, I'm carrying around this wrapped up bottle of whiskey every time I go over there and Pasquale's wondering why I need so many guitar lessons a week. I'll have to think up some other way to get Pasquale to fall for me, but it's getting later and later and my "friend" hasn't come, and I'm pretty sure I'm, you know, I can't even say it or even think about it or it gets me so depressed. I have to face it—I'm definitely, definitely, uh, in trouble. Then, I panic. What am I going to do? My brain starts doing that crazy thing again—forcing me to deal with the problem. "Father, Father...." And then I think, Father Milani—maybe that's why I keep thinking that crazy chant in my head. I need to talk to Father Milani. Confess? I'm not so sure.

I'm afraid Pasquale might think I like his brother and that would kill my plan. Gino's lurking again. Pasquale must tell him when I'm coming over for a lesson because he's always right there hanging around just outside the door. I just manage to dodge a date request from him when Pasquale takes the guitar to put it back in the case. I pretend I have to be somewhere and dart out of the Corso house. Actually, he's a really nice guy and I feel bad to hurt his feelings. That's usually how I've been treated by guys. Oh man, if anyone knows what that feels like, it's me, and with all my other problems that's the last thing I need, another thing to feel like crap about, but he's definitely a road block and I don't have time for a detour. I head straight towards the church after my guitar lesson.

I pause in front of the church considering that I'd rather just go home, but I figure I got this far and nothing else in my plan has worked so I might as well give it a shot. Confession is supposed to be a way for God to help you solve your problems. I don't know if I believe that God can help but what other choice do I have?

As I walk in the massive arched doorway, each step is a major accomplishment. It's all I can do to force myself to move forward, and then just past the holy water receptacles I turn and start back towards the door to exit. Father Carmichael steps forward from the side of the foyer. I don't really know him well. He's only been with the parish for a few months, and when I gawk at him with a shocked expression, I see that he's young and more gorgeous than any priest I've ever seen. My experience with priests is that they are grey-haired and feeble, like Papa Vito, but up close, this Father Carmichael looks like maybe Pasquale's age, and actually, he looks something like Pasquale. Oh man, how can I tell him I'm in trouble?

"Angelina, that's your name, right?"

"I just came… I just, uh, was looking for Father Milani, but that's okay. I, uh, just wanted to pray for my grandfather."

"Very nice. Your grandfather?"

"Vito Campisi. He died a year ago."

Now, I feel worse. I know this Father Carmichael can see I'm lying—another sin chalked up on my slate and right here in church. What could be worse?

"I'm so sorry, Father Milani is visiting his family Upstate for a few days. Would you like for me to pray with you?"

I bow my head and fight back tears. I'm such a bad person and a hopeless one at that. "No, no, that's okay. I have to hurry home to help with dinner. I almost forgot."

The nice Father puts his arm on my shoulder. "If there's anything you want to talk about you can always speak to me."

I nod and then dart out the door. I can feel the sweat rolling down my neck as I exit the church. What was I thinking? How can a priest help me find a father for my baby? And then, when I think the actual word, baby, and it actually sinks in to my consciousness that it's a real baby in me, I slow my pace from a hare to a turtle. What in the name of God am I going to do with a baby? I feel like jumping in the lion's cage over at the zoo and be done with it—everything.

• • •

I still have the whiskey bottle in my tote when my plans fall through again. Somehow, each day I get a renewed focus on solving my father problem. Frantically, I march back over to Our Lady Mt. Carmel and go directly to the confession booth. Is it Father Carmichael in there, or maybe Father Milani has returned? But no, there's a notice up on the bulletin board by the door. He's out in Italy with the Pope for some meeting or whatever, just when I need him most. I chicken out again, this time at the booth. Who knows who's behind that window—it could be one of the priests who knows Mama and Papa, or Father Carmichael who I would be embarrassed to tell something so intimate, so much like Pasquale and all. I kneel at the pew and, with tears, pray for a father, and I pray that there is no baby, and I pray that I am a little kid again, and that I never met Ford. And then I pray that Papa and Mama and none of them would ever have to find out about me. I begin to sob out loud, and the sound of my sadness echoes in the church so I must leave immediately before anyone notices me. A few people interrupt their prayers to glance at me as I slip out the back door. One of them is Nonna. That's all I need.

• • •

And, each day it seems like I start out with a positive goal in my mind and something happens that I realize I'm stuck. There's no solution, and then I go to my lesson with Pasquale and Gino doesn't seem to be around and we're there alone in Pasquale's parents' house and we're cuddling on his couch, strumming the guitar and he looks into my eyes and I smile at him and he pauses and it's like he really sees me and it's like he likes me in the way a husband would like a wife and in a way that you know he's a wonderful father and in a way that I know he cares and will love me forever no matter what and he will protect me and our child and make me happy and make everything okay and in fact, he will make everything perfect and wonderful and there's nothing in the world that can be better, there's no problems and he is happy that we are having a child and we will be married and everyone will be so thrilled. I kiss him on the cheek just as his mama enters the house through the front door.

He turns from me and goes to her, "Mama, let me take those bags." He turns and smiles at me and back at her, "Angelina is a great musician, so enthusiastic."

"Yes, I see," Josephine Corso says with curiosity in her eyes. So now I am convinced that everything will work out with Pasquale. A new plan is concocted in my brain in an instant as I bobble down the street on a cloud of passion. This must be what it feels like to be on some of those psychedelic drugs. No, it could never feel this good.

CHAPTER 31

Maria

Instinctively, I knew there could never be anything to worry about with Pasquale and Angelina, but I find myself wondering about how I could have gotten so absorbed with this man, and each day, I agonize more and more about how I behaved so "out of character" from my normal self. I can't seem to shake the obsession with the fact that I got, not only physically involved with him, but that he got under my skin emotionally. I have been so angry at myself for letting this happen. And then I think of him with Angelina. Never. I will not let that happen, but he has not been to the house since. I haven't heard a thing from him since that day, not working at the house or coming by on Sunday. Nothing. But as ridiculous as it seems, I'm still obsessed with wondering if he ever did care about me—if he really was attracted to me. Did he ever think and dream about me the way I fantasize about him? I consciously make an effort to fantasize about Luigi that way. He used to be so romantic and sexy, but then, he comes home and his "stones" are bothering him and he's ready to bite everyone's head off. What's there to fantasize about that?

As we trek over to Francine and Giuseppe's for Sunday dinner, I think about all the changes in me over the past month or so. Just like the clothing I alter in Tia's shop, my existence has been altered. I have not only committed adultery, but I have lusted over another man without shame or concern. But, one of the obvious things about me that I'm sure is apparent to those around me is the change in my appearance. Luigi is the only one who doesn't seem to notice—at least, I don't think he notices. I hardly ever ask for his approval anymore and he doesn't usually say much about what I'm wearing or how I'm fixing my hair like he used to do. Could he be interested in someone else? No, of course not.

I get Tia to help me find an inexpensive ring in her friend's costume jewelry shop connected to Gianni's Hair Salon on Belmont. As we are heading back over to Tia's shop after purchasing the fake ring, we walk by Maurizio's Pawn Shop and right there in the window is a ring I swear is my wedding ring. How can that be? The shop is closed with a sign that says something about a funeral in the family but I decide I will come back in a few days to check out the ring. Tia insists there is no way it's my ring but my instincts tell me there's something about this ring. Replacing my heirloom ring with a fake was easier than I thought. Maybe that's why I feel so sure the pawn shop ring is the real thing, and now every time I look at the fake ring on my finger, my heart breaks that I lost the ring that Luigi was so proud to give to me on our wedding day.

Once I get the ring issue temporarily taken care of, I get into solidifying my style, as Tia says. I purchase four new dresses from her shop, with a discount, of course. I feel more in with the current fashion and I know everyone notices because all my neighbors comment when I walk in the bodega or the bakery and of course, Francine always has something to say about how I look like one of the kids who call themselves "freaks." But, she has eased up a bit and finally allows her two girls to dress more fashionable, within reason, that is. And, oddly enough, Angelina seems to be dressing a little more conservative these days. But, on Sundays, Rosa and Lita have to wear their traditional Sunday dresses like Francine's mama made her wear back in Italy. We hear this every Sunday at least once. The girls roll their eyes and Angelina and I snicker. I never did find a way to approach Angelina for our girl talk, but she seems mellowed out a bit with a certain sense of maturity that I have to admire. Maybe things are getting back to normal in our family. We agree that she will be considerate and tell me where she's going and when she'll return when she goes out with her friends. I think she realizes that it's just because I don't want to worry. She knows that our little agreement is between us, nothing to do with her papa, who would go through the roof if he knew of her gallivanting around.

We each carry a portion of our family's contribution to the dinner on our walk over to Francine and Giuseppe's. With both hands in mitten pot holders, Luigi totes the pot roast. I carry the serving dish, Angelina has the bread that Luigi picked up earlier at Terranova Bakery, and the boys each carry a bag of vegetables. Nonna arms herself with her wooden spoon. As we approach the house, Jen and Celia come along on the walk. There are whispers between the girls and Angelina. My ears perk up like radar. Usually, Luigi pays little attention to his daughter's friends but one of them ruffles his feathers.

"Meet us around eight," Jen says. Angelina nods. Her eyes move to see that her papa has heard.

"Angelina stays home with her family on Sunday night," he demands and marches up the steps to his brother's apartment house. He turns back to Angelina, "You respect your papa."

I can tell Angelina is upset all during the dinner. She doesn't say a word while we prepare the table and chatter about who is doing what around the neighborhood. Even to her two cousins, there is no chatter and excitement as usual. And Luigi even lets her sit at the adult table since Giuseppe's table is bigger than the one at our house.

I'm busy bringing in the food in serving bowls, and just about to sit down and serve myself, when I hear Luigi and Angelina arguing in the dining room. I hurry in with the gravy careful not to spill any, but I have to dodge Angelina as she scuffs her chair back from the table and leaps up facing me on her way to the front door.

"I'm going to Celia's," she announces to me.

"You do as you are told," Luigi demands. He stands up and throws his napkin down. Angelina ignores him and darts out the door without saying goodbye to her aunt and uncle.

Luigi plops back down in his seat mumbling something about respect.

"My, she's fresh," Francine says.

"I'm sorry for her actions," I say, taking my seat at the table.

"You sorry?" Luigi looks at me with hate in his eyes. "Sure, you train her."

"I train her to stomp out of here?" I say feeling hurt like he has to lash out at someone when he's upset and it's almost always me.

Then Nonna gets into it. "You stop sass a' my son." She shakes that spoon at me. Sometimes I feel like grabbing that darn spoon and snapping it in two.

Now, Luigi is really fired up. "Stand up!" he yells pointing his finger at me. "Show your family how you dress now, like the floozy at the dress shop. You think I don't notice how you act a little crazy these days?"

I feel like crying. I feel like leaping up and stomping out and following my daughter out the door but instead, I just hang my head.

"My girls want to dress like Angelina now," Francine complains.

"We will no' put up with it," Giuseppe insists.

With my head still lowered, I move my eyes enough to see the expression of anger on Luigi's face. His forehead is all scrunched up and his mouth is set in a downturned frown. "You shame yourself."

This final remark has upset everyone at the table. They are all silent and cease eating—all except Nonna who sits with her head down shoveling in her food like it's an eating contest to see who will finish first.

I glance around the table at everyone and think that they would be much happier if I was not here joining them for the dinner. I can't take it anymore and I completely lose control. Sobs wail from my inner core. I hold my napkin to my face and dart away towards the bathroom by the back door, but I slip on a throw rug and fall sliding across the floor to the wall where I bang my head like a hammer on the wall.

Francine hurries to my side. She packs a dishtowel with ice and applies it to my head. I compose myself and sit perfectly still on the floor. Something changes in me. It happens instantaneously, like a stab in the heart. I wipe my face and gently push Francine away. My tears are gone now. I stand up, straighten my hair, reach for my purse hanging over a kitchen chair and I walk directly out the front door without saying one more word. I don't wait to hear the belligerent reactions. But I do hear my controlling husband when he realizes I'm actually leaving. He yells, "Get back here. Where you think you go?"

I take a deep breath of the warm summer air as I slowly walk away from Francine and Giuseppe's and away from my whole family. I have never done this before—just walked out. I usually absorb the criticism and put up with the disapproval and degradation. I stop and touch my bruised head for a minute, and that's when I notice Nonna along the side of their house heading towards the sidewalk. So that's why she was eating so fast; she has a purpose to be somewhere. I stand in silence holding my bruised head for a minute and watch her quietly, then, I decide to follow her.

Nonna obviously has her own agenda and somehow manages to sneak out of the house while no one pays attention, probably during the ranting and raving about all the commotion of Angelina storming out, and then me and my weeping temper tantrum, or would Luigi have called it my lack of respect. What does it matter?

As I ease along behind her, every once in awhile, Nonna senses someone following, or is it my imagination? I slip into a doorway out of sight when she slows. We continue for blocks, me in pursuit of Nonna, in a quest for her ultimate destination, when suddenly she darts into a dinghy-looking Italian men's hangout, The Bronx Men's Club. I don't believe my eyes.

Suddenly, I am apprehensive about her safety. Does she know where she's going? There are gangsters in there—mafia men. I rush up to the door that has slammed behind her. There is a worn sign that says, "Bronx Italian Men's Club-Members Only." I search around the outside of the building for a window to peek in but I don't see any way to see a thing, so I knock hard with a closed fist on the door Nonna entered.

I hear heavy footsteps. A deep gruff voice answers, "Who's there?"

I stand bravely, "My mother-in-law just came in."

A middle-aged man, wearing a newsboy cap and chomping on the stub of a cigar, opens the massive wooden door just a mere crack. Through that little sliver of an opening, I get a picture of the place. The room is smoky, so fogged up it's hard to make out images. But, I see men assembled in the room playing cards, looking mean and tough with bottles of liquor on the tables. And there's Nonna, gripping her spoon with a tough but innocent expression, standing next to a tank of a guy with a big round head to match his belly, more hair on his scruffy chin than on his head. I'm careful not to show my fear and clueless as to why Nonna would, seemingly on her own account, just simply walk into a place like this. And, why would they admit her when it is clear as glass that they aren't letting me in so easily? "Men only" the sign says.

"Nonna, what are you doing here?" I yell out. The door man appears startled that I am so bold.

She furrows her brows and shakes the spoon at me, "You go away."

"No, I'm not leaving here." But, the doorman is definitely not letting me in.

The door is now open enough for me to see all around the room. Nonna takes a hold of the burley guy's arm and moves towards me slightly. Her expression softens a bit and her tone changes.

"I just stop to see a' my friend, Vincenzo from a' bingo on Sunday night. You remember?" She smiles a rare smile and so does tank-man, Vincenzo.

I can hardly believe what I'm hearing and seeing. I can't leave her in this place alone. I scan the dinghy room that has become silent since my appearance.

"Nonna, you shouldn't be hanging around here. Come on over to Giuseppe's. Your sons must wonder what happened to you."

"It's a' Sunday. I walk a' down to bingo with Vincenzo. Go on home."

The beefy man around Luigi's age smiles protectively and nods his head. Nonna is definitely in charge. She looks up at the man.

"Come on Vinnie. We leave a' now."

Tank-man, Vinnie looks at Nonna like he's confused, "But, we, uh…"

She slaps him on the back of the head with the spoon.

"Vinnie is a' fine. Go on now Maria."

"Yes, yes, we go now," Vinnie mumbles and shakes his head up and down like a bobble-head doll.

Something does not feel right to me, but Nonna definitely

knows these guys, and even though she hasn't totally convinced me, I decide to leave.

"If you need a ride, call home."

Typical of Nonna, she spouts back at me, "I call a' my son if I need a ride."

When I leave, I head towards home. I'm not going back to Francine and Guiseppe's. I'm deep in thought when I walk up the front steps to the house. I can't help but see the bag of cannolis placed on the porch swing, and there's a note attached. I anxiously tear off the note from Pasquale and read it, "Sorry I missed you this Sunday."

I hold the bag and the note up to my face trying my best to fight back the tears as I enter the house. I set the bag on the dining room table and run up the stairs to my bedroom where I stand in front of the full length mirror in the corner of the room. I stand there and examine myself, and I fix my dress and my face and my hair. Then, with purpose, I rustle through my closet. Something sexy, I think. I change three or four times until I get it right, and I fix my hair, parted on the side so it drapes down over one eye. And, I put on lipstick and a touch of eye make-up. What am I doing, I think, and sit on the corner of my bed, the bed I share with my husband. I am slouched there like a miserable heap. But then, I have a view out the bedroom window to the back yard, and there is the picnic table where I first had lunch with Pasquale. I can't help but smile. For a second, I glance over at my wedding picture on the bureau. There in a silver frame is me and Luigi on our wedding day. For good luck, I had tucked dried palm leaves from Palm Sunday Mass in the corner of the photo. I leap up and out of the room. I dash down the stairs, grab the bag of cannolis and scurry out the front door. I can't wait to get to Pasquale's house.

I am out of breath when I reach his house. I have only been here once before to drop off the payment to Mr. Corso for some of the work they did at our house. I pause to compose myself when I notice Pasquale's van parked in the street. In plain daylight I'm here, not sneaking around like a secret lover. I have come to see the man I'm crazy about, and I'm no longer ashamed. I pound on the door, stepping from one foot to the other nervously. It seems like no one is home. I pound again and it seems like endless time passes. Maybe he went out with his brother, or with his parents to a family dinner somewhere else. I look over at a guy fixing an old car next to Pasquale's van. It's Gino, his little brother. He watches me, like he's also waiting for the door to open. I wave and he waves back. Well, Pasquale could be anywhere. But then, just as I am about to leave, I hear movement inside. My heart throbs so loud like a drum and then, the door bursts open and Pasquale stands there in front of me.

I hold up the bag of cannolis, "I didn't want the cannolis to go to waste."

"What about your husband? He likes them."

Pasquale does not seem like his normal self. His mouth is twitching, and I can see nervous shifting in his eyes, and I'm standing there slightly embarrassed that I've come to a man's house like this, and why doesn't he ask me in or something? I had pictured it to be different, for him to sweep me up in his arms and hug me and kiss me and tell me how happy he is that I've come to see him. But, like a robot, he reaches to give me a peck on the cheek. I have not seen this shy side of him. I blatantly kiss him on the lips with passion right on his front step, right in front of Gino. Then, I laugh in a flirty seductive giggle.

"You're suddenly shy with me?"

Pasquale's eyes are wide and I notice that Gino has approached the house and is watching and listening to us with interest.

"I, uh," Pasquale says.

"I'd like to share more than cannolis with you. Do you still...? Uh, I mean, my marriage, it's unhappy and I..."

I gape, unable to continue. "Wha…?" I am speechless, embarrassed. There's a woman with him—another woman.

From the darkness in the house, Angelina's face appears as she comes up behind him holding his guitar.

"Mama, what are you doing here?"

"Me?"

I glare at Pasquale. Then, I step inside his house and grab my daughter's arm.

"Maria, please, I…" Pasquale mutters.

"Mama, Pasquale is my friend. He's teaching me guitar, remember?"

I am rough with Angelina as I pull her away from the house. I drop the bag of cannolis not even looking back at Pasquale. Gino picks up the bag, pulls one out and takes a bite as he watches us leave.

"Angelina?" Gino says.

• • •

As far as I can see, Luigi's life is quite simple. He goes to work. He comes home for his supper and he watches the news or *Bonanza* on TV. He never gambles or plays cards like his papa, but he will sometimes hang out at the pool hall or saloon down the block. There's a bunch of Italian guys from the neighborhood who hang around there after dinner. There's the pool hall and Tucci's next door where Tony Tucci tends the bar. The two local hangouts are connected so the guys go back and forth from playing pool to drinking and talking about whatever Italian guys talk about when they're all together away from their families in the dim-lit saloon. I don't think there're any famous pool players around there or anything, it's just a bunch of local guys hanging out, shooting-the-shit and complaining about their dull lives. I always hear them talking about it, down at Tony's, this and that. It goes something like this:

Luigi sits at the bar looking glum while chatting with Tony

who is busy cleaning glasses and putting them on the shelf. That's what they say, he's always cleaning the glasses.

"The women are crazy these days," Luigi probably says.

"So, what's new?" Tony answers.

"I don't know, ya work to put food on a table an' pay the bills. No respect. What's a guy gotta do?"

I can just picture this whole scene. I know it by heart. Luigi comes home and repeats his conversation with the guys every time he goes out. What does he want me to do?

So, I come home a little later than usual from taking Nonna for her check up at Dr. Marcianno's, and since I don't see Luigi's lunch tote on the hook by the kitchen door, I figure he stopped off at Tony's before dinner tonight. But, I'm thinking Angelina should have started the dinner by now. She's not in the kitchen and the boys have made a mess. The place looks like a hurricane hit. Usually by this time, I look up at the clock and its six o'clock, dinner is almost always started. I thought I told Angelina this morning when I left what to make for our dinner. The boys are sprawled out in the living room watching TV with peanut butter and crackers and glasses of milk.

"I'm out only a few hours for Nonna's check up, now look at this mess. What're you two doing?"

Nonna is right behind me. "Waste a' time, stupid doctors."

She plops down in a chair and searches through her black click-top vinyl faux leather purse. I'm wondering what the devil she's so anxiously searching for.

"Just gettin' a snack, Ma," Louie says. He jabs his brother when he thinks I'm not looking and Johnny kicks him back.

"Ma," Johnny whines, "He won't leave me alone."

I turn toward the kitchen with the feeling that something's not quite right, and before I am able to interrogate those boys, they're up and out the back door. The door swings back in a loud slam and I hear them arguing outside. What the heck are they up to? Nonna starts fixing gravy and penne for dinner. I pick up the wall phone to call Jen Riley's house. It seems like Angelina has not returned from a sleepover at her house last night, and I know she won't be with Celia who's upstate New York with her family this week.

"Can't keep control a' your own kids," Nonna mumbles as she peels the carrots.

I focus on the phone and when Mrs. Riley picks up, I say, "Oh, hello, it's Maria Campisi. I thought Angelina was coming home this morning but we haven't heard from her."

Jen's mother says, "I was at work. I didn't see Angelina with Jen."

I apologize to her for the bother and scan through the phonebook in the drawer under the phone trying to think who to call next just as Angelina comes zipping into the kitchen with her overnight bag. She must have heard me on the phone with her sneaky expression, head down and looking humble and guilty of something.

I plant my hands on my hips, "Where have you been?"

CHAPTER 32

Angelina

I can't wait to get home to talk to Mama, but that urgency changes when I encounter her attitude. She has no idea what I'm going through; she's just like all the rest of the adults in this world. She doesn't understand what it's like. If she only knew what my night was like, but she's like a drill sergeant and I'm so disappointed I could scream. Should I even bother to tell her my life is ruined? She's my last resort—someone I think will help me. The minute I see her face, I know it's useless. I turn toward the stairs. My hair is matted and nasty. My clothes are disheveled. I'm tired as hell and she takes a hold of me like I'm a kid, yanking on my arm.

"Where have you been," she asks. If she would let me explain, that's what I want to tell her. I want to sob in her arms and tell her my life is over and all the horrible things I don't know what to do about. But, no, she doesn't give me a chance.

"What do you think you're doing?" she demands. "I asked you a question."

When she finally releases my arm, I drop my bag next to the table and drop myself, like a ragdoll, onto a kitchen chair. "Mama, what do you think? I was at Jen's."

"I thought you were coming home early to keep an eye on the boys. Look at you." Now she's pacing in her old-lady apron ordering me around like I'm a slave. "What did you girls do last night?"

Like I'm going to tell her anything now, the infantile way she's treating me. "What, you don't trust me?"

Then, I panic. The phone rings and she turns to pick it up. I leap out of the chair.

"Jen, yes she's here. She was…"

"Give me the phone, Ma." I take the phone out of her hand before she realizes what's going on and I spout out to Jen into the receiver, "Let me call you later," and I hang up the phone. I glare at Mama who is now gaping at me.

"What's gotten into you? You know I have work and errands. At least you could watch the boys while I'm out."

"Ma, the boys don't listen to me, or to Nonna, and they're old enough."

Nonna's got her spoon positioned and giving her two-cents, "Whadda I tell ya?"

This family is crazy. I'm tired and I haven't slept and my life is ruined. I pick up my bag and run out of the room. I may be shedding real tears, but just in case and for more of an effect to keep my whole family off my back, I add a howling vocal cry to my tears as I dash up the stairs. Mama watches me but she only comes to the foot of the stairs.

• • •

I have not figured out what to do. Somehow, Jen found the bottle of whiskey I've been carrying around for ages. I couldn't tell her why I had it. She wanted some —a thrill, and so, we got drunk. I've never gotten drunk like that and I never ever intend to touch booze again. I don't even remember half the night and ended up waking up on Jen's terrace. Jen is definitely not the one I can tell about my situation. But then, maybe I told her and don't remember. That makes me feel even crappier.

Celia is probably the only one who will understand my circumstance, my ruined life. She might know what to do but she's still away with her family. I think maybe Pasquale will know what to do. We have become so close lately, even though I never did give him the whiskey. Oh man, did Jen and I drink the whole bottle?

• • •

In a couple of days, when I'm feeling a little better after the crazy drunken night with Jen, I find out that she doesn't remember anything—same as me, so it's nothing to worry about, at least the fact that I might have told her I am in trouble and my plan for Pasquale and all. I tell myself that Pasquale is so much older, that he will understand if I explain everything to him. I decide to talk to him, but I don't want the boys to listen and they're home being annoying. If only they'd just go out and play for awhile but they will want Pasquale to play ball with them, so I sneak around and bring Pasquale up to my room to talk. I figure, if he really does like me it will be the first time we really get a chance to be alone and make-out. Why not, I think? Perfect. I don't know why I didn't think of this from the start of trying to seduce him.

The boys lay on pillows on the living room floor in a messy room with soda bottles and bags of chips on the coffee table. I make a mental note to make sure I clean up the mess before Mama gets home from work, but for the time being, my attention is on Pasquale. I just let the boys lay there watching a rerun of *American Bandstand* on TV. What I don't know is that Papa is off work early and he walks in to find the boys lounging around and the house a mess. But, I've convinced Pasquale to come upstairs to my room for a guitar lesson so that the boys won't distract me. I'm stretched out on my bed purposely giving him a minor beaver-shot because my mini is a little too short. He's sitting in the chair by my window and I coax him over to the bed.

"You're not uncomfortable, are you?" I ask.

"My Angel, I am not usually hanging around in a beautiful teenage girl's bedroom." He snickers.

"It's so hot today," I say and remove my blouse.

"Whoa," he says.

"Oh, it's just a bikini top, not a bra." I strike a seductive pose something like I'd expect Jen to do in a case like this. "You afraid to sit by me on the bed?"

"Afraid?" he says as he eases over and sits next to me. "Where's the guitar?"

At first it seems like he's just humored by me—a silly teenage girl, but, suddenly, I must seem like a woman to him. His expression and body movements change. I ask him how he kisses. I know that sounds childish. He sort of laughs but I drape my arms on his shoulders. What choice does he have?

"I want you to teach me something else," I say in a voice I've heard Jen use on the guys.

"Something else? Something on the guitar?"

"I want you to teach me," I pause hardly believing the words that are flowing out of my mouth, "to French kiss."

He looks confused but does not answer. His eyes are

popped wide like he's seen a ghost, and I take that expression to mean he's excited to kiss me, not that it's something scary or weird. Maybe he has always wanted to kiss me but was shy about it. Maybe he didn't realize it was okay.

"Show me," I say with my face right in front of his.

"You're kidding?"

"No," I say and I press my lips to his, and then we are kissing. I stop and remove my bikini top so that I am naked from the waist up. The look on his face is like he's hungry as a bear, like he can't control himself.

"Oh, my Angel," he says. We are kissing now and I loosen his pants. I can tell he's a little apprehensive but I have gone this far and I have almost achieved my goal with him. I never thought I'd have the nerve to reach in and tough a guy's penis, but that's what I do, and it's as hard as a baseball bat. His hands are instantly on my breasts and it feels good, not like with Ford and I'm not thinking of the boys downstairs or Mama and Papa and Nonna. I'm with Pasquale in my bed. Why didn't I think of this before?

I do not even notice when Papa slowly creaks open my bedroom door.

"You are there with your girl friends?" he says peeking in.

What is he thinking? He never walks in my room without knocking. God, can't I have some privacy? And then, it's chaos, absolutely crazy. We all gasp, me and Papa and Pasquale—all shocked to see the other. I am on the bed with Pasquale and he's partially on top of me. Papa's barging into my room is at the most passionate moment. It's like Pasquale finally let loose with me, like he's finally expressing himself with desire and lust for me and I'm ready to give him all of my love. When Papa walks in Pasquale's hands are on me, on my buttocks and my breast. And then, it all comes to a halt with the unexpected shock of Papa in the room. We scramble to straighten ourselves. Pasquale leaps to his feet. I cover my chest with my fluffy pink bedspread.

Papa yells, "WHAT GOES ON HERE?"
"Sir, I'm sorry, I…"
Papa points his finger towards the door, "GET OUT!"
"No, Papa."
I leap off the bed just as Mama arrives in a state of panic at my bedroom door.

CHAPTER 33

Maria

The minute I open the front door, I know something's wrong. The boys sit like perfect angels and Luigi's voice from upstairs shrieks with alarm. I dash up the stairs. It must be Angelina. Something must have happened to Angelina. I drop my bag and cover my mouth with both hands at the sight of Pasquale in my daughter's bedroom—her little girl innocent pink bedroom now tainted with male lust, and Luigi, he must have caught them together. Together, it doesn't register in my brain.

"Oh my God, how could you?" I scream and Luigi is screaming and its lunacy. I rush to Angelina and push her against the wall.

"You pervert," Luigi screams. "Get out of my house."

I face Pasquale in disbelief, "You, and my daughter? You!"

I don't even think. An angry force takes over my body. I pick up one of Angelina's go-go boots and swing it wildly hitting Pasquale as many times as I can, on his chest and his head and on his awfully gorgeous arms—where ever I can make contact. He tries to grab my wrist to retrieve the boot, and Angelina is fighting, too. She manages to get the boot from me because I am losing my strength from my emotional rage.

"Stop," Angelina wails. "You don't understand."

Then, the boys are there gaping at the dramatic scene in their sister's bedroom.

"*Lei e matto,*" Luigi howls. "You are old enough to be her father."

Pasquale tries to make his way out of the room, "I am sorry, Sir." I step forward regaining my calmness and I slap Pasquale across the face as hard as I possibly can manage—so hard that my hand stings with pain. But, at that moment all I feel is painful emotional torture and I don't care if I have more anguish. How can anything ever hurt worse than this agony?

"What have you done?" I howl. "Get out!"

"I don't want to see your face again," Luigi yells as Pasquale makes his way out of the room. "You stay away from my Angelina, my poor child. *Stare lontanoda mis figlia povera. Uscire dalla mis casa. Lei e undisonora. Lei e pervertitita.*"

Pasquale glances back at Angelina who is in a fit of tears, and then he looks at me. "Maria, please?" he pleads.

Angelina cries, "Please, Papa, I love him."

Luigi pushes him out the door and screams even louder, "GET OUT YOU PERVERT! *USIRE DALLA. LEI PERVERTE!*"

One more time my ex-lover pleads, "Maria, please, let me explain." Then he turns to my innocent, or maybe not so innocent daughter and begs, "Angelina, tell them."

But, Angelina just howls, "No, No, No. NO!"

I am sobbing now with my arms wrapped around my quivering body. I glare at Angelina refusing to lay eyes on Pasquale. "How could you do this after our....?"

Luigi pushes him out the door and down the stairs and we are all right behind him, and there by the front door rocking in her chair is Nonna who has conveniently returned in time for the drama. She sits smiling at Pasquale as he walks out.

"I knew you were sexing someone in this house," she says shaking her wooden spoon. Pasquale glances at her quizzically and then darts out the door. I drop down on the top step of the stairs holding my head and tearing at my hair. It is unbearable that my innocent young girl has been involved with this man; the same man that has made me a sinner has spoiled my daughter, and it is all my fault. God is punishing me.

• • •

I am not speaking to Angelina. My anger is crawling around just below my skin like the red ants that come out in the spring, and I simply can't face her. Luigi has already punished her so she can't go anywhere or do anything. She must work in the kitchen cooking or clean the house or sit in her room alone with no friends or phone calls. But I have to work and partially I dread going, but there's something inside me that knows Tia will get me through this, and I want to cry to her about Pasquale and Angelina and about our whole complicated situation.

I'm at my machine hemming swirly, printed bell-bottoms for the rich girl who lives over by the park. Her Mama buys her anything she wants even if it's too sexy for a teen-aged girl. I wonder if that girl has been involved with any slick, fast-talking older men who manage to coax themselves into her expensive bedroom and ruin her virginity. What would her mama do? Tia walks in the back room and plops down on a chair. She kicks her feet up on a stool.

"Whew," she says. "My feet are killing me."

She starts rubbing one foot at a time humming one of the songs I'm sure Angelina listens to on the radio. I know I have a miserable face on as I sew the pants.

"You okay?" she asks, and that's it. I stop sewing and cover my face with both hands. Tears dribble down on the pants.

I hear Tia kick off the other shoe and tiptoe over to me in her stocking feet. She pulls the pants away and hugs me. "Oh, Honey, what is it?"

"My Angelina was with the roofer, in her bed."

"Oh dear." Tia hands me a tissue and I wipe my eyes. She holds my hand and squeezes it. I know I can tell her everything that's happened and she will understand. I look up at her and try to smile but tears form where my words try to explain.

She is patient and pulls a stool up next to me, and I tell her, "What a fool I was about Pasquale. I thought he, you know, fancied me, but all he wanted was Angelina."

Tia hugs me close to her, "Oh sweetie, you don't know that for sure." She hands me the whole box of tissues.

"A thirty-year-old man with my little girl; it's no wonder the way she flaunts herself."

Tia crinkles her brow and looks at me, "Pasquale?"

"The roofer, you know, the worker, his name is Pasquale Corso."

"Oh my," Tia says concerned. "Anthony Corso's son? Oh, dear."

"You know Pasquale?"

"Pasquale Corso sings with my ex, you know, Freddie's band."

"Are you sure?" I ask. "Oh Tia, I feel like such an old fool."

"A real smooth charmer, that one. He's the one you did it with?" She smiles at me like she totally understands.

"He was always flirting and..."

A bell jangles at the shop door. Tia turns and walks over to the door to the main portion of the shop and peeks out. There's a customer in the shop but I can hear Kate helping her. Then, Tia closes the door again, sits down pulling the stool closer to me.

"I'll give Freddie a call tonight. Let's see if he can convince Pasquale to stay away from Lina."

"Good. I think Luigi might kill him. Maybe I'll kill him."

If I thought Pasquale would just go away and stay out of my family's lives, I wouldn't worry about it, but I know that no matter what Luigi says to Angelina, she will fall for smooth-talking

Pasquale no matter what. Look how easily I fell under his spell. But, if Freddie talks to him, maybe he'll listen. It's worth a try.

I take the long way home. I walk over to the pawn shop on Belmont and decide I will buy the ring. Even if it's not mine, and of course, there's no way it could be, but I will find out how much it is and give a deposit so Maurizio will hopefully save it for me until I have enough money. At least it's probably a real diamond. When I reach the store I gape in the window and the ring is gone. I go in and speak to Maurizio.

"Sorry, the owner came back for the ring," he says trying to brush me off.

He doesn't even try to sell me a different ring, which seems odd. These guys are always trying to sell you something. But, I have to face it, the ring is gone now and all I have left on my finger is the fake rhinestone ring.

CHAPTER 34

Angelina

Now my life is really ruined. There's absolutely no one to talk to; no one who understands me. I could try to call Celia or Jen, but I don't, even when Mama is at work. I'm so embarrassed. What would I say? And, I have not seen Pasquale or anyone other than my family for days. I just want to die. My so-called friends have probably just forgotten about me anyway. Plus, they're all better off without me in this world—all of them.

I lie on my bed leafing through a magazine but not really seeing the pages. Mama opens my door without even knocking. She peeks at me like a spy and then tiptoes in like I'm so fragile that I'll break. She sure didn't act like that when she lost her temper and pushed me right in front of Pasquale. I definitely wish she'd go away but she comes right in and sits on the edge of my bed. I can smell the gravy cooking for dinner as soon as she opens the door, and she's wearing that ugly apron. The aroma of garlic and olive oil and fresh tomatoes wafts in through my open bedroom door. I feel craving, but more than a hunger for food, I feel sick to my stomach and empty.

"You're sick?" Mama asks.

"I'll be fine."

"I must speak to you about Pasquale."

"Never mind, Mama." I close *Seventeen* magazine and turn towards the wall.

"Please, he's much too old for you."

"You don't understand. I love Pasquale and he loves me."

Mama gasps. I knew she would. Good. Let her think I'm having a love affair with Pasquale. Maybe she'll realize I'm old enough to make my own decisions. And, if she knows someone like Pasquale will love me, then, maybe she'll have more respect for my feelings. She leans over and puts her hand on my shoulder and for a fleeting second, I consider telling her about my condition. More than anything, right now, I want to tell her but something in me resists.

"Believe me, I know about these things. Pasquale is just having a little fun with you." She sounds critical and upset now. She stands up and I turn and sit up in my bed bracing for a verbal battle.

"You're wrong," I tell her with no question in my mind.

"Come down to dinner," she demands like I'm her slave.

I turn back toward the wall. "I'm not hungry."

She stomps out and slams my door. Now what am I going to do? But, she doesn't leave right away. I can hear her outside my door. She must be leaning against the wall. What is she doing? I must have really upset her and I feel bad, and now Nonna is hobbling down the hallway near my bedroom door probably nosing around to see what we're talking about. I hear the thump-and-drag of her cane. Oh God, I've gotta get out of here. No one around here understands me.

• • •

I must have fallen asleep. I'm drowsy and I realize that it's almost dark out. They must have had dinner without me. I get up and carefully open my bedroom door, peek out, and listen. They're all downstairs at the dining room table eating dinner. They must be just finishing. They're scraping plates and I hear them talking. I inch out and sit on the top step to listen.

"As soon as I'm old enough, I'm joining the Army," Louie announces.

"You're crazy," Johnny says. "War is bad. You'll end up dead in Viet Nam like Cuz."

Then Mama says, "If you two are finished, take your plates to the kitchen." The boys argue some more, but I hear them get up and take their plates to the kitchen and then head to the stairs. I dart back into my room so they don't see me. And then I'm back sitting on my bed bored, as you can imagine, like in a jail cell. The boys have stationed themselves in their room playing with their army men, attacking each other in play armies.

I sit there and wait and wait until I can't stand it any longer. Is it my mind that can't take anymore? Or, is it my stomach crying for food? Or, is it my heart yearning for understanding and love? I walk out of my room in my stocking feet and slowly meander down the stairs and into the living room where Papa sits in his chair watching the news. Mama is in the kitchen washing dishes and I don't know where Nonna has disappeared to. I walk into the living room right up to Papa. At first, he acts like he doesn't see me. His frown deepens, so I turn to go.

"You are never to see that Pasquale again," he announces.

That's when I lose my temper. I spin back around and face him. I stare at him like I never do. "No Papa."

He sits up and slams his fist against the coffee table,

"What's a' wrong with you?"
"I love Pasquale."
"I kill him," he screams. "I forbid you." He turns away from me and waves his arms at me as if to dismiss me from his sight, and I run to the door where Mama appears from the kitchen. I brush past her and back up to my room.

• • •

My mind is stirring again, trying to think of a plan. I remember at my last guitar lesson, Pasquale had been so excited looking forward to a temporary move into Freddie's apartment up in Yonkers while Freddie travels to London to work on some rock band album. He has to take care of Freddie's cat, Patches. I know Freddie from when he was Tia's boyfriend. We all thought she would marry him so we included him in some of our family get-togethers. But, Freddie was never popular at our house, especially with Papa who could hardly keep his mouth shut about him. His face would turn red with anger and he would growl under his breath. It was clear he couldn't stand Freddie. And, personally, I also think he is sort of a jerk, but I guess he's a good bass player. That's what Pasquale says anyway. But now I realize that that must be what's keeping Pasquale so busy lately. He must be at Freddie's, alone. Perfect. This is my opportunity.

I pull out one of the old suitcases from the hall closet, and when Mama's at work and the boys are down at the park with Nonna and Francine, I leave home. It's a trek to Freddie's apartment but I've been there with Tia, and my memory is one of my best assets, especially now with everything else wrong with me. The problem is, I'm burdened with a suitcase and it is a million degrees outside and I'm sick to my stomach, but I am determined. I head out of my neighborhood as fast as possible. What would I tell Mrs. Pazzo who noses around the neighborhood always butting into everyone's business? Seeing me with a suitcase would be like teasing the pigeons with breadcrumbs. She would be right on my case. I head to the Fordham Road station and take the train toward Grand Central Terminal. Then, I switch to Metro North to the Croton line and get off at Ludlow Station in Yonkers. It's a lot of switching trains in boiling hot stations, but I keep telling myself that I can handle it. Anything's better than putting up with my family. It takes me over an hour with all the transfers, and now I'm almost out of money. I guess I'll be losing my job at A&W, being that this will be the second time I don't show up for work. I walk over to Freddie's apartment over on Morris Street only a few blocks from the station in Yonkers. I am determined to be with my love.

Its Saturday afternoon so I know Pasquale will be around getting ready for his show in the evening, or at least I hope so, and when I enter the tiny foyer, I push the button for the buzzer to 5W. I'm so overjoyed when he answers that I can hardly believe it. So far, everything has gone according to my plan. I enter and tuck my suitcase behind the staircase on the first floor landing. I don't want to freak him out like I'm moving in or something. I dash up the steps two at a time and there he is with the door open waiting for me. It looks like he's ready to leave. He's got his guitar case next to the door. But, he lets me in obviously curious as to why I'm at his door.

"My little Angel, there's no lesson today, and what are you doing all the way up here?"

"Oh, I know. Please won't you just let me stay here? Mama and Papa are treating me so mean after the other day, you know last week in my bedroom."

I can feel the love. He tells me to make myself at home, that we will figure out what to do, and then, the bathroom door opens and there's a woman in the room with us—a very pretty Italian woman who could be Mama's age. Why is she here with my Pasquale? I am shaken, but Pasquale is very calm and smiles.

"This is Patty," he says and he goes on about something to do with singing together at the club.

"Patty?" I meekly shake her hand and she smiles with warmth.

"You sure you want to stay here? It'll be lonely." She gazes over at Pasquale.

"We'll be late," Pasquale explains. "Won't your parents be worried?"

"No. No. Please don't call them. I promise I won't be a bother. I'll just wait here. Please?"

"Okay, if you're sure," Pasquale says slinging his guitar case over his shoulder.

I'm baffled, in a state of shock at the sight of Patty in the apartment with Pasquale. And, I feel humiliated the way they talk to me and treat me sort of like a child, seeing if I'm hungry and showing me how to use the TV. Then, they leave and go to the club to sing.

I sit there on the couch alone once they're gone and scan the studio apartment. I plan it out. I will make a bed on the couch so Pasquale doesn't think I'm being overly aggressive. I prop the door open so I don't lock myself out and I hurry downstairs to collect my suitcase. While Pasquale is out singing, I settle in like it's my own place, but mind you, this is real, it's not "playing house." I lie on the couch and daydream about how I will seduce Pasquale when he returns, and I'm praying really hard that he doesn't bring Patty back here when he returns.

CHAPTER 35

Maria

For days Angelina has been acting strange. She's not herself, the fifteen-year-old that I'm so used to, so carefree and jovial and stubborn. Instead she secludes herself in her room—no singing and dancing and dressing up in her wild and crazy clothes; no begging for me to let her go out and be with her friends. I'm convinced it's all because of Pasquale. I wish he'd never come into our lives. As I walk home from work, I try to think what I should do—what is the best thing to snap her out of her infatuation with Pasquale, get her back to her usual teenage self. Tia says that Freddie laughed when she showed her concern about Pasquale's involvement with an under-aged girl. He thinks it's ridiculous to worry, that Pasquale has women swarming around him like he's a beehive.

"What's he going to do with a fifteen-year-old? That would be like looking at the jail cell," that's what Tia says Freddie told her.

I agree with Tia, about his reaction, but I'm still worried. I saw the two of them with my own eyes and my gut tells me it's more serious. Usually she would already have another boy she'd be showing an interest in, like one of Celia or Jen's boyfriend's friends or some other boy from the neighborhood. But she mopes around so serious with a droopy sad expression. She doesn't even want to go out.

I arrive at home suddenly feeling overly tired. I hear voices of play from the boys upstairs as soon as I open the door, and Nonna's sleeping in her rocking chair in the dining room by the front door. At least I don't have to worry about where she's gone off to. I set down my purse and tote bag and yell out, "Hellooooo?"

Louie peers down from the top stair, "What's for dinner?"

Then, Johnny is right next to him. His hair has grown so much. It looks long and shaggy like some of the hippie teenagers. Nonna notices, too. She's suddenly awake. "Your son looks like a girl."

The boys bound down the stairs. "Hey, come on, Nonna," Johnny complains.

I grab my apron off the hook and head into the kitchen.

Nonna follows and sits at the kitchen table waiting for me to hand her vegetables to cut up. The boys are practically under my feet.

"I'll get the scissors after dinner and trim your hair," I tell Johnny.

"No, Ma, I like it this way."

"He's a fairy," Louie says.

"Rock stars wear long hair," Johnny says. "Pasquale said he'd teach me guitar."

I pull the vegetables out of the refrigerator and slam the door. "You stay away from Pasquale. Do you hear?"

I hand the vegetables to Nonna while she's laughing at Johnny, "Heeheehee. Maybe you want to pin your hair up in a bun." She's absolutely hysterical at her own joke. I try to ignore her.

"Tell your sister to come down and help with dinner."

"Haven't seen Lina all day," Louie says.

"Angelina's got love on her mind," Nonna announces. "Can't do much to change that."

I slam down the bottle of milk and it sloshes all over the counter, "What are you talking about?" But, I know something is wrong. I have that feeling inside.

"Lina's been gone all day, Ma," Johnny says in a concerned tone.

I pick up the phone and start dialing. And that's what I do, I dial and I ask and I dial and I ask, calling up every single person I can think of who would know where Angelina has gone, but I have no luck. When Luigi walks in ready for dinner he finds me in a ragged mess, infuriated and tearful.

Somehow Nonna and I manage to throw together a pasta primavera and salad for dinner, but I can't eat. I go out back and sit at the picnic table sobbing. Nonna must know something. She's doesn't even appear to be upset. At least she doesn't show it. When they all finish and Luigi's fuming and mumbling in the living room, I clean up the dishes and then I realize that Nonna has disappeared. I tear off my apron, grab a head scarf and dart out the door.

I search the neighborhood streets for signs of Angelina and her friends. I pass by Celia's house and then over by the high school and on over towards Jen's house. I spot groups of teens hanging out, smoking and drinking and talking, playing music and flirting but no one that Angelina hangs around with. Do I darn walk over by the Corso's? Instead, I head over to the bingo hall by the parish looking for Nonna, but she's not there. Could she possibly have gone back to that men's club? First, I tie the scarf from around my neck up around my head and knot it under my chin like a rural peasant. Then, I walk on the opposite side of the street by the club hovering there for a bit. The neighborhood is sketchy and I'm watching my back not sure what could happen around here. Two tough looking guys approach the door to the club. I watch like a spy as the doorman lets them in. I inch closer crossing to the side of the street where the club is, but I duck out of sight slightly behind a big black Cadillac. A limo pulls up and I stoop lower behind the car as the driver exits. He walks around to the opposite side and opens the door for his passenger, a mean-looking guy who struts out and up to the door. The driver knocks on the door. The door immediately swings wide open and I can see inside as everyone in the place seems to be greeting the guy in a black suit like he's someone really important.

Right straight across the room is Nonna sitting at a table playing cards with a group of rough looking Italian men. She's the only woman in the place playing cards, except for two sleazy looking, possible prostitutes in slinky, revealing outfits. My jaw drops. One of the girls brings drinks to the table where Nonna plays; the waitress smiles all friendly and familiar with my crazy old mother-in-law. Vincenzo sits at another table talking, but also watching the table where Nonna seems to be winning. She guards a pile of chips on one side and a pile of cash on the other.

There is a musty stillness in the evening air—an eerie quiet before the storm. It's all dark and cloudy, but I can hear crisp conversation from inside the smoky place even with the whir of fans from inside the obviously humid club.

One guy, standing outside by the open door says to the doorman, "The old bag's getting a little too lucky lately."

"Looks like the lady's winning again," Vincenzo laughs from inside. The others look serious and possibly a bit angry.

"It's skill, Sonny," Nonna says with authority and confidence. "You should know. I learned from my dearly beloved Vito." She crosses herself and looks up at the ceiling. One card player tries to sneak one of her chips, but she swats him with her spoon. "God rest his soul."

No wonder she's always got that darn spoon. I ease closer to the door that is now propped open, probably for some ventilation. The room is packed and smoke filled, and there's lots of cursing and drinking going on. Almost everyone stops whatever they're involved in to greet the man who arrives in the limo. Suddenly the doorman slams the door shut.

I stand there numb not knowing what to do. I turn and hurry toward home. Should I tell Luigi? He will blow his top especially since Angelina has disappeared as well.

I rush in the house and face Luigi's ranting and raving and wondering where I've gone off to. He's red with a swollen up face like a balloon ready to pop. I drop into my chair in the living room as he puffs on his pipe and continues to pace. "Everyone wants to leave this house. And my mama, now she's gone, too, and in the middle o' the night."

"Middle of the night?" I say. "It's eleven o'clock. How do you expect me to keep track of your mama?" I don't dare tell him where his mama spends her time, especially when he approaches me and raises his fist. When he's in this mood, it's impossible to have a conversation with him.

"Watch your tongue, woman."

I turn my face away and pull my legs up wrapping my arms around them. "I've called everyone, Jen and Celia and all of them that I know. I didn't call Pasquale."

"Gregory Rigoletto said to me that he saw our Angelina with Pasquale an' he had his arm around her. I told him he was crazy, that his eyes were going bad."

"It's probably true. I can't figure where else she would be."

Luigi puts out his pipe and heads for the front door. "I go to the Corso house. If my Angelina is there I bring her home and have that pervert thrown in jail."

"We should call the police," I say. "What if something happened to her?"

"Bah," he grunts marching to the door.

I grasp Luigi's arm and glance at him with a pleading look as he prepares to leave. I know he will only cause trouble at the Corso's. "No, please." He pulls away and stomps out the door. The sky opens up with lightning, but I follow after him in the pouring rain. Thunder booms in the distance and I try to cover my head with my arms but it is no use. Rain pours down in buckets and I run to keep up with my husband.

By the time Luigi has almost reached the Corso house I have caught up to him. He is out of breath now that he carries around so much extra weight and never exercises. He acts like I'm not there right behind him as he pounds on the Corso front door in the thunderous rain storm. The house is dark and then suddenly, the lights flick on and Mr. Corso is at the door. His wife, Josephine peeks out the window. Both are in their night clothes and certainly startled awake by Luigi's intrusion. He stands there sopping wet with a scowl on his face, fists clenched by his side. I rush up beside him as the door opens and Anthony peeks out.

"Is the middle of the night," he says.

"Where's your son, Pasquale?" Luigi screams.

"Pasquale? What happened to Pasquale?"

"Your son is a pervert. He has my Angelina. She's just fifteen."

Josephine meekly gazes over Mr. Corso's shoulder at Luigi.

"You crazy. Go away an' leave us alone." He attempts to close the door but Luigi pushes him. Mr. Corso pushes him back.

"Luigi, no," I bellow.

"Go home," Luigi yells at me, and then back at Mr. Corso, "Let me speak to your son."

"Pasquale is not here."

"I have him arrested for this. *E Un pervertito.*"

"Go away crazy old man. *Andare via il vecchio matto.*"

Luigi punches Mr. Corso in the nose. Suddenly there are neighbors all around in their robes and night clothes with umbrellas. Mr. Corso slips and falls on the porch. In a flurry of worried neighbors and Josephine, there is craziness as everyone tries to help poor Mr. Corso to his feet. I pull at Luigi to get him to go but he pushes me away. I slip on the rainy sidewalk and fall to my knee in a muddy spot. Luigi hardly notices. We are all falling down and wet and muddy and miserable. We are quite a sight. That's for sure.

"Have you lost your mind?" I say.

"I fight for my daughter's honor."

"You insult my son. Pasquale is too good for a daughter of a crazy old man."

Josephine manages to get her husband's arm and pull him away from my raging husband. He glances at her softly with love and concern. And then, Gino appears groggy from sleep but ready to assist in the fight. When he realizes that things are under some control, he glances at me quizzically and it makes me uncomfortable. He knows way too much about his brother and my family, specifically about me and his brother and maybe about Angelina and Pasquale as well. He must know where Angelina is. He stands by his father with fists clenched ready to knock out Luigi if he causes any more problems. I turn away from him. I can't look him in the eyes when he whispers something to his mother and points at me. Josephine frowns at me.

"Go home now," she announces to the neighbors. "There will be no more of this tonight." She waves the crowd away but keeps a hold of Mr. Corso, lovingly shielding him from further harm. I pull Luigi away down the sidewalk as everyone watches us all wet and muddy and exhausted.

Through the crowd that begins to dissipate, I see Nonna rushing along the street dodging everyone and hiding her face with Louie's floppy yellow rain hat. She scampers away ahead of us toward home before Luigi is able to spot her. One of the tough guys with a mean scowl from the club, or maybe from somewhere worse, follows her in anxious pursuit. Luigi and I walk home behind her a half a block away. He grumbles all the way, not realizing his mama is just ahead of us. I turn to see Gino still standing in the middle of the sidewalk watching to make sure we are gone. I wonder what he's thinking; what he knows. And as we trudge along I'm not listening to Luigi's yelling and complaining, I'm thinking of how I could figure a way to speak to Gino alone.

"Angelina is probably home by now and all this fuss for nothing," I say.

When we reach our front door, I kick off my shoes all muddy and wet, but Luigi just tromps right in. And there, sitting in her rocking chair is Nonna pretending to be asleep like we wouldn't have noticed she was ever gone. I look down at her soaking wet shoes.

"Mama, where you been?" Luigi demands. She pretends to awaken from a deep sleep. She should be on the stage the way she puts on an act.

"So, what are you sleep-walking right out of the house?" I say sarcastically.

"None of your business," she says.

Luigi faces me with a crinkled forehead, "Don't speak to Mama like that."

I turn away as the boys come running down the stairs. Nonna rises silently and hobbles toward the stairs.

"Did you find Lina?" Johnny asks.

"Your sister is fine. She plays a trick on us just like Nonna. Now get up to bed," I tell them.

"Can't we wait up?" Louie asks.

But they both race up the stairs when Luigi yells, "Go. Now. *Andare.*"

Once the boys and Nonna have gone up to bed, Luigi picks up the phone. I look up at the clock in the kitchen. It's 1:45 AM. I sit myself down wringing my hands at the kitchen table as Luigi stands by the counter on the wall phone dialing the police. The phone is turned up so loud, I can hear the whole conversation.

"I am Luigi Campisi. My daughter, Angelina has disappeared. Maybe she is abducted by this man, Pasquale."

"How old is your daughter?"

"Only fifteen, sir."

"Did you argue with her?"

"We argue, yes, but my Angelina is a good girl."

"My guess is she'll be back before you know it. You know how these kids are."

"I don't understand. Our Angelina may be in danger."

"Sir, please, there's nothing I can do tonight."

Luigi paces in front of the counter for as long as the cord will stretch and then back again in the other direction. I begin nervously putting things away in the kitchen.

"You don't help us? What kind a crazy place you runnin' down there?"

"I don't need another trouble maker tonight. Good night, Mr. Campisi."

Luigi slams down the phone and stomps around. "I kill

Fifteen

Pasquale." He heads over to his chair in the living room and I follow as he slumps down. Then, it's like he just notices that I'm present during this whole ordeal. He points his finger at me. "This mess is your fault. You are the mama, you should know where your own daughter is."

"My fault? Stop this. Let me get you some hot milk with maybe some grappa?"

He crosses his arms and looks away, "I don't want nothin'."

I don't think I can sleep knowing my daughter is off some place and I have no idea where, but, I'm emotionally exhausted and fall fast asleep. When I awake the next morning I quickly jump up and rush to her bedroom but she has not come home. I run down the stairs in time to see Luigi heading out the door for work. Nonna and the boys sit at the kitchen table eating cold cereal. I watch as the boys giggle and Nonna flips silver coins in a coffee cup like a magic trick. I frown at them knowing where the coins came from.

"You call me as soon as you hear from Angelina," Luigi demands.

I turn to the boys and Nonna. "Where'd you get all these silver dollars, Nonna?"

"You mind your own business," she grumbles. I hunch my shoulders and go up to get ready for work. Maybe Tia will know where I might look for Angelina.

When I come back down, the boys are still playing with Nonna and the silver coins that now fill two coffee cups, one for each of the boys.

"You boys call me at Tia's if you hear from your sister. Do you hear, if you hear anything?" I hate to leave them with Nonna knowing how unreliable she is but I don't know what else to do. I could call Francine but I don't want to face her about Angelina's disappearance, at least not yet. Plus, I'm sure Angelina will appear with a lame excuse surely some time during the day.

I walk into the shop looking tired and distressed. Tia stands at the counter with Kate and a new girl discussing business policies and I know she notices me and the distraught state I'm in. She watches me out of the corner of her eye as she continues her meeting. I head into the back.

"Use these hangers for the sweaters, here on the bottom shelf. The blazers go on the curved ones."

It's not even five minutes and I'm getting settled at my machine when she bursts into the room, closes the door, and comes right up to me. I stare at the machine and can hear the muffled voices of the girls out in the shop.

"Oh Sweetie, is it Lina?" She hugs me. I cover my face with my hands and sob. This is becoming a habit. She reaches for the box of tissues that still sets near my machine from the last time she consoled me.

"She's gone."

"Gone?"

"I called all her friends. They're worried, too. Maybe she's with Pasquale."

"But, Freddie didn't think..."

"Maybe Freddie knows where she is."

"I don't know. I doubt that she's with Pasquale. Freddie left yesterday for London. I know Pasquale's staying at his apartment. I don't think he'd let Angelina stay there."

I leap to my feet facing Tia with my clasped hands over my mouth. "Of course, that's it. Maybe Angelina's there." I look hopefully at Tia.

Tia shakes her head. "I could call her there but, I don't think so, Honey, not just yet. And Pasquale won't be there now. He'll be at work. If Lina's there, I doubt that she is, but if she's hiding, she won't pick up the phone."

"But, I need to find her and speak to her. Why can't you call? Please, Tia."

"Sweetie, if Lina's gone to the trouble to run away with this man, then, I don't think she'll speak to you so easily. She's probably not even there, probably with a girlfriend somewhere."

"Could you just call? I don't know where else she could be."

Tia is deep in thought. She rubs her chin. "I'll give it a try and if I reach her, I will be very diplomatic."

"Diplomatic? Just get her to come home."

Tia takes a hold of my arm and pulls me to my feet. "You need some rest. Go home and take a nap, Sweetie. No work for you today. As soon as the girls leave and we close up the shop, I will try to reach her. Let me try to talk to her."

I want to stay and listen to the conversation, if she gets Angelina on the phone. But, it may just be a hunch. Angelina might already be home. I rush home, but she's not there. I go up to my bedroom and lie on the bed staring up at the ceiling. At least Nonna has not run off again. She's still downstairs with the boys. As I close my eyes, I hear their laughter and I'm visualizing Tia sitting at the café table, kicking off her shoes and hoisting her feet up on a stool in the backroom as she dials the phone to try reaching Angelina.

CHAPTER 36

Angelina

After much dramatic pleading, I manage to convince Pasquale to let me stay here in Freddie's apartment over night. I can't help but think how everything has gone so crazy this summer as I sit here in this strange apartment. It was only something like a month ago that I was still hanging out with Celia and Jen and we all had our boyfriends and were making plans for the summer—all the carefree fun we had planned. Now, my life is totally wrecked and I still don't know what to do, where to turn. I haven't even spoken to Jen and every time I talk to Celia, she's busy with her new boyfriend down in the city. I don't know what happened to Carlo. None of them even know I'm here in Yonkers and it's a good thing because it's not like I thought it would be. I'm just so confused and I miss my room. This place doesn't even have a fan and it's dark and smells like dirty feet. I haven't been here for very long, only a day and a half, but it seems like ages and Gino comes around a lot which complicates things. He's the one who talked his brother into letting me stay longer. It's not just an inkling that he likes me, I know it now, but it's Pasquale that I love. I just have to convince him. It's nothing like I thought it would be, but I'm in trouble. I'm trapped and what else can I do?

Pasquale went out earlier to buy bagels for breakfast and he returns with the stale bagels and Gino. I can't believe how disappointed I am when I see the two of them and the bagels are nothing like our fresh bagels from Arthur Avenue.

It's late afternoon and I'm stir crazy sitting in this stuffy place all day. I'm anxious to make some headway with Pasquale but the situation is complicated. He sits on the edge of the bed that has the saggiest mattress. I'm sitting cross-legged in the center of the bed and Gino is in the bathroom. Actually, I'm so freaked out that Gino found out I'm here. How am I going to manage to seduce Pasquale with him snooping around? But, at least Patty has gone. Sometimes I actually think Pasquale thinks the reason I befriended him is because I like his brother, even after we almost did it in my bedroom. Oh man.

Pasquale's trying to say something to me but I'm not interested in listening to his parent-type lectures. "You should at least call your mama." He fiddles with a pencil like a nervous papa when the phone on the night stand next to him jangles. I hear the female voice on the other end of the phone.

"Hello?"

"Freddie's not here," he says into the phone.

Fifteen

I'm trying to figure out whose voice it is on the other end of the phone. I recognize it, but then, it doesn't make sense to me. It sounds like Tia, but why would she be calling? And then I remember, oh yeah, this is Freddie's apartment. She's trying to reach him.

"I know," she says on the other end of the line. "Angelina's mother works at my shop and…"

"Maria?" Pasquale says and he really looks disturbed. There is a crucifix on the wall and he stands up and stares at it.

"We're all so worried about Lina. You must understand that."

And now I know it's Tia on the phone and that she's looking for me.

"Angelina is fine."

"But what about her family? It doesn't matter how they feel, that they're worried?"

Pasquale sits back down on the bed and kicks the wall by the window. The room is way too small. At home, at least I have my own bedroom.

"I have no choice, she came here. What could I do?"

It's almost like I'm not in the room and he's talking about me. I leap off the bed, walk over and stand in his face and mouth the words, "Don't say anything, please."

"You could send her home."

"Mr. Campisi doesn't understand. He's an old man who can't remember what it's like to be young."

"Lina doesn't know her heart at fifteen. Let me speak to her?"

"Fifteen?" Pasquale glares at me. "I thought she was older."

Gino walks into the room with his hands stuffed into his pockets. You can tell he idolizes his big brother just by the way he respectfully listens to what he says.

"I simply want to arrange for her to talk with her mama, that's all." Then, there is silence on the line. Pasquale hands the phone to me and I shake my head, but then I figure it's no use. She already knows I'm here.

"Tia?" I say into the phone.

"Lina, thank God you're okay. Promise me you'll speak with your mama. Honey, you shouldn't be staying out with a man. You two could get in so much trouble."

"What kind of trouble?" I say sarcastically and then I remember how cool Tia has always been to me and I feel bad for snapping at her. "My parents don't understand me."

"Give them a chance Sweetie."

I look over at Pasquale and then at Gino. Pasquale takes a hold of my hand and nods. I say into the phone to Tia, "Okay, I'll call Mama."

"You could meet them at a coffee shop and talk."

"Not with Papa, and I'll only meet Mama if you promise not to let Papa know. I hate him."

"Fine. Meet your mama at Red Hill diner over by Van Cortlandt Park at 7:00 tonight. Have Pasquale walk you over and drop you off."

"Tonight? I was thinking of tomorrow."

"My sweet Lina, I love you and I love your mama. She is sick with worry. How can she sleep without speaking to you?"

"Okay, I'll meet her but if Papa is with her, I'll leave and they won't ever find me."

I hand the phone back to Pasquale and he says goodbye. I roll my eyes at him and then lean back on the bed. Oh, what the heck. I guess it won't hurt to speak to Mama.

CHAPTER 37

Maria

The door to my bedroom is closed. This is the only place I feel I can relax and release my mind from the emotional exhaustion that has invaded me lately. I stare into space as I lie here totally clothed in the same navy straight skirt and the now crumpled pink blouse printed with mini-bows like dots that I wore to the shop earlier. It's dark in this room and cool, good for sleeping. I close my eyes and try hard not to think of Angelina, but that's all that dances in my head, and I imagine her kissing Pasquale—what it's like between them, and my eyes pop open. Why Pasquale? I can't help but grit my teeth in frustration. My whole body tenses at the sudden knock at my bedroom door. I hadn't even heard anyone come up the stairs. And then, without my reply, the door eases open and Nonna peeks in and enters without my consent.

"You gonna lie here all day?"

"What is it?" I raise myself up on my elbows.

There's no relaxation in this house—not even in my own bedroom. She growls something complaining, probably about me, and then, "The floozy woman is on the line."

I sit up, swinging my legs to the floor and turn on the lamp on the night table. The extension phone is there and I quickly pick it up. Nonna listens as I speak to Tia and I realize that she found Angelina and I will have a chance to speak with her. I try not to say anything out loud for Nonna to hear. I stand by the bed cupping the receiver with my hand. She will go right back and tell her son, but who knows what she'll tell him—certainly a different story no matter what I say. When I hang up, Nonna walks out.

"Start the dinner, I'll be right down," I tell her but then I sit back down thinking of what I will say to Angelina when I see her. Nonna hobbles downstairs and I can hear that Luigi has arrived at home. The boys are watching a re-run of *Gunsmoke* on the TV and I can also hear Luigi and Nonna's voices as I make my way down the stairs.

"Where is Maria? Did Angelina come home?"

"I don't see Angelina. Your lazy wife lies in a bed upstairs."

"Maria. Maria," Luigi yells up to me. Nonna must be heading out the door because he says, "Mama, don't you dare to go out. You take one of the boys if you wanna walk. It's time for dinner. No one makes my dinner?"

"Dinner?" Nonna says like she forgot it's that time of day. By the time I enter the kitchen she has her apron on and announces, "I make the dinner. For once you get good Italian food."

When I appear at the kitchen door, Luigi starts right in on me. "No dinner? And, no Angelina? An' my poor mama is doing all the work here; the old woman who was preparing to dash out the door."

"Relax, I'll make the dinner," I run my fingers through my messy hair, then, fix it into a quick bun with a clip from my apron pocket. With my back to Luigi, as I prepare some lasagna, I say, "I heard that Angelina is fine, that she is with Pasquale for sure."

He steps forward towards me. "What? She stays the night with that pervert? I kill him." Now, he is out of control pacing around the kitchen and I'm looking at the clock thinking how I'm going to get his supper ready and on the table and get myself out the door and over to the diner by 7 PM. Impossible.

"I'll try to get her home."

"What? Are you crazy? I want her home now."

Somehow I manage to get him to go out to the pool hall for an hour so I can get the supper ready. I tell him it will relax him with all the aggravation, but as it turns out, that just causes more problems later when I hear about it from Mrs. Pazzo.

I always run into her when I have no time to listen to her gossip, and of course, there she is when I'm heading out to meet my daughter. God, if she only knew. Maybe she does. She acts like she knows everything about everybody in the neighborhood. She stops me to tell me about Luigi at the pool hall the other night.

"I don't have time tonight. I'm late," I say, but she rambles on to me anyway.

"Luigi's over there shooting pool and Tony Tucci tells him he could swear he saw you out in a restaurant with Pasquale Corso. He's Anthony Corso's middle son, but you probably know, the gorgeous one. Forgive me, God, if I was a younger woman, if I didn't have to put up with Frank. You know what I mean. Well, what can you do?"

I nod. It must have been the night I went with him to Telly's because that's what Mrs. Pazzo says, that it was a while ago. I know how agitated Luigi gets over anything to do with Pasquale since that day with Angelina. So then, Mrs. Pazzo tells me that Luigi says to Tony that it was Angelina that he sees with that pervert. She can't see why anyone would call such a perfect male specimen a pervert but everyone is entitled to his opinion. And Tony says 'no' and they get into an argument. Finally, Tony tells Luigi that maybe he's mistaken, that Angelina looks similar to me, but he tells him he's still pretty sure it was me. And then she tells me how angry Luigi got, that he missed a shot in the pool game and lost some money and now he says it's all my fault. I'm looking at Mrs. Pazzo wondering how she gets all this information and thinking what a pain it's going to be to listen to Luigi about this when he gets around to confronting me with it.

I glance at my watch and its 6:45. I don't want to be late to meet Angelina so I just leave Mrs. Pazzo alone on the sidewalk still telling me the story and raving about what she would do to get Pasquale's attention if she was young and single. And, I still hear her as I'm rushing away.

"Balls go flying, and he points the pool stick at Tony and he calls him a crazy man, and…" She's still talking and I'm waving as I head down the street towards the subway. I must meet Angelina on time. I only have this one shot at this and I don't want to mess it up.

Red Hill diner is packed. I don't know why I thought no one would be having dinner here. It must be that I only notice this place during the day when people have lunch or in the afternoon when friends meet for coffee. I'm shaking like a bag of nerves, and I go into a panic when the hostess tells me I have to wait. What if Angelina arrives and there's no seat? She won't want to talk to me, she'll just run off.

I ask the girl again, "How about that table over in the corner?" I point to the table as a young couple approach and are seated by someone else. But then, the girl seats me by the window in a cramped booth for two, and it's really hardly big enough for one person. And then I think that this is good—I will see Angelina walking in with a perfect view of the door.

"Just one?" the waitress asks.

"No, there'll be two of us." She hands me two menus.

"Something to drink?"

"Thanks, a coffee, please."

I watch each person as they walk in the door, each time yearning for it to be Angelina. I'm actually feeling sick from the smell of fried chicken and buttery mashed potatoes. I fidget grasping my purse. I pull out my compact and apply light pink lipstick. Maybe I will look more like a "cool" mama, one that my daughter would want to confide in. Then, I find myself wringing my hands. I pick up the menu like I'm reading it and I'm thankful when the waitress returns with my coffee—something to occupy myself with. What if Angelina doesn't show up? I glance at my wrist watch and sip my coffee, glancing and sipping and looking at every single person until I think I will go out of my mind. Then, like a light bulb turns on, I know that my daughter is not meeting me here in this ridiculous coffee shop or diner or whatever it is. I don't think she's ever been in a place like this. What was Tia thinking? I pull open my purse and take out my wallet. My coffee is finished. I get up to pay and decide I will get out of the place as fast as I can. That's when I spot her at the door glancing around. I stand there by the little table waving at her. When she spots me, her eyes look away like she's ashamed. Is she ashamed of me? She approaches the booth and slides in keeping her head down so I can't read her expression. I stand there with a joyous expression, arms stretched to give her a hug, but then, I realize this is going to be a lot tougher than I'd thought. She definitely has her own mind and its set on a course that I'm afraid to even try to comprehend. I slide in across from her.

Angelina sits there with her purse tucked under her arm like she's ready to bolt at any minute, and she won't even look at me. I lean over the table toward her.

"We've been so worried."

"I'm fine, Ma."

"I know you're smart and all but fifteen is too young to be on your own without your family."

"I'm sorry, Ma, but Pasquale will look after me now."

The waitress comes to the table with a pot of coffee and pours more into my cup. She addresses Angelina like a robot.

"Something to drink?"

Angelina doesn't even look at the waitress. "Coke, please."

"What could you possibly think, to stay with a man twice your age?" I say.

"Mama, you wouldn't understand."

I reach for her hand but she pulls away. "What do you know of life with a man? What about the boys at school? Didn't you say just recently that you were crazy for Ford? Then, the next week it's someone else. It will be the same with Pasquale and then what?"

She slides out of the booth ready to leave and stands there clasping her purse like it has gold or diamonds in it. She looks down at me and now, I see her eyes red from crying and scared like a baby animal lost in the woods. But she tries to be bold and strong and is a bit too loud in responding to me in this crowded cold environment.

"No, Ma. Pasquale is who I want to be with always."

I sit as calmly as I can finding it hard to comprehend that she really feels this way about Pasquale who I am convinced tricked her into feeling this for him. I say in a soft tone what I remember always worked when she was a tot, "Mama is all ears. Please, sit down."

She looks around at the customers, now gawking at us and eavesdropping on our domestic quarrel right in their midst. She slides back in the booth to avert their attention, and I quickly grasp both of her hands. Her purse drops in the booth seat next to her and she leaves it. I force her to look into my eyes, but keep my voice low, almost to a whisper.

"All I want in this world is happiness for you. You have just started high school and remember, you wanted to go to design school?"

"I can still go, Mama." She looks away but I know I have her ear now even though it was my ears that I'd offered for her to spill her heart's troubles to me.

"If Pasquale really cares about you, he'll understand that you are too young and this is so wrong. If he cares, he will send you home to be with your family."

"Pasquale is so sad now that Papa hates him. He's worried that Papa will call the police and get him in trouble."

"And Pasquale is not sad about me? He has not mentioned me?"

The waitress brings the check and lays it on the table. I look at the robot waitress who has suddenly become the eavesdropping waitress, sensing a drama unfolding, like I'm ready to bite her head off.

"Anything else?"

"No." I pull out a ten and hand it to her and she walks away.

I turn back to Angelina. "Pasquale is breaking the law now and yes, he could be arrested."

"I don't believe that. He has done nothing wrong. It's all Papa's fault. Please, you must talk to him. He is a crazy old man, Ma. Even you say that."

"A crazy old man, eh? Yes, I say that, but I put up with him. He is my husband."

I pause and turn my face away from my daughter. Something about Luigi, and about Pasquale, has touched me on the inside and I look out the window next to me, struggling to continue. I cannot help the tears that well up in my eyes no matter how hard I try, but I turn back to my daughter. She must understand about life. The decisions she's making will affect the course of her life.

"Sometimes I wish I married a younger man, someone my own age. Your papa and I don't have so much in common, but he provides for his family."

I pull a tissue from my purse and dab at my eyes, and then, I look back into Angelina's eyes, "And, what about you when you are Pasquale's age and you desire to enjoy life, then he will want to slow down like your papa now?"

"It won't be like that Ma. Pasquale's not like Papa."

"What, you think your papa was always an old man? I didn't marry him because he was an old man. I married him because he was charming and experienced and full of life. He just got older and grumpier, not just in his body but in his head and I'm still full of life wanting to do more."

Tears stream down my face and I drop my head down onto my folded arms on the table. I hate it that I'm breaking down in front of my daughter like this. I want to be strong. I take a deep breath and sit back up noticing all the customers around staring at me. My tissues are all gone, so I pull a napkin out of the silver napkin holder on the table and I dab at my eyes. Then, I notice that Angelina's eyes are glossy with sadness as well.

"Oh Mama, I'm sorry, Mama."

"It's okay. I didn't mean… Why don't we take a walk? It's a nice evening."

And then we are out on the street walking and we're both silent, just walking by the park. We take a seat on an empty bench like two women out together enjoying the warm summer night.

"It's good to talk. We haven't talked for such a long time," I say.

"Oh Mama." She breaks down in tears again, my little girl. I wrap my motherly arms around her and she hugs me back. The relief I feel in my heart is gigantic—like I'm positive that everything will be fine. Everything.

"Come home."

"Maybe for awhile, at least until I finish school." I tilt my head to gaze at her and I see a scared little child, clueless about the world but so determined to be strong. There is a bonding that occurs between us in that moment. I know she realizes that I understand more about her than she had thought, and that I am here for her with empathy and understanding.

"Always remember, Mama is all ears whenever you want to talk."

"Silly Mama, it's you who has done all the talking."

I must get back so Luigi doesn't blow his top. I put Angelina in a cab to go and get her things from Freddie's apartment. She assures me that Pasquale will be more than happy to see that she gets home to the Bronx. I'm hesitant to let her out of my sight, but she has proven to me that she is growing up and will do just as she says. I kiss her on both cheeks.

"I will keep some dinner warm for you. Hurry home." I close the door to the yellow cab and watch it drive away.

CHAPTER 38

Angelina

When I come back to get my things from Freddie's apartment, Pasquale is in the living room pacing back and forth. He's frantic with worry just like he's responsible for me. I think he knows I was meeting Mama, but right away he's yelling at me like he's my papa.

"Where you been?" I plop down on the corner of the bed to pout.

He calms down a little and stands anchored in front of me with his hands on his hips like he's the boss and I begin to cry. I don't think he intended to get me so upset. But he doesn't realize that it's not just his yelling that has me upset, it's everything. I'm just confused and all. I turn away packing up my stuff and set the suitcase by the door. I'm thinking how I really can't wait to get home that there're lots of clothes I forgot to pack that I'd really like to wear, like the new acid green jumpsuit Mama let me buy for my birthday. Pasquale would like me in that. It makes me look at least five years older. And, how could I forget to bring the tie-dyed tunic with the sunburst in the center? That would be perfect for me now. I especially need some clothes that are a little big around the middle.

"It's best for you," he says like he's the papa. "What're you gonna do around here?"

"Oh, Pasquale, I love you. I want to be with you always." I go right up to him and grasp him around the neck hugging him and I try to kiss him but he pushes me away gently.

"My Angel, you only think you love me. You will see."

Fifteen

I sit back on the bed with my head down and sob. Not even Pasquale wants me. He kneels down on one knee and grasps my hand. With his other hand, he tilts my head up gently by my chin and gazes into my teary eyes. I must look like a snotty-nosed little kid to him.

"My sweet Angel, it will be okay. I promise."

Just then, the buzzer interrupts us. Someone is at the front door. It must be Gino and I'm thinking that his timing is plain lousy. Pasquale goes over to the intercom but he is unable to detect who is there. The sound is all static.

"Who? I don't understand."

He pushes the button to release the front door. We hear footsteps of more than one person tromping up the stairs to the apartment and then there is loud pounding on the apartment door. Pasquale glances over at me. My eyes are wide in anticipation. Now what? He opens the door and they burst into the apartment shocking both of us. It's Papa with two policemen.

"Where is my daughter?" He is raging mad and I am too stunned to speak until I realize what is going on. It's something about Pasquale. It's about Pasquale and me.

"No, Papa."

"Pasquale Corso?" one of the policemen asks.

"Yes, but let me explain, sir."

The two officers take a hold of Pasquale and cuff him. The other one says, "You can explain down at the station."

I cannot believe this. What did Pasquale do? Why is Papa with the policemen? I'm so angry and astonished that I can't think what to say. I just pull on Pasquale and keep saying, "No. No. NO."

Then, the first officer says, "You're under arrest for the abduction of a minor and statutory rape." He's reading him his rights as they yank Pasquale out the door and I'm thinking, rape? Who did he rape?

Papa has a hold of my arm. "Get your things."

I pull out of his grip coming to finally realize that it's Papa who brought the police here and it must be Mama who told him where I was. I pound on his chest yelling, "No Papa. I hate you. I hate you." I didn't think my life could get any worse. Everyone I love has betrayed me.

CHAPTER 39

Maria

It looks like rain. When I go out back to bring in the cloth bag of clothes pins on the picnic table, I look up at Angelina's bedroom window. I can see her sitting there looking out like an old woman with nothing better to do. It has been almost a week since she came home and she won't talk to any of us. Of course, it was her papa's stupid plan to bring the police and arrest Pasquale. I hadn't even been able to tell him that she was coming home on her own. He somehow found out about Freddie's apartment from one of the patternmakers at his job. He thought he'd be the big man and save his daughter from the big bad Pasquale. And, even though he deserves it, I feel bad that he's still sitting in jail. His mama and papa don't have the bail money is what I hear.

Anyway, I don't know what Luigi was thinking but now our little girl won't speak to any of us, and I can't even convince her that I had nothing to do with telling her papa about Freddie's apartment. She just sits there in her room. Maybe she nibbles on leftovers when we're not looking but she refuses to eat a dinner with us. I just hope she will get over it and maybe hang around with Celia and the girls like she used to. I even try to call Celia's mom to convince her daughter to invite Angelina out or something, anything.

I peel the carrots daydreaming. The boys are out back playing army men on the picnic table. I think about the fact that they will be teenagers soon. Oh God, what will that be like?

Luigi comes in from work and washes his face and hands at the kitchen sink. Nonna sits at the table cutting the carrots admiring her son. He ruffles his thinning hair making himself look less attractive—all worn out and hopeless, and it seems I'm feeling the same way lately. I wonder if it's rubbing off on me or if I'm just getting older, too. He watches the boys out the window and I wonder if he's thinking about them the way I am—as teenagers.

"Where is our daughter?"

"Where do you think? In her room and silent for the whole week."

I stir the marinara sauce at the stove and then wipe my forehead with the skirt of my apron.

"I put a roof over her head and food on the table and she treats her own papa with no respect."

"You must earn respect. What do you expect?"

"Agh. She doesn't talk to those girlfriends of hers?" He sits down at the table across from Nonna and grabs a carrot to chomp on. Nonna sits there slowly chopping with her head wobbling like she doesn't hear a word we're saying.

"How should I know?" I say.

"You are the mama," he stands up and walks over to the bottom of the stairs and looks up like she will magically appear because that's what he desires. "You should know these things. I have much to think about with my work and all."

I slam down the pan and sauce and oil splatters all over the stove and on the floor. Nonna comes to life, picks up her spoon and shakes it at me. "You," she says, but I ignore her. I leave the mess and walk over to face Luigi.

"Look at you, you, the big man. What does it matter if anyone is happy in your home? Look at your sons. They're afraid of you. You yell at them. You take no notice of them. They will be teenagers soon and then what?"

He pounds his fist on the wall. "That is enough. Clean up this mess."

"Who do you think will clean it up?"

Now, Nonna is on her feet and standing next to her son with the spoon ready. She points the spoon at me, "You clean a' this up."

"I make a decent life for you. You are as bad as the rest. No respect."

"No respect, eh? Look at your daughter. She refuses to speak to you, to have a meal at the same table. She tells me she hates her papa but I stick up for you, you, the big man. How can she respect you? You don't talk to her. You boss her around like a possession."

"So this is what you think? You know so much?" He picks up the newspaper rolled up and he smacks it into his other hand over and over.

"You are a stubborn old man. You don't want to listen to no one. You hide behind your mama."

Something sinks in to Nonna. All of a sudden she is sad. She sits back down at the table and stares at her spoon. I can't help but notice the change in her all slumped down, defeated. Is it because I finally spoke up to her son right in front of her?

"This Tia, she puts stuff in your head."

"It's me, Luigi. You don't even care to know your own wife. When have you ever asked my opinion? When have you ever said, 'What would you like to do? What do you feel about this or that?' After all these years, what do you know about my passions?"

He hurls the newspaper across the kitchen into the splattered sauce and oil. Then he grabs me roughly and stares daggers into my eyes with his uncontrollable rage.

"Passion?" He yells and his saliva spits in my face. "I'll show you passions."

He pushes me away and I slip in the spilled sauce, but I catch a hold of the counter and do not fall. I stand strong and straighten up with dignity. I rip off my apron and discard it on the floor amidst the sauce and oil and newspaper, and with determination, I walk out of the room almost knocking down Angelina, who stands in the doorway of the kitchen listening to all the squabble and quarreling between her parents.

CHAPTER 40

Angelina

Poor Pasquale. He doesn't deserve to be in jail. Man, jail is like for drug dealers and killers. But then, I feel like I'm in my own jail—my room. My life just keeps getting worse and now, after I finally felt I was getting through to Pasquale, that it seems like he sort of almost wants to be with me and, oh God, this has to change. I feel cursed. I decide to sneak out to see Celia. It's not that Mama wouldn't encourage me to see my friends, but out of spite, I don't want her or Papa to think I'm doing anything at all. Right now, it seems like Celia's the only friend I can trust. Sure, there's Jen but sometimes, I just don't know about her. Celia and Jen have called me over and over but I haven't even taken any calls—another way to punish my family. Let them feel bad that I'm so depressed. Why should I care? Anyway, it's not like I'm going out to have fun—it's just that I feel like I really will lose my mind if I don't talk to someone, and Celia is the absolute only person I trust right now other than Pasquale, and there's no way to talk to him. I'm about to burst. I need to tell my problems to someone.

I listen for them to leave—first Papa goes off to work, then Mama and the boys. I hear Nonna puttering around in her room. That's when I slip on my shoes and sneak out and rush down the street to Celia's house. I knock on her door, and as soon as she sees my face, it's obvious that she knows there's something seriously wrong.

I say hello to Celia's mama and Celia quickly grabs my hand and leads me upstairs to her bedroom like we have a big secret and she doesn't want her mama to know anything at all. If she only knew!

"Oh man, what happened to you? I've been trying to reach you for a week."

"You just won't believe what's been going on."

She plops down on her bed and I sit in the beanbag pillow chair printed in the most gaudy lime green and orange swirls. "What? I mean, is it true that you got raped?"

"No, no," I say, but then I think about Ford. "I mean yea, sort of."

"How do you sort of get raped?" And then, I realize she's heard something about Pasquale being thrown in jail.

"I don't have much time. I made an appointment with Dr. Parker. He's all the way down at the end of Belmont. I gotta be there in a half hour."

She sits up looking concerned, and in a bit of shock, like she doesn't even know her own best friend, at least I hope she still considers me her best friend. "You're not sick are you?" She stands up and covers her mouth with both hands. "Or hurt? Are you hurt?"

"Celia, promise not to tell anyone?"

"Are you kidding?" She sits back on the corner of her bed facing me. "Of course, I won't tell."

I put both of my hands on my belly. "I'm in trouble, I'm pretty sure anyway."

She gasps and again, she covers her mouth with both hands. "Pregnant?"

"Sh, sh." I nod and drop my head. She jumps off the bed and cradles me in her best-friend arms, the best thing I've felt for ages. Why is everything so messed up?

I don't go into the details. I don't tell her it was from Ford. I just tell her I can't talk about it now that I haven't even told Mama and Papa and I just needed that hug and someone to listen. She insists on walking me over to Dr. Parker's office and when we go downstairs to leave, she acts like nothing is wrong in front of her mama and just tells her we're going over to Jen's to fix our hair.

Celia's mama yells out from the kitchen, "Lina, you okay honey? Your mama's been calling me."

"I'm fine, thank you. I'm fine."

"Bye Mom," Celia says and pulls me out the door.

It feels so good to have Celia there with me at the doctor's. She waits in the waiting room, leafing through old magazines, and when I come out in tears, she hugs me again. We don't need words between us. She knows why I'm here. She knows that I would not be tearful if Dr. Parker told me there was no baby, but, there is a baby and it's all so real to me—so overwhelming and scary.

"Yes?" Celia says. I just nod, and that's when she hugs me. I can't get out of that place fast enough and I know that if I don't get home soon, Papa will be there and asking where I've been and all of that. I don't think I can deal with any more stress. Celia walks me home. I tell her I don't want her to come in, just in case someone like Papa is home and will question why I'm so upset. So, she leaves but makes me promise to call her later in the evening. I have every intention to call her, but it doesn't work out the way I plan.

I stay in my room during dinner again until I can't stand to sit in there a minute longer. When I finally come down and have figured out how I'm going to present my life situation and convince Mama and Papa to see things my way, I time it totally wrong. They are arguing again. And for what? What's the use of being married? But, I know for me and Pasquale, things will be different. After all, Pasquale did let me stay there in the apartment at Freddie's even though we didn't do anything sexual—not yet, anyway.

I watch as Mama rushes up the stairs and Nonna hobbles after her. You never know what Nonna is up to. I want to follow them because now I'm faced with Papa alone and an angry Papa on top of it.

"Angelina, come here."

I turn just enough for him to know I hear him, so I'm trapped. He holds out his hand to me. "Let me speak to you."

I glare at him. "What's wrong with Mama?"

"With your mama, that is between us." I don't like his tone so I turn to leave, wondering why I came down in the first place. He takes a hold of my arm but he doesn't realize that I am not his property. He can't stop me. I will do my own thing and it's better that I speak up for myself so he understands. I won't put up with it like Mama.

"You will go to school and do things with your friends like before."

"That's not going to happen, Papa. I came down here to speak to you; to ask you… I'm not going to abandon Pasquale. He's in jail because of you. I'm begging you to drop the charges, to set him free."

He is a stubborn old man, my papa. He turns and heads for the living room rejecting my request. He waves his arm at me as if to dismiss me from the room. But, I don't turn away now. I am down here in the living room face-to-face with him. Finally, after almost a week of thinking of how to speak to him, how to convince him to change his mind, I am facing up to my problems. No matter what he likes, I will speak my mind. I follow him into the room where he plunks down in his chair and kicks his feet up on the ottoman. With bold intent, I walk right up to his chair.

"Please, you must drop the charges. I'll do whatever you say, but you must tell them to release Pasquale."

I sit on the corner of the ottoman pleading with him and I see how his body softens by my nearness. I know he cares about me. I am his little girl, but he turns his face away.

"Please, Papa, please."

He stiffens again and crosses his arms glaring across the room like I'm not there next to him. Can't he look at his daughter? How will I ever get him to understand that my life is ruined? And to think that just a few months ago I was carefree like a child in this family. Nothing will ever be the same. How can I tell him that?

CHAPTER 41

Maria

I sit on my bed, the only place of solace in my house. I dab my tears with the hem of my skirt. I had been waiting all day for a chance to speak with Angelina and she had actually come down stairs. I could have pulled her aside to talk, to show her I can be understanding, and all she sees is me and her papa quarrelling and bickering. This is not how it should be.

There is a weak tap at my door. It must be her. I try to maintain my composure, to be there for her, but I turn and it's not Angelina, it's Nonna at my door entering my sacred space without my acknowledgement. Now I am so furious with feelings of disappointment to the point that I cannot control myself.

"What?" I turn toward the window by the bed so she can't see my face. Why is she bothering me, up here rubbing it in that I'm a bad wife or something? Why doesn't she leave me alone? But, she has a hurt puppy expression that really confuses me.

Fifteen

"Go away. Leave me alone for once." I give her an evil-eye glance.

But, she doesn't go away. Instead, she quietly closes the door behind her and approaches the bed where she sits down hesitantly. I turn around and face her enraged.

"Go on down with your son. You don't ever see how I feel."

"Why you never tell Luigi when you find me at that club?"

I crinkle my brows, "What are you talking about? You wanted me to tell him you were at a men's club alone with a pack of mobsters?"

"Thank you for not telling him, that's all." She hangs her head.

"Forget it," I say bowing my head as well. I turn and look out the window.

"Luigi is turning out just like his papa. I know how you feel." As quietly as she entered, she gets up and hobbles out leaving me with a stunned expression. Now, she's nice? Now, after all the years I've tried to be close with her? You never know what that old woman will do. I get up and head down stairs as well. What about Angelina?

When I reach the bottom of the stairs, I realize that Angelina is quarreling with Luigi. There are angry words and she is rushing away when I come in. She sees me, stops, and then, she runs to me in tears, hugging me with her head buried in my bosom like she would do when she was a young child. Her whole body shakes from her sobs. I run my hand down along the back of her silky hair that smells like Prell shampoo.

"It's okay," I try to assure her.

But, she breaks free and halts between me in the doorway to the living room and her papa, who sits like a log in his chair. She holds her head in a frantic pose. What is wrong, I think. I frown at Luigi looking for a clue as to why she is suddenly in such a state. It must be something he said.

"It will NOT be okay. Don't you see?" She howls.

I approach her and try to calm her again. I wrap my arms around her, but her face is swollen and red with frustration. She thrashes in my arms like an animal fighting to be free.

"You'll see. There are so many other boys and you'll fall in love one day and marry one of them."

"No. No, I won't. I'm in love with Pasquale." She pulls away and turns to run out of the room but then she whips around with her face even redder than before. "Don't you see? I'm going to have a baby."

"You're pregnant?" I say with a voice so hoarse it's hard to recognize.

"Is not possible," Luigi mumbles. Now, he is out of his chair.

"Yes, yes. It is possible." She holds her belly with both hands. "How can you live with yourself to have the father of your grandchild locked up in prison?"

She runs out of the room and up the stairs just as the two boys run in the room playing and romping around loudly. They spot their papa and immediately quiet down—just the look on his face is enough to scare them into silence. Luigi says nothing, he just stares at them. And then he turns to me. He points to the kitchen.

"And you," he says.

"What?" I am annoyed with him and in total shock about Angelina's news. What more could be wrong that needs to be discussed at a time like this? Maybe she is being dramatic. Maybe there's a mistake. I look towards the kitchen like there is something I should see that has to do with the fact that my fifteen-year-old daughter is pregnant. Pregnant! It has not sunk into my lunatic brain.

"You have no sense of responsibility. You leave your wedding ring in that wobbly dish by the sink. You don't realize how easy you could lose something that means so much to our family. It was my auntie's and you leave it sitting in a cheap dish by the sink. One of these days it will be gone—down the drain just like your daughter's life."

With my right hand I grasp my left hand and can feel the fake ring on my finger. I speed over to the sink and gawk at the ring in the dish where I always leave my ring, where I left my ring ages ago, where it disappeared and now, it has re-appeared like magic. Am I losing my mind? I take the ring, holding in tight in my palm unable to comprehend what has happened in this house. I scurry up the stairs to speak to my daughter, but it is no use, she will not speak to me for now. In the evening, I lie in my bed while Luigi snores like an electric saw, and I wonder how my ring miraculously re-appeared. Was it Angelina? Could she have taken it, or Luigi, or what about Nonna? And then the fact that my little girl is going to have a baby with Pasquale as the papa, invades my mind, and that does it for me. I lie awake all night, and every once in a while, I hear Angelina sobbing in her room. How are we going to fix this one?

• • •

In the morning I call Tia to meet me in the coffee shop. She will know what to do. I know I must look sick with worry, but when Tia approaches the table, I notice that she appears unusually tired and unhappy as well. Even when I'm telling her about Angelina she doesn't have much to say—none of her genius ideas or insights. We sit and drink our coffee. "I don't know who else to talk to," I say, hoping she'll tell me just what to do that will fix everything, but she just sips her coffee deep in thought.

"You okay?" I ask.

"Yeah. Yeah. It's just, sometimes I kind of wish I had a dull normal life, but gosh, we all got problems."

"Me, too." I drop my head down. Tia reaches over with a dim smile. She takes my hand and I'm thinking, my daughter is pregnant at fifteen, what can I possibly do? Her life is broken

and I don't know how to fix it and even Tia doesn't know."
"This ring sure looks like the real thing, Doll."
"It is the real thing. There're too many weird things going on in my house lately."

CHAPTER 42

Angelina

I don't care what my family thinks anymore, and I don't want to stay cooped up in my room either. It's time for me to take some action. I call Gino to ask about his brother. Even though he seems depressed about the situation and sort of angry with me, I finally convince him to tell me where Pasquale is held in jail.

My need to speak with Pasquale is like an itch I can't reach to scratch. I decide that I will tell him about my condition. The whole conversation plays out in my head and I visualize him hugging me and telling me that he will protect me and take care of me and for the time being, once we get him out of jail, I will be able to stay with him and we can zip over to the justice of the peace and elope and then no one will be bothering me about what I'm doing, where I'm going or any of that. I have daydreamed and played this out in my head over and over—different ways this could work with Pasquale; all the different ways he could react and how it may happen. I've got it worked out in my head for the most logical way it will go, once I figure out a way to speak directly to Pasquale. It's my hope that after I discuss everything with him, he'll arrange for me to stay at Freddie's until we can get him out of jail. I stayed up all night deciding exactly what to take with me to stay at Freddie's apartment. Even if Pasquale's not sure, someone has to water Freddie's plants while he's away. So, I'm packed and ready to go. I pull the piece of paper with the address for the jail out of my purse as I trudge along the sidewalk. I feel like I might faint in the ninety-five degree temperature, plus I've got this back pack that weights a ton clamped on my back, and my purse is extra heavy, draped over my shoulder. I probably look like a street person. Finally, I make it to Brooklyn after switching trains twice. I look up at the building and see that this is the address Gino gave me. Now, I'm nervous, but I trudge up the steps of the police station or holding area, or whatever it's called. I stuff the sheet of paper back in my purse and look around the lobby. I go right up to the policeman at the desk that says, "Information."

"I'd like to see Pasquale Corso." I let my back pack slide off onto the floor.

The uniformed officer at the desk hardly looks at me; he's bored and he couldn't care less that my life is ruined. How would he know? He picks the dirt out from underneath his fingernails with a plastic straw, "You related to Corso?"

He seems to be bothered that I've interrupted his precious time, but then, he stares at my backpack sitting on the floor next to me. "What you got in there?"

"Oh, just my stuff."

He nods and turns to leaf through a folder. Is he looking for information about Pasquale? Maybe Pasquale has gone home already, or maybe he has a list of people he is authorized to let in to see him. I suddenly feel very young and naive, having never had to deal with anything like this before.

"Aw yes, He's here alright."

I think if I act older he'll listen to me. I puff my chest out. "I'm his wife. I must see him."

I almost wilt on the spot when he chuckles and his gigantic belly bounces around like Jello. "His wife? Let's see some ID."

You can't lie to a policeman, the fuzz, some say, "pigs" so I stick to my story. "My ID is back at our place. Please, it's important; a family issue."

"You tote around all this stuff," he points at my over-stuffed back pack, "and you don't carry no ID?" He raises his eyebrows and stares at me.

I shake my head.

"Alright, alright. Just have a seat." He points to a bench on the other side of the foyer as he gets up not taking his eyes off me.

I hobble over practically dragging the heavy back pack and sit on the bench with my purse poised in my lap and my heavy bag next to me. It's 10:05 according to the enormous clock by the marble stairs. Honestly, I'm glad to sit down for a minute since I'm feeling like crap all of a sudden. I need to compose myself before I speak to Pasquale and then I'm thinking, can they arrest you for lying about being married. I sit there and sit there and suddenly there are dozens of officers milling around like they're meeting there for something important. There are also men in suits asking questions at "Information," and suddenly, so much is going on. I just sit and observe, but finally I'm wondering if that bored cop remembers I'm here waiting to see Pasquale. Now, it's 10:26. When the group of officers finally leaves through the front door, I go back over to the first jelly-belly officer at the desk and now there are two of them.

"Can't let you see Corso, Miss."

The second cop is standing there and he adds, "This is a holding station. There's no visiting area, only for meeting counsel and stuff."

I feel like I'm going to cry. I wasn't expecting this and I can hardly look them in the eye. They're both standing there staring like they just want me out of their hair.

Finally, I get up the nerve to squeak something out. "Can I leave a message for him?"

The two cops exchange glances and I feel like I'm in the principal's office getting punished. Jelly-belly says, "Fine. We'll see that he gets it."

"Do you have a pen and paper?"

Jelly Belly rolls his eyes then reaches in the drawer and pulls out a notepad and pen. I stoop down, covering what I'm writing, as I scribble a note to Pasquale. I hate it that they keep staring at me. I'm trying to think exactly what I want to say to Pasquale. When I finish, I fold up the note and Jelly Belly holds out his hand.

"You got an envelope?"

"Come on, Miss. We don't got all day," the other cop complains. He pulls out a roll of tape, takes the note from me and tapes it shut. "Write his name on it. No one's gonna read it."

I clearly print Pasquale's name on the note and hand it to the officer. "You sure you'll get it to him?"

"I'll give it to him personally."

I hoist my back pack up on my back and turn to leave. As I walk away some instinct tells me that they're laughing at me. I go through the rotating glass doors and just as I'm about to walk down the stairs outside, I think of something else, and I go full circle back through the doors and to the foyer. It doesn't seem like they see me at first, but then when they do, the second officer keeps looking over at the trash pail by the desk.

"Oh yeah, I just thought I'd ask; they didn't tell you if they thought they might let Pasquale out anytime soon, did they?"

They both stand there shaking their heads no. Once again, I turn to leave. That's when, out of the corner of my eye, I see one single thing in the mesh metal trash pail next to the information desk, and that's definitely my note to Pasquale. I slow my pace as I walk back to the door. What good would it do to confront them? I tell myself to face the fact; they're not going to tell Pasquale I was here.

The day has been wasted and I have no place to run away to. As soon as I get back home, I lock myself in my room with my desk fan blowing on my face. I had it all worked out to be with Pasquale. How did it all get so messed up? I'm sure I could convince him to be with me, but then I lie there and wonder what I had been thinking toting around that back pack all day like it was my marriage trousseau. My mind is a mess, swirling around, trying a cope with the heat and figure out what I'm going to do about my situation. All sorts of things enter my mind and I can hardly stand it anymore. I wonder if Celia told Jen, and when the kids at school find out, oh man, I'm going to get the worst reputation as a slut. But then, I think, what about all this free love talk. Everyone seems to believe it. Maybe they'll think it's cool that I'm pregnant. Love is free after all, right? Maybe it won't be so bad. I imagine all sorts of scenarios of how I could deal with my problems. Nothing seems to make any sense.

I hear Mama come in downstairs. She yells up the stairs, "Hello. Boys? Angelina?"

The boys go tromping out of their room and down the stairs like a herd of elephants. If I have a boy, I'll never let him go tromping around like an inconsiderate clumsy ox.

"Where's your sister?"

Louie opens his big mouth and yells up to me, "Lina."

I pat my eyes with the bedspread hoping it's not totally obvious that I've been crying, and I slowly walk over to the landing and look down at Mama. She looks up like she understands what I'm going through. She must get it, what it's like to get pregnant when you're still a teenager. She was pregnant with me when she was my age. Oh God, not like Mama. But, it's different for me. She had Papa who married her right away and pretty soon, everyone forgot that they had to get married. If I think about it honestly, it's not like I even want to get married right now. But under the circumstances, I guess I do. I'm baffled about the whole thing. I wasn't planning on this happening to me, and still, the more I think about it, the only one I would want to marry is Pasquale. I just can't think of anyone else on such short notice. The trouble is I don't think he has the slightest inkling of my intention to marry him. And, all the schemes and plans I've concocted haven't even convinced me 100 percent. I was going to work on him, get him to fall in love with me since he's from an old-fashioned Italian family, and if I could get him to have feelings for me... Oh what's the use? I feel myself tearing up again. I don't know why I'm so darn emotional all of a sudden. I'm inching down the stairs and Mama has her eye on me again like she can see right through to my brain.

She looks over at the boys, "Go on and play outside for a bit. Dinner will be ready in awhile," and then to me, "Come help with dinner." Oh man, if that isn't a cue for a private talk. I roll my eyes.

Before I get to the bottom of the stairs there's a knock on the front door. Mama's already in the kitchen so I open the door to Tia, not appearing like her normal bubbly self, but more shabby and tired than usual. When she sees me, she approaches me with a warm hug and then she seems like the old Tia I'm so used to.

"Lina, sweetie. You're just the girl I came to see. Come on down to the pet store with me."

Mama must have set this up with Tia ahead of time—very well thought out—like Tia really needs my help in selecting a puppy pal for Pumpkin. I don't want to let them know that I am clever enough to see their plan. Actually, I really need someone to talk to and Tia is perfect for that. Why didn't I think of talking to her earlier?

So, it's hot as hell and we're walking along Arthur Avenue towards the pet shop.

"I really need your opinion," she says.

"Right. I know, should you really get a puppy to keep Pumpkin company?"

"You love dogs. Who's better to help me pick one out?"

We walk along in silence and I get a feeling that something is not quite right. I can't put my finger on it. As we walk by the square I break a twig off a bush that protrudes onto the sidewalk. I diddle with it breaking the little branch into tiny pieces and scattering a trail of quarter-inch sections as we tread along.

Out of the blue, Tia announces, "I know you're pregnant, sweetie."

"I figured Mama told you," and then, I don't know why, because I really do think my mama probably does understand some of what I'm going through, I say to her, "She doesn't understand anything."

"I know your mother a long time. I remember when she was in love, years ago before you were born."

"I can't ever imagine her in love."

"Well, she was and I'm sure she still loves your papa. It's just that things change as you get older. Your papa used to be quite the charmer."

I laugh right out loud at that one. Does she think I'm stupid, that I'm falling for this?

"You've got to be kiddin'? Come on, you don't have to tell me that."

"Honey, you just can't even imagine, can you?" She slings an arm around me for a quick hug as we walk along. "He used to bring her flowers for no reason at all but that he loved her, and he used to make her laugh. I remember all the stories when she'd come in the shop and we'd laugh. Your papa would do anything to make your mama happy. Anything. One time he even got stitches from a guy punching him—just because he wouldn't take any crap from other guys talking negative about your mama."

"That's where he got the scar on his right eyebrow?"

"Sure thing. I was sort of envious of their relationship. My hubby back then, he didn't do anything romantic. And, oh man, he never stood up for me like that."

"Then, why don't they understand about me and Pasquale?"

"Oh Lina, you're so young. You need to live life as a teenager and not worry about a husband and a baby and a home. Not yet, sweetie."

"But, I'm having a baby."

She stops and takes a hold of my shoulders turning me towards her to look in my eyes. "I know, but be honest with me, is this really what you want?"

I try not to look at her, to turn away and keep walking to the pet store but just as I thought, this is not about a puppy, it's about me having a baby.

"What do you mean?" I say and fling the rest of the broken twig from my hand.

"Wouldn't you rather be hanging out with your friends, going to the prom with that boy, Ford or another boy? And, did I hear that you fancy Gino?"

"What? I love Pasquale."

"Is it really Pasquale's baby?"

"Pasquale's perfect for me, plus, Tia, the prom is way over with, and it's not cool anyway, and the only reason I've been around Gino lately is that he's Pasquale's brother."

We continue to walk and I'm much more defensive now that I know the purpose of our meeting. And then a young mother comes rushing toward us on the sidewalk pushing a baby carriage with a screaming baby, red-faced and kicking wildly. The young mother has a lonely and hopeless expression of sadness and frustration and it hits me, there's no such thing as daydreams, this is reality. That could be me in six months. The mother whizzes by and I burst into tears with Tia next to me hugging me on the street.

"I'm so confused. I'm afraid to have a baby."

"You could always have another baby."

"What do you mean?" I look at her with my forehead crinkled and my face all puffy and red. She hesitates and looks away then back at me like she has a secret for the perfect life or something. She pulls me over to a bench by the bus stop. I can see the pet store right across the street.

"Have you thought about an abortion?"

I spring to my feet and grasp the glimmering gold cross around my neck. That's an unthinkable sin.

"How could you even think I'd kill my baby? Never." I plop back down on the bench and she's got her arm around me again.

"You're right. I'm sorry. I'm just trying to figure a way out of this."

She pulls a tissue out of her bag and hands it to me, but then I see that she's got a tissue, too. She is also crying.

"Oh, Tia, why is everything so difficult?"

"Honey, God has his way for teaching us our lessons." She kind of stares off towards the pet store in a melancholy mood.

"Yeah," I mumble.

"It's getting late. Let's go see that puppy."

CHAPTER 43

Maria

Luigi, grouchy and hungry as an old bear, is home from work and anxious for dinner. So are the boys—they're starving, they tell me. Nonna is here in the kitchen with me exhibiting no sarcastic drama for once. I keep my eye on her anyway. Her recent apologetic behavior baffles me. I set an extra seat for Tia, but they're not back from their walk yet and I feel nervous that Luigi will start making a big deal of everything like, why did I get Tia to have a talk with our daughter, and I just wish they'd get back already. I peek out the dining room window for the thirtieth time. Finally, I spot them heading toward the house with arms wrapped around each other's waists. I rush to the door to meet them. Angelina kisses Tia and darts inside. I stare at Tia like I will read from her expression how the talk went, but what I read is sadness and depression.

"How 'bout some dinner?" I say.

"I better go. We had a nice talk." She turns to leave.

"Wait," I say. I step out on the porch and pull the door shut behind me. "Something's wrong. Come sit on the swing a minute."

We are friends for almost thirty years. By now, we can pretty much decipher each other's thoughts at almost any given moment, if we pay attention. I let my dramatically starving family wait on dinner and sit for a minute with my good friend. She forces a weak smile.

"It's that damn Freddie—gave me the disease, and now he's off in London again infecting God knows how many helpless women. Darn men, I can't seem to make the right choices."

"But, I thought you broke up with him months ago."

"I did, love, but he knows exactly how to shake me; rock and roll me and inject me with the clap."

"I'm sorry, Tia, but what's the clap?"

She stands up to leave and pats me on the shoulder. "Oh Sweetie, it's V.D., you know, gonorrhea. No big deal."

Angelina actually joins us for dinner so I'm sure Tia said something to her to make her feel better about her situation—her pregnancy. But then again, maybe she's just getting sick of sitting in her room. I'm wondering if Celia and her friends know about her condition. I haven't seen any of them around lately, and I'm just about to ask her about it. With a full belly, Luigi retires to the living room to watch *The Lawrence Welk Show* and smoke his pipe. I figure I'll talk to her in the kitchen while we do the dishes.

Luigi yells in, "You sure one of the boys walked Mama over to bingo?"

"Louie said he'd go."

There's a knock at the front door.

"Who comes here so late?" Luigi complains.

I remove my apron and open the door to Anthony and Josephine Corso. Angelina looks on and follows as I lead them to the living room to Luigi. I'm wondering what the Corso's know of Angelina's pregnancy. It's blatant that they know something the way they glance with tenderness at Angelina and smile.

Luigi drops his feet to the floor and turns in his chair to see his daughter. He points to the stairs and dismisses her like a possession or a pet dog.

"Go upstairs."

"But Papa…"

"You go now."

What can I do? I can't go against my husband in front of the Corso's. They are here in our house and I must be gracious, but I feel for Angelina and glance at her with tenderness. At the same time, I'm curious as to why Pasquale's parents would be here at our house at this time of night.

CHAPTER 44

Angelina

What does my papa think? Does he really think I will just go and sit in my room and not listen to what the Corso's have to say? Actually, I've decided exactly what I will do, but first I sit on the stairs out of sight fully able to hear the conversation in the living room.

"We come about our son," Mr. Corso announces with dignity in his voice even though it cracks as he tries to get those simple words out.

I peek down and although I can't see their faces, I can see that he holds his wife's hand in a humble stance. I'm sure he's standing there with his head slightly bowed.

"Pasquale is a good boy," his mother says in her heavy Italian accent. "Please Mr. Campisi, you must understand."

"I know what kind of man is your son, the kind who ruins my child," Papa stammers.

"I am sure is only out of love," Mr. Corso says.

"In this country, is against the law to love a young girl in this way."

Love, I think? Did Pasquale tell them he loves me? My heart soars.

"My wife is twenty years younger than me," Mr. Corso states. "After many years and many children, we are happy together."

I can almost see them glance at each other with love as a couple, although I can't see them anymore from where they have moved. Maybe they're actually sitting down but that doesn't seem possible under the circumstances.

"She was fifteen when we married in Italia. It's normal to marry a young girl. We had the blessing of our families. It should be the same with Pasquale and your daughter."

As I sit there, suddenly, I feel so much better about Pasquale. Yes, it is true; he does love me. He must feel that way if his family knows about me. But it's confusing to me. How would they know I'm pregnant? I haven't even told Pasquale yet. And then, I think of the letter—the note in the garbage pail. Pasquale must have somehow received the note. How else would he know? I try to remember exactly what I wrote in that note, composing it again in my head:

Dear Pasquale, I wanted to tell you in person that I'm pregnant. I want you to be the papa. I don't mean to shock you and I hope this makes you happy. My Papa will have to give in. I will continue to beg him to drop the charges against you. Love always, Your Angel.

I can hear Papa on his feet stomping his foot like he needs to pound in his words.

"Is not the same."

I'm sure Mama helps him back to his seat since I hear the springs squeak as he plops back down. She says, "No, it's not the same, but it's something we must deal with."

"Thank you," Josephine Corso says. "Mrs. Campisi, you must understand that our Pasquale means no harm. You were friends. My son, Gino sees you at our house with Pasquale."

"I, I, we were all friends with Pasquale."

I can hear the anger in Papa's voice and I'm angry, too. What was Mama doing in the Corso's house and speaking to Pasquale. Did she try to convince him to not love me? But, Papa growls my questions, "You were at the Corso's house? What do you think...?"

I inch down and peek into the living room. Mama's wringing her hands. She only does that when she's really nervous about something.

"I, I returned his guitar. I, it was..." Then, she faces the Corso's.

Anthony says, "Please, we ask you to drop the criminal charges against our son. We have no money for the bail."

And, Josephine adds, "It seems that Pasquale will be father to the child no matter what." So, it must be the note. I haven't even spoken to her.

"It's not possible to forget," Papa grumbles. "Your son disrespects our family."

"Let us celebrate a new life to be born in joy and not in sorrow," Anthony pleads.

I watch them with embarrassment and fury. Papa crosses his arms like a stubborn old fool. He is firm but Mama tries to pry him loose from his bitterness. "We'll speak about the situation with your son, him being in jail."

Papa stands up and points to the door. "Go on. Go home."

Josephine takes Anthony's arm and they move towards the door with Mama who graciously opens the door like they are special guests in our house.

"We will discuss this," Mama says.

But, from across the living room, Papa yells, "No woman, I am the boss here. I will decide what to do."

Before they leave Mr. Corso says, "What is the use. You are old and stubborn and miserable. You no think of joy, just bitterness."

They step out the door and I can see out the dining room window as they make their way down the street, as Josephine dabs her eyes with her lacy hankie.

Now, there's no hiding from Mama and Papa. I am right there and Papa stomps over and slams the door. He glares at Mama who glares back.

"He is right. You're a bitter old man."

I walk right up to both of them. "How could you Mama? You went to the Corso's to turn Pasquale against me."

"No, Angelina. No."

I'm so angry that I refuse to listen to a thing she has to say.

"How do you dare to treat me this way?" Papa says to her. "You turn against me. You go to the Corso home. Disgraceful." And then he turns to me. "No one listens to me. I told you to go to your room."

As I dash up the stairs, I hear the back screen door slam and obviously Mama has run out the back to sit at her favorite place to sulk—the picnic table, like she always does when she's upset. I decide that I will not put up with any of this anymore, especially now that Pasquale must have found my note and told his parents about me. How can I face him? How can I face anyone? There is no choice for me any longer. There is only one way out.

CHAPTER 45

Maria

There's no tears left in my body, only anger remains, and it's rage at myself for not seeing that this could happen to my daughter, and for me not being content with a life with my husband and my perfect family. Even with Nonna—have I ever really tried? Maybe if I was a better daughter-in-law, a better wife and mother. Oh, what's the use? I don't want to think of any of it anymore. I open the closet and spot a box of our old family photos. I pull it down and tote it over to the bed where I spread out old albums from the box. There's one large picture of me and Luigi when we were young over at Van Cortlandt Park before we had the boys. Angelina must have been there with us, but in this picture we were alone. We were so happy. And then there's one of our wedding, and one with me and Luigi, and Angelina at Orchard Beach, and there is even one with Nonna and Papa Vito when we were all happy together. Maybe it was me who didn't make the effort. Nonna has a look of pride with her hand holding mine—the two of us women standing in front of our men. I stare at the pictures analyzing them—one at a time. Yes, we were happy. How content and easy life was. When did it all change? When did our family turn bitter and cynical and disgruntled? Or, could there have been something I could have done to make things better? Suddenly, all our family troubles seem to be my fault.

I arrange the photos and albums in the box to put them away, but one slips out and slides off onto the bedroom floor. I pick it up and look at the picture of Luigi's 1956 Buick. He shared the car with Giuseppe and Papa Vito, but when Luigi had the car we had the best times. In the picture we are sitting on the back of the shiny, esteemed vehicle, but it is not the automobile, it is about our carefree love that I notice. It's smeared all over our faces and in our posture and stance. I sit back on the bed and lean on the pillow staring at the carefree photo. The necklace I'm wearing in the photo is the same one I still wear today. I reach for it clasping it in my palm, and I close my eyes remembering the day Luigi gave me the cherished necklace as a gift. It was the most memorable day.

• • •

It was over fifteen years ago in this same house. I can picture myself in the kitchen downstairs sitting on a chair by the table. Jovial Luigi made me close my eyes as he opened a gift box.

"Don't peek," he said with such enthusiasm, "Just one more second."

And, I'm so excited, I'm giggling.

"Come on," I say kicking my bare feet. "What is it?"

And then, he puts the necklace around my neck and clasps it in the back.

"Okay, now you can look."

When I open my eyes, I feel the necklace but it's Luigi that gives me the most pleasure. He stands there in front of me with an enormous bouquet of my favorite pink roses and lilacs, and he's so pleased with himself. I wrap my arms around him and kiss him. Only then do I run to the hall mirror to admire my new necklace and then, I kiss him again. His kisses are like drugs to me.

"It's so beautiful. Oh, Luigi you are so good to me."

"And you my *Piccolina*, my darling wife, I love you more than the sky is high."

It is my first Mother's Day since Angelina is born.

"I am so lucky with the man I love and now a beautiful baby."

• • •

And I remember I could hear Angelina in the upstairs nursery as she woke up crying for attention.

Luigi had said, "My sweet Angel, she calls for her mama."

And I think about Pasquale when I remember the way Luigi always said, 'my sweet Angel.' It was just the same, in the same tone that Pasquale referred to my daughter as, 'my sweet Angel.' No wonder it upset me so much. Oh God, will Angelina ever feel true love for a man the way I felt for her father? Will she ever have a loving husband to care for her and her tiny baby? There is a gloomy feeling deep in my heart that it will not be like that for her. For her, things in the world are so different. She has had a taste of women's liberation. When I was her age, I knew nothing else. I expected nothing more than to be a wife and a mama in an Italian family in the Bronx. I believed that I'd live happily ever after in a life like that.

I reach for the necklace around my neck. I unclasp it and put it in my jewelry box on my bureau and then I carefully replace the box of photos in the closet. I don't deserve the love that was given on that Mother's Day so long ago.

In the evening Luigi and I are back in the bedroom getting ready for bed. He climbs into bed and I stand at the end of the bed watching him in my simple plain nightgown. I outline my body with my hands but he pays no attention.

"You no longer find me attractive?"

"What do you mean?" he says but does not even look at me.

"I mean as a woman, I uh, mean sexually."

"We are older now. Is different."

"I'm not so old. Sometimes I wonder if maybe a man might find me attractive. You used to."

"You get crazy things in your head. What's wrong with you?"

I get into bed next to him and we both lie there looking at the ceiling for a few minutes before he speaks.

"I have much on my mind. I'm an old man now." His tone is soft. I know him so well after all these fifteen years of marriage. I know that what he says means that this is life; this is the way it should be between a couple married for so many years.

"We used to laugh. Can't you remember those times?"

"I remember." He reaches over and pats my hand before rolling over on his side facing away from me.

In a careful delicate tone I say, "We should drop the charges against Pasquale. It will cause fewer problems for Angelina and the baby."

"I am tired. I don't want to discuss this now."

"We could keep him away from her. That could be the condition. She can continue at school and eventually she will have a normal life."

"How can she have a normal life? Now, she is spoiled from him."

"It's the right thing to do."

"I will think about it. Go to sleep."

I reach over and click off the lamp by my side of the bed. I lie there thinking in the dark knowing he will listen and do what I ask as long as he makes it his decision. That is one thing I know about him for sure.

The next day the situation seems like it will work out. Somehow, it just makes sense that Angelina will get on with her life. I will take care of the baby, but the baby can stay in her room and Pasquale will go on with his life and do whatever he wants away from our family. Then, when I think of him, it brings my spirit down. I really did think he cared for me. How could I be so stupid and self-centered?

I hurry into the kitchen with the groceries from Teitel Bros., and I put away the fresh meat from Peter's Meat Market as the phone rings. I'm out of breath when I answer.

"Hello." It's an unfamiliar male voice.

I say, "Who?" and he asks for Angelina, but I tell him I'm

not Angelina, that I'm her mama. He has a sense of urgency in his voice.

"I've been trying to reach your daughter all day. We received the results of blood work we did on Tuesday. We have very serious concerns for your daughter's health and that of her unborn child." He says his name is Parker, Dr. Parker.

I drop down in a kitchen chair and say into the phone, "What? What could be so serious?"

My heart thumps in my chest so hard that I feel it pounding in my ears.

"Please, there's no need to panic. Your daughter should be fine. It's just the position of the fetus that concerns us, and some toxicity. With treatment, she'll be fine. But, I'm afraid the fetus could be in danger if we don't treat this immediately."

I am breathing in gasps into the phone. He pauses and then continues, "I'm on the way to the hospital now. Please bring her down right away. Have them call me from the front desk when you arrive."

"The hospital?" I say.

"It's just that I will be there with my rounds."

"Right away doctor," I promise. "I'll bring her right away."

When I hang up the phone, I run up the stairs two at a time. Now I am really out of breath yelling as I'm running, "Angelina, Angelina." But, she doesn't answer. No one answers, not even the boys. Where are the boys?

"Where are you?" I yell. The house is completely empty. I stop for a second on the stairs and listen to the quiet, the stillness that is never present in my house. I run through the kitchen to the back door and yell, "Angelina, Johnny, Louie." But, nothing. No one is around. I stare at the picnic table and yell at it, too, "Fucking picnic table. Fuck. Fuck." I never say that word. I never swear like this. I turn back to the house to the dining room and there is Luigi home from work.

"Why are you yelling?"

"Luigi, oh my God." I pull at my hair. "Where's Angelina? And the boys, where are they?"

"The boys? Don't they go to baseball on Friday? Angelina, I don't know."

"Something is wrong. We need to get her to the hospital right away."

• • •

Why, when there is something so wrong does Angelina decide to disappear? Or, did something happen to her and she's hurt somewhere? We are frantic with worry and now in the evening no one has eaten supper. That's the last thing on our minds. No one knows where Angelina has gone. Even Nonna has returned and sits by the window in her rocking chair looking worried. The boys are still in their dirt-streaked baseball uniforms and sit quietly with the rest of us. I notice out of the corner of my eye that Nonna is perceptive to the two mobster-type guys walking by the house. She's trying to be sly about peeking out at them from her chair like no one will notice. She seems concerned as she gets up and checks the lock on the front door. Is it for Angelina or is she worried about the mobsters? Maybe the mobsters have something to do with Angelina's disappearance. Oh God.

And then, before I find the opportunity to question Nonna in private about those mobsters, I see her slipping out the back door just as there's a knock at our front door. I don't want to rile up my husband about some phantom mobsters. I want to confront my mother-in-law in confidence especially since her attitude towards me lately has been so much more gracious and understanding.

Luigi orders the boys to go upstairs when the officers and Dr. Parker arrive at the door practically at the same time. After hours of trying to find our daughter, we called the police and Dr. Parker and now they're here to help. What could they possibly do to help, with no Angelina? Johnny and Louie sit together at the top of the stairs listening to our conversations downstairs with the police and the doctor at the house. We pull kitchen chairs into the living room.

Pretty soon with all the drama we have a full house for a police investigation under the circumstances of the health issue. There's Francine and Giuseppe and their kids, and the boys have crept downstairs now, too. Tia is here, of course, and Celia and Jen, too. They look scared as rabbits. No one seems to notice that Nonna is not present. They probably think she's napping upstairs, and what would she know anyway? Luigi paces back and forth in front of everyone. I wish he'd sit down but Dr. Parker is in his favorite chair.

The officers question Parker about the seriousness of Angelina's condition.

"It's not life-threatening as long as she's treated," he explains. "We just need to get her in for some tests and simple medication." Then, he stands up, "If that's all officers, I'm needed at the hospital."

I walk him to the door. What more can he do? What more can any of us do but find out where Angelina has gone?

One officer is writing a report and Luigi points at the other one, "If that bum had something to do with Angelina's disappearance, he will pay." He quickly grabs his sacred seat, where Parker had been sitting, before someone else might decide to sit there.

"Sir, we just came from the Corso home. That was the first place we searched for your daughter. We understand that you dropped all charges against Corso and that maybe he tried to contact her."

As I walk back into the room, the second officer questions Celia, "Did she indicate anything to you? Any place you think she might go?"

"Only the friends that we listed," Celia points to a sheet of paper the officer holds on his clip board. He looks down at the list.

"Any indication as to why she would run away? Anything you might think of? Well, anything other than the fact that the father of her unborn child was incarcerated and was just released?"

Celia looks over at Jen, then, she glances at Luigi who turns away like he's disgusted with all of them. "She was angry that her father wouldn't drop the charges on Pasquale. I don't think she knew he was released."

Luigi leaps back up to his feet and shakes his finger at her. She cowers. "I was a stupid man, but I dropped the charges and now, the pervert is out of jail."

Francine stands up. "Maybe she ran off to my brother, Carmine in California. They were always so close."

We all look at her like she's nuts, but then I think, you never know with Angelina.

"Her uncle, right? Why would you think she would go see her uncle?" the officer asks.

"No, she would not go to California," Luigi complains.

"But, she always said she wanted to go out to see her uncle," Giuseppe says.

The officer writes down Carmine Campisi's phone number and then we see Francine already out in the kitchen dialing the phone. What's the use, I think.

"Well, let's see what we can find out here," the second officer says. "I believe you were the last one to see Miss Campisi, around noon, correct?" he says to Celia.

We had learned earlier that Angelina dropped off a jacket she had borrowed from Celia around that time. Celia nods.

"Did she give you any indication as to where she was headed?" He asks. "Was she depressed? Sad? Angry?"

"She usually tells me everything," Celia says with tears forming in her eyes. "I knew something was bothering her but she just said, 'I wanted to make sure you got your jacket back' and she gave me a hug and left."

"Okay, technically, we can't list Miss Campisi as missing yet, but because of the dire urgency of her medical condition, I'll put out a request to look out for the girl. That's about it."

Both officers stand to leave like it's part of the practiced choreography. That's about the same time Nonna sneaks in from the back door and enters the room surprisingly in the mid-summer heat wearing a full-length mink coat. We all gasp at the sight of her. This is a gigantic, extravagant mink coat grazing the 4'10" woman's ankles with a matching pill-box hat like the ones Jackie Kennedy wears, and she's wearing new Italian leather shoes and calf-leather gloves and has a hold of a designer handbag so shiny you can't miss it. I look at her like she's lost her mind, like I've lost my mind, like we're all seeing things. She just sashays into the room like it's a party or something. Isn't she worried about Angelina like the rest of us? And, where did she get all this stuff?

"Excuse me but I saw Angelina no more than an hour ago," she announces, and it seems like that's about how long ago Nonna has been gone. I'm thinking of the mobsters again.

"Ma, you been outside walking again?" Giuseppe says.

Luigi looks at me and then at his mama. "We thought you were upstairs."

We are all so shocked, we don't know what to say but Tia stands up and goes over to Nonna right away. She glances at us knowing that now, we've got more problems and maybe she better think of something to do to help, but Nonna's not budging.

"I'll go make some coffee." And she exits to the kitchen. The officers glance at each other with suspicion like maybe our family is a little nuts and Luigi and I both get up and go to Nonna, one of us on each side.

"You saw Angelina?" Luigi asks.

Fifteen

"Where, Nonna?" I ask.

I look over at the police when Nonna takes off the expensive coat. I pet it like I need to take care of it—like it will come alive and purr or something. Are they going to arrest her now? That's all we need.

"Getting on the subway," she says like it's no big deal and all this commotion is for nothing. "I said no that she could take a cab, and I gave her a hundred bucks."

"Yer crazy, Ma," Luigi says, eyeballing the officers out of the corner of his eye. Of course, no one believes a word Nonna has to say. "Where'd you ever get a hundred bucks? An' where you get this coat and stuff?" He looks over at the officers who are obviously interested themselves, and they look pretty much puzzled with Nonna, but they get a call on their hand-held radio about another emergency and seem in a hurry to get going so Luigi walks them to the door. Actually, he's practically pushing them.

"She doesn't know what she's talking about," Giuseppe says.

"Who says?" Nonna argues.

I whisper to Nonna, "They'll arrest you for stealing, Nonna. Go on in the other room 'til they leave."

But, they are gone and we are partially relieved temporarily, at least with what is going on with Nonna. How she got this stuff out of a store is beyond me, but we will have to get it returned in the morning, and why she would lie about Angelina is baffling. Where would she go in a cab anyway? Right now our main concern is finding Angelina, and her friends sit here in the living room still nervous, looking like we're holding them against their wills.

And now there is another knock at the door and I'm thinking they're coming back for Nonna, that they thought about it and realize she must have stolen the coat and stuff or they got a call that an old woman with a fancy fur coat got away with thousands of dollars of merchandise worth a year's wages. Louie runs over and opens the front door to Pasquale who steps in meekly and right behind him are the same two officers.

Luigi balls his fists when he sees him. "Get out a' my house."

Tia enters the living room and examines Nonna's coat and rolls her eyes. "Coffee's ready." Then she looks up and sees Pasquale and looks over at the coat and says, "Boy, we got trouble here."

"Please, sir, I want to help, to find Angelina. Maybe she looks for me."

It feels like steam is pouring out of my head. I approach Pasquale and Tia is right next to me instinctively knowing I need her support.

"How dare you come here after all you've done?" I turn away and Tia tends to me with her arm around my waist for protection. Even Tia is baffled by this crazy situation.

"I never meant to hurt anyone, especially you. I did nothing to Angelina."

I spin around and sarcastically laugh. I slap him across the face as hard as a can. I have never hit another person in my life, not even when I was a kid on the playground. I've never dared to or even thought about raising a hand to one of my children or my husband, but it is like a reaction and I have no control over my actions at the moment, and this is the second time I've slapped this same person. Then there is silence in the room. Everyone is watching to see what I'll do next, even the two returning officers are a bit stunned and baffled.

"You call it nothing? You, with your smooth talk and sneaky tricks?" And now, fully in control of my slapping arm, I slap him again and he just stands there taking it like a man. It's not the officers who step in to stop me, but Tia, who has the good sense to pull me away or I probably would have continued to slap him. Maybe I would have punched him and kicked him and God knows what, right in front of the police officers and my family.

The second officer looks at Pasquale and says, "I don't think this was such a good idea you coming here."

"If I could have a list, I will go to each home of Angelina's friends until I find her," Pasquale offers.

I have my back to Pasquale and tears are welled up in my eyes but I spin back around facing him, "No. I will look myself. She is my daughter."

"That's a good start," the first officer says as he motions for Pasquale and the other officer to leave. "Let's go Mr. Corso."

Pasquale turns back and with tenderness he says, "I will take Maria to help look for her daughter."

Luigi squints with a suspicious smirk. I can tell he thinks this is a good idea no matter how ignorant and stubborn he can be at times. I know that he realizes this is serious and the best bet at locating his daughter and bringing her home is by luring her with this man she claims to love. And Luigi knows it is me who would be more apt to convince Angelina to come home or at least to find her and make sure she is safe.

"I should be the one to go," Luigi says but it is a weak statement and I know he can be talked out of it. "I am the papa."

I lay my hand on his shoulder, "It's okay. It's better if I go. You stay here with Nonna and the boys. We'll call you."

Pasquale has a hold of the front door knob. He nods, "I will get the van."

Once he is out the door, going for his van, with the police officers following him out, we all turn our attention to Nonna who sits on the couch. The boys pet the coat like it is a live animal, maybe a dog or cat. Tia pulls it away and holds it up for examination. Out of the sleeve she pulls the price tag still attached but pinned up so it doesn't show.

Tia looks down at Nonna, "Sweetie, we've gotta take this stuff back. You can't just take stuff, that's stealing." She looks over at me and shrugs her shoulders.

"Ma, how'd you get this coat outta the store? How could you do this?" Giuseppe grumbles.

"Nonna, did you really steal this stuff? Wow," Johnny says.

"This coat's worth thousands of bucks. Look at the tags. Grand Larceny, at least. If ya didn't steal it, where'd ya get it?" Tia says.

"I bought it at that fancy store in the city, Bergdorf a' Goodman."

Luigi spins around and slaps his forehead with the heel of his palm. "Oh no, now I know we got trouble. Ma, you gotta take this stuff back before the police come back an' take you to jail."

Nonna produces the wooden spoon like a magic trick and shakes it at Luigi, "Pipe down. You getta yourself all wound up in a knot."

She opens up her designer bag and pulls out a wad of papers. "I got all the receipts. See." She waves the receipts in the air. I take the receipts from her, and Tia reads them.

"Oooo. Weeee. She's got the receipts alright."

"Ma, where'd you get money for all this stuff?"

Nonna crosses her arms with a stern expression. "Earned it fair and square."

Tia and I just stand there with our eyebrows raised but Luigi is pacing again. "Ma, you're crazy." Giuseppe and Francine stand with arms crossed.

"Why don't you tell them how you earned it," I say. I'm probably the only one in the room who gets the picture, has seen the old bird in her element as a card shark.

She glances at me as does everyone else in the room. Then, they all look over at Nonna and back and forth between the two of us like they're watching a tennis match. She smiles at me, but says out loud to everyone in the room, "Poker."

Now that the secret's out, Nonna's in a jolly mood. Maybe she knows where Angelina is as well. She reaches in her bag and pulls out hundred dollar bills. She hands one to each of her grandchildren, and one to Tia and me. She even hands one to Celia and Jen and Giuseppe and Francine.

In unison, the boys say, "Gee thanks, Nonna."

"Is only money," Nonna says and she turns to her precious son, Luigi and shakes her spoon. "You'll get yours too, when you start to act nice to everyone."

What a reversal of attitude. Tia and I sort of inch out of the room.

Luigi says, "Whadda you mean, Ma?"

Just then we hear the horn from Pasquale's van and I hurry out the front door to look for my daughter with her lover, who was once my lover. How did everything become so complicated all of a sudden?

For the most part, we drive around in silence. I hold the list of new places to check, and friends we might not have thought of in our earlier search. We decide to cover the neighborhood again, more thoroughly this time, all the places or people we think that Angelina might have gone to, the ones we've already checked, but maybe they've heard something from Angelina. We drive all around the immediate area of the Bronx especially Arthur Avenue and around the park, the school and the zoo. Certainly Nonna didn't know what she was talking about seeing Angelina getting in a cab, or going down in the subway. We knock on doors of friends from Girl Scouts and church and friends of friends of Celia and Jen and their boyfriends and again, we check with Ford's family, not realizing that he's in a correctional rehabilitation facility. We walk and look and drive and look, and if one friend says we should look somewhere, we go there. We even speak to the janitor from the school and the bus driver, who are on summer vacation but out on the street. We ask them if they've ever seen Angelina with someone from outside of the neighborhood. We go to Freddie's apartment in Yonkers, and Freddie's back from tour and he says, "no" he hasn't seen her. We expand our search outside of the Bronx area. Could she have actually taken a cab or the subway? We cross over into Manhattan because one of the kids mentions a Girl Scout camp friend, Shirley McCay, who lives in the city, in

Greenwich Village. I remember Angelina was writing pen pal letters back and forth to her. It's an easy address to remember 311 West 11th Street, so we drive there. By now it's dark, and I'm losing hope that we'll be able to find her. I don't know where to go after this. It's the last place we can think of. I climb the steps to the building and Pasquale sits in the van with the window open, watching as I ring the buzzer. I pound on the door but what's the use? It's an exterior door and no one will hear, but it's the right place. I see the family name next to the buzzer. I stand outside the building and look up at the windows. Most of them are dark and my mind feels dark now, too. I feel hopeless and sad as I trudge down the cement steps back to Pasquale's van.

We are both tired and upset, but Pasquale does not let up on his positive attitude.

"It's no use," I say, "I don't know where else she might be."

He looks out the window deep in thought and then back at me, "But we must find her. There must be somewhere else. Think."

"I've been thinking. What if someone did something to her?"

"She's a smart girl. She'll be fine. Let's go for coffee. We'll try to figure out what to do next, and you can call home, see if they've heard from her." I nod and he points the van in the direction of the Bronx.

It's not long before we reach our neighborhood. We pull up to a diner that I've never been in before. What does it matter? We go in to the poorly lit café with only a few customers and elevator music streaming through the dismal place. An enormous clock over the kitchen entrance area reads, 10:05 PM. Pasquale and I sit across from each other at a table by the front door. We order coffee and then, I spot a pay phone.

"I'll call home. Maybe she called." I suddenly have hope as I approach the phone booth. Pasquale watches me and doesn't take his eyes off me. He really is concerned. But as I speak into the phone, he must know by my expression that there is no word from Angelina. I must look so sad and he does, too. I sit back down with my elbows on the table, sipping my coffee and staring right into Pasquale's eyes, but I say nothing, I just stare.

My hands are wrapped around the chunky coffee cup. Pasquale's puppy-dog eyes are on my hands.

"I see you have your ring."

I nod.

"It looks just like the one at the pawn shop."

Something stirs in my mind; something about Nonna. No, that's not possible. She certainly would never take my ring to a pawn shop. And then I look up at Pasquale.

"I want you to know that I will do whatever you wish once we find Angelina," he says.

And now I think to myself, "What am I doing here with this man?" I look away saddened.

"I know you don't believe it, but it's impossible for this baby to be mine. But, if you want, I will marry her because of the baby."

How can he say this to me? And especially now when I am so worried about my child, my missing child? With fury, I say, "Because of the baby? You don't even love her?"

"She has a teenage crush, that's all."

"She knows no better at her age, and you seduce her and take advantage of her."

"That's not the way...."

"No, then how was it?"

"Maria, you were so important to me. And Angelina, oh, I don't know. She made me think of you, so lively. But, there was never..."

I can't listen to another second of this. I stand up to leave. I will take a bus or walk but I don't want to be anywhere near this smooth-talking, lying man. Does he think I am stupid or what?

I look back at him and spit words, "Men. You don't think

how you hurt women. You're all the same, flirting and sashaying around with compliments and teasing. What is a woman, a girl to think? When she hears words of seduction from a man, how does she know what's true?"

He reaches for my hand and I don't know what else to do but to sit back down, but I pull my hand away. He has the most calming, sexy voice. I could just kill him. It hurts so darn bad.

"How does she know?" he says with butter in his voice, the way he first spoke to me at the picnic table, "She can feel it, and the man can feel it." And I remember that first lunch with him.

But, I want to shoot myself as I sit here with this man in this awful situation and all I want besides the safety of Angelina, is for his hands to be on me and to give myself to him completely, but I say, "You know I am 34, only four years older than you. Do you think I can feel it when a man flirts with me and takes me to his bed? Or, do men only think girls of fifteen can 'feel it'?"

He grasps both of my hands before I can put them up to hide the tears in my eyes, "Oh Maria." I pull away but he still continues, "I didn't... I offended you. No, no, I think of you as beautiful and I admire you so. Really, I don't know what happened with Angelina."

"Yeah, it happened alright."

CHAPTER 46

Angelina

Better off dead, that's what I think. I struggle with a possible way to achieve this, and all that makes sense is: Drugs—it's the only way out for me. So, I make an effort to figure out how to go about this drug overdose idea. If I was still friendly with

Ford and if he wasn't in rehab, I could get some drugs from him, but what kind of drugs would kill me and how much? Why does everything have to be so complicated? But, just the way that crazy idea gets stuck in my head, it floats away like a feather in the wind when I feel the baby kick in my belly. What is wrong with me? I can't kill my baby.

    I'm plunked down on an uncomfortable bench at the Port Authority right in the center of Manhattan. Suddenly, I'm completely exhausted like after running the mile in gym class on a day following an all-night sleep-over with Jen and Celia. I don't know what has come over me. And, once I stop to unwind for just a second, my mind begins to spin with images. No matter how hard I try, I can't manage to get the thought of my bedroom out of my mind. When I was back in the Bronx, everyday just sitting there trying to find a solution to my problems, it felt like the room was closing in on me, like a pressure, a weight like the anxiety to be popular in school or to find the right boyfriend for the summer. And what do I end up doing almost all summer long—sitting in that room like a jail cell dreaming of my break out, yearning for adventure, not knowing what I really truly want. The only real logical plan I come up with is to be with Pasquale. There was a glimmer of hope when his mama tried to convince my family to forgive their son, that he is the father of my baby. What was I thinking anyway? He is going to be so angry if he thinks I'm telling people that he's the papa. It's hard to face the fact that he has no interest in a serious relationship with me. I'm like a kid to him. Why can't I see that, just accept it? And, now everything is so complicated. Stupidity, that's it, I'm practically brainless, and here's another dim-witted thing I've done. Why didn't I call Shirley? Why didn't I plan my escape, my adventure? Some brilliant escapade, nothing like I thought it would be, but I had to get away. I think I'm ready to die, but I'm plain old chicken. And still, the thing is, nothing is solved. There is still no one to help me. Even when I told Celia I was pregnant she was like, you can't let my parents find out. Her parents? God, those are the last people I will tell. Now everyone in school probably knows, even though its summer, and Ford, oh my God, he's probably ready to take out a contract on my life, even though he's probably got worse problems up in the rehab. He probably doesn't know anyway—that he's going to be a father. And, Pasquale probably thinks I'm totally nuts and mad as a hatter, thinking I tried to frame him into fatherhood.

My mind goes full circle sitting on the hard bench, avoiding eye-contact with all the creepy people milling around. Now I'm back into the thought of a drug overdose. It all keeps coming back to the same solution. If I just disappear, it will be the best for everyone. God should erase me. And then, my daydreams take me off on a tangent of what it will be like if God decides to erase me. Why doesn't he do that with all the evil men, like the murders? How will it work? Will I disappear a little at a time, or suddenly like on *I Dream of Jeanne*? Will it hurt, or will he just flush me like a toilet, down into hell?

I have to get up and walk. I can't stand to sit in the bus station a single second longer. There're just too many scary people, probably on drugs. I wouldn't want to die from anything they're tripping on. I manage to get on a subway train headed downtown and I get off in the village. I'm thinking and thinking and thinking and now I'm walking down in the village and it's really dark and late and I'm out here on the street all alone and I'm a little scared. Where am I going to stay? I stop at every phone booth along the way. Shirley always says I should come stay with her, that she has bunk beds and I can come anytime, but I keep calling and no one answers. I think, if I just go straight to her place she will be there and we can talk and her parents will understand and everything will be better. She'll know what to do, for sure. But, this is my second time coming back to her apartment and there's no answer. Maybe the bell is broken. Maybe I have the wrong address. No, I remember its 311 West 11th Street, plus under the buzzer it reads, 'McCay.' This is where I send letters and she always writes back. This has to be it, but where is she? Her parents, where are they? I decide that this time I will sit on the stoop and wait for her. I can't be traipsing around the neighborhood now that it's dark and my bags feel like I'm carrying around boulders.

    I circle the block again and use the phone booth at the corner of Hudson Street. This time, when I reach her address, I look up hoping to see more lights in the windows on the third floor—3B, that's where she lives. Maybe 3B is in the back. Of course, 3A must be in the front. They're probably home from a family day out and I'll bet they're sitting down to a late supper in their kitchen overlooking the courtyard. I'll bet there's a table and chairs out there with one of those huge umbrellas. Heck, I don't even know if they have a darn courtyard. What am I thinking? I trudge up the stairs and ring the buzzer. I convince myself that the buzzer doesn't work. I ring it like twenty times and then decide to plop myself down on the middle step. I count the steps—seven. I sit on the third one and prop the large backpack against the iron railing and stick my other bag under my legs. I pull out my plaid newsboy cap and pull it down over the top of my ears, and I lean against the bag—not too close to the street and not right by the door in case someone comes out. I'm feeling queasy sitting here, and the idea of crawling into my own bed in my own previously described jail-cell bedroom really appeals to me. My mind concocts an image of my bedroom like it's the Garden of Eden. No, I don't feel like Eve, okay, maybe just a haven. In any case, it's like the only place I can imagine in the whole world that I'd like to be right now. I doze off visualizing the pinkness of my bedroom and scents of olive oil and tomatoes cooking down in the kitchen.

    I'm sitting on my bed with the latest Nancy Drew book, and all my dolls and stuffed bunnies are arranged around me.

Mama's cooking meatballs and I'm starving and anxious to go down to help set the table and have family dinner when someone kicks me. Is it Johnny? Again, whack, I am kicked this time much harder and the bag under my legs goes tumbling down the steps. A nasty looking man with an enormous afro stares down at me with his hands on his hips. Am I in hell?

"What the fuck; you sleepin' here? Get away or I'll call the cops."

I open my eyes and gawk at him.

"I was just waiting for my friend. I have no place to go."

The man's expression softens a bit. I guess he didn't realize I was a girl and pretty young to be out on the street alone, but he is still pretty stern.

"How old are you anyway? Hey. Who's your friend? She lives here?"

I get up and retrieve my bag that had rolled down to the sidewalk.

"Yes, 3B."

"Oh, yeah," he scratches his whiskers. "That girl and her parents got in a cab this morning with suitcases, like they're going away for awhile."

"Oh no," I say.

"Well, you can't sleep here. There are shelters. Go on now."

What can I do? I can't ask the man for any favors like to use his phone or anything. I'd have to go in his apartment and he doesn't look like the type of guy I'd want to be in an apartment alone with. I sling the giant backpack on my back and pick up my tote. As I make my way down the steps and away from the building, I turn back to look and there he is inside the foyer peeking out probably to make sure I leave his precious steps.

I'm not even a half block down the street when I start to feel really sick to my stomach. I stop and set down the tote and lean over grasping my stomach. A moan of pain involuntarily escapes my lips, but I force myself to walk almost aimlessly down the sidewalk practically dragging my tote. If I can just get to a store or something, maybe someone can help me. Maybe someone will let me use their phone if they see that I'm only fifteen.

As I near to next corner, three young greaser guys with slicked back shiny hair and tough-looking skin tight tee shirts and leather vests strut around the corner towards me. They stop when they spot me. At first I think they're going to help me, that they see I'm young and sick and they want to do a good deed, but then, when I get a closer look, I realize that they have rage in their eyes and I'm afraid. I really wish I wasn't here. I have no time to fantasize about being secure in my pink bedroom.

"Hey, sweet thang," one says blowing out cigarette smoke towards me.

The three of them encircle me preventing me from moving in any direction without coming into contact with one of them. They stand with cocky attitudes smirking, and the antenna of my brain tells me that this is a dangerous situation I've managed to get myself into.

A second greaser with a scratchy voice says, "This chick's rare, like in meat, man."

They snicker some more and the third one says, "I'd say more like raw, man."

Now, I'm really terrified and they laugh out loud swigging booze out of bottles in paper bags. I can smell it. The smell reminds me of Ford.

"Leave me alone," I demand.

"Think she wants to have some fun?"

"You into free love, baby? We got lots a' free love?"

They are cracking themselves up from their antagonizing comments and each of them tries to hug or grab a hold of me. One pulls at my tote, another pulls off my backpack and I struggle to get away. I swing the tote as hard as I can and hit the biggest one right in his knee. But, when the third one pulls out a shiny switch blade and flicks the blade open right at my face, I panic and take off running down the street as those mean guys stand there laughing. Now, they have everything I own, but they don't have me, I think. I turn the corner and realize that they're not behind me and I fall over doubled up in pain.

I lie close to cement steps leading down to a lower apartment. I crawl in underneath the steps out of sight. The greasers search for me. I can hear their inebriated laughter, but I'm hidden in the doorway in the shadows. They walk by with my backpack and tote bag still cackling with drunken humor.

"Come on baby. We didn't get our free love. Where are you baby?"

I stay there crouched in the dark corner until there is no trace of those guys. I feel like I have to sleep or I will pass out and I don't want to stay in that spot in case another mean guy comes out and does something even worse to me. I wander around on the street until I reach a subway station. Is it the IRT? Will it take me home to the Bronx? I don't remember, but that song by Petula Clark invades my brain, the one about sleeping in the subway. It seems like a good idea. I'm so tired and sick, so I wander down and find a corner just past one end of the platform where I think I can just lie down and get a few hours sleep to get my strength up before finding someone to help me call Mama.

There are at least three or four people already sleeping there. I don't know why this doesn't surprise me. One of them is an old woman. At first I just sit down and try to assess the situation. At least three of them are already sleeping.

"You got no blanket, girl?" the homeless woman says.

I just shake my head. She hands me a smelly tattered blanket and says, "Go to sleep. Don't bother no one and they won't bother you."

I can hardly keep my eyes open. I curl up and fall asleep

dreaming of my own luxurious pink bedroom, but what if I'll never be able to be there anymore? I really messed things up.

CHAPTER 47

Maria

Pasquale asks me questions until my head feels like it will explode. There is nowhere else I can think to search for Angelina. We leave the diner. At first, when we reach his van, we just get in and sit there. I feel his eyes on me, gazing at me, trying to be subtle. Is he thinking what a bad mother I am? So what! What could Angelina possibly have told him about me? Is there anywhere that he's not telling me, anywhere she could be? He's so sure she is fine—safe. It gives me some comfort, but right now, I just want my daughter home where she belongs. I turn and look right into his eyes, the eyes that are unexpectedly sorrowful and true. He reaches over and takes my hand.

"Things can be so painful," he says.

"You know, I don't think I feel anything for Luigi anymore," I say to this man I should hate, and as soon as this slips from my lips, I feel shame. Why am I confiding in this man; this man who may become my son-in-law; this man who I will have to deal with as the father of my grandchild for the rest of my life? But, from my heart, I must speak to him. I must tell him what else is on my mind.

"When we made love that day, I really thought you felt something for me."

"Oh, my sweet Maria, that was the problem. I felt too much for you."

"I'm sorry to deceive you—you know, about me being married, and Angelina." I am so embarrassed that he still holds my hand and we sit in his van like teenagers. "Did you really think

Angelina and I were sisters?" I look up at him terrified to look into his eyes, but needing to read what his eyes would tell me.

"At first, yes, but then I played along because I was so drawn to you. I suspected something the way the boys and Angelina had such a motherly respect for you, but I didn't want it to be true. I told myself it was not possible. You were like a miracle to me—just the kind of woman I wanted in my life and I didn't want to lose you. Once it was out, that you were Luigi's wife, I couldn't live the lie anymore. I had to let you go. And then, there was Angelina, a young version of you. She was always right there, anxious to grow up. I could tell she had a crush on me, and I really wasn't interested especially because of her youth. And then, there is my little brother, Gino. He is crazy about her. She was so tempting to me, always cuddling. I'm sorry, I don't need to tell you all this."

"No, I want to know. You are the father of her child, my grandchild. I want to know."

"Maria, please, you don't understand the situation. I am not the father of her child."

I pull away from him. What are we talking about anyway? And now after he is starting to make a little sense, he just outright lies to me. I'm getting some answers of how we ended up in this mess, but he won't face his responsibilities and I'm out here in the van being sucked into his smooth talking garbage again.

"Please take me home right now."

I turn away from him and close myself from him, from any further discussion. I stare out the window. He starts the engine and we drive towards my house in silence.

Even though it is really late, maybe midnight by now, I can't go into my house. I pretend to open the door and go in so Pasquale will drive away, but I stand there until his van is gone and I dart away down the sidewalk. I will walk around the neighborhood just to see if I can figure out where Angelina might be hiding or God forbid, hurt and in need of help. I walk down 183rd street and then down Arthur Avenue. I don't want to be on a main street so I head off down a side street. I walk near the men's club where I had found Nonna that day. What a crazy old woman, and I think of my daughter how much she is like her grandmother. I stop in my tracks. There is Nonna out at this late hour. Of course, she snuck out again. What is wrong with that woman? She's easy to spot in her big fluffy mink coat especially in this hot summer weather. Even at night, it's around 75 degrees.

I am quiet and can hear her talking to the guy at the door. Two other mobster-type guys and a scantily dressed young girl come up to the door, but they're not letting her in and they're angry.

"Look at this," the girl says, "hot as hell and Granny's got on her fancy mink coat."

"No need for you thugs sniffin' 'round my house. Can't steal no money, spent it all." Nonna does not back down. She doesn't even act scared, but knowing her, I'll bet she's dying to get in there and play some more cards.

"No room in here, Grandma," the biggest mean-looking gangster says, and they slam the door in her face. I hurry to get around the corner so she doesn't see me and I head back home as fast as I can so I'll beat her. I'm out of breath when I leap up on the porch, but I sit there on the porch swing waiting for her to arrive.

CHAPTER 48

Angelina

I'm twisted in a scratchy blanket reeking of sweat and mildew. I've been sleeping in a mangled mess, but now I'm awake in a groggy sort of pain. Something is wrong. Is this a dream? I try to awake—to speak, and then I realize, I am awake but I can't vocalize words, just sounds like an injured animal.

"Awwwgh. Oh, help me. Awwwgh."

When I hear the sounds coming out of my body, the agonizing moans, I realize it must seem like torture to these homeless people around me. But, I can't see anyone. The old woman is gone. My hair is matted and foul smelling. I have thrown up all over myself, maybe while I was sleeping. And, I'm wet and shivering. I couldn't have peed in my sleep, but it's streaked like blood. That's not possible. What is wrong with me?

A uniformed man comes rushing over—a fireman, no, a transit cop. Oh no, he will throw me out and where will I go? But, I can't move like I'm drugged. I just want to sleep a little longer. I can feel his breath on me as he leans over. He has a hold of my shoulders. Is he going to hurt me? I whimper. Maybe it's the greasers trying to trick me—hurt me.

"Wake up. Wake up. Ugh, vomit. Get paramedics down here right away. We've got a young girl hurt or sick. Not responding." I hear footsteps tromping towards me.

I try to focus on the greaser's face, or is it a cop's face but my eyes fail me. I pass out to the blare of sirens—louder and louder and then, nothing.

• • •

I struggle to open my eyes. I feel sluggish and strange. I thrash around but my body is not responding to my brain. Somehow, I realize I'm in a bed. Maybe I died, but this doesn't feel like hell and its sure not my bedroom—the jail-cell bedroom that I cherish and wish I could magically be transported back to in time. Is this heaven? No, it must be hell for all the sins I've committed. And there's a pungent antiseptic smell. I don't want to be here. I don't want to open my eyes, but there are people around—voices, voices—louder and then softer. My brain is fuzzy. It can't be those greasers. I yell out, "No No. Leave me alone. No."

The people scurry over to me and suddenly my eyes work and open wide. It's a nurse. I'm in a hospital. What's wrong with me? A nurse reaches up and adjusts something, a tube going into my arm. I try to pull it out. Her tender face relaxes me a bit. She puts her palm on my forehead like Mama always does when I'm sick.

"Shhh. It's okay, honey. It's a dream. You're awake now."

I just stare at her. My voice is gone, now.

"You're in Saint Vincent's Hospital. Remember?"

"No," I manage to whisper, "I don't…Am I hurt?"

"You just need a little rest."

I crinkle my brows. I remember things—bits and pieces. I try to sit up but it's useless. I feel my stomach.

"I was sick. I was in pain and I…"

She touches my shoulder like a caring older sister might do.

"You have no identification. Who can we call to notify that you're here?"

And then I remember, "My purse, my bag; the greasers took them. What's wrong with me?"

"You were pregnant, honey," the nurse says and then another nurse is there and a doctor and they're all demanding information from me and questioning me. "You had a miscarriage. I'm sorry. What's your name? Where're you from?"

I can feel the tears welling up in my eyes building like a volcano. She takes my hand and with my other hand, I hold my belly—my childless belly.

And then, more questions come, one after the other from the doctor and the others in the room. The questions echo in my head and the room spins.

"What's your name? Who's your doctor? Where do you live? Did you know you were pregnant? We need to call someone. Honey, your family must be so worried. Why were you in the subway? Are you homeless? Did you fall down? Did someone hurt you?"

I pull away and try to roll over on my side but it's no use, they're all around my hospital bed.

"I don't have a name," I announce and squeeze my eyes closed.

I want to disappear but this is even more like a jail. There's no way to get out of here. I have a tube in my arm and no clothes or shoes and I can't even sit up, but now I make up my mind. I will not talk to any of them. They're all around my bed—strangers—all frantic and demanding until someone with a soft voice says, "Everyone out of here. Let her rest."

I lay there whipping my head from side to side crying until the soft-spoken woman sooths me with tenderness by swabbing my forehead and speaking softly to me, "It's okay. You're fine. I'll help you. Just relax honey. Relax."

I lie still letting her pamper me. But, the rest of them are out in the hallway whispering about me. They are in a tizzy about what to do about me, but I am just so tired.

This goes on for days. I'm finally able to sit up but I still have the tube in my arm, and I scoff down the bland food like I'm starving to death, but I decide I will not speak to them. The soft-spoken woman is gone and I haven't seen or heard her since I first awakened. I don't know what I'll do but when they give me some clothes and shoes I'll just walk out the door and into the street and I'll wander around until I can find a job and a place to stay. I don't even know where I am—this hospital, that is. I close my eyes and think about my life. I will protest the war and be an artist. I will go to Greenwich Village and find a commune and I'll work there and live with all the hippies, and then, I think that this hospital is in Greenwich Village. It will be easy. What can I wear? It'll be easy to snatch some slippers, tie a sheet around my waist as a hippie skirt. Maybe I'll hoard some food just in case I get stuck wandering around with nothing to eat. I'm stumped on the thought of a shirt to wear. The "no bra" situation will not be a problem, and I've heard that hippies don't wear underwear anyway. I imagine life at the commune with a long-haired rock-and-roll boyfriend who will play ballads at the Bitter End down on Bleeker Street, and I will forget about my old life. I will choose a new name, something like Marybelle or Natasha. I spend my time laying there mute to the hospital staff, expanding my daydream until it's a concocted life that could never come true, even in my wildest dreams.

A mean nurse with black hair brings a tray of food to me. "It's been three days. They'll have to release you today." I stare up at her and realize my daydream of living in a hippie commune is ridiculous, especially since the only person I know down in the village is away on vacation or gone somewhere for an unknown period of time. Plus, I miss my family and my neighborhood. That's all I'd be thinking about if I was living at a commune. I would always be thinking, what are they doing now? Are they having Sunday dinner at Aunt Francine's or at our house? And, would one of the boys take over my pink bedroom and paint it blue or green? And, what about Celia and Jen and all my friends? They probably don't want to be friends with me anymore. I feel so embarrassed and sad.

There's a second nurse in the room who is cleaning up and preparing the other bed for a new patient. "Psychiatrics will get involved. They won't just release you. Is that what you want?"

Then, the doctor who's been treating me shows up at the door. He's out in the hall and he's got someone else with him. They're in a serious conversation and I realize it's probably about me but I can't make out what they're saying. He motions for the other guy to come into my room. It's another doctor. "She's in here, Parker." I look up and there's my doctor, Dr. Parker. Now what?

What choice do I have? I'm actually feeling fine physically, like nothing ever happened to my body. It's my brain that's messed up. I don't want to go home. I don't want to live, actually. I want to go somewhere far away. I definitely don't want to see Celia or Jen or anyone from school and I've had it with Papa. I can't face him. But, now that they know who I am, I have to leave. I would have had to go somewhere else anyway, but, where would I find a commune, and I'm sort of relieved in a way, but I'm firm that I'm not going back home to the house I grew up in.

By the end of the day, they tell me they've spoken to Mama and that they agree it will be good for me to go somewhere else for the time being—to Tia's, they say, so I agree to cooperate.

• • •

I look out the window of the hospital room. It's pouring with rain and the sky has darkened. I think what it would be like if they released me with nowhere to go, but to search for a commune. Oh my God, where would I go in a storm like this, not in the subway, that's for sure. My forehead leans against the hospital room window up on the third floor. I watch as Tia's car pulls up to the front entrance below with her and Mama inside. Mama bolts out of the car like she's late for an appointment, and she darts through the front door of the hospital below my window. I hear the elevator door and then I see Mama. She's out of breath from hurrying to me, but she slows at the door and stops. She peeks in at me sitting in the visitor chair next to the stripped hospital bed. I am dressed in the clothes that I ran away in. Someone at the hospital washed them for me. She enters the room slowly like I'm a breakable doll or something. When I see her face, I realize how much I love her and could never live without her. She comes right over to me and I stand up. We hug each other so tight like we want to make sure we never lose track of each other ever again. I feel like I'm already in the pinkness of my bedroom, like I'm a little girl and my mama has come to make things better— to save me.

"You okay?" she says in a tone that makes me feel like everything will be alright.

"I'm fine."

She releases me and looks into my eyes. "Your papa dropped the charges against Pasquale. I guess you didn't know."

"I didn't know, but I just can't go home. I don't want to see Papa right now."

"Dr. Parker explained everything and Tia is thrilled to have you at her house for awhile. I hope that's okay."

I nod.

She wraps her arm around me and motions towards the door. I stop her before we leave. "Oh, and Mama, I don't want to see Pasquale either."

She looks at me thoughtfully and tilts her head, "Oh?"

"I don't think I really loved Pasquale," I admit. I had to let her know everything, or at least the important part. "It was Ford's baby. I wanted it to be Pasquale's but it was not possible."

Mama sits down on the bed like her legs give out on her. I didn't want her to know about Ford—about his forcing me. I didn't want to be pregnant with Ford's baby. I wanted it to be someone else's baby, someone like Pasquale who would be a good papa. But, I don't want to tell her all that, at least not right now. Look what happened to poor Pasquale because of me. I owe him an apology.

"What do you mean, 'not possible'?" Mama asks, her voice cracking.

CHAPTER 49

Maria

Luigi paces around the living room like a bull ready to charge the matador. Thank God I'm not wearing red, I think. And then I realize it doesn't matter what color I'm wearing, I could be traipsing around completely naked, it wouldn't matter, my husband always blames me and I'm fed up to my ears with it. We had to do what is right for our daughter and even though he desperately wants her home with us so that things can be back to what he thinks is normal in his world, that's just not possible right now. Under the circumstances, Angelina is best off staying with Tia for a little while.

Nonna and the boys sit at the kitchen table playing hearts. As long as the old bird's playing to win, she's happy. I've just dropped Angelina off at Tia's and made sure she's settled, and I walk in not wanting to speak to any of them. Nonna puts on the pot of gravy so we can have left-over spaghetti and meatballs for supper. The pot simmers on the stove and I go for my apron. Luigi stomps into the kitchen.

"She would not come home? Not even to say hello?"

"Not yet. I told you."

Luigi comes right up in my face. "You go against me. I don't agree with this decision. How do you dare to let her stay at the floozy's house?"

"She doesn't want to see you right now, that's why," and I point my finger right in his chest. Okay, I shouldn't do that—it's too bold and he's sensitive about the subject, but I am so tired of his bullying. He pushes my arm away, and not surprisingly, Nonna hops to her feet. But instead of taking a stance next to her son against anything I have done, she hobbles over to my side to show her support to me. This is something unexpected and quite surprising to me, to say the least. She drapes her left arm around my waist and holds the spoon ready to attach her son in her right arm.

"Go sit down, Mama," Luigi demands.

"You gonna push me too?" Nonna asks shaking the spoon.

"Nonna, go have dinner and watch the boys for me," I say as I untie my apron. The boys are already seated in the dining room and the table is all set. I dish up the food and carry it into the dining room and then I walk right out the back door.

"Get back here..." Luigi starts toward me but is interrupted by Nonna. I see her out of the corner of my eye as she crosses herself and looks up to the ceiling—the heavens.

"God forgive me," she says with a determined expression on her face. I thought I'd never see this from her. She's actually reprimanding her son and making things right in the world of her family. Where did this side of Nonna come from?

As I walk around the side of the house for my exit, I can hear her reprimanding Luigi like he's a little boy, as I pass by the open window at the side of the house.

"You want to be a' center of the universe and be a nasty, mean man, then no one wants to be near you. You need to learn what's important. You sure don't know now."

Whatever has gotten into Nonna, it's definitely for the best. I am frozen just outside beside the window because I can't believe what I'm hearing. And then, I don't wait to hear more. As a smile smears across my face, I rush away from the house, down the street and I'm thankful that I grabbed my sweater as I left. This is the first cool night of a premature autumn, so I wrap myself in my sweater, heading straight for Pasquale's new apartment. I don't know what propels me in that direction, except that I haven't spoken to him since Angelina was found. I feel a rush of excitement shiver down my spine.

Tia told me Pasquale has moved into a new apartment over on 185th Street. I know the building—it's the same one Carmine lived in years ago. When I reach the apartment building, I lose my courage. I stand there at dusk staring up at it like it's something from outer space. I count up to eight floors. He's at 8B, Tia had said. I look to see if there's lights glimmering up on the eighth floor, but it's a big building and who knows where 8B is located. I notice the scent of autumn—of falling leaves and the cooler air, and oddly, I think, that there will be few days left in this year to sit and relax at the picnic table in the back yard where I first got to know Pasquale. I sit on the bench across the street and fix my eyes on the building wondering if I lost my mind back in my kitchen.

There will be a new Maria, I tell myself. I will stand up for myself. I will be understanding and kind but I will not be pushed around and treated with disrespect. I am here because what I want is to speak to Pasquale. I wrap my arms around my body as a breeze whips the air spraying dust and bits of litter around. I shiver, then with determination, I get up and walk straight over to the building and find Pasquale's buzzer and ring it. I'm promptly buzzed in with no speaker request to announce me, just the 'zzzz' and 'click' of the door. I enter and push the 'up' button by the elevator and before I know it, I'm sitting on Pasquale's couch.

The apartment is small and plain with mix-and-match furniture and practically no decoration. He is no longer the intimidating, flirtatious irresistible man I first met. Here in his humble abode, he is meek and shy—slightly embarrassed of his lack of hosting abilities. I ask for wine. Why not? He hands me a glass of red wine in a tumbler with a confused expression. He joins me, straightening up and apologizing for the mess of papers tossed on the couch along with a few articles of clothing. Then he sits with a glass of wine as well, and waits with apprehension to hear the reason why I have made the bold decision to visit him alone in his new apartment, unannounced after the emotional ups and downs our two families have encountered over the last few months.

"Don't be nervous," I say. "It's just that I felt I needed to speak to you."

The worry seems to melt from his body. He relaxes in a chair across from me and takes a sip of wine.

"I couldn't even sit down and eat with my family. I had to

get out of the house. Things are going to change. Definitely."

"What can I get for you? You must be hungry," he says after I've expressed my frustration.

"No. I just came to tell you about Angelina, that she is with Tia."

"She's fine then?"

I nod and sip my wine. Then, I lean forward and look into Pasquale's eyes. He is still uneasy, a little surprised to see me, of all people at his door and sitting here drinking wine with him like it's no big deal. I can tell he's curious and maybe not really too happy to see me, after all he's had to deal with regarding my family. God, he was in jail because of Angelina's lies, and the accusations against him and his family. He has every reason to despise us all, but, once he sees I have not come to him with accusations and problems, he gets up off the chair across from me and sits on the couch next to me.

"Angelina doesn't want to see you," I say. "Just like you said, a teenage crush. I'm sorry you got involved."

"I understand," he says with compassion in his deep husky voice. Frustration returns to me along with infatuation for this handsome man.

"Why couldn't Luigi connect with me like this? Why can't I talk to my husband like I can talk to you?" I bow my head. As I stick my nose in the wine glass and sniff, there's silence between us. And then, I blurt out, "I think I hate Luigi."

He looks a bit stunned like he doesn't know what I will do next.

I set my glass of wine down on the table next to the couch, and I stand up to leave.

Like a copy-cat, he does the same, standing and gently laying his hand on my shoulder. "Did I do something wrong? I will make you a little bite of supper, or I will take you out someplace to eat."

"No, I must go."

"I'm concerned," he says, "Are you going home? I will walk you."

"No, please don't worry," I say as I rush to the door. I leave with an empty pit in my stomach. I wonder if it will ever be filled with satisfaction and love.

I stay overnight at Tia's in the room with my daughter, and the next day I go to my house and get clothing while Luigi's at work. Nonna agrees to watch the boys while I'm gone until I can figure out what I'm going to do, but, of course, she seems concerned. I hate the idea of leaving the boys, but I know Nonna will make sure they're fed. I think she actually feels useful that I have put her in charge of them. But, something has changed in me. For the first time in my life, I've decided to live my own life and make some of my own decisions. I'm going to be on my own for a while and see what it's like.

It is just me and Nonna at the front door as I'm ready to leave with my small suitcase. She reaches up and lays a wrinkled, bent old-lady hand on my shoulder like she needs for me to wait a minute. I lean down and kiss her on the cheek and give her a hug. Usually, she doesn't want to be bothered with such emotional displays of affection, but now, she takes my left hand and looks down at my wedding ring, the ring that had disappeared and then re-appeared so mysteriously.

"It was me who took the ring."

"What?"

"I pawned the ring for gambling money. It was because of you, your wedding ring that I won all that money."

I can't believe what I'm hearing from my mother-in-law, that she actually had the gumption to steal my ring, and pawn it with the chance she might never get it back. I stand there at the front door of my house—yes, it's my house, too, and I have a hard time comprehending what I'm hearing. You never know with this old woman. She comes out with some pretty amazing things, but this is something I could not have imagined in a lifetime.

"How could you do that? What if they sold it to someone else? Then what?"

There are tears in her eyes but she will not succumb to them. She is a tough old bird, but maybe I'm the only one who can actually understand her, and I think she finally realizes that after all these years. I can see in her eyes how hard it is for her to tell me the truth, to apologize.

"I am sorry. I just want you to know that I was wrong and you can hate me for the rest of my life." She bows her head, but then she is her determined old self. "I will make it up to you. I promise."

I actually chuckle. I'm so glad she has confessed to me but I decide to give her a bit of her own medicine.

"Huh. You think I didn't know you took it?"

The expression of shock on her face is worth the white lie. She must know how much I agonized over the loss of that ring, but something in my heart simply knows that we will always be close from now on. I hug her and then I leave.

• • •

After the first difficult night away from home, Tia decides I need to get out and enjoy myself. She plans a night out for the two of us. I don't want to leave Angelina at the apartment alone but she insists on us leaving her, that she's tired and that she is dying to watch a movie on TV that's a re-run she missed from last spring. Finally, I agree to leave her alone in the apartment while we go to a café for salads. We will bring her back something to eat. It's a good idea to get out and not mope around. I wondered what it would be like to live Tia's lifestyle as a single woman. That first night I'm sad and it's difficult and strange to be away from home, but I'm determined to make the most of this time that I've dedicated to finding myself, figuring things out and just simply being with my daughter in a different environment. But, my face is as long as a yard stick as Tia gives me suggestions of what I should do, like taking some fun classes or going bowling with the girls, and she tells me not to bother cooking, that I should go out to eat in cafés or bars every night to see what other singles do. Most of what she says makes me feel uncomfortable except the suggestion to go back to school. I am too miserable that first night to think about the possibility of anything new, or to take any of her suggestions seriously.

Then, the next morning we're sitting in Tia's kitchen drinking coffee while Angelina's in showering. We have a shopping trip planned—just for the fun of it, and we plan to have lunch along Arthur Avenue afterwards.

"I know what you really should do," Tia says, "Why don't you go back to F.I.T.? Get a degree in fashion design or something."

"At my age?" I say but there's a sparkle in my eyes. I can feel it. Actually, there's a switch that turns on in my head.

"Hell, yeah. Why not?"

"Phew," I exhale thinking of what Luigi would say. "I don't know."

"Definitely. You can sew like a pro. Jeez, you're always zipping up all sorts of fun stuff for the shop. Why not? I know you'd be damn good at it—much better than any a those young kids outta high school who don't know a straight stitch from a zig-zag."

I chuckle at Tia's dramatic bobbling about just as Angelina comes in with her hair wrapped in a towel. "What time we leaving?"

Tia darts to the bathroom for her turn in the shower, and now my head's spinning with possibilities for my future. Suddenly, I'm invigorated.

After a couple of days, we are settled in like three college buddies. We cook dinner together and laugh like carefree friends living together in an apartment. This is really living, I think, no pushing, no condemning or criticizing and no degrading. It's like a vacation in a way. I try not to think about Luigi or our home. I make a point to see the boys every day while Luigi is at work, and they suddenly show concern that I'm not at home, and that Angelina is here at Tia's as well. I tell them that things will work out, that it will all be fine and not to worry. I just need a little time.

One night I go out with Kate and Tia to Ricco's Pub on Hughes Avenue. Men actually flirt with me. It's funny, I've never been an adult woman out in a bar like this. I dance with a couple of the guys on the small dance floor, but I'm a lousy dancer so mostly, I sit and watch as Tia dances with some guy named Rock who looks close to Angelina's age. I guess I should have thought about it ahead of time—that I could get drunk and act a little foolish. I'm not used to drinking alcohol—especially not "screwdrivers" and I get a little out of control that night. It's like I can't stop giggling and acting silly. I haven't giggled like this since I was a kid; no, since my brief time with Pasquale.

Tia has to guide me back to the apartment later that night and literally help me to bed. All I remember is Angelina sitting on the bed next to my cot and staring at me with wide eyes. I'm a little embarrassed for her to have seen me drunk so the next day I'm anxious to speak to her, to try and explain or apologize. I was certainly not acting like a good mama, and truth be told, it is not the way I want to act for myself.

CHAPTER 50

Angelina

I'm trying to muster up some feelings of being cool, just sitting in Tia's tiny living room waiting. I've braided my waist-length hair Indian-style and wrapped a beaded band around my head.

Then, around my neck, I dangle a seed-beaded necklace that Mama bought for me from a street vendor during our shopping trip a few days ago, and the peace sign on a rawhide strap, like the one Jen always wears. I'm dressed in my new striped bell-bottoms with a gauzy peasant blouse I couldn't wait to wear. I'm all jittery and anxious when Celia buzzes the door bell. I know it's her, and for the first time ever, I feel nervous to see her. All that changes as soon as I ease open the door and gaze into the glorious face of my best friend in the whole world. I can feel the apprehensive eyes of Mama and Tia watching me from the kitchen where they're making lasagna. I've been a loner for the past few days since I returned from the hospital. I know they're concerned about me, worrying if I'll be okay, wondering if I'll resume my teenage life. For some selfish reason that I guess is just part of growing up, I didn't think of my family and friends during the ordeal I experienced this summer. People really do care about me and it fills my heart up to the brim with a warm cinnamon-like joy that feels something like I imagine true love feels. It feels safe and indestructible. One major thing I've learned is that I don't know a darn thing about real love between a man and a woman. Why did God make it so confusing?

    Celia peeks in tentatively like she's afraid I will be angry at her, or maybe that I won't accept her. I wrap my arms around her and we giggle like little kids who have no worries and are loving life. It's like nothing happened, no rape or pregnancy or hospital ordeal, and I know that this is a friend I will always have by my side. In one second it flashes through my head that I can trust her with anything and that, God forbid, anything happens to her, I will be there by her side just like Mama and Tia.

• • •

    I want to clear up all the fragments of my broken summer and the toughest thing for me is to face Pasquale. Oh man, he must really hate me. Celia and I are out on Arthur Avenue looking in the windows at the new merchandise in the shops, new fall clothes and school supplies.

"What do you think I should do about Pasquale?"

"What? What can you do?" Celia shrugs her shoulders.

"I feel so bad about trying to rope him into being the father of a child he had nothing to do with, and man, he went to jail because of me, and you know, Gino hangs around with us, and the family, they must hate me. I was thinking I should apologize or something."

"You should apologize," she says in a very matter-of-fact adult voice.

Mama had said the same thing to me that first night at Tia's, and as soon as I get it in my head that I have to face him before I put this part of my life in the past, it's like an itch, like a poison ivy itch that has to be scratched. The next morning, I get up before anyone else. It must be like six o'clock. I want to get over to his house before everyone goes to work. Tia told us that Pasquale moved into his own new apartment over on 183rd Street since Freddie is back from London with a new girlfriend and obviously taking up all the space in his Yonkers pad. I guess Pasquale realized it was time to break free and get his own place. But, I know he still works with his papa and he will be over there picking him up for work, and I know they should all be there at the Corso family house only a few blocks away from Tia's having breakfast.

Mrs. Corso answers the door with a disappointed expression when she sees me. It makes me tremble even worse, but actually, I don't blame her a bit. I can hear them all in the kitchen eating breakfast.

Mr. Corso hollers, "Who's there, Josie?"

"It's the Campisi girl."

The chattering in the kitchen stops and whispers of concern are all I hear, that and the anxious thumping of my heart.

"I came to apologize."

Pasquale, Mr. Corso, and Gino appear in the foyer, all still chewing food and holding their napkins. I look over at Pasquale who frowns at me. "Especially to Pasquale," I say and a smile miraculously appears on his face. He comes over to me like a big brother and slings his arm around my shoulder. I must look like a scared rabbit.

"Everything will be okay, my Angel. Thank you."

"I'm so sorry for all the problems I caused." And, I feel phenomenally better, and even the family that I caused so much pain in their lives, they even show concern and caring for me. I can tell they forgive me. And when I leave, I glance at Gino and I think it's the first time I really see him for who he is—a really cute guy from a really nice family.

CHAPTER 51

Maria

Angelina has connected with her friends in the neighborhood and everyone seems to be treating her like nothing happened over the summer. Jen and Celia are with her as usual talking about school that starts in a few weeks, and boyfriends and the usual teenage stuff. I see her approach Tia's apartment building with some of the kids, as I sit in the living room feeling ill from a nasty hang-over that I swear I will never experience again as long as I live—no more "screwdrivers" for me. Angelina's with Celia and Jen and two boys. I peek out the tie-dyed curtains with caution so they don't think I'm spying. I take a closer look just to be sure that everything's okay with my daughter. It's Rudy and Gino with them. Maybe it's the alcohol still affecting my thinking, but I feel suddenly hopeless and sad for myself. At least I'm relieved for Angelina. She appears happy for the first time in months. I'm glad to see my nephew, Rudy with them, but Gino—he sparks feeling, reminding me of Pasquale. Suddenly, I yearn to be with Pasquale right this minute.

As lousy as I feel, I must keep it up, this new life. I must be the new Maria—bold and self-confident. I walk over to the phone table by the couch. First, I stare at the phone and then I quickly pick up the receiver and call Pasquale. I'm surprised when he answers on a beautiful day like this, but when he does, I don't falter from my intent.

"Oh, hello," I say almost stuttering with a loss of words. "I, uh thought you would be at work."

"It's beautiful outside. I took off early."

"Oh."

"Is everything okay?"

"Well, yes," I say. "Sort of, I mean, I miss you."

Pasquale says we will do something together, that he will call me in a day or two. Is he avoiding me? I certainly don't blame him if he is, and I'm uncomfortable in a school-girl way wondering if the boy will actually call. I hang up the phone as Angelina enters jovially chatting about school registration and what classes they will take and who teaches what class and who's in this class or that class. I realize that I must get the boys ready for school soon, that I am probably neglecting them a bit. I sit down on the couch by the phone and try to think sincerely from my heart. Am I happy?

* * *

I go home to see the boys and make sure they have clean clothes. The house is warm and inviting with the comforting aroma of chicken soup simmering. It feels like I belong there but I keep my focus on what needs to be done. I take the boys to register for school. Louie is going in seventh grade and Johnny will be in fifth grade already. I feel lonely to be away from them at this time of year, but I'm sure Nonna is feeding them properly. They are wondering what the heck is going on that their mama is sleeping at Tia's and their sister, as well, but they're busy with boy stuff and school and I'm sure they're just fine.

"You staying, Mama?" Louie asks. Johnny just stands there full of smiles waiting for my answer.

"Not tonight boys."

"We could use another hand around this place, you know," Nonna says, and I know she's really just fine without me, but that she's anxious for me and Angelina to come home, too. She glances up at me as if to try reading my intent from my face. I know she's concerned for me and I'm touched. We have a secret bond between us now. It goes much deeper than the disappearance of the ring. I don't know what went on in that old bird's head recently, but if she will only remain like this, she will be a heck of a lot easier to live with. And, I'm pretty sure that is the way things will be.

I go up to my room for a few things and there's Luigi sitting on the corner of the bed rummaging through the picture box. I'm startled to see him home from work and even more surprised to see him doing something so sentimental. I've never seen him so much as peek into the box of pictures I keep up on the top shelf of our shared closet. He brims with smiles when he sees me. I'm ready to turn and dart out when he holds up a photo of a bunch of us at Papa Vito's retirement celebration. He holds up the photo so I can see but he doesn't move from the bed.

"Look at this. You are always the most beautiful one in the room."

I glimpse at the picture avoiding Luigi's eyes, then I amble over to what was my side of the bed, where my bureau stands, and I pull open the top drawer for a few pieces of clothing. All the while, he surveys my every move without saying a nasty word. He watches with a crooked smile, with an odd sort of admiration like he's sorry for being such a bully but doesn't know what to say. I'm confused by his actions. He's sort of flirting with me, but I don't want to deal with him right now. I grab an armload of clothes and hurry to leave. Out of the corner of my eye, I see his smile turn downward. I wonder what he's doing home. Is he sick? I should be the one making him chicken soup.

The emotions surfacing in my unreliable brain as a result of my new life situation have found me in a perplexed state of mind. I thought I'd feel different—carefree and cheerful to be away from criticism and judgment, but doubt and confusion cloud my thinking. There's nothing in my life that is more important than my family. That I know. Even so, I am determined to enjoy this life away from my husband, the tyrant, Luigi. A few smiles and flirtatious eyes will not move me.

• • •

On Tuesday, Pasquale calls me at Tia's and asks me on a proper date, a dinner rendezvous at his apartment. My emotions are a battlefield in my heart and mind—a mix of excitement and guilt and nervous confusion. I decide not to tell anyone about the date—not even Tia. I pretend I'm meeting with someone to talk about design classes in the city. Tia knows I have an appointment at F.I.T next week, so it's not surprising to her that I want to find out a little about what to expect if I sign up. And then, I'm there at Pasquale's on a rainy Tuesday evening sitting at his tiny kitchen table while he cooks. The lights are dimmed—all but the bright stove light—and candles illuminate the apartment adding a romantic touch. He whistles one of the songs he sings at the club as he prepares the macaroni. I sip red wine. This is what I wanted, why am I not "over the moon" with passion and joy? I watch him with my head propped on my elbow, like I'm yearning to see something that's not visible with the human eye. I analyze him as he's cooking and chattering away about something to do with fishing upstate New York. He's the perfect example of what I fantasize to be the most handsome, sexy man alive. Something eats at me as I watch him standing at the stove in an over-sized apron. He reminds me of something—someone. He's not old and stogie but wears tight bell-bottom jeans that stretch just so across his perfectly toned butt, and even a peace sign around his neck. I don't remember him dressing so youthful and stylish when we first met. His skin is tanned a golden color that glistens around his strapping arms, and I can see the muscles in his perfect legs right through the stylish jeans. How does he have such style all of a sudden? And, I don't remember that he had a mustache. Why does he want to cook for me? There must be thousands of girls he can date. I take in every little detail as he works, every once in a while, turning to smile at me. I love his hands and his silky black hair, now a little longer than when I first met him, and he is barefoot. He has a dish cloth stuck in his back pocket. What is it about him? I try hard to think of whom it is that he reminds me of as he sets the table with the plates and silverware and now the food that he has cooked. He removes his apron and joins me at the table. He pours more wine and lifts his glass to me with a glow in his eyes that makes me melt.

"To my beautiful Maria."

We touch our glasses and sip the wine. He serves the food, sits down across from me and begins to eat heartily, but I am having difficulty. I can't mask the perplexity dancing around in my ridiculous brain. I pick at the food. The thought of digesting food makes me nauseous. He looks up at me and abruptly stops eating.

"What's wrong?"

"I'm sorry, Pasquale."

"Is it the food? Is it not good? You're not happy?" He puts down his utensils.

I take a deep breath, stand up and push in my chair. It pains me to look into those inviting eyes. I retrieve my jacket from the hook by his front door and put it on quickly.

He has a shocked expression on his face as he too rises.

"I just can't...I don't know what's wrong with me." I bow my head avoiding any glimpse of him. I have made up my mind.

"But, you wanted...you called. I thought we..."

"I am so sorry. I must go home."

"Oh Maria, I was hoping..." He steps towards me like he will take me in his arms, but I put my finger to my lips as if to quiet him. I can't bear to hear another syrupy word from those sensual lips. I turn and walk out.

As I hurry back to Tia's I'm thinking as hard as I can. I'm free to make love with Pasquale, my fantasy man, and what do I do? I walk out. What is wrong with me? And, all of a sudden I remember who Pasquale reminded me of standing there cooking. Oh my God. I stop in my tracks on the corner of 187th Street—it was Luigi when we first started to date, when we were so madly in love. Oh my God, it was Luigi!

For the next few days, I try to just enjoy myself at Tia's, at work and being with Angelina. I never tell any of them about my date with Pasquale. I want to move on from that experience. There's no need.

I glance up at Tia's calendar next to her unorganized, practically empty pantry. It's August 30. School will start soon but for now, the three of us prepare dinner together. Angelina and Celia have joined the Future Homemakers group at school. I don't think Jen is in on that, but Angelina has become a phenomenal baker testing out homemade goodies on me and Tia for the Ferragosto street fair in a couple of weeks. Tia and I are corralled by an enthusiastic Angelina to help bake for the event. Tonight's a marathon night of creating delicacies together. I'm trying so hard to work through some of my sadness and despair. I don't tell them today is special for me, or, was special.

Celia arrives. She goes right to the cupboard and grabs an

apron, ready to get started. Tia and I are already covered in flour and egg yolk. I'm kind of in a daze immersed in my own thoughts when Angelina tells some joke about what happened at "The Dumps" on Friday night. I laugh with them but my mind wanders. I don't really know what I'm laughing at when the doorbell rings.

"Yikes, who's that?" Tia says heading for the door. "I bet its Gino looking for a date," she says giggling and directing her dig to Angelina. It's only in the last couple of days that she has admitted she fancies Pasquale's younger brother.

When she opens the door, Tia's laughter stops. Angelina darts out of the room and I stand there shocked to see Luigi hovering in the doorway awkwardly holding a bouquet of pink roses. Tia magically disappears and it's just the two of us as he hands me my favorite flowers.

"You don't think I forget our anniversary?" He wears that crooked smile that was one of the things I fell in love with about him so many years ago.

I accept the roses with a weak smile. "Thank you."

"I couldn't get the lilacs to go in the bouquet."

"It's fine. The roses are beautiful." I stick my nose in the bouquet and fill my head with the scent. It feels comforting to see my husband, and to know he didn't forget our special day.

We are both uncomfortable. He never knows what to say. "I better go." He turns to leave then spins back around. "We miss you at home; both of you." Angelina must be peeking in from the other room. His eyes scan over to where she exited the kitchen, and then back at me, "I wish you would come home. Is not the same without you."

He pauses as if he is hanging on the moment, that I might say something convincing him that everything will be good between us. I hug him with little passion—just a thank you gesture. He grips me tight but I pull away and turn from him. I hear as the door shuts behind him.

Luigi's visit puts a damper on the rest of the evening's baking merriment. Tia jokes and carries on. She even pretends to be drunk on the Amaretto that was supposed to be for the almond cookies, but Angelina and I mope around like it's a chore to work in the kitchen and Celia leaves a little earlier than usual. I can tell my daughter misses being at home, maybe as much as I do. And, I actually wonder if she doesn't miss her papa a little bit, too.

Later, once we're all in bed, I lie on the cot across the tiny room at Tia's trying my best to be still and not awaken Angelina in the opposite bed. She seems to be adapting to everything that's happened to her much better than I expected. The fact that she could have died is what I believe has given her a new will to live, and to live with a new energetic vitality.

I must have fallen asleep in the wee hours of the morning. I didn't even hear Angelina rise. When I open my eyes, the apartment is eerily still. I pop up and pick up my watch on the table between the beds—10:04 AM. I have never slept this late. I leap out of bed. Even though it's my day off, this is the day I have made my appointment for the interview at the Fashion Institute of Technology in Manhattan. It was Tia who got me going on this idea, saying I need to find something I enjoy and go for it. She reminded me that I have the knack to concoct all sorts of garments and that's a way to start, a sort of indication that I have a spark of talent. Well, we'll see. But, I've been looking forward to this appointment ever since I left home and came to stay at Tia's. The plan is to get signed up and start classes at the end of September. I will need to get a student loan, but Tia promises to help. But now I'm late and I scurry around like I'm an industrial sewing machine.

I dash around like a maniac. First, I have to stop at the house and the boy's school for their assigned classrooms, and by the time I get the train into the city, I will just barely make my appointment. What I had planned to wear just doesn't look right. I'm supposed to be applying for fashion design and I look like a ragamuffin. What was I thinking? Oh, man, have I totally lost my mind?

It's funny how I get myself all in a tizzy over something so simple. By the time the end of the day rolls around, I've miraculously made it through all the day's stresses. I actually made it to my appointment on time and it all worked out perfectly. I had no idea it would be so simple to sign up for classes at a college. Even in my dreams, I didn't expect to be able to attend college, and design school at that. My head spins with ideas of draping classes and sketching and being right in the middle of the exciting garment center.

I walk out of the counselor's office on 27th Street and Seventh Avenue and I head up towards 34th Street—the center of the garment center. I take it all in—the garment workers rolling racks and carts through the streets and the people hustling and bustling through Fashion Avenue. I examine each interesting person I see on the street and make up in my mind what I think they do as a job in fashion. I notice some of the older patternmakers hanging around along the street in front of 530 Seventh Avenue smoking and flirting with the sexy models with legs up to their chins and I wonder if my husband is there among them. I wonder if Luigi fantasizes about some of these gorgeous young girls, so perfect they look, with porcelain faces and perfect hair and bodies showing everything in this unusually chilly almost-fall day. Their blouses open to show cleavage and their mini's almost showing a little too much. I sit on a bench to absorb more of the beautiful people. I'm right by the A-train at 41st Street where everyone is heading home from work, and then I guess I could easily catch a glimpse of Luigi. He takes this same train and it's just a block away where he works. What would he think to see me sitting here? I panic at first but then I think, so what, I'm in charge of my life. Like the kids say, "Do your own thing." I'm doing my thing, but all I can think about in this crazy moment of my life is Luigi. I day dream of him trudging toward the subway station all bent over and miserable like he usually is these days. And then, I think of him cooking in the kitchen instead of Pasquale, all joyous and happy like he used to be. I think about him at the core of his character, the Luigi I fell in love with years ago. Maybe I could have made him happier. I could have thought more about making him smile instead of moping around complaining about all the things I had to put up with. There are so many wonderful things I love about him, and I sit there remembering good times—not dwelling on the difference of our ages, but, the sameness of our hearts.

I'm so mesmerized by my day dreams and people-watching that I don't realize how late it is until I peek at my watch. It's already past 6 PM. It's supper time. Something wild and crazy clicks in my brain. I hurry like everyone else on the street and blend in with the mass exit of workers as I roll along with all of them down the subway stairs and on the train that will take me back to the Bronx.

I rush in to find Tia and Angelina watching a re-run of *The Beverly Hillbillies*. Tia's newest young boyfriend, Rock is there with them, but I can tell the way Tia speaks to him that she's tired of him already. Angelina has a pad of paper in her lap and works on how much the Future Homemakers will make at the street fair while barely watching TV. Tia and Rock are bickering on the couch. She turns attentively as I come in the room.

"Hey Love, we were worried. You okay? It go okay at F.I.T.?"

"Great. It was really great. Sorry I'm late."

"Dinner's on the stove."

"Angelina, pack your stuff. We're going home." I still stand there with my shoulder bag slung across my shoulder.

Tia leaps to her feet. "What is it, Love?"

Angelina doesn't budge but I can see in her eyes a certain

glimmer of relief. "I don't think…"

"Tia, you've been great but it's time to go."

"You sure, Sweetie?"

"Our family is broken up. That's no way to live." I hug Tia, then reach over and lay my hand on Angelina's shoulder. I can see that Tia gets it; she sees it in my eyes. I glance at my daughter. "You've had some time. Now, let's go home." She gets up smiling at me like it's all okay, in fact, I get the feeling that she's been waiting for me to make this move. I don't even pack my stuff. I tell Tia I will get everything tomorrow. It takes us less than ten minutes to grab a few necessities and head for home where we belong.

Perspiration streams down my neck by the time we reach our house. Angelina's practically jogging next to me all the way from Tia's. "What's the hurry, Mama?" She keeps asking.

"Its dinner time," is all I say, out of breath.

We march up the front steps and in the front door. Johnny is right there and Louie comes running. They hug us and even Nonna in her sauce-stained apron hobbles to the door to greet us, as if we've been on a long vacation and finally home to tell of our great adventures.

As I remove my jacket in the dining room, I glance at the family portrait over the buffet and I smile remembering that happy day years ago just after Johnny was born. Angelina was only eight and Louie was four. Papa Vito was still alive and vibrant, as was Nonna—feisty as ever. We were younger then and our family has weathered plenty of stress and difficulties since. But, we are a family and life happens. We have to stick together because we have love for each other—we have the sameness in our hearts. That is what I'm grateful for—that is what I want in my life. Even Nonna expresses that new, cherished respect for me. She hugs me like a daughter. I melt in her arms. I have yearned for this for such a long time—acceptance.

We are given such an appreciated homecoming, but only

when I see Luigi in the doorway admiring all the love and hugs does my heart skip. He steps boldly up to Angelina and hugs her. Then, without shame or selfishness, he possessively takes me in his arms like I'm his lover and he hugs me and he kisses me, and he won't let go until the boys and even Angelina and Nonna are snickering at us. Nonna pulls a hundred dollar bill out of her apron and stuffs it in Luigi's shirt pocket. He knows what that means. He smiles.

"Now, we are a family again," Luigi announces, "Finally, you came home."

And, it smells like home. It must be a late dinner, almost like they expected us to come barreling in after 7 PM.

"Smells good. Come on Angelina, let's help Nonna with the dinner."

CHAPTER 52

Angelina

I hadn't realized how much I missed Uncle Carmine. We've always had a special connection—I think most people are like that, they have a particular relative that they just know they must have been together in a past life, or they're just plain alike in their thoughts and personalities. Well, that's me and my uncle. I had forgotten how upset and confused I was when he moved out to California. Why? Why would he desert me like that? One good thing, at least for me, that came out of all my summer drama, is that Uncle Carmine was so worried about my disappearance that he made a trip back to the Bronx just to make sure I was fine—to see me in the flesh. And the best part about that is that he's staying here to live and work as a travel agent, all because he came here because of me. I couldn't be happier. I guess things happen for a reason. Sometimes you wonder what the reason is when you're going through the tough parts, but I've got my uncle back and to top it off, he's hiring me to do filing and paperwork in the office three days a week after school.

So, I'm sitting on my bed writing a letter to Shirley, who must be back from vacation by now. I tell her about my adventures in the city and how I tried to reach her so I could stay with her family for a little while. I stop to think—I guess I'm a daydreamer like Mama. Lately, when I'm sitting in my "pink" bedroom, I feel a whole new sense of gratitude. My whole way of thinking about life has changed over the summer. It's kind of like the before and the after—not about my pregnancy, although that sure must be part of it, but of growing up and appreciating things, especially my family and friends, and understanding more about life. It's like I'm becoming more of a woman than a kid. Don't get me wrong, I still think I'll stick to being a kid (or, at least a teenager) some of the time, but thank God I don't have to think about living a totally adult life just yet.

Writing to Shirley and recalling all the craziness about sitting on her step and being harassed by the greasers and sleeping in the subway makes me really think about my life. There are so many people in my family who love me. What was I thinking? Did I actually think I would be happy to go live at a commune? I missed my bedroom and all my silly stuff from when I was a really little kid. I missed being here with my bratty brothers and with Mama and Papa and Nonna. I missed being home. I didn't want to tell Mama when we were at Tia's, but when she came in and said we were going home, my heart smiled.

And then, my mind wanders to Pasquale and Gino's family. The kind forgiveness expressed to me by the Corso's inspires me. After all the trouble I caused, they excuse me for my awful childish actions without even so much as an explanation. I can't get that out of my head, and so, I decide to give it a try in my own family by forgiving Papa. I rattle my brain to think from his perspective. One thing for sure is: he doesn't know how to control his feelings and his temper. I know he loves me and that is why he acts wild and crazy sometimes, not because he wants to be mean and make me feel miserable. It's all because he cares. And, I care about him and all my family. What a lucky girl I am.

• • •

Ford was at a re-hab for 30 days and now he's back home and planning to go to school again with the rest of us. He heard all about me and actually apologized and wants to be my boyfriend again. That's just too much for me. There's no way that's happening, but I'm glad he has the courage to tell me he's sorry about how he treated me. It seems like apologizing is catchy around here these days. But, it makes you feel better about yourself to admit you were wrong and say you're sorry. It's like you can go on with your life without feeling completely foolish. And now, my summer ordeal is old news with everyone. It's time to get back to school and everyone's got plenty of new stuff to deal with. That's a big relief to me, not to be the center of attention, especially since I'm really into Gino. Why didn't I see him, really see him before? This time when he kisses me at "The Dumps" on Friday night, I just about melt off the chair. I lay my head on his shoulder all through the movie that I don't remember anything about.

When I'm at home lying in my bed, I can't control my daydreaming, which is still one of my favorite things to do. It's funny how dreams change. Now, it's dreams about being with Gino and what we will do and say and where we will go and how much he will love me and on and on, but today I think about Mama. She doesn't know that I found out she went on a date with Pasquale. My mama with Pasquale—that upsets me, so I'm doubly grateful to be home where Mama is with Papa like it's supposed to be. If Mama thinks she was upset about the thought of me with Pasquale, oh man, she is only half as upset as I am at even the slightest thought of her even going out on a measly date with him. I can't even imagine. What was she thinking?

But, one of the things that always sneaks into my mind with the rest of the concocted daydreams I have for my future is the dynamics of the Corso family. Mr. and Mrs. Corso are still so in love, the way they look at each other, and stick up for all their kids even when other people accuse them of doing something bad. They're tight. They're a family that cares for each other, like they never give up on each other. I'm thinking they never give up on others outside of the family if they believe in them, like me. Gino never gave up on me even after…. Oh man, I don't want to think about that anymore. And then, it occurs to me that my family is not so much different. The Campisi's are a family to be proud of being a member of, too. Didn't everyone in my family believe in me when I messed up? And when Mama left, Papa just waited for her to come home. And Nonna, I'll never figure her out even though she's probably the smartest of us all.

CHAPTER 53

Maria

A new attitude of life has swept over me. It's like someone waved a magic wand and sprinkled fairy dust over my family. I stroll along the street on the way to work at Tia's. In the past few weeks I've created some of my own new clothes—my versions of the current trends and I'm wearing my new corduroy bellbottoms that I just finished last night. I feel good about myself, freer, and every time I think of it, I can't believe that I'm actually a student at the famous F.I.T.

There's the sound of hammering in the distance, maybe a block away. For an instance, it enters my mind that the neighbors are preparing their houses for the upcoming winter season, then, I think of Pasquale and sure enough, as I walk closer, I see him up on the Morales' roof working away. I hadn't thought much about him since that day in his apartment when I realized I must leave, when I knew I must go home because that is what I really desired.

He doesn't notice me as I near the house and then, the hammering stops and I can hear his voice. He stands on the edge of the roof on a ledge with his hip jutted out and the hammer positioned in his hand. His hair is longer. He must be trying to be in style, and his t-shirt is soaked with sweat even in the cooler weather. I wave but he doesn't notice me. He focuses on a pretty Italian woman, around twenty-two or twenty-three. Her dark brown hair is braided in a single strand down her back to her perfect waist and she wears a mini skirt and platform shoes so high I think standing next to Pasquale, she is probably a few inches taller. Ever so slightly, she rotates her hips as she speaks to Pasquale on the roof, and she cocks her head to one side. He is obviously panting with desire as she teases him. If she gave the word, it looks like he would be sliding down that ladder and into bed with her before she knew what happened. I snicker to myself and then just as I'm passing the Morales' house, there he goes, down that ladder. He gazes at the young woman with such intensity that he doesn't even notice that it's me walking by. I stop for a minute thinking I would yell out a hello to him, but I decide not to bother. I turn and walk with a lively step toward Tia's.

A few days later, we celebrate Angelina's sixteenth birthday. We rent out the hall connected to the parish over on 187th Street and invite all her friends from high school. After all, it's a special birthday—she's a full-fledged teenager and now, Luigi tells her she can actually date boys, but only ones who meet his approval. We all know that he's not too thrilled about this, but at least he's sticking to his word and I'm sure it will have to be good Italian boys that Luigi knows. It seems he's abandoned the idea that his precious daughter is "ruined." And, it's Gino that Angelina is crazy for. Even though my husband knows Gino, he's still not thrilled with the idea of his only daughter dating Pasquale's brother.

Francine, Nonna, and I and a few of the other women have made the food and carried it all over with decorations for the party. Angelina, in her special new dress of pink lace and satin is beaming with delight. Giuseppe and Carmine hook up a stereo and Rudy acts as DJ. We kind of split up into groups: the teenagers in the main room with the dance floor, the younger kids in a middle area, and the rest of us, the older relatives and parents in the alcove off on the side with tables to sit and chat. We're all sitting around the tables stuffed and groaning from so much food and we haven't even had the cake and gelato and all the pastries that Tia brought over from Terranova. We're in a lively conversation about how all the kids are so grown up all of a sudden, and then, it seems like all the adults are arguing about whose kid has grown the most and what kid is the cutest and the smartest and so on.

I listen to the younger kids at a table near ours. I just want to make sure I pay attention to what our kids are thinking and doing.

"You can't go in the Army without a buzz cut," Johnny says.

"I'm not goin' in the Army. I'm goin' into politics. That's the only way to change the world, dummy," Louie says.

"Like Nixon? You won't see me hookin' up with any a' those clowns," answers Johnny.

"After the Army, I'm going to work at Cuddlecoat. You can make plenty of money as a patternmaker," Rudy says as he walks by the younger boy's table all sweaty from dancing with the girls. I can see that Francine is so worried that another of her boys is joining the armed forces when she hears this.

And, Giuseppe is not willing to tolerate this from another son. He follows him towards the men's room. "So that's why you cut off your hair. You forget about it. You come work with me an' make me proud."

"Leave him be," Francine says and pulls her husband back down to sit at our table. "Let him enjoy the party."

Luigi says, "You think I should not be proud a' my boys? An', Angelina and Maria, they go to design school, first Maria and then my Angelina. You see, they be the boss of Rudy."

Usually Tia would have plenty to say about the controversial subjects of war or fashion, actually, just about any current subject that is brought up in a lively discussion, but I glance over to the end of the adult table and there she is sitting quietly listening to the rest of us.

And then the conversation criss-crosses and voices rise and there's some more arguing. There's peace and then there's war—back and forth. That's what it always is in our family. Then, Nonna speaks up, "These kids have their own minds. Is good."

It's me who starts in about gratitude. It is the mama in the family that is the center of the family—who needs to organize things like this. I have learned this since all the changes of attitudes and craziness this summer. I have learned to be strong, and most of all, I have learned what is important in life. Oddly enough, I finally feel like the master of my own kitchen. Why is it that I feel I learned all this from Nonna?

"Enough, enough," I say and I stand up. "We go around the tables and we each tell what we're grateful for," I explain, and yes, some of them complain but once we're started, each one of us tries to top the others. The gratitude discussion is catchy. Everyone has to top off the one next to them.

"Okay, I will start," I say. "I am grateful for a beautiful sixteen-year-old daughter who makes her family proud." Everyone claps and cheers.

Carmine goes next with, "I'm grateful that I come back to the Bronx."

As we go around the table to hear from each one in my family and our friends, I think back to a year ago. Every one of the kids has grown at least an inch or two. Louie has actually grown his hair slightly longer, and Johnny has his hair trimmed. Rudy has a buzz cut. Francine's girls are dressed somewhat like Angelina was last year and Angelina is actually toned her style down quite a bit, and you'd never know by looking at her today, what she's gone through recently. I glance over at her dancing to a slow song with Gino and it reminds me of myself at that age. This is her day and it's time for the cake.

Tia prepares the cake all ready with the candles—all sixteen of them, and we're ready to light the candles and switch off the lights for singing the birthday song and for making wishes when I notice Carmine right by Tia's side. I pause in the doorway to the parish kitchen privately tucked behind the dance floor. The two of them are giggling and flirting as they prepare the serving dishes and the cake and gelato and pastries. In a secluded nook of the kitchen pantry they embrace and kiss. Oh my God, Tia and Carmine, who would have ever thought of those two together?

Soon we are clearing the tables, piling plates and preparing for the big clean-up. The teenagers are making big plans to go to some outdoor music event—a rock festival, they say. I can't take my eyes off Tia, and stuck to her like a magnet is Carmine. Why hadn't I noticed this before? I could have fixed them up on a date years ago.

Johnny goes over to Nonna's seat, "Nonna, want me to walk you to bingo?"

"I'm done with all that. The money's not worth much, you

know. How 'bout we get some fresh air, then you kids maybe wanna play a game a' hearts back at the house? See if you can beat old Nonna."

"Sure, Nonna," Johnny answers.

Carmine and Tia have disappeared. There's me and Luigi and Francine and Giuseppe standing there just about ready to leave. We all sort of giggle at the idea of Tia with Carmine, and then Nonna goes for her coat from the coat rack and the boys slip into their jackets. I notice that Nonna's got her old coat and hat. I guess I was too involved in all the party planning to notice earlier.

"Nonna, what happened to your mink coat and hat?" I say.

"Lucky I kept the tags. Returned everything but the gloves. My hands always get so cold."

We all stare at her in surprise.

"Ma, I thought you wanted that coat an' stuff?" Luigi says.

She waves her hand. "Ah, it don't mean nothin'." She picks up her old snap-top vinyl purse and opens it. She pulls out an envelope and waves it in the air.

"I guess now's as good a time as any to tell you all," she pauses, crosses herself and glances up as if to communicate with Papa Vito in heaven. Then she announces, "Traded all that useless stuff in for tickets to visit Italy, for all a' us together."

"Ma, you're kidding?" Luigi says.

"That's what you wanted, right?" She looks right at Luigi, and I remember how many times he always told me it was his dream to take me back there to the village where his family lived for hundreds of years. That's what was important to him for all these years, to show me about family ties.

"Well, yes, Ma but we never thought..."

Totally surprised and excited, we all hug Nonna and she brushes away the extra affection like it's nothing. Then, Luigi hugs me. There is something about that hug. It makes me feel like I am where I belong—that I am loved and valued and appreciated.

"Ah, come on let's go on home. Come on boys. Let's walk," Nonna says.

I watch them out the window as the boys dart around her and she hobbles toward the corner. She pushes them away when they try to give her a hand. I chuckle to myself as we leave the parish. Then, out of the corner of my eye, I see her stop at the corner awaiting the cross-walk sign. She opens her coat and from the inside pocket she pulls out the battered old wooden spoon. She holds it over the garbage can like she's going to toss it in. That is something I thought I'd never see. But instead, she stops and yells to the boys waving her cane.

"Forgot something," she says and hobbles back inside. Quickly, I pretend not to be watching her and straighten the curtains where I'd been peeking out. She comes right up to me and hands me the spoon. "Here, maybe you can use this."

It's her cherished wooden spoon, the one she reprimands everyone with, the one she never lets out of her sight. She has given it to me. "Thanks," I say and tuck it in the pocket of my apron. It's one of the most precious gifts anyone has ever given me.

* * *

Soon, we are all back at the house. The teenagers have all gone home to change their clothes into something more casual—mostly bell-bottom jeans and colorful tee-shirts. They never fail to be entertainment to my heart. You never know what to expect. Gino comes like a gentleman to the door, just like his brother did this past summer. But, he is more fitting as a date for our Angelina. He politely shakes hands with all of the adults and thanks us for a lovely party. I must say that Luigi was a bit apprehensive of him considering all Angelina has put him through, but he doesn't complain and pick on him. He is more accepting. Gino actually appears a little nervous around Luigi, maybe it's because he's seen him in livid action. He arrives with

Jen and Ford who it seems are now a couple—couple of crazy teenagers I think. And Celia is the fifth-wheel, at least that's what I think until Rudy jumps up and slings his arm around her, and then, I remember back at the party that they were dancing together. It's hard to keep them straight.

So, the teenagers leave for the rock concert. The boys return with Nonna and play hearts. Me and Francine clean up and pack away all the leftover food, and Francine's girls leaf through *Seventeen* magazines in the living room where Luigi and Giuseppe smoke and watch the news. They're trying to figure out what happened to Tia and Carmine. I just smile to myself. Before long, Giuseppe's family packs up and heads for home. They take Louie and Johnny to sleep over with their cousins. I check to make sure they have what they need, and soon they are out the door. Suddenly, after a long, exciting day, I am so tired, but in a good way. The party has been more than a success. And now, it's just me and Luigi alone in the house, except for Nonna. I want to speak to her about the trip to Italy. You never know what that old bird will do, but Luigi says she's tired and gone up to bed. This is actually the first time since I've returned to my home that the two of us have been alone together to have an adult conversation. Yes, I have been sleeping in the same bed with him at night but he is always tired and snoring by the time I slip under the covers, and Luigi has never been much of a conversationalist. But now, here we are, the two of us. In a way, I'm nervous. How could I possibly not know what to say to this man I've lived with for more than sixteen years?

In the quiet of the house, I put away the last of the serving dishes and I gaze out the window over the kitchen sink at the picnic table. I smile with a vision in my head of me and my young family years ago, all sitting around the old picnic table that I've had to paint at least five times since.

I remember a time when Angelina was around seven, and

the boys were toddlers. Angelina plays mommy to the boys. Luigi tickles me as I serve the food and I giggle with pure delight and then, I remember I used to clean up the dishes in the very sink I am standing at right this minute and he would come up behind me and hug me. I exhale savoring the thought.

"Are you still working in the kitchen?" he asks.

I turn to see him in the doorway. I smile as he comes to me and hugs me for no special reason at all. I dry my hands on the dishtowel hanging on the rack inside the lower cabinet and follow my husband into the living room where we take our usual seats—me on the couch and Luigi in his chair where he always sits. I kick my shoes off and rub my feet before curling my legs under me. I pick up a random magazine from the rack next to my seat. For a minute, I lay the magazine on my lap to rest my eyes, and with surprise I look over at Luigi who is staring at me intently. The TV is on tuned to a low volume, but he's staring at me—just staring quizzically like he's trying to look right inside me.

"What?" I say. I hunch my shoulders and give an uncomfortable laugh but he doesn't answer at first.

"What is it, really?"

"You left, and then, you came back." He pauses and then rises and turns off the TV. "Why did you come back?" He stands looking at me.

"What about why I left?"

My husband comes and sits next to me on the couch where I don't think I've ever seen him sit, and we face each other. He takes my hand and I turn away. "It's hard to live with an old man like me," he says.

"I won't argue with you on that, but now I see that it hasn't been easy for you," I turn back to face him. "I thought it was just me; that I needed more in my life, maybe that I wanted a different kind of life."

At this, I rise and wrap my arms around my body as I pace

in front of the couch where he sits like an injured animal after hearing my remark. I feel sad to hurt his feelings, but that is just how he is, how he reacts.

"Our family, we couldn't live without you. You are the center of us all." He stands up and faces me to stop my pacing.

"We are a family. That's what's important."

"I know sometimes I don't think about how you feel. I am sorry for that." He takes both of my hands and cups them in his large masculine hands that I've always loved so much.

"Sometimes I think of how happy we used to be; us, together. We used to laugh a lot. I was so proud just to be your wife."

"And now, you are not?"

"Oh Luigi, I am proud." I reach my arms up around my husband's neck. He is rigid at first, looking as if he feels sorry for himself, but then, when I smile at him seductively, he holds me firmly.

With my head tucked into the crook of Luigi's neck and the comforting feeling of his protecting arms holding me, we drop down together to sit back on the couch. Softly, I say, "That's why I came back. I don't want a life like some young girl. I already have what I want."

When he kisses me with a passion I have rarely felt these days, I see out of the corner of my eye, Nonna sitting over by the stairs smiling with a glimmer in her eyes. Like mother, like son, I think.

I wouldn't trade this kooky family for anything in the world.

THE END

ACKNOWLEDGEMENTS

Some of the most worthwhile things in life are those things we achieve through a "we" effort. In my life, I have found this to be true. I'm sincerely grateful to all those who have made an effort, or taken the time, in one way or another, to make my first novel a reality.

Thank you to my friends who have read and critiqued bits and pieces of this story over the years. Some of these friends include: Terese Dana, Jeanne Talbot, Melissa J. Peltier, Susan Hansford, Vincent A. Cea and Andrea Cea.

Thank you to all the members of The Nyack Library Writer's Group and original leader, Chris Enchaure-Baldino. Additional thanks to all the members of the Piermont Library Book Club who have helped me hone my craft in writing through reading and discussing fascinating literature.

Much thanks to the multi-talented, Bob Aulicino, who designed the cover and interior for this book and gave me advise along the way. Thank you to my editor, Erica Goebel, and to designer and artist, Janis Wilkins for her artwork and website development.

And, most recently, I am enormously grateful to the 96 who contributed to publishing this novel through my Kickstarter crowdfunding campaign: Michael, Maxine, Joseph, Deborah, Richie, Nancy, Karen, Angelique, Pamela, Debbie, Angela, Marian, Elaine, Janis, Michelle, Kathleen, Gina, Deborah, John, Simone, Jessica, Marcia, Nick & Laine, Karen, Kim, Haydee, Teri, Bonnie, Elizabeth, Sarah, Judy, Mark, Aunt Eleanor, Aunt Maryanne, Mary, Joan, Mary, Sheri, Walter, Beatrice, Janet, Harvey, Linda, Angela, Sharon, Mercedes, Eileen, Dianne, Linda, Andrea, Anne Marie, Mimi, Barbara, Betsy, Elaine, Olivia, Barbara, Chris, Barbara, Edwin, Sharon,

Veronica, and Gemma. An extra thanks to the following for their excessive generosity:

Gary & Mary Michelsen
Tara Estevez
Tony Rubio
Carolla Dost
Melissa J. Peltier
Anna Alemany
Jeanne Talbot
Barbara Scholz
Siri Smith
Lisa Johnson
Michael Simon
John Gray
Kathy DeSellem
Barbara Levy
Rosemary Newhardt
Arlette Mooney
Mara Purl

Travis Schweiger
Susan Hansford
Marie-Eleana First
Alex Garfield
Maximino Vazquez
Donna Hesselgrave
Rita J. Louie
Terese Dana
Tom & Nilda English
Don Bracken
Rosselyn Alemany
Rhea Vogel
Leslie Slauson
James McSherry
Iris Montaldo
Jordan Feuer

Finally, I am most grateful to my family for always being there for me.

ABOUT THE AUTHOR

Carolyn Doyle, a former fashion designer in NYC's fashion district, has used many of her fashion industry experiences to develop plots and characters in this, her first novel, *Fifteen*. This is the first in a series of four novels set in and around the Garment Center between 1967 and 2001. The second novel in the series, *Dance to Fashion*, is set to release in 2015. Carolyn is a graduate of the Fashion Institute of Technology in NYC. In addition, she earned a Certificate in Screenwriting from New York University, and is a previous student of Creative Writing at The New School in NYC.

Dear Reader:

Thanks for reading my first novel, *Fifteen*. I sincerely hope you enjoyed the story, and would be most grateful if you have the time to express your views, write a positive review, or make a comment about the book at: Amazon.com, Goodreads.com, or to me personally at: Carolyn@Skydancepress.com. I would love to know how you liked the book and I welcome your feedback, comments, and questions.

Best Regards,
Carolyn Doyle
www.skydancepress.com
@SkydancePress for Twitter
Skydancepress.com for Facebook

DANCE TO FASHION
By Carolyn Doyle

CHAPTER ONE

Disco music throbs through our buzzed and wired brains like we will die here on the dance floor like dead "energizer bunnies" if we don't catch up to the phantom-images in our drippy-nosed heads. The music pumps, faster and faster, louder and louder in our alcohol soaked minds. Right this second, it's only about the dancing. It's me with Alice and Roxy dancing on the crowded dance floor of thick raised latex that is lit up with flashes of neon orange, fuchsia, sunshine and day-glo green under our spiky platform heels. Glitter on our eyes, shaggy teased hair, me and Roxy in vintage velvet halter dresses, and Alice in body-revealing pants. We dance like our lives depend on it, each one of us performing our dance steps to the beat of 1973, trying to top each other, just trying to have fun. It's vibrant, lively and exciting—the newest disco craze, after more than a decade of pure rock-and-roll. And, this is the place to be (the only place, really) on a Saturday night in Madison, Wisconsin—The Scene Discotheque and Bar.

The Christmas lights draped around the bar area twinkle like it was the plan to match the festive decorations to the unique dance floor lights. The D.J. melds Gloria Gaynor's song, "Honey Bee," with The Jackson Five's wildly popular, Dancin' Machine. You can't have a night in a place like this without the extended version of that pulsating hit. I step off the six inch high dance floor, bend over and shake out my shaggy Jane Fonda inspired hair. I hadn't realized how out of breath I was, but Alice and Roxy urge me back on the floor.

"Come on, Zoe Hill," Alice whines with eyes lit up to match the glittery Christmas decorations. She pleads with me to get back on the dance floor with her sing-songy voice pronouncing my full name like its one word with accent on the e. "Zoeeeeehill," she summons, "get your sexy ass back over here." She rotates her shoulders and does a full body-roll, her favorite dance move. A college kid gyrates with her from behind trying to keep her frantic rhythm. Alice plays along for a couple of beats swiveling her hips and torso with the boys like they're toys, and then, she gently pokes one in the chest adding a wink, and turns to the biggest, tallest black dude I ever saw. He's hot, mimicking her moves but with a style all his own and definitely much more sophisticated than the boy toy. He really knows how to dance in a rhythm and blues style. I've got my eyes on those two as Roxy and I move to the beat.

Dancing sends me into another world—one where no one can touch me, hurt me, disappoint me. My spirit soars. I am lost in the music; I'm one with my movements.

Roxy cocks her head and grinds her hips towards three conservative guys trying, with no dance skills, to flirt with us, to partner up. Yeah, right, I'm thinking. Way too straight for me—for us, probably more college students trying to be cool. I glance over at our table at the end of the bar where my stoned-out husband, Hick and his loser friends are planted. I've given up on Hick ever wanting to dance with me. One of the straight guys wears a Santa hat. We play with them, kind of dance like wild slutty girls with no boyfriends or husbands sitting a few feet away. The Santa-hat guy looks familiar. I can't imagine why, and I'm trying to figure out how or where I would know a guy like that. He has no style—a buzz cut under the corny hat and wears clothes I'd imagine were no good but to use for washing your car. Even though he looks like a teen-ager, he's probably not even any younger than me, but he's not my type at all. I would never be caught dead with a guy like that. Well, I'm married, but if I were single. How can you wear khaki pants and white socks to a discotheque?

By the time the song ends, we are a little bored with the guys and ready for a break—another vodka and orange and a toot of coke in the bathroom. Actually, I'm not a coke-head or anything like that. Drugs are big in Madison which is known to be one of the coolest places in the mid-West and everyone who is cool does a little of this and a little of that. I keep a small vial in my purse, one that has a twist-off cap with a miniature spoon attached. A snort in each nostril is all I need to get a buzz on. I know when to stop, not like most of the jerks around this town.

The D.J. announces something about Christmas and most people scatter from the dance floor for a breather. I head to our table and there's Hick slouched down in his chair with his angry expression pronounced by his bushy fu-Manchu moustache. He twists his silver and turquoise ring (a sure sign that he's not getting enough attention) and runs his left hand through his shoulder-length stringy hair. I know that inevitable quirk of his, it means he's pissed off. Next to him is Paul, his side-kick who mimics Hick's pissed off attitude. That, too, is predictable.

As soon as I approach the table laughing with my girlfriends, Hick stands up glaring at the three straight guys. What's he gonna do, hit them or what? His chest is all puffed out like he's itching to cause some trouble. I pretend I don't notice when Paul and Roxy's boyfriend, Keith each take a hold of one of Hick's arms. He sits back down turning his chair away from where the young guys are now leaning against the bar. He waves his arm in their direction like he can't be bothered. I pretend not to notice, but what pops into my head is what it used to be like with Hick. God, that guy was so fabulous, so romantic and thoughtful. I would do anything for that old Hick. I might even sit there just to be next to him instead of dancing with my girlfriends. But, things have changed over that past three years—drastically.

We're definitely drunk and way too wired by now. It's past midnight; maybe even 1:00 or 2:00 AM. The music is blasting again and Hick's pouting with his arms crossed until he sees Johnny Junk by the door who motions with his head for Hick to join him outside. Everyone knows Johnny is the biggest junkie in town. Hick struggles into his purple leather jacket, at least a size too small. I've got my eyes on him as he eases outside with Johnny. My lively party mood has dwindled to a glum place in the bottom of my heart. I really don't need any problems with Hick tonight. It's always something lately.

I peek out the window by the coat racks and there's Hick shivering in his thin jacket snorting what I assume is coke. Hick counts out money and then hands Johnny a small package. Johnny pats him on the back and disappears around the corner hunched over like an old man. Hick does another quick toot of coke and turns toward the door just as I'm thinking how fabulous he used to be, how he used to be all about making me happy. Back then, we couldn't do enough for each other, but now as he approaches, I rush away from the window before he sees me and plop in a chair at our table. He's really hyper. I can see it in his eyes.

"Hey, Babe," he says in his sexy, but possessive tone, purposely shedding his recent anger. He scooches his chair up next to me wrapping an arm around my shoulder and runs his other hand through my hair. He gazes right into my eyes and I can see his frenzied eyes up close, almost as if the pupils are darting back and forth so fast he can't control them, but it's the coke. I know how that is. I hate that feeling because you know eventually you're gonna crash and then, it's the worst feeling in the world no matter what.

I let him kiss me, but then, I brush him away. I'm ready to go home to sleep. He nibbles on my ear and whispers in his liquid voice, "I've gotta have you, Babe. Let's go."

The place is winding down and the only ones on the dance

floor are the drunken dancers who were too shy to dance earlier until they got plastered enough on booze or drugs. I get my jacket ready to split, but now, Hick's in conversation so deep with some guys from the head shop on 5th Street. He doesn't even know what he's talking about. It's the coke. It wraps your mind up into a tight spring and when it uncoils, there's no stopping the chatter about anything that comes up.

"Come on, Hick," I moan. "We've gotta pick up Nessa." I wave good-bye to Roxy and Keith, and Alice and Paul and the others we hang with. They're all leaving now. I slouch down in my seat waiting for Hick to uncoil. There's no coke-chatter left in me and I'm crashing—done for the night.

All I can think of now is my two-and-a-half-year-old daughter, Vanessa. I doubt that I'd put up with Hick's craziness if it wasn't for her. I want her to grow up with a daddy, not like me. My sweet, single-mother struggled over every darn thing in life to raise me. Nessa's over at my mom's (where she usually is when we go out) and I told Mom we'd pick her up around midnight. She knows by now that we're never on time. I start to feel bad about the fact that she probably thinks I'm a lousy mother. But, really, I try. No one could love a little girl as much as I love Nessa, but hell, I'm only twenty-two and still learning how to do my life. I'm still searching for a path in life, and I know that's no excuse, but the fact is, most of my friends don't even have kids yet. Most of them aren't married. I wonder if I would have married Hick if I wasn't pregnant. No, I would have married him. We were so crazy about each other. But, would he have wanted to get married if I wasn't pregnant? He's turning wilder and wilder and totally changing into a different guy than I dreamt of as a husband. I don't want to think about this. There is no way out. I just want to get out of the bar and get Nessa. All of a sudden I miss her like crazy.

We're one of the last to leave *The Scene*. Hick gets his 1969 black charger while I stand by the entrance shivering in my thin

1930's velvet dress with the slit up to my hip. My fake monkey fur cropped-off jacket was made for style not warmth. The car rumbles up and I step in. Hick's doing another toot of coke. That means he'll be up all night mauling me into all sorts of sexual positions.

"God, Hick, what the hell?" I say when I'm in the car and he's speeding away.

"Here, take a hit," he says handing me his vial.

"No, I did enough. I'm tired. Who's gonna get up with Nessa?"

Hick pulls the car up in front of my mom's house on Elmwood Drive. It's the same house I grew up in, the tiniest bungalow on the street tucked back behind two overgrown bushes almost as high as the roofline. On the side of the driveway there's the same raggedy swings hanging limp and snow-covered where mom used to swing me as a kid. Now she spends her summer afternoons swinging Nessa in the same spot. Seeing my mom with Nessa brings back memories of my own childhood and I appreciate her so much more than I ever did when I was a kid. I am so grateful for her, and that she's always anxious to babysit her granddaughter. Yes, Deborah Jean Wilham is the best mom and grandma a girl could ask for, but I didn't think so as a wild teenager, always drawn to the kids who lived life on the edge. I regret my rebellious attitude toward her back then when I thought she was just being tough on me for no apparent reason. Now, I cherish her like she's a saint—the perfect grandma—my best friend. Without her I don't know how I could deal with the problems Hick causes. She's there for me and Nessa (and Hick when his behavior is appropriate) without judgment, only pure love.

Just as I'm about to get out of the car, Hick reaches over and kisses me, a sloppy tongue kiss that tells me what he has in mind. "Ask Deborah to keep her for the night."

"I can't do that." I get out and run up the walkway. Mom

always hears us coming in that rumbling car of Hick's with the noisy muffler. She's standing in the doorway, her slightly chunky body wrapped in her white terry cloth robe and pink puffy rollers in her hair. It looks like she's been sleeping on the couch worrying about us. She flicks on the foyer light. I step in and close the door. Hick's car radio is blasting rock music in this quiet neighborhood so late at night that I'm sort of embarrassed.

"Hate to wake Vanessa. It's late," Deborah says.

"Sorry, Mom." I give her a hug. "You should be in bed."

Mom follows me into my old bedroom where Nessa sleeps tucked in the Barbie comforter in the same twin bed I slept in my whole life.

"Go on. I'll bring her in the morning."

I stoop down next to Nessa and kiss her lightly. "Sleep tight, sweet girl," I whisper and then exit the room pulling the door partially closed, then, I hug Mom. "Thanks," I tell her and really mean it.

I run back out to the car in my spiky platforms and almost slip on the icy walkway. I look back and wave and I'm thinking how tired and weary Mom looks. I visualize a mirror-image of myself in twenty years. Is it my distorted vision because I'm crashing on the booze and coke? It hurts to think her gloomy expression is because she's disappointed in me. I have to stop thinking and just get some sleep.

I head right up to the bathroom to wash up. Hick's snorting more coke in the bedroom when I step in ready to snuggle up in my bed. He's got two joints rolled on the edge of a mirror with four lines of coke, a couple of pills, and drug paraphernalia on the night table. He uses a razor blade to chop the tiny crystals as he sits there on the edge of the bed with his pants unzipped and his shirt stripped off.

"Wanna hit?"

"God, no. I'm beat." I slip in under the covers on my side of the bed.

"It'll pick you up, babe."

I've managed to slip in under the covers, but, he rolls over on the bed to face me and whips the covers off. He's got his tongue in my mouth and his hands all over me within seconds. What's the use? I try to be receptive to his lovemaking. We make out and he has practically torn my nightgown off within seconds. It's not really lovemaking, its drug induced sexual urgency and he's so wound up and hungry like a starving dog. At first I figure I'll just go along—get it over with so I can go to sleep, but, although I don't think he realizes it, Hick gets rough and demanding and it completely turns me off. I push him away and glance at the alarm clock next to my side of the bed. It's 2:34 AM.

"It's late," I complain.

It's like he doesn't hear me. "Come on, babe, over here like this." He grabs a hold of my waist and forces me into position as he kicks off his pants, but I push him away again and slink to the floor next to the bed. Now, he's riled up and pissed. He sits up with his legs wide apart and holds himself.

"You're not leaving me with this all night."

I turn away from him but he takes a firm hold of my head with his fingers snarled in my hair and guides me into position to give him a blow job as he sits on the edge of the bed. Tears leak out of my eyes. I know this is not the real Hick that I married, the real guy I was in love with. This is the drugged out Hick who I'd only recently gotten to know. It's easier to go along with his mood than to fight him, and that's usually what I do. But, I'm sick of it—like, I don't want to put up with this anymore.

I try to slip back into bed hoping that is enough to satisfy my husband, but he grabs a hold of me rotating me like a cylinder onto the bed.

"I'm not done with you," he says and rolls me over. I fight him with hesitation at first and then with more determination.

It's like that turns him on and he's even more horny and sex-crazed. He's got me pinned crosswise on the bed and when I struggle to get free, he accidently elbows me right in my eye. I see stars, but he doesn't realize he hurt me. "I like it babe," he moans, and I know he thinks it's a game that I'm into.

By the time he's finished with me, the sun is peeking up on the horizon. Hick takes some pills and rolls over to sleep. I slip out to the kitchen for some ice. I make up an ice-pack and take it to bed with me but I can't sleep. Melting ice and tears soak my pillow and I'm thinking it's a good thing that Nessa stayed at my mom's over night.